NOT WITH
A BANG

NOT WITH A BANG

A BANG

Temi Oh

solstice

London · New York · Amsterdam/Antwerp · Sydney/Melbourne · Toronto · New Delhi

First published in Great Britain by Simon & Schuster UK Ltd, 2026

1 3 5 7 9 10 8 6 4 2

Simon & Schuster UK Ltd, 1st Floor
222 Gray's Inn Road, London WC1X 8HB

Simon & Schuster Australia, Sydney
Simon & Schuster India, New Delhi

www.simonandschuster.co.uk
www.simonandschuster.com.au
www.simonandschuster.co.in

The authorised representative in the EEA is Simon & Schuster Netherlands BV, Herculesplein 96, 3584 AA Utrecht, Netherlands. info@simonandschuster.nl

Simon & Schuster strongly believes in freedom of expression and stands against censorship in all its forms. For more information, visit BooksBelong.com

A CIP catalogue record for this book is available from the British Library

Hardback ISBN: 978-1-3985-3325-7
Trade Paperback ISBN: 978-1-3985-3326-4
eBook ISBN: 978-1-3985-3327-1
Audio ISBN: 978-1-3985-3328-8

This book is a work of fiction. Names, characters, places and incidents are either a product of the author's imagination or are used fictitiously. Any resemblance to actual people living or dead, events or locales is entirely coincidental.

Typeset in Sabon by M Rules

Printed and Bound in the UK using 100% Renewable Electricity at CPI Group (UK) Ltd

MIX
Paper | Supporting
responsible forestry
FSC
www.fsc.org   FSC® C013604

*For Keche, who I missed,
before she was here.*

BRIAR MINTON

Is it possible to want something so much that the force of your longing pulls taut the fabric of reality until it bursts? Our father had imagined the end of the world so often that, for a while, he believed that he summoned it.

It was a couple of months before we discovered the extent of his prepping. It began the summer before, with tinned cans and non-perishables, rice, pasta shells and powdered milk, puce tubs of pickled cabbage. My sisters and I returned home from school one day in September to find him cooking venison stew on his new rocket stove, a tower of propane canisters spilling from rain-spattered Amazon boxes piled on the porch. He rigged the house with alarms. Stockpiled hunting knives and hatchets. By spring, we weren't allowed to drink the tap water in case it was poisoned.

In February, he built a bunker. A utilitarian monstrosity. We watched from our kitchen window as it was lowered into the ground. Inside were hastily assembled bunk beds, a compost toilet and medical supplies: ventilators, iodine pills and codeine. We were instructed to participate in drills that could happen at any hour – although usually at the smallest. Tannic taste of adrenaline as the doomsday alarm dredged us from sleep with its urgent mechanical bawling, all the lights off and Dad shouting. We'd fumble blindly for our dressing gowns and jackets, then run. Sometimes our bedroom doors would be locked, and we'd have to find another way out. I would climb out of the window and clamber down the trellis. Land, bruised and shin-scratched, in the shrubs below, just a few seconds left to sprint down the weed-choked garden path.

We were urged to bring something we loved. The first time, I'd dashed back to get Digit from her dog crate, but it had been empty, and I'd run about the house with a torch, tears in my eyes, calling her name until I saw her retinas flash at the bottom of the garden. Dad had shouted at me for the delay. In the real thing, like us, she would have to run or die.

By the fifth time, we only brought our phones. Not that they ever worked once he closed the airlock.

Some nights, I wake and I'm still there. The February chill, shafts of grass like glass snapping under our heels. The doppler of the siren as we ran. Dad standing sentinel at the end of the garden, looking as if he'd been there since the start of time. The figures of his Casio luminous. Six minutes, he would say. Four minutes. Three. He'd smile if it was less than three. His teeth piano keys in the moonlight.

Chantale would always glance over her shoulder at the neighbours' houses, the glass eyes of their unlit windows, their bedrooms quiet as tombs, and ask the same question every time.

'If this was the real thing . . . ?'

'If this was the real thing, would they be . . . ?'

'Dead?'

'Yes.'

Then we'd lie on our bunk beds in the dim glow of the propane lantern and discuss it. Weeks of fallout, millions dead. Poisoned rivers, bellied fish floating like Coke bottles downstream. We'd survive, of course. We'd emerge to raid the abandoned shopping centers. Tanice fantasized about pulling designer clothes off the deserted racks at Harrods. 'They won't cost anything,' she'd say.

'They won't be worth anything,' Aaliyah would remind her. 'You think the corpses will care how fashionable you are?' But Tanice would shake her head and smile at the thought of white-knuckling it through the nuclear winter in Max Mara mink. Chantale, who was seven, would tell stories of moving into the Natural History Museum, playing hide-and-seek among the dust-veiled bones of dinosaurs.

Dad would laugh. It was never a nightmare for him. I realize this only now. It was a *dream*. The Mintons, victorious. Persistent as roaches.

In my memories of those nights, Mum was almost never there. And when she was, she was stonily silent. She'd dry swallow a sleeping pill and slip into unconsciousness. By spring, she had stopped coming at all. If this disappointed our dad, he tried not to show it. His behaviour intensified. He began paying careful attention to the movement of celestial bodies. Particularly Hero, a rogue planet set to swing past Earth that summer. He took lessons in bushcraft. One weekend, he told us that we were only allowed to eat food that we had foraged or killed.

In the weeks leading up to June, there were drills almost every night.

Of course, when it actually happened, it was nothing like the drills. There was no time to grab the things we loved, no hope of making it to the bunker.

Dad had been right about some of it. He had imagined the squeal of tyres, the polyphonic clamour of car alarms, dogs howling, birds splattering across the pavements. A strangled ringing from the blood vessels in our ears. He hadn't imagined it would be beautiful, though. Hadn't defined the particular colour of the sky, feathered with auroras and chrome-coloured clouds, an awful light.

Almost everything that I didn't live through, I would learn later from witness reports and testimonies. I have examined everything in its entirety, more than once. Some things I can only imagine. Like my father's expression the morning it happened. His gaze drawn up by the sound. Red capillaries scissoring the whites of his eyes. Reflexive terror, confusion, realization, then – *hadn't he dreamed of this? Hadn't he numbered our days?* – finally, smiling, delight.

PART ONE

Before

KIMONA MINTON – 5 DAYS BEFORE

My mother would spend a couple of minutes every morning imagining what it would be like to lose everything she loved. The way some might count sheep, she counted backwards: the bed, the walls, her house, her husband, her daughters, one by one.

She'd picture the bed kneecapped by termites, white paint flaking off its four posts. The house snatched up in the blistering maw of some freak electrical fire. Steel herself against the thought. A bed was just a bed. A home was just a home.

Except she used to tell us that that bed was the loveliest thing she owned. That she hoped to be buried in it, hoped we'd lash it to a raft, her cool body under its quilted duvet, and set it sailing down the Thames.

'The Princess Bed' our father teasingly called it. It was maximalist, bombastic, ostentatiously feminine, completely impractical – like my mother.

Five days before the world ended, she had been dreaming of an army of carpenter ants riddling holes into the magnificently carved headboard when her phone buzzed and startled her into wakefulness. She snatched it off the dresser.

An unidentified number. 'Hello?'

'Is this Ms Kimona Minton?' Leopard-skin dapples of sunlight fell on her muslin sheets.

'Doctor.'

'Sorry?'

'It's *Doctor* Minton.'

There could be damp in the walls, in the joists and rafters. The house could crumble all at once like a diseased tooth. She tongued a familiar gap in her gums and imagined it.

Maybe it would be a relief. She'd never imagined she would grow old in the place where she had watched her own mother die, too young, of a tumour that had spidered through her skull.

'Claire? Is that you?'

'You have to answer these questions for security.'

'14 Albert Road, Clapham, SW11 ...' She trailed off, glancing at the clock on the wall. It wasn't even 7 a.m. 'Isn't this a bit early?'

'Sorry.' The voice on the phone was a little sheepish.

'Didn't you say to expect a letter? That if the results were clear, I would get a letter. Not a call. A call is ...'

'Yes ...' Claire sounded hesitant. 'Dr Minton, the results from your biopsy—'

It was something about the tone of her voice. Kim felt a sick swoop in her stomach, terror and dread. Sweat needling the tips of her fingers. 'Wait!' Slightly breathless. 'Once you tell me, it will always be true.'

There was an arc to these stories, Kim knew. They began with some innocuous symptoms, headaches that were usually worse in the morning, fatigue, slight muscle weakness on her right side, a perfunctory visit to a GP, and ended with ...

'Can I just hang up now and save my life?'

'You know it doesn't work that way,' Claire said, not unkindly.

'It's just, today is almost the worst day. My eldest daughter, Aaliyah, is getting married this weekend, and on Thursday we have this fancy rehearsal dinner and ...'

'This is urgent.' Claire sounded as if she was losing her patience a little. 'The sooner we start treatment ...' she continued, but Kim stopped listening. She could taste bile in the back of her throat. Her eyes flitted out to the untended garden. Yellow sprays of dandelions across the sun-struck grass. Aaliyah had insisted they celebrate Kwanzaa the previous year, had decorated the house extravagantly in red, green and black bunting that still hung on the washing line, cracking in the wind like her heart against her sternum. The sight was so familiar and suddenly strangely dear.

'Briar wants me to watch Hero's approach with her ...' I had set up a telescope on the porch ready for the night when the planet would hurtle into view. I had told her, 'It's a once in millennia event,' when I'd asked if she could take the night off work to watch it with me. 'I'll catch the next one,' she had replied breezily.

'This will only get worse if you ignore it,' Claire warned.

'Look, I'll call you back later.' Kim moved to end the call and said, 'By Sunday, it will be over.'

She meant the wedding.

For a long time, I believed that I hated my mother. If you'd asked me that summer, when I was seventeen, I would have given you a dozen reasons why.

She'd worked abroad for a couple of years when we were younger, leaving our father and grandfather to raise the four daughters she'd left behind. Motherless years of going to school without brushing our teeth, of matted hair and mismatched socks. After which, she'd returned a stranger to us.

It seemed to me that her whole self was a palace she built and rebuilt again every morning from the ground up. And always slightly differently. Stage makeup, mannerisms, hair. She had a variety of wigs that she kept on foam stands in her closet. There was the short black bobbed one she'd wear to parents' evening, the auburn one she took on holiday, the ombre blonde for nights out. My favourite was the afro she wore once to Notting Hill Carnival, which made her look like Erykah Badu. I can't remember when I first discovered that they were wigs. But I do remember how, aged ten, I opened her closet to find those blind polystyrene heads lined up on a shelf like Bluebeard's dead wives. Startled, I'd whispered, 'Oh,' as if at the answer to a riddle I already knew.

It wasn't just her appearance that changed; her entire personality shifted depending on who she was around. Her accent was full of cut glass when she spoke to her colleagues or the other parents at our school. But it grew round and undulant when she logged into Zoom calls with her cousins in Kwara State.

Sometimes she was a great mother, sometimes she wasn't. Sometimes she was needy and affectionate, sometimes she was prickly and reserved. Her moods always seemed to affect the temperature in the house. That quicksilver crackle of her laughter from downstairs could coax the sun from behind a cloud. She could give something a sideways glance, and I'd go from loving it to despising it. I hated the power that she had over me. More than anything, because I was convinced that she didn't love me. I used to try to get her to admit it.

One evening, a few months before the wedding, I said it quickly so as to catch her by surprise: 'The house is on fire, who do you save?'

I was sure it would be Aaliyah. Longed-for Aaliyah, who they'd conceived after a couple of devastating losses. Our grandad used to joke that Aaliyah might as well have been gold-plated, and, for most of her life, they'd treated her as if she was. When I was ten, she'd won a scholarship to an exclusive tennis academy. She'd been on track to win her first Grand Slam title when she'd broken her wrist in a skiing accident a week before the Wimbledon Championships. A complicated fracture with severe ligament damage – specialist surgeons had told her she'd never play tennis again. At twenty-two, she'd remade her life, impressively, immediately. A couple of months later, she returned from a date to announce that she was engaged to the millionaire cousin of her former tennis coach, setting the wedding date so soon after her engagement that we'd initially – wrongly – assumed that she must be pregnant.

'I wouldn't choose any of you,' my mother reassured me when I asked. 'I love you all equally.' I was sure this was what the parenting books instructed her to say. She didn't look up from her laptop.

Four years after Aaliyah was born, Mum had returned to school to study for a PhD, but she'd had to drop out when she discovered that she was unexpectedly pregnant with me. She said that she'd cried during that first ultrasound because she'd been so hopeful. After all that waiting and the losses, there was almost nothing more terrifying than hope. Watching the little early flicker of a foetal heartbeat projected on the screen in the clinic, she'd felt like a homeward-bound astronaut glimpsing the Earth for the very first time.

'Okay,' I tried, posing the question a different way. 'That planet, Hero, has peeled away from its orbit and is trundling like a bowling ball right for us. The collision will grind all our bones to salt. But there's a space shuttle scheduled for launch just in time to save only one of us. Kim, which daughter would you choose?'

'That's ridiculous,' she scoffed. The UK Space Agency had released a short press statement, claiming that Hero would pass through our solar system at a distance of approximately 0.08 AU. *Current modelling indicates no risk to Earth.* 'And I hate it when you call me Kim.'

It never seemed possible that Tanice, my younger sister, could be her favourite child. You might have seen her eyes behind a visor in that historic photograph. That summer, Tanice had just turned sixteen. She was the most beautiful, the most like Kim. But they argued too much. The perfect symmetry of Tanice's face might have destined her to move through the world with a kind of ease, but she was too acerbic and impetuous, lacking in some essential empathy.

I tried again. 'You open the door, and a woman who looks exactly like you makes a claim on your life. She'll only leave if you feed her three children. Which do you choose?'

I should have guessed that she would probably save Chantale. Chantale, the surprise, late-in-life baby, her heart's complete delight. When she played that game with herself every morning – mentally pulling apart her life as a boy might pull the wings off a fly – her stoicism always crumbled at the notion of losing Chantale. Who was seven. Who was scared of everything. Whose front teeth Kim still kept in her purse. Although she claimed she didn't have a favourite, it was clear to see that when the promised floodwaters came for our house, Chantale was the one she would fling onto the life raft first.

'Briar?' she said, finally looking up. 'Why are you doing this?'

Do you think of them as the 'Before Times' as well? My memories of the beginning of that summer possess a kind of nostalgic loveliness. It was June, and exams were over. There was a heatwave coming, and the air smelled of pollen and petrol. If the year was a Ferris wheel, we were at the highest part, the end of the beginning, the longest days. Aaliyah's wedding to look forward to. Summer holidays. I wouldn't have said I was happy then, but I should have been.

It would be over before we knew it, and if we'd been scouring the news that week, we might have noticed some of the signs. Those plane crashes in Jaipur, the freak weather in San Francisco, the power failures on the space stations, those people on the Reddit forums who claimed they were all dreaming the same dreams.

For Mum, it began with the birds. When she hung up the phone that morning, the vacuum-sealed silence of the house was unnerving. It was Monday. Tanice should have been taking too long to get ready, playing her music obnoxiously loud in the downstairs bathroom. I might have been braiding Chantale's hair in front of early morning children's TV.

Kim pulled on her dressing gown and headed downstairs. When she called out our names, there was no reply. It was as if her family had been raptured.

She opened the front door to check for the car out in the driveway, and when she did she saw Hannah, the single mother from Flat 7C across the road. She was standing on the tarmac in slippers and a nightshirt. Blood spattered on one shoulder. She seemed shaken.

'Are you okay?' Kim called, but she didn't seem to hear.

She put on her slippers and walked out towards Hannah. As she did, her sole crunched something in the parched dirt of our driveway. 'Ew.' There was a smear of blood across the beige rubber. For a second, she thought it was ketchup. A fried chicken bone some kids had tossed. But when she looked up, she discovered more corpses, strange explosions of blood and meat splattered across the hot asphalt.

'One hit me,' Hannah said, tilting her head to her shoulder.

Kim looked up at the sky, shielding her eyes against the sun, which was waxing behind fleecy clouds, as if she could plot the dying bird's trajectory.

'Some kind of avian flu?' she suggested. There had already been an outbreak that year, and it was still difficult to get hold of eggs at the supermarket.

'Oh. Does this mean I'm infected, too?' Hannah's eyes widened with concern.

'No, no ...' Kim said, when in fact she had no idea.

Gabriel – our other neighbour, from the new-build mansion whose outdoor bins were mainly filled with takeaway boxes and empty cans of protein powder – had been trying to pull his car out of the driveway when he noticed them. He wound his window down.

'Looks like someone shot them all,' he said.

'Do you think we should call someone?' Kim asked. The birds looked, to her, as if they'd made a suicide dive at high speed for the pavement.

'Pigeon funeral directors?' Gabriel teased. Hannah had tears in her eyes.

'No,' Kim said. 'The council. Or environmental protection? DEFRA?'

'Yeah,' he said and rolled his eyes. 'You do that.' They watched him drive away.

'Are you okay?' Kim asked Hannah again.

She wiped her eyes and nodded.

'It's just the lack of sleep, you know ... At first, I thought I was dreaming this. A rain of dead birds. Gross.' She shuddered.

'It gets better,' Kim said lamely. Hannah's son was almost two. *But then, there's always some new shit*, she didn't add.

'Do you think it has anything to do with ...' Hannah looked up at the sky. 'The comet that's coming?'

'You mean the planet,' Kim said. 'Hero.'

'Right, yeah. That's what they're calling it now?'

It wasn't possible to see yet in the sky.

'It's not "coming",' Kim reminded her, the way the news anchors and scientists did. 'It's a flyby. It'll be in our sky for a little while and then gone forever.'

'Yeah ... hopefully ...' Hannah said.

'Not "hopefully",' Kim said. 'Certainly.' Hannah just nodded and continued gazing upwards.

In the beginning, my mother had treated the bunker like an illness Dad just needed to get over. It had started in February, a couple of days after his suspension, with digging. He'd woken one night as if from a bad dream, put on his gardening shoes and an old headlamp from the camping gear, grabbed a shovel from the shed. By morning, he'd dug deep enough to make his own grave.

Every time Kim's gaze flitted to their wild lawn and the hatch in the ground, her gut clenched with fury at him.

The morning of the dead birds, we were all underground in our bunk beds. The hiss of the airlock woke us. Kim leaned down the hatch and said, 'You're going to be late!' She started making her way down. It was impossible for even Chantale – the lightest of us – to descend that ladder without a cacophony of squealing metal and groaning wood.

Our mother turned when her blood-stained slippers hit the ground. We must have looked like voles to her, three pairs of jet eyes in the gloom. The bunks rocked and whined as we rose.

Kim discerned the cyan glitter of her husband's eyes at the back of the room.

'Marcus.' There was steel in her tone. 'You said you wouldn't do this anymore.' She was thinking about Tanice, who a few months ago had sprained her ankle so badly climbing out of the bedroom window that she'd had to use crutches for a week.

'I said I wouldn't do it on school nights.' He'd just woken up, and there was sandpaper in his voice.

'Today is Monday,' she said, working hard to swallow back her fury. He'd been losing track of the days of the week a lot recently.

'It can happen at any time, Mum,' Chantale said, rolling out of her bunk and rubbing the grit from her eyes. The sight of her almost broke Kim's heart. She wore an oversized camo jacket – Dad's – on top of cartoon-print pyjamas, and there were a couple of healing scabs where brambles had scratched her bare feet.

'Okay, sweetheart, I know.' Kim ruffled her hair and said, 'But if you don't start getting ready now, you'll be late for school.'

'It's not like I asked for any of this,' Tanice said, rubbing her arms against the early morning chill. I wondered then if she was referring to the drills or our family in general. She'd fallen asleep in her basketball gear, baggy shorts and a pink-and-black jersey that said RAINMAKER on the back. Yesterday's mascara made gummy smudges down her cheeks.

'Aaliyah's back on Wednesday,' Kim said. She'd been in Portugal for her hen party. 'Then there's the rehearsal dinner on Thursday ... Can we put a pause on all this until after the wedding?'

Dad was hunched in a camping chair, on watch. 'These evacuation procedures,' he said, taking off his glasses to rub at a scratch, 'need to be second nature.' Then, his old motto, 'We don't lose anything by being prepared.'

'Don't we?' I asked. For once, I was on my mother's side. I had been thinking of the cold. Of Tanice's fear of heights. Of how I couldn't move into my own room because Chantale was jolted awake by terrors every night and kept sleepwalking into my bed, mumbling about the gas cloud, the solar flare, the whiplash of lethal power from our sun to our sole Earth. Of how Aaliyah's rushed engagement was probably a sign of how desperate she was to escape our family.

'When the sh—' Dad bit back the word. 'When things get bad up there, we're going to want to be down here.'

'Dad?' Chantale asked. 'When it's the "real thing", can I bring a friend?'

'This isn't going to be a sleepover, Chantale!' he hissed, then through gritted teeth asked, 'Who?'

'My friend Isla?'

'From Brownies?' Kim asked.

Tanice rolled her eyes. 'If we have to spend the rest of

our natural lives listening to the two of them talk about ponies ...'

'Isla has a family of her own,' Marcus said. 'A father. It's his job, really, to be prepared.'

Kim examined Marcus then, as if for the first time in a while. The problem with marrying someone born the same year as you is that you get to watch yourself grow old. His face had been like a Dorian Gray portrait of her own. There were the silver hairs she tucked under her wigs, there were the creases their years of money worries had etched into his brow, sunspots from every heatwave, bags under his eyes from four children's worth of stolen sleep.

Chantale's muffled sniffs were the first sign that she had started crying.

'Hey ...' I reached down to hug her and felt how cold she was.

'But what if they're *not*?' she said, pushing me away.

'What?' Dad asked. She was properly sobbing then.

'*Prepared!*'

Mum snapped and ushered all of us out of the bunker. Told us that if we were ready in twenty minutes, she would drive us all to school. Tanice helped Chantale out, still sniffling, and they headed into the house. I lingered outside in the grass, by the hatch, listening to the voices that echoed up its makeshift shaft.

'I told you,' I heard Mum say as soon as she thought we were out of earshot, 'not to talk like that in front of the children.' I could imagine them at opposite ends of the bunker, their long shadows thrown across the steel floorplates.

Kim used to believe that my father had changed more than she had. Physically, perhaps. I've seen a photo from the first night they met, at the eighteenth birthday party of a friend, and, in it, Marcus looks like Kurt Cobain. He was too proud to wear his glasses, and so there is a faraway look in his short-sighted eyes. She had spotted him on stage, covering for the drummer in a cover band, and when she went to compliment him after the performance, he had been so embarrassed that he'd almost choked on his beer. He had been shy but kind. She'd loved the way he flicked his dirty blonde locks out of his eyes. He was the sort of white guy her friends used to tease her that she would probably end up with. She used to list in her head the things that she loved about him. He was a good cook, a good dad, a good dancer. He was honest, almost to a fault. He was loyal. A true romantic.

And yet.

'We can't keep doing this, Marcus.' He searched her face as she said, 'You know that thing that people say about frogs boiling? How they don't notice the water getting hotter if it happens slowly? It's like all of this. Ever since you lost your job – the drills, the conspiracy theories. The nightmares.'

'They're not nightmares,' he argued.

'You think something terrible is about to happen. But maybe it already has.' My mother was thinking about everything that had happened last summer and that had led to his eventual suspension. But, as usual, my father swerved away from the topic.

Marcus said, 'Have you heard of Flatlanders?'

'What?'

'They live in two dimensions; we live in four . . .'

'What are you talking about now?' She would have appeared especially tall because of how low the ceilings were. Flanked by neatly organized shelving units, labelled boxes of rice and pickles, packs of egg replacer and Angel Delight.

'Three dimensions of space, one of time. Imagine time, flat as a sheet of paper. And a little crease in it that allows us – me – to see . . .'

'To see what?'

He said it quietly. 'The future.'

There was a stunned silence. I can imagine the incredulity on Mum's face. Or maybe, by then, it was only disappointment.

How has this happened? she thought, a sinking in her gut. How had she ended up married to a man who'd built a doomsday bunker?

'More than ninety-nine per cent of the species that have evolved on Earth are now extinct,' Marcus continued. 'Extinction is the rule! What makes you so sure that we will be the exception?'

'I don't know,' Kim sighed. 'Tell me which of those species built rockets or cultured penicillin or eradicated a virus?'

Marcus puffed in contempt.

'Is this about Hero?' Kim had seen the tabs open on his laptop, watched him late at night with his amateur astronomer's star chart.

'I don't know . . . Maybe,' Marcus replied a little sheepishly. 'What if the disaster *is* coming, and I'm the only villager shouting in the shadow of Vesuvius?'

Kim winced. 'How many men in history believed that they knew the day that the world would end?'

'And aren't the doomsayers *always* right . . .' he pressed.

'. . . eventually?' Kim raised an eyebrow.

There was a calendar on the wall behind him with big crosses through the days we ran drills. Almost everything else in his life had fallen away, other than this. *How long until he exhausts this morbid fervour?* Kim asked herself, as she did almost every day. Running drills and stockpiling cans. Waiting for the world to flip around for him again. Waiting in agony, preparing, practising for something dreadful that would never actually happen.

'Maybe the thing that terrifies you,' she said, 'is not disaster, not eruption or fallout.' She saw it clearly now, what was on the other side. 'It's *this*.' She gestured at the air, towards their inherited house – the one in the city he'd always longed to flee – the challenging daughters, the naysaying world. Maybe it was true for her, too.

'This life. Your little life.'

BRIAR MINTON – 5 DAYS BEFORE

I first heard about Ruby's disappearance the year before, on the WhatsApp group for jazz band. It was mid-December, and I was doing my homework on the living room floor when Ruby's face flashed up as a notification on my phone. When I clicked the thumbnail, there were only a couple of lines: 'Hopes and prayers,' said Fiona McClellan, the fifth-form trumpet player. 'SHARE WIDELY.' The first forty-eight hours are crucial, apparently, when a person goes missing.

It was never hard to miss Ruby Barker, because there were about three Black girls in the upper school and one of them was my sister.

Ruby always looked, to me, like an actress playing a student in a Nineties teen movie. Slightly too old, maybe, as if she had already grown into all of her features. She wore her hair in waist-length braids with clip-in beads that glittered and chimed when she walked.

She had saved my life once. I had been distracted on the busy crossing between Lavender Hill and St John's Road. Not far from school. She had yanked me so hard out of the way of an oncoming car that we'd both collapsed onto the pavement together.

All I really remember is the explosion of the traffic lights across my vision, and then all the air was knocked from my lungs as my body slammed into the ground. And her face. I remember that, too. Her dark eyes and little teeth – she had two tiny canines, the size of pearls, that I heard were baby teeth which never fell out. She pulled my headphones from my ears as I fought to catch my breath. I think she said, 'It happens so fast.' Words that have taken on a couple of meanings for me since. Or she said, 'They go by so fast.' The cars? Down the hill? Or had she said, 'It goes by so fast'? Our time on this Earth, as Dad was always warning? All I had replied was, 'Yeah,' my nerves still jangling as if they had been struck by a tuning fork. That was two weeks before she disappeared.

By the next morning, I had read that MISSING PEOPLE bulletin almost forty times. Ruby was a bundle of facts the way everything on my phone was a series of ones and zeros. I kept combing over them as if they would yield something new.

She had just turned eighteen. She had won a scholarship to our exclusive school. She had been in foster care for a couple of years when she was younger, but she lived with her grandfather now, in a flat in Brixton. By the sounds of it, they had a turbulent relationship. Rumour was that she had tried to run away twice.

'It's got to be her grandfather, right?' said Ella Henry, the second trombone. 'Isn't it always the grandfather?'

He had been the last to see her. Friday, 15 December. She'd told him that she was going to stay with a friend for the weekend. Which was why, he claimed, he didn't call the police until Monday night.

It hadn't been difficult for me to find his Facebook account. His profile picture was of a snooker table, and he shared updates about the poor quality of the local drinking water and petitions to block the refurbishment of the South West London library. In the 'Friends of Brockwell Park' group, one user had commented, 'Anyone know of any good assisted living communities in the Surrey Hills? 81, no dependants.' He'd replied with a thumbs-up and a 'Following!'

And then, just one week after Ruby's disappearance, I'd seen on Facebook that he had listed their flat on Rightmove. In the pictures, her little box room was completely cleared of any belongings. I zoomed in, looking for traces of her – the wrinkled lipstick kiss at the edge of the mirror, the discoloured patches that her torn-down posters had left on the wall.

Ruby herself had a pretty scant social media presence. Which, Tanice insisted, should have been the first warning sign. There were only two pictures on her Instagram page. One was of her sandalled feet on a sunlit pavement dusted by cherry blossoms. 'Hi, I'm new here.' One like. And a selfie, dated nine months later, in which she wore a pendant necklace featuring the phases of the moon. The caption said, 'Are you ready?' I wondered if she was referring to the lunar eclipse, which was represented with a flashy black opal on her necklace and had taken place over the weekend she disappeared. When I refreshed the page that morning, it had triple the likes and a stream of comments. Mainly heart emojis, red and black, that one with a bandage across it, yellow crying faces. Pleas for her to come home, the usual, a number to call. 'SHARE WIDELY.'

The same blurry thumbnail boomeranged through all my group chats.

'Wasn't she in your year?' Tanice asked.

'The one above.'

Tanice's eyes flitted back to her phone. 'All the interesting things happen to you guys.'

The next day, in assembly, the headmistress announced that she had some terrible news to share. I thought she was going to say that Ruby had been found dead, but she only told us what we already knew: that she had been missing for three days, the teachers we should speak to if we had any information and the email address of the school counsellor. She said a perfunctory prayer for Ruby's safe return. It was a Catholic girls' school, St Clotilde's. Everything there happened under the sorrowful gaze of that ancient queen, who was rendered delicately above our heads in stained glass. We'd been told that her sons' feuding had threatened to divide the kingdom, making her the patron saint of brides, queens and disappointing children.

Later that week, we all watched the police escort Nico Costa – a student from the neighbouring boys' school – from tech rehearsals for our schools' joint production of *Oliver!* into their patrol car, which was parked in the driveway.

Of course, after that, rumours swirled that Nico had something to do with Ruby's disappearance. The two of them had dated for a couple of months, but she had recently broken it off with him. Fiona claimed she had seen them arguing at the school's gates a few weeks before Ruby disappeared. But Nico had allegedly been camping with his stepfather that weekend.

I spent all December thinking about Ruby. By mid-January, the investigation had begun to lose momentum.

Although she remained listed as a missing person, the police seemed to have downgraded the urgency of the case. At eighteen, Ruby wasn't classed as a vulnerable adult, and her history of running away had led officers to believe that she had likely left of her own accord. There were no signs of foul play – no body, no phone activity, no evidence of coercion – and without a clear lead or last known location, the investigation drifted into silence.

Still, not everyone was willing to give up. The school chaplain organized a candlelit vigil, gathering classmates, teachers and neighbours together to pray for Ruby's safe return. I attended out of curiosity and some strange sense of duty.

Her friend Soo-Jin – president and, by then, sole member of the school's Astronomy Society – read a cryptic poem that Ruby had once published in their shared zine. The choir sang, and everyone cried except for her grandfather, who remained stonily silent until the end of the service, when he stood up, pointed at Freya Mínervadóttir in the back pew and shouted, 'She knows! She knows!' Before he was escorted out, he yelled, 'Tell them what happened to my Ruby!'

If this were the 1600s, Freya was the kind of girl that Puritan villagers might have conspired to burn. She was the groundskeeper's blind daughter, and she was always hanging around, collecting rainwater in urns or leaving shards of bone inside mushroom circles. At eighteen, she was in Ruby's year. I saw her once, through the hatched window in the door, writing, 'But what makes it a monster?' on the whiteboard in our chemistry classroom.

She was almost six feet tall and had spectacular platinum hair, locks that curled like a nest of silver sand boas all the way down to her thighs.

I'd heard that she'd gouged her own eyes out with a tablespoon, that she had vanished for a couple of years and returned the same age, that she had the power to take away pain. By the time I joined St Clotilde's, she'd already amassed a small group of loyal followers: girls from the school, as well as mystics and misfits from the local area who would attend her self-proclaimed 'healing sessions' and night vigils. That year, the chaplain had broken up a gathering of forty in the woods at the end of the school's grounds and said that St Clotilde's was no place 'for the occult'.

In spite of the warnings, the sessions had continued in an abandoned church somewhere in Wandsworth, drawing crowds. Ruby's grandfather claimed that she had been among them. Immediately after breaking up with Nico, she had begun dating Laurie St James. He and his sister Beth were loyal followers of Freya's. Two months after Ruby's disappearance, I'd heard Beth in a music practice room, explaining to Amy Snape, the fifth-form pianist, how Freya could heal the tendonitis that had seen her struck from that term's musical.

'Is it true what they say about her?' Amy had asked in a breathy whisper.

'Everything,' Beth promised.

'Have you seen it?'

'I've *felt* it.'

I was trying not to seem like I was eavesdropping, while examining a broken saxophone reed.

'Is it true that she can ... ?' I imagined Amy making some kind of a gesture with her bandaged hand. A silence. Did Beth nod?

'You've seen it?' Amy asked.

Beth whispered, 'Yes! It was only *this* much off the ground, but . . .'

A soft gasp from Amy. 'But still.'

'Yeah, still . . .'

I dropped the box of reeds then, and the crash halted their conversation. I cursed myself for it, but later that evening, after school, I saw Soo-Jin, Beth and Amy greet a group at the school gates, climb into a dark car and drive away.

Curiosity overtook me at the sight of them speeding down the road. I could see Amy in the rear window. Her stringy ginger hair which she liked to suck. During practice, I would watch as sticky globs of saliva dripped onto her starched collar.

After Ruby's grandfather's accusation at the vigil, the police reportedly brought Freya and a couple of members of her group in for questioning, but they were quickly dismissed and then Amy was somehow on the summer term's production list for *Into the Woods*, playing Sondheim's impossible counterpoint on the piano, her tendons healed.

As the months passed, I became convinced that whatever had happened to Ruby had to do with Freya and the Group. I waited to hear that Freya had been charged with murder, or that Soo-Jin had finally broken and led the police to some shallow ha-ha ditch where Ruby's body was decomposing. Maybe Beth knew that there was a dungeon-like grow house where Ruby languished in a sedated stupor.

After the Easter holiday, everyone seemed to have decided that Ruby was dead. Students decorated her locker with paper cranes, cards and flowers. For a while, theories abounded. The usual: suicide, homicide. She had liked a picture of Wat Rong Khun; perhaps she had saved up money from her weekend job at Waterstones and used it to run away to Thailand? A vocal minority believed that she had been abducted by aliens.

Anyway, in May our exams were coming up. All the flowers on Ruby's locker wilted and shrivelled and were swept away. By June, it was almost as if it had never happened.

For everyone but me.

Five days before Aaliyah's wedding, I discovered Freya asleep on the grass behind the swimming pool. Curled like a foetus in the gloaming.

'What happened to Ruby?' I asked, hoping that catching her by surprise would startle the truth from her.

She rolled over slowly. It was the closest I'd ever been to her. To the scarred craters where her eyes would have been.

She stood, with some effort. Her skin was translucent, and I could see the blue vessels that spidered beneath it. Her unusual height meant that she was almost a head taller than me.

'Can I?' She held out her hands, lifted my head between them, ran her fingers along the low bridge of my nose, my cheekbones with their smattering of pimples that I'd covered with blue, daisy-shaped blemish stickers, my hair which I had bleached – to Mum's horror – and dyed pale pink that summer and was fashioning in space buns on top of my head.

'Briar Minton,' she said with a smile of recognition. It sounded like a spell in her mouth.

She put her hand on my forehead as if checking for a fever. 'There's something in there.' I stepped away quickly. 'Oh no,' she said, 'it's your mother . . .'

'What?'

'Something's sickened her.'

'That's ... not true.' I was discomfited by her mention of Kim, but thought she was distracting me, as a magician might. I asked again, 'What happened to Ruby?'

Her demeanour stiffened subtly.

'Have you ever seen an impossible thing?' she asked.

I was the granddaughter of a pastor. I'd grown up hearing about miracles, healings, prophecy, resurrection. I used to think that God spoke to me. I enjoyed a certain enchantment that faded by the time I turned thirteen and noticed that for years all I'd heard was silence.

'No,' I told her.

'Really?' Freya probed. While our mother was gone, Dad stopped taking us to our grandfather's church, Providence House. By that summer, I'd defaulted into an arid agnosticism that – at times of crisis – had offered me no comfort at all. 'What about last April?'

I frowned and then recoiled in surprise at the specificity of Freya's knowledge. It was as if she had reached her cool fingers into my psyche and pulled the memory out unbidden.

Around the Easter holidays, the year before, Tanice had shown me a video which had just gone viral. I remembered it vividly because Tanice had screamed when she saw it.

Have you ever seen an impossible thing? The video is called 'Man levitates outside the 42nd Street Y'. He has a beard and shaggy sable hair. He wears oil-stained jeans that are scuffed to shreds at the ankles and a polyester jacket that was once black. He's not floating very far off the ground. But it's far enough to see the light peer right underneath the soles of his battered trainers.

No way to explain it. He isn't holding anything, there are no wires that anyone can see. Tanice and I kept rewinding it and watching it backward, at .5 speed. The thing that makes it feel real is the reaction of the people around him. It's a crowded street. A woman in heels struts past, turns as if checking him out, then squints, confused. Someone drops her bags. Someone else reflexively makes the sign of the cross as if to ward away a demon. A man points and laughs, then, after examining further, leans over and vomits. That's how the clip ends. A kind of horror dawning in the face of every onlooker. The comments beneath read 'WTAF?' and 'Who *is* this guy?' Apparently, no one knows.

'Ruby didn't disappear,' Freya told me that evening, 'she was shifted.'

'What?' I squinted at her.

'You believe a body is solid, but Ruby was mostly empty space.'

That year, I'd been struggling through A-level physics, so I already understood this to be true.

'The atoms in her body were examined, including their positions, types, energy states and quantum properties, and converted into pure data.'

'What?' I said again. This claim seemed mind-blowingly wild. 'Like teleportation?'

'More elegant,' Freya clarified. 'Ruby was ready. Her waveforms collapsed. She became information.'

'So ... she died?' I probed.

'The ones who witnessed it say it was more like "transcendence". Her atoms have likely reassembled in a higher dimension. The fifth or maybe sixth. She's just pattern now, waiting.'

I didn't know what to say in response. I was so baffled by this claim that I simply turned around and began to walk back home.

'It happened to me!' Freya called out to my shadow.

When anyone asks me now, I tell them that I never believed any of it. Even after everything that happened. Except
that evening, when I walked past the crossing at Lavender
Hill where Ruby saved my life, I thought I could picture
it: onyx-eyed Ruby with her Rapunzel hair. She might
have smiled at me the way she had across the lunch queue.
She might have looked like a text bubble with the opacity
turned right down. Like the Cheshire Cat. Maybe I'd have
reacted like that man in the video, whose amusement cur-
dles abruptly into horror.

What would she have said – *It goes so fast* – as she
evaporated?

MARCUS MINTON – 4 DAYS BEFORE

'"*Your old men will dream dreams, your young men will see visions!*"' The man balanced on the upturned crate outside the Asda supermarket shouted into the afternoon sun. He had the kind of wild eyes that had seen civilizations rise and fall. He looked as if he'd lived too long to expect that anyone would believe him now.

Something about the man reminded Marcus of his father-in-law, my grandfather, Pastor Abiola. Except that instead of an Armani pinstripe, he wore a frayed gabardine raincoat. And whatever essential optimism the Pastor possessed – about the future of humanity and our condition – this man radiated the opposite.

'"*I will show wonders in the heavens and on the earth!*"' The man turned and pointed straight at Marcus, who gave him a wide berth on the way to the cash machine. He'd lived in this city long enough to know the protocol: don't make eye contact, don't respond, even to provocation.

That was the day that Dad discovered he was running out of money. Although he'd been withdrawing his daily maximum amount in order to store small denominations for future bartering, he'd thought he'd make it a couple of weeks longer on the insurance payouts and settlements, on the overdraft and credit card balances, but that afternoon, the ATM disgorged his card with a disappointed sound.

'"... *blood and fire* ..."'

He tried again with another, but the screen read 'Insufficient funds'.

Marcus swore under his breath.

'"... *billows of smoke* ..."'

He was almost at the shop's entrance when a delivery driver careened past, the wheels of his electric scooter skidding over the pavement, zigzagging between pedestrians, mainly pensioners and women with children at that time of day.

'"*The sun will be turned to darkness and the moon to blood* ..."'

'Hey, watch out!' Marcus shouted as he swerved by. 'You're not allowed to ride here!'

'"... *before the great and dreadful day of the—*"'

A crash. The driver collided with the old man, first with his rickety newspaper stand of handwritten tracts and then with the upturned plastic crate he'd been balancing on. He groaned as he hit the ground hard enough to break a hip, his pamphlets fluttering like confetti around him.

Marcus dove to his rescue, crouching down beside him. 'Are you all right?'

The delivery driver swore at both of them as he picked up his branded thermal bag and reattached it to his scooter. He looked like a teenager. *Too young*, Marcus thought, *to be working*. 'Move it!' the kid shouted through a bleeding lip as he leapt up and rode away.

'I'm all right,' the stranger wheezed, reaching for one of

the pamphlets that had landed in the gutter. Marcus helped to gather them up before too many were stepped on by passersby. 'Used to it,' the old man said. With real effort, he got to his feet.

Marcus examined one of the stepped-on tracts then. 'Enjoy it while it lasts!' read the cover of one, its title blocky word art that he'd clearly hand-drawn and then photocopied. A cursory flip through it revealed a couple of different headings: 'How long will the millennial reign last?'; 'How to reject the Mark of the Beast'.

'What were you talking about just then?' my father asked him, against his better judgement.

'"*And everyone who calls on the name of the Lord shall be saved*,"' the man replied.

'You said the sun would be turned to darkness . . .'

The man muttered something under his breath and turned back towards his newsstand.

'What did you mean?' Marcus pressed as he started to push rumpled leaflets back into the stand. 'A solar flare? An eclipse? The nuclear cloud?'

The man turned suddenly and grabbed Marcus's wrist, his bony fingers bird-light and cool.

'I woke up a couple of months ago,' he said, 'with a taste at the back of my mouth.'

'Like . . .' Marcus swallowed. 'Blood? Or copper?'

'Like dread.'

Supermarkets always made Marcus nervous. They reminded him what a thin bubble of civilization modern life was precariously balanced upon.

My father couldn't look at the garnet skins of vine-ripened tomatoes without considering the thousands of miles they had been air-freighted to reach the artificial, floodlit aisles of the store. He knew that the UK imported almost half of its food: bananas from Central America, grains and rice from Asia, out-of-season asparagus from Peru, wine from New Zealand.

I think the origins of Dad's prepping truly began during that first lockdown of 2020, when he'd seen the supermarket shelves empty and had felt that old childhood dread of hunger. Of empty cupboards and weeping fridge shelves, of pushing a fist into his gut to quiet its growling. My grandfather would tell his congregation about Filipino villagers who would offer ten per cent of every bag of rice to the Church. In a similar fashion, Marcus began to devote ten per cent of his budget in every food shop to his future self. Over time, he'd built up a store of non-perishable items to last our entire family more than a year.

If the people on the Reddit forums were to be believed, this could be his last shop for a while. His final chance to load up on the fresh foods, meats and veg that would be the first to vanish from the shelves in the face of disaster. Last chance to buy cooking oil, batteries and paracetamol, soap, water filters and dog food. Coffee, vitamins, duct tape and protein powder. The Butterkist popcorn that I loved, Dr Pepper and my favourite cereals. Pot Noodles and low-fat yoghurt for Tanice. A dozen packs of fizzy strawberry laces for Chantale. The baklava that Kim liked.

At the till, the cashier, a Black woman with a silver septum piercing, looked at him suspiciously. Eventually she asked, 'Are you him?' and Marcus felt sweat needle at the back of his neck. He didn't answer. Once she finished scanning all his items, the sum flashed up in electric green digits. £718.43. Flustered, he handed her his debit card.

'That police officer?' she continued. Ice crystallized in his veins as she pushed the card terminal over for him to type in his PIN. He shook his head. 'It says rejected.'

Marcus cursed himself. He'd forgotten that his account was empty.

She swung the device back around. It was the way she had said it. '*That* police officer', like something foul she'd discovered sticking to the sole of her shoe.

'Want to try again?' She reached for his card.

'No – I've got it,' Marcus said.

In the child seat of the shopping trolley was the duffle bag he had started bringing everywhere with him. Inside were wads of twenty- and fifty-pound notes, precisely counted and tied together with rubber bands. He calculated the sum quickly and handed it to her.

The cashier looked even more suspicious then. But Marcus kept his head down as he packed the last of his items, trying to shake off the nauseating sense that everyone in the supermarket was looking at him. That at any moment someone would shout at him and toss a paper cup of boiling black coffee at his head again. *Impossible*, he reminded himself. He'd grown a beard since then. Lost three kilograms.

Once he'd finished, he walked away quickly, but she called after him that he'd left his card in the reader. He leapt back to grab it – too late. She pulled the plastic out, and the embossed initials caught her eye. *M. Minton.*

'It *is* you,' she said, with chilly loathing in her voice. Her tone seized the attention of the people in the queue. Marcus felt the world rock a little under his feet.

He snatched his card and shoved it in his pocket in a hurry. Before he could leave, he heard her shout, 'Murderer!'

BRIAR MINTON – 3 DAYS BEFORE

It feels different every time. Sometimes my blood typhoons from my head to my gut. Sometimes I open my eyes and my face is plastered into a carpet. Or fluorescent lights sparkle like comets' tails and I hear voices. My sisters', most often. Time bends. I say things that I regret.

The first time it happened was on my thirteenth birthday. I watched as faces warped behind candlelight and fuchsia wax dripped rivulets into buttercream. The first thing I saw when I woke was my mum. The light fixture behind her made her look as if she was some violent goddess who could eat me whole.

Whenever you stand, an average of about eight hundred millilitres of blood wash down to your feet. Astronauts notice this acutely upon returning to Earth, especially after prolonged space flight; their blood pressure is lower, and they struggle to walk. Biologically speaking, gravity can be a challenge. It can take a while to adjust.

''scuse me? Excuse me? Can you hear me?'

'Does she need help?'

'Has anyone called an ambulance?'

Voices filtered into my consciousness.

'She said not to.'

Roar of traffic, shouts of school children, bikes and dogs. Limpid morning light.

'We're all we have,' I heard myself say.

A concerned, middle-aged woman in running gear leaned over me. My cheek was pressed into the wet concrete of the pavement, and a small crowd had gathered. A man in a navy suit pointed two fingers together and offered to check my pulse again. A woman with a pram was on the phone, describing the street to someone. A dog-walker offered me her chewed-on plastic water bottle. A couple of students in uniform were hovering awkwardly around. I immediately recognized them as members of Freya's Group. There was Bethany St James and her blonde brother, Laurie, with their matching buzz-cut blonde hair. Soo-Jin Lee and the red-headed contralto who was playing Jack in the school's production of *Into the Woods*. I guessed that the boys had been on their way to tech rehearsals for the summer play, as I had been.

'Where does it hurt?' Beth was leaning over me.

'My arm . . .' I mumbled.

I'd scraped the skin off my elbow, which was bleeding and felt as if someone was holding it over a stove. Beth took my hand, squeezed it tight.

'I'm taking it from you,' she said quietly. I felt the pain travelling up my arm, through my nerves and into the bones of my hands, fingertips, fingernails, finally replaced by a cool numbness. I let go and looked at my palm in surprise. She smiled.

'Maybe someone should take her to the nurse.' Soo-Jin was close behind her. We were on the corner of the

Common, a couple of metres from the school gates, where the tidal wave of pupils rushing for registration had stemmed abruptly into a trickle, the clearest sign that we were late. Soo-Jin looked stressed out about it, her eyes darting between me and the gate as if she was debating the merits of abandoning me to run.

'I can go myself.' It took some effort to peel myself off the ground. It had rained the previous night, and now half my blazer was wet.

'We'll take her to the nurse,' Beth reassured the adults, who dispersed reluctantly.

'Does this happen often?' asked Soo-Jin.

'All the time,' I said. It was a condition I'd had for a couple of years – postural orthostatic tachycardia syndrome.

'Do you see anything when it does?' the red-headed boy asked, and a stillness came over the four of them, a cautious attention.

'Sometimes,' I said carefully.

The cardiologist had called it an 'aura'. That Wednesday morning, before I collapsed, the sky had looked as if it was raining diamonds, and I'd seen sparkling clouds before the ground had heaved and my vision turned black. Soo-Jin flinched, Beth and Laurie shared a meaningful look.

'I can't always remember . . .' I hedged.

'Do you feel something . . .' Beth reached over to touch my chest, and I could feel the blood pulse in her thumbs and fingertips even through my school blouse. '. . . here?'

'Sometimes,' I repeated, swallowing.

'Does your watch always stop?' the boy asked. 'When it happens?' I stared at the frozen digital figures. It only took a rough shake for it to start again, but I was disconcerted.

A sudden embarrassment set in then, like a chill. I

mustered my strength to shake everyone off. 'Actually,' I declared, warmth rushing up to my face, 'I'm fine. Really.'

They looked at each other, unconvinced.

'I'm fine.' I tried to get up, but my legs still felt like jelly. 'I have a minor heart condition. It causes orthostatic hypotension. Causes me to faint sometimes. It gets better or worse ...' Worse, lately. I seemed to be having episodes every week.

'Do you take anything for it?' Soo-Jin asked.

'Yes,' I said, thinking of the blister pack of white pills I hadn't swallowed in weeks.

'Was your heart damaged?' asked the red-headed boy, who was staring at me the most intensely. I wasn't enjoying this questioning. I wanted to crawl out of my skin, to escape from the keen light of their gaze. I started walking off, towards the gates.

'Hey.' The red-headed boy started running after me. 'You forgot your bag.'

I didn't want to look at him, I just kept walking.

'Briar!' he called. 'Briar Minton!' I turned then, wondering how he knew my name.

'You don't remember me, do you?'

I stared. The boy was about my height, with rarely blinking blue eyes under brows and lashes that were so pale that, from a short distance away, they looked as if they'd fallen out. He wore a string of pearls under the collar of his school shirt and painted his nails black. He looked like a sickly egret that needed to be nursed back to health.

'I'm Anderson Xavier ... ? Axel?'

'From ...' My chest tightened as I registered the name.

'High Tower,' he said. Did the words still taste of high-calorie protein shakes, bile and bread buttered duvet-thick to him?

'How long has it been?' I asked.

'Four years, almost,' he said. 'I kept hoping I'd find you again.'

'We thought you'd died,' I said. The last time I'd seen him, he'd weighed less than six stone and had no hair; we'd all crowded around the window, our breath steaming on the glass as paramedics wheeled him into a shrieking ambulance.

'I did ...' He unbuttoned his shirt slightly to reveal a thick scar, which ran down the length of his sternum. There were little staple marks on either side of it, a sight that made me feel nauseous. 'I was dead. For five whole minutes. That was the first time it happened.'

'You look ...' I flailed for the word, 'better.' Then I hated myself for saying it. Even now, in recovery, I still hear the word 'better' as 'fatter'.

'I *am* better,' he said. 'And I'm ... thankful. Every day. They saved me.'

'Who?' I asked carefully.

Axel smiled as if he suspected I already knew the answer. 'Briar!' he said. 'The Tau.'

I used to have this black canvas tote bag that said 'I'm with Sondheim'. Mum bought it for me from the theatre during a West End revival of *Follies*. For a long time, Stephen Sondheim wasn't just a person to me, he was a hero. His musicals were a place I could retreat to. Victorian London, the Upper West Side, Ancient Rome. There was the summer of *Follies*, where I performed the whole thing from beginning to end in my bedroom, in front of the mirror, almost every afternoon. Later that year, in autumn, I was obsessed with *West Side Story* and couldn't get out of the car in an underground parking lot without thinking of Riff commanding the sweaty gang of Jets to be 'cool' after that murder. The first time I was hospitalized was during the winter of *Sweeney Todd*, when I'd gaze out at the parking lot and imagine myself the imprisoned Johanna.

Axel was one of the few boys on our ward at High Tower, and he was the first person I met who loved Sondheim as much as I did. I'd first heard him singing in the toilet stalls. A contralto, with a voice bright and lovely as quicksilver. Axel was singing 'Giants in the Sky' from *Into the Woods*, the ballad that Jack performs after his descent from the beanstalk, a song full of the dread and awe of the newly discovered realm beyond the clouds. I had loved to sing it on my own, it felt like skating down a trick staircase, surprising and then exhilarating. At some point, every pre-teen boy involved in musical theatre will have to perform it. To sing that song well, though, is to do something astonishing. And he did.

I crept into the bathroom stall next to his, but as soon as he heard the creak of the door, he stopped. Desperate to make a friend in that place where I'd felt so lonely, I started humming the saxophone part to 'It Takes Two', the song that the Baker and his wife sing when they discover they'll need to work together to break the curse. I hummed the first bars quietly at first, but then he joined in and started singing again.

When I was younger, I used to believe that there was a country where all the musicals were filmed. Some utopian community where every citizen sang and the sky was Technicolour and magic was real. I was poised and practised, ready to fit right in. Singing with Axel felt the way I'd imagined it would to flee there. I still remember the glimpse

I caught of his bare feet on the linoleum. The white marbles of his toes, which he clenched when he sang, the blue veins that spidered up his high arches. It was a delight to hear our final harmony echo off the stalls. We burst out laughing and threw open the doors.

In the movies, I always wonder about the seconds after the song ends. Often, the scene cuts. Sometimes the actors shake off their final posture, slip back into dialogue, climb off their pedestals and continue with their day. In *Seven Brides for Seven Brothers*, after the women sing about getting married in June, pirouetting under the farmhouse rafters, they freeze in a final pose like porcelain dolls. After the camera fades to black, do they turn to each other and giggle hysterically? Or do they leave with a morning-after kind of embarrassment, as if waking from a dream, a shared madness evaporating?

Axel kissed me. When I told Tanice about it later, it had been impossible to explain that he hadn't kissed *me*. He had kissed the Baker's wife, who had been growing weary with monotony, disappointed by her childlessness.

Axel stepped back. Under his ruffled painter's shirt, he was all bones. He looked a lot sicker than I did, I noticed with – I'm ashamed to admit it now – a pang of jealousy. He'd managed to lose a huge amount of weight before his parents noticed. He'd been sectioned, put on feeding tubes, in and out of hospital, and by the time he'd found his way to High Tower he looked like a prisoner of war. Impossibly thin, maybe the thinnest person I'd seen alive.

I blushed, my heart beating wildly. I searched for something to say. 'Don't you think that Jack's actually the villain?' Axel smiled, and I saw that he'd lost one of his front teeth. 'So,' I continued, 'he breaks into a house and sees this giant woman—'

'A "terrible" giant woman,' Axel reminded me.

'According to Jack. Maybe she was just an ordinary giant woman? And she was kind to him! It's Jack who was terrible. He stole her hen and killed her husband.'

'Self-defence,' Axel said, 'or . . .' He shrugged in concession. 'Maybe Jack was just dumb.' He pulled a vape pen, the fluorescent yellow of a highlighter, from the pocket of his pink corduroys. 'Do you mind?' he asked. I shook my head and watched his grey tongue as he blew three perfect candy-floss-flavoured smoke rings in my direction.

'That's not it,' I said, about Jack. 'He mistook kindness for permission.'

In real life, we were only friends for about ten days. And only in the bathroom, where Axel would vape and we'd sing together. At mealtimes, we didn't know each other. Meals at High Tower were always tense. They mostly passed in a silent hour where we slowly ate whatever the nutritionists ordained be put in front of us. Meals several times the size of what we'd forced our bodies to grow used to. Axel and I never spoke to each other then; we didn't even make eye contact.

One night, the sound of sirens lanced my dreams. I shared a room with Joanne Ridley, who claimed she never slept more than ninety minutes at a time because she was always cold.

'Who do you think it is?' I asked blearily. Joanne just shook her head, her hazel eyes flashing in the moonlight.

In the hall, all the lights were on, doors were open and a couple of people were shouting. We crowded around the bay window in the rec room and watched as his limp body was pulled on a gurney into the shining maw of the ambulance.

Axel may be one of the reasons I decided to get better.

This is the prize for being the thinnest, I'd realized then. A hospital bed, a mortuary slab, a grave.

That Wednesday, by the school gates, Axel explained how his life had changed that night, too. That he'd had a personal encounter with an alien consciousness. Although the tale seemed absurd to me, it was difficult to deny the obvious change I could see in him.

'What did it feel like?' I asked. He paused for a moment; he looked like a time traveller trying to describe the birth of a star.

'Love,' he said, 'awe, terror. I felt like They knew me, had been watching me with keen interest. They didn't just want me to recover, They wished for absolute healing. No more pain, no more despair. I woke with something like a ... *knowing*. Meaning I longed for but hadn't hoped to find in this life. And as the nurses and the doctors intubated me and put me back under, I could hear the blood in my ears and Their hope making it possible: *live, live, live.*'

'Wow,' I said, moved and concerned. His story had the cadence of a testimony. The kind that the happy congregants at Providence House would line up to deliver.

'And that's what ... all of you ...?' I was astonished to discover this new fact about Freya's Group.

'We've all had some kind of experience with Them, yeah.'

'And Ruby, too?'

He looked surprised that I'd mentioned her, and the silence expanded.

'Yes, Ruby, too,' he eventually replied.

Axel could answer all of my questions about 'Them', a race of beings whose peaceful interplanetary empire spanned the solar system around one of the most luminous stars in the Andromeda Galaxy, 2.5 million light-years from Earth. Axel claimed that their home planet was called M31-AF-614b, though the group had shortened it to M31. Axel explained what a miracle it was that They had evolved at all on a planet so uniquely uninhabitable: an ice giant, far enough from its main sequence star that methane condenses in its upper atmosphere into clouds that roil in perpetual storms. If you were to lance a probe through them, you'd discover that as temperatures soar, methane breaks apart, releasing carbon molecules that bond into graphite. Further down, intense pressures and heat from the planet's core squeeze the graphite into diamonds, which fall like glittering hailstones, plunging through the atmosphere until they eventually vaporise or accumulate in molten diamond oceans on the surface.

'How can the Tau survive that?' I asked, arrested by the image. How the storm-laden sky would dazzle as lightning glittered off diamond hailstones.

Axel explained that the Tau were five-dimensional beings who had developed as a conscious neural network in vents in the ground – think something like the biofilm that might float like scum on the surface of a pond. 'Or actually,' he quickly corrected himself, 'don't think of Them at all.' Imagine communion with another mind. One that sleeps for thousands of years in the chaotic dark, has traversed the universe on the backs of meteorites, is watching Earthlings with the loving attention of a beekeeper, waiting to make contact.

'And They *do*?' I said.

'With a select few,' Axel explained. 'And only sometimes.'

He said that it normally took a near-death experience, or NDE, for them to be able to make contact. Apparently, during an NDE, the brain is prised open, and they can speak directly into it, fold a human consciousness through time and space, over vast distances or thousands of years – although their favourite thing to do was pull the person back through their own life.

'That's why you see it flash before your eyes.'

'Is that what happened to you?' I asked.

Axel nodded. 'Time collapsed. I witnessed entire millennia. I saw the heat death of the universe. But you know what I mean, don't you?' He looked at me then, invited me into his confidence.

'What?'

'Well, doesn't it happen to you?' The tone of his voice implied something recent. I realized that he was referring to the fainting incident.

Suddenly, I spied an opening. A way into the Group. If I claimed to be one of them, I could get to know them better and hopefully discover what had happened to Ruby. Maybe uncover some evidence about her disappearance, bring her back or, at the very least, seek justice. It felt important to me that someone carried on looking for her, even though her case had been abandoned.

I nodded. And this is how it began.

TANICE MINTON – 2 DAYS BEFORE

Tanice could tell it was about to happen before I did. She'd seen it more times than she cared to count.

'What should I say?' I asked.

'Anything!' Carmen, Aaliyah's heavily pregnant maid of honour, shouted from halfway down the aisle. 'We're just testing the sound system.'

Tanice was distracted, staring at her phone.

'I could tell you about the planet,' I said into the crackling mic.

I was standing in front of the lectern, which was set up under the pergola, its pine rafters heavy with wisteria, lilac stalactites in full bloom. Lines of chairs stretched back across the grass. Chantale and Tanice were seated in the front row. It was a beautiful set-up for an outdoor wedding, on the grounds of Aaliyah's future in-laws' Buckinghamshire estate. Glassford House, they called it. Tanice had let out a low whistle that morning when our car pulled up on the shingle drive.

'Lucky Lia,' she'd said at the sight of it, a white-stuccoed mansion that looked like a buttercream cake in the June sun.

'Lucky Hugo,' Dad had replied. Aaliyah's fiancé.

The rehearsal was taking place on one of the vast lawns. In less than forty-eight hours, a hundred and fifty guests would be gathered on it. Chantale, Tanice and I would march up the aisle to the sound of the string quartet exactly the way we had spent the evening practising.

Chantale sneezed theatrically, projecting little droplets of spittle all over Tanice's face.

'Quit it!' Tanice snapped, shoving her.

'Hay fever!' Chantale said.

Tanice's eyes were beginning to feel like sandpaper as well. She'd had enough of everyone by then. The heat, which hadn't let up even as the day waned; the muggy air; the suffocating tension between our family and Aaliyah's in-laws. We'd learned that morning that Hugo's parents were on a wine-tasting holiday in Provence and wouldn't be back in time for the wedding. They'd said something about a new virus variant – we'd not met them yet, but they were old, in their seventies apparently, and had been convalescing from a couple of illnesses in the warmer climate. Everyone suspected that they were actually just disappointed by the match. Their son and our sister.

'You're not close enough to the mic!' shouted Carmen. She was Aaliyah's school friend and had also appointed herself wedding planner, taking her maid of honour duties to the extreme.

I had to stand on my tiptoes to reach it. My bottom lip brushed the cool grating on its head, making my voice sound breathy and tremulous over the speaker system.

I said, 'Another time of year, another half a million miles, and Hero would have been on a collision course with Earth. Instead, it will pass us by at escape velocity. It will slingshot around the sun and then it will be gone forever.'

Tanice's phone vibrated in her borrowed clutch purse, and she scrambled for it. A message, finally.

'Is it your boyfriend?' Chantale asked.

'Shut up,' Tanice said. It was. I'd suspected that Tanice had been dating someone for a little while. She'd been glued to her phone more than usual. She kept slipping off after school or breaking curfew and sneaking into the house late somehow without setting off any of our dad's over-sensitive alarm systems. That spring, I'd accidentally picked up her school blazer instead of mine, and the jagged foil edge of a Durex wrapper slipped out.

She'd been compulsively checking her phone all afternoon. She and Sydney were in the middle of an argument, and when she had called him to try to make up, he'd ignored her, simply texting 'Working tonight. Busy.' He was a waiter for an events company. Tanice couldn't shake the feeling that he was avoiding her.

'Did you see that?' Chantale grabbed her shoulder and pointed up at the overcast clouds.

'What?'

'Something just fell from the sky.'

But Tanice was distracted then by the sight of me. Silver sheen of sweat on my upper lip, a kind of faraway look in my eyes.

I continued. 'By tomorrow night, we'll be able to see it. By next week, it will be visible in the daytime.'

Tanice could hear my breathing coming more heavily through the speaker system.

'Who will we be when it arrives?' I said. 'Will anything change . . .' Then, my mouth was too far away from the mic for anyone but my sisters in the front row to hear. '. . . after?'

I don't remember this, of course, but the way that Tanice

described it, my eyes drifted up to where Chantale had pointed. As if some absence in the sky seemed to hold my attention for a breathless moment before I collapsed like a string puppet on the ground, my head bashing the lectern with a sound that made everyone wince.

Aaliyah had returned home from her hen party the night before the rehearsal. Tanice heard her crying in her bedroom early that morning and crept in to check on her. She couldn't shake the strange sense of trespass as she pushed the door open. Whenever Aaliyah was away, the room seemed to take on the status of a museum. There was our oldest sister on the cover of a couple of teen magazines, newspaper cuttings, print-outs. Tennis trophies glittered under a string of fairy lights, burnished salvers and gilt cups, a signed racket, gathering dust. Aaliyah kept it locked when she travelled – correctly convinced that Tanice would try to steal her things.

'These are happy tears,' Aaliyah said, on seeing Tanice in the doorway. She was curled on her patchwork quilt, wearing our mother's wedding dress. Checking the fit, one final time. Tanice had only ever seen it in pictures. Kimona's dark collarbones between the swooping neckline of that delicately embroidered bodice, ivory charmeuse, a storm cloud of soft tulle. On the bed, the dress was a magnificent explosion.

Aaliyah had done her makeup already, and her mascara stained inky trails onto her pillow.

'That's okay, then.' Tanice entered the room tentatively and shut the door behind her. 'If they're happy.'

One of Aaliyah's false lashes had slipped off and was hanging like a third eye on the pillowcase. Tanice climbed into bed with our sister, forded layers of lace and tulle to wrap her arms around her. Breathed in the smell of her. The base notes of her perfume, musk and mandarin and something sweet.

'I'm happy you're home,' Tanice said.

'Me, too,' Aaliyah said.

There were some girls – like thoroughbred-obsessed Emily Blackwell, or Flick Ashbourne, who had little diamond earrings it was rumoured her mother stored in the family safe at night – that Tanice imagined had emerged from the womb destined to marry a man like Hugo. She had never thought that Aaliyah was one of them.

Tanice had imagined that our eldest sister might elope with that tennis star she'd been photographed kissing after a match, or that tattooed musician she'd travelled to Bali with. Not someone like Hugo, who worked in 'insurance-something-something' as Tanice always described it. Ham-faced Hugo, whose small talk was almost aggressively boring. He was sallow and as portly as someone who slathered his toast with cognac butter. Once, during a family picture, his hand had accidentally brushed against hers, and Tanice had felt the soft, uncalloused fingers of a person who only ever touched tempered glass and butterfly keys, Egyptian cotton and eiderdown.

Hugo had the breezy confidence of someone to whom nothing bad had ever happened. He was sure that everyone 'meant well really' or that everything would 'come good in the end'. And maybe it would, for him.

'D'you remember,' Tanice asked, 'all those Christmases when we'd walk Digit past the big houses by the Common?' The ten-foot fir trees and all the presents they could see through the windows. 'The way we'd tell each other stories of the people who lived in them?'

'I still catch myself doing that sometimes,' Aaliyah confessed. 'I used to think that they must be the happiest people in the world.'

'And by Sunday,' Tanice reminded her, 'you'll be one of them.'

Aaliyah was silent for a moment.

'Right,' she replied after a pause, wiping her eye. Maybe she was thinking, then, about her registry. That Tiffany Blue De'Longhi toaster she had wanted for so long. She and Hugo had argued over which Le Creuset Dutch oven to list when the woman at Selfridges had said, 'They're great. I registered for one, too. Lasted longer than my marriage.'

'Maybe you'll have everything,' Tanice said.

'That's what I want,' Aaliyah laughed then. 'Everything.'

At the wedding rehearsal, Carmen screamed at the sight of my blood smeared across the lectern.

Everyone rushed to action.

Mum was first, getting up from her seat and striding imperiously up the aisle. 'Give her room,' she commanded.

The string quartet, who had been practising, sputtered to a halt. I was slumped on the grass, blood matting my hair.

'This happens all the time,' Tanice said, as everyone apart from our mother took a step back.

'Really?' the photographer – a skinny white man with dreadlocks – asked with a frown.

'Can someone get some water!' Carmen demanded with a wave of a hand.

'Can someone call a doctor?' another person asked.

'I thought that *she* was a doctor.'

'She just needs a minute.' Mum was by my side then, her hand on my face. She looked tender.

'Yeah,' Tanice said, 'Briar's "blackouts". They used to happen all the time. At church or the dentist's office. At school once, in assembly.' Tanice shuddered at the recollection. 'In front of *everyone*. I used to think she was doing it for attention.' There was a crowd around me by then. 'I really think that if she took control of how weird she allows herself to be, life would get a lot better for her. And me.'

'Urgh ...' The photographer grimaced and sat down heavily.

'Are you okay?' Tanice felt obliged to ask.

He took a deep breath and said, 'It's just all the blood, you know. I'm not good with blood.'

'Yeah ...' Tanice did feel a little concerned when she glanced at the lectern. 'My dad's the same.'

'They say that head wounds bleed the most.'

'She shouldn't fall asleep, isn't that right?' Carmen was kneeling near the lectern, nodding at Kim for approval. 'Think of something happy, Briar. What makes you happy?'

'The Fol-lies,' Tanice claims she heard me mutter.

'Aren't you supposed to be getting ice or towels or something?' Eugenia, Hugo's sister, appeared behind her, holding her phone as if it was a sword.

'Am I?' Tanice asked.

'Make yourself useful,' she snapped.

Tanice bristled slightly as she headed towards the house. Her heels kept sinking into the lawn. Finally, she took them off and strolled barefoot up the majestic limestone steps which led to the house.

The door was open, and Tanice stood, sunblind for a moment, in the double-storeyed atrium. Rich people's houses always smelled lovely. There was a dramatic floral display on the marble-topped console table to her left. Mock orange and stargazer lilies listed open.

Someone was having an argument in the billiards room. Through the gap in the door, she could see Paris, Hugo's younger cousin. He looked like Gatsby, in a pink seersucker suit and dark aviators, a film of sweat on his upper lip.

'You're really going to go through with this?' he was saying.

'Of course.' It was Aaliyah's voice behind the door. Tanice shifted to get a better view. Lia was leaning over the billiards table, turned away from him. Her backless ivory gown gave the impression that she was half-naked from Tanice's vantage point, the bones in her spine subtly visible. 'There's only forwards now. By this time on Saturday . . .'

Paris touched her back. 'Or we get in a car and just drive. By this time tomorrow, we're in Saint-Tropez drinking Aperol and letting our phones sink in the Riviera.'

Aaliyah flinched. His hand moved down.

'We post "Wedding cancelled because of cold feet" on your fancy website, take a train to Gatwick, by this time tomorrow we're in the Masai Mara watching zebra from a 4x4.'

Aaliyah shook him off like a bad dream and stepped back.

'All these people are coming. A hundred and fifty. Some of them are here already. And the flowers were so expensive. And my parents—'

'Come on, Lia,' Paris said.

'Maybe we take a bus back in time,' she said, 'and I see myself coming off-piste at Cortina and grab myself before I can fall.' She touched the jagged scar at the base of her wrist. Paris was silent for a moment.

Aaliyah's hazel eyes flickered up, and Tanice ducked

away. Too late, though. For a brief moment, the sisters made
eye contact.

'You little—!' Aaliyah rushed to the door, her teeth gritted in a familiar fury. Tanice tried to run but, in her haste,
tripped, and they found her on all fours on the rug.

'Tanice.' Paris glanced worriedly out at the sunlit lawn.
'Aren't you supposed to be—?'

'Briar had an accident when they were doing the sound
testing,' she blurted out.

Aaliyah's face was flushed.

'Is she all right?' Paris asked.

'She hit her head. There's a lot of blood. Eugenia told me
to get ice or something.'

'I think there's a first aid kit in the ...' His eyes drifted
down the hall. 'I'll get it.' He turned to Aaliyah before he
left. 'I meant what I said.'

There was a stormy look in Aaliyah's eyes as she pulled
her sister into the billiards room. They listened to the echo
of Paris's shoes as he disappeared.

'You didn't ... ?' Aaliyah ventured, a rill of sweat rolling
down her temple. Tanice affected a clueless innocence.

'What?'

Aaliyah stared at her. The way she had, years ago, when
she'd discovered Tanice's infuriating habit of picking up the
downstairs landline and eavesdropping on phone calls. We
all hated her for that.

'It was just ... talk,' she admitted feebly. Tanice shrugged
as if she had no idea what our sister was referring to.
'Anyway.' Aaliyah glanced back out at the hall, where the
sunlight streamed in. 'What happened?'

'That fainting thing.'

'I thought Briar had grown out of that,' Aaliyah said,

turning to the window, where the porters were setting up for the al fresco rehearsal dinner. Tanice could see them through the gap in the velvet curtains, wheeling out iced buckets of drinks and lush flower arrangements. Apparently, Eugenia took great pride in her 'tablescaping' and had printed a couple of diagrams for them to follow.

'Guess not,' Tanice said to Aaliyah's reflection in the glass.

People were always complimenting Aaliyah on her looks. She had skin like silt, smattered with freckles. Eyes that were almost green in the right light. Our nan – Marcus's mother – had said once, watching her on television, her voice light with wonder, 'With her hair like that' – straightened and pulled up tightly behind a sweatband – 'you'd never be able to tell.'

'Tell what?' Tanice had asked, and our grandmother had caught herself. Blushed a little. It was a chameleon trick that Tanice, who looked the most like our mother, whose hair grew in the tightest jet curls, would never be able to pull off. Did she want to? Only sometimes. Only when she beheld the magnificent facade of Glassford House and thought, *Of course Lia, green-eyed Aaliyah, she of the 'good hair', would stumble into this inheritance.*

Tanice had decided long ago that she would never marry for love. 'Is this what "love" gets you?' she would say to our mother when she caught her biting her nails over a credit card bill. Or arguing with our father over the hole in the roof. As soon as she was old enough, Tanice hoped to marry for something she could hold on to. Money. Or fame. Or a Spanish colonial in Montecito. She'd explained this to Sydney when she first met him.

Sydney, who had nothing at all, not even a father.

For a long time, I didn't understand what could possibly have drawn the two of them together. Had they encountered each other by chance or had she sought him out?

Tanice told me that they'd met just after the incident at our father's work the previous summer, when she had decided to change her name and pretend she was from a different family.

She'd joined the local girls' basketball team, cornrowed her hair and wouldn't acknowledge any of us if we ever waved at her when she was with her new friends on the court, leaning against the hot chain-link or practising a viral dance or sharing a paper box of off-brand chicken after a match.

Her basketball friends knew Sydney because his father had been an elder at the local Baptist church. He'd achieved an unlucky fame among them, and they'd lower their gaze if they ever mentioned him.

Tanice must have seen him, too, on the news, making a statement after his father died. A lonely pallbearer in faded black.

Sydney was tall and uniquely cool. He wore oversized turquoise glasses and dashikis, or jumpers with slogans like 'Black – by popular demand'. He had melancholy eyes and a hi-top fade. He wanted to be a cinematographer. He searched antique stores and charity shops, eBay and market stalls, for old film cameras, which he repaired.

She'd met him before a match once, at a bus stop outside the leisure centre. When he'd asked, 'Are you ... ?' she had told him her made-up name. When he said, 'But you look familiar,' she replied, 'I will be,' and smiled her lip-glossy smile. 'I'm going to be famous.'

He'd laughed. He was three years older, an age gap that might as well have been ten to her.

'I'll remember that when I see you again.'

'That's good,' Tanice had said, 'I won't.'

He'd been surprised to bump into her later, sitting on benches by the court's chain-link fence, gossiping with her friends. He came over to congratulate her – their team had come third in the competition. They were all wearing their medals around their necks, putting on their makeup, still humming the victory song they'd invented, breaking into spontaneous harmonies and excited laughter, still jittery from adrenaline and Pepsi Max.

'Hey, —.' He'd said her made-up name. The one all the girls knew her by. Every person who said it made it more true. Sydney was holding a restored SLR camera and, when she turned to him, he'd snapped a picture of her.

'I wasn't ready!' she said.

'I know,' he laughed.

She held onto that photograph, though. With half of her makeup applied, she looked as if she was wearing half a mask. One eye glittering with eyeshadow, the other flashing with vulnerability. Acne-scarred cheekbones, her lips parted in a moment of particular loveliness.

Does it count as love when you're sixteen? Tanice said it did. She said it happened like a fever, all at once. She knew it would be a mistake, but she'd been wilful and foolish, tempted by a dream. She couldn't explain it, but when she was with him, she didn't have to be a Minton and she didn't have to be ashamed.

By the time she returned with a bowl of ice, everyone was gone. The house staff had wiped the blood off the hard edge of the lectern and the exposed wood of the pergola. You could only see it if you looked for it, a dark patch on the ground. The guests were gathered on the patio for the rehearsal dinner. The jazz band was playing 'I've Got You Under My Skin'. Stars were erupting in the sky, and Tanice thought she could see Hero – she was wrong, of course, she was looking at Polaris – hurtling towards us.

The night before the rehearsal dinner, Sydney and Tanice had argued. He'd revealed to her that he often fantasized about killing the person responsible for his father's death. Imagined turning up at his door with an Amazon parcel and a baseball bat or mowing him down with his uncle's truck. The conversation had felt like slipping on black ice. It had turned quickly into a fight, and Tanice had hit him – not hard, she insisted – then regretted it immediately. Had sent him a couple of rambling voice notes apologizing.

Her phone buzzed again, and her heart fluttered. It was only Mum, though, wondering where she was. Disappointed, Tanice made her way over to the party. Although the shadows were lengthening in the garden around her, the dinner area was forgivingly illuminated by candlelight, brushed bronze candelabras and the colourful paper lanterns strung between trees and wooden posts, swaying gently in the wind. The trestle tables were elaborately decorated with lace appliqué linens and fresh-cut wildflowers – purple loosestrife, meadowsweet and foxgloves – in fluted vases.

Aaliyah's shoulder blades were sharply defined above the low back of her dress. She and Hugo were seated at the head of the table. Her fiancé looked so happy, holding our sister's hand.

Eugenia was on their right, in a hydrangea-print summer dress that matched the placemats. Carmen sat with her husband, Paris, holding his hand under her rib with a smile, so he could feel the baby move. Opposite them was our family.

Mum looked queenly in her kente cloth dress, with her hair
tied up in a scarf. Heavy diamanté earrings that glittered
like chandeliers. I was slumped next to her, already holding
a bag of frozen peas to my head, which Tanice registered
with annoyance, discarding her bowl of ice on the nearest
serving table. Chantale was on her iPad, and there was an
empty seat between her and Dad. He always managed to
appear scruffy, even on the rare occasions where he took
the time to get ready in the morning. His salt-and-pepper
hair had come loose of the gel he'd applied, and he wore
a black shirt under a sports coat that meant he kept being
mistaken for a waiter.

From that vantage point, though, in that golden hour, we
almost looked happy.

Marcus stood as the song finished and raised his glass
for the first toast. Nearby, Tanice heard one of the catering
managers scolding the staff because he could see that not
everyone had a champagne glass yet.

Something made her want to slink back into the house
or to retreat entirely. Back home, back to the new friends
she'd made who didn't know her real name, back to Sydney,
whose forgiveness she longed for. Mum had spied her,
though, and flashed her a look of irritated impatience.
Tanice knew that she should be sitting with us. She should
be shading her eyes from the setting sun and watching our
dad raise his glass of tonic water – he had stopped drinking
by then – to the couple.

'Whenever people told us, "Marriage is hard,"' Marcus
began, sweat beading on his upper lip, his thrifted tweed
jacket the wrong choice for the weather, 'I'd think, "For
you". I was sure it would be different for us.' Kimona
winced at that. 'And now ...' His smile faltered.

Everything is different now, Tanice thought.

'Hey, —.' A voice she recognized behind her, dulcet baritone. He said the name that she had made up, and she turned.

'Sydney?' He was dressed in a black shirt and trousers. Holding a tray of champagne, he regarded her with happy surprise. Their argument was temporarily forgotten.

'What are you doing here?' he asked.

'I—' Tanice reflected his joy for half a second before her blood turned to ice. 'What are *you* ...?' Maybe there's a moment, just before, when your brain registers the trajectory of a turn, calculates the braking speed, long enough to know that a car crash is about to happen but not long enough to stop it.

He said, 'I told you I was working tonight.'

'Right.'

'Do you know ...?'

'To the happy couple!' Our father's voice filtered in behind them. 'May it last forever!'

The sound of cheers and applause, shouts and laughter came up like a wave. At the sight of our father, Sydney turned grey. He would have seen Marcus before. On TV. In court. Many times during the uncertain months before he was officially discharged. Tanice had even seen his face at the supermarket on the cover of the *Daily Mail*. 'People like that make me sick,' the shop assistant had said. So had the girls on her basketball team who didn't know her name ('Fuck the police, right?' 'Yeah ... sure.').

Sydney's hands stopped working, and he let his steel tray of champagne flutes clatter to the floor. An explosion of glass and wine like Molotov cocktails. Everyone turned.

Tanice reached out to grab him, too late. He bounded

forward, hurdled over the table and slammed Marcus's body onto the ground. Blood spilled from Marcus's nose. Sydney was taller than him, but our father was twice as strong. Everything in him was always coiled like a spring, anticipating an attack. It wasn't long before he'd tackled Sydney to the ground, pinned his arms down, pushed an elbow into his throat.

Everyone was screaming by then. Aaliyah tore her dress as she jumped up suddenly, catching it under a chair leg. Chantale dropped her iPad and watched in horror as its screen splintered under someone's stiletto. Tanice jumped on top of Marcus and tried in vain to pull him off.

'Dad! No!' His back felt like a brick wall.

Sydney spat in Marcus's eye, and Marcus let out a roar of long-stifled rage.

'Marcus!' Kim grabbed the lapel of his sports coat. 'He's just a child. He's—'

'My friend!' Tanice said, tears in her eyes, hysterical. 'He doesn't know!'

Marcus leaned back and wiped his face with a clenched fist. His fury melted as he looked at the young man beneath him again.

'*You?*' He was ashen then, as if he'd seen a ghost. He loosened his grip completely.

'Sydney doesn't know,' Tanice sobbed, wishing the ground would swallow her or that Hero would smash into the Earth at that exact moment, taking everyone with it. 'I haven't told him.'

'Yeah,' Sydney shouted as he pushed Marcus off, his voice razor-edged with loathing. 'My dad wasn't enough for you, huh? You wanna kill me, too?'

AALIYΛH MINTON – 2 DAYS BEFORE

I sometimes wonder if it was impossible for Aaliyah to be a compassionate person because life had worked out so well for her since childhood. Up until that summer, the arc of her life had mimicked the sublime parabola of a served tennis ball. Predictable forces, the pull of the Earth, the slap of the air, impossible velocity, clear light, victory, everything subordinate to her own perfect will. For years, she'd believed that she could have anything she wanted if she only tried hard enough. Almost anything.

But that day, the rehearsal dinner was ruined and she felt nauseous with humiliation. Clouds were rolling across the treeline, threatening a storm. Aaliyah couldn't see the patio from the upstairs guest bathroom, but she could imagine the rain soaking the table linens, heavy drops filling the blown-glass charger plates, flaying petals off the golden-rayed lilies she'd picked out so carefully.

'How could you be so *stupid*?' she said to Tanice, who sat crying in the empty claw-footed bathtub in the middle of the room. The four of us were hiding out in the bathroom from the chaos downstairs. A police car outside the front of the house strobed red and blue light across the black marble tiles on the floor.

Damp seeped through the silk lining of Aaliyah's ripped dress. From her vantage point by the window, she could see the group gathered on the driveway: Sydney, sat with his feet out in the back of Hugo's BMW, holding a sopping dishcloth full of ice to his swollen cheek; Kim and Marcus talking to a police officer; Carmen with Paris's salmon-coloured dinner jacket draped over her shoulders. She looked round as a blueberry to Aaliyah, or a tick, fat with blood.

Her phone kept pinging. Someone had suggested that Hugo take Sydney to A&E to check for a concussion. Someone wanted to know if they should store the leftover crates of wine in the cellar. All the broken glass had been swept up from the patio. Was she okay? Did she need anything? 'It's impossible to find good help these days,' one of the bridesmaids teased on their WhatsApp group.

Marcus looked miserable and ashamed. With a thumb pressed against the cool glass, she could make him disappear.

'She made a mistake,' I said, coming to Tanice's defence, kneeling at the end of the tub. 'She can't have known who he was.' I couldn't fathom at the time that she might have sought Sydney out, lied deliberately and caused this suffering where it so easily could have been avoided.

'It was lo-ooove . . .' Tanice said through tears.

'People aren't your playthings!' Aaliyah hissed. 'Everything isn't just a game.' I peered at her in the darkness, thinking about how I had seen her arrange the seating plan, moving chess pieces around little paper notes with everyone's names on them, like a general arranging her troops.

'Haven't you ever made a mistake before?' I snapped at Aaliyah, who reflexively said, 'No!' and then caught herself.

'Is Dad going to prison?' Chantale asked. She had been sitting quietly on the toilet. When I looked over at her, I saw that her eyes were wide with terror.

'No one's going to prison,' I promised.

'I'm not sure who called the police,' Aaliyah said.

'Probably Hugo,' I guessed.

'Well,' Aaliyah came quickly to his defence, 'a waiter assaulted a guest at his house.'

In the short silence that elapsed, we heard a car drive away, the delayed yawn of the gates opening. Aaliyah whispered to the glass, 'Maybe Dad *should* go to prison.' And was met with three dark pairs of eyes. She gritted her teeth.

'You're just upset they ruined Eugenia's perfect "table-scaping,"' Tanice said. Aaliyah glared at her.

'I'm upset about everything!' she yelled. 'I'm upset about ...' She struggled with finishing the sentence. 'I've been thinking for a while that this family would be better off without him.'

'How can you *say* that?' I gasped.

'Mum can't cook,' Chantale said.

'Yeah,' Tanice agreed. 'Without Dad, it would be nothing but M&S ready meals and cold cuts.'

Aaliyah made a feeble defence. 'She does cook ... sometimes.'

'Like when?'

'That Father's Day brunch last year.'

I snorted. 'She Uber Eats-ed a Full English and then hid the packaging.'

'Work smarter, not harder?' Tanice snickered in spite of herself.

'Work more *expensively*,' I said. 'They charged four pounds for a cup of baked beans!'

'Come on, guys,' Aaliyah said. 'He's ruined *everything*. It's not just the rehearsal dinner or the bunker or that weekend he turned off all the electricity and told us we could only eat what we could kill ...' We all shifted uncomfortably at the memory. 'It's that they're all distractions from the fact that we can't talk about what he did last year. And how nothing's been the same since.'

'That's not true,' I said, more quietly than I'd intended.

'I know you don't like talking about it, either,' Aaliyah responded.

'Because there's nothing to talk about,' I said, though I could feel my gut twist as it always did when this topic came up. 'It wasn't his fault.'

'It was an accident!' Chantale shrieked, gripping the toilet seat under her bum.

'It could have happened to anyone,' I said.

'It didn't, though,' Aaliyah replied coolly. 'Importantly, it happened to *him*.'

'Why are you bringing this up now?' Tanice asked, pulling the skirt of her dress over the gooseflesh on her upper thighs.

'Because.' Aaliyah turned away from us and took a deep breath. Her eyes flitted to the reflection of us all in the mirror. In the dim light, her gilded earrings glimmered like church bells. 'I don't want him to come to the wedding anymore.'

There was a stunned silence. Tanice, Chantale and I stared back at Aaliyah in horror.

'*What?*' Tanice gasped.

'You know that would break his heart,' I said. Aaliyah

looked resolute, though. She always was stubborn once she'd set her mind to something.

'Today was the last straw. He's a real ...' I thought she would say 'embarrassment', but instead she settled on, '... distraction.'

She glanced back outside again, and saw that Sydney was gone, along with Hugo's car. Rain pelted the stones that lined the driveway.

Tanice started to cry again then, and we turned.

'What?' Aaliyah asked. 'I thought you agreed with me.' It was rare to see Tanice cry, and we were all a little alarmed by this fresh torrent of emotion.

'He already lost his job. He can't lose you as well as Mum,' she sobbed.

'What's wrong with Mum?' I asked.

'Haven't you noticed that she's been acting differently?' Tanice said through her tears.

I thought about it for a second. Kim and I weren't very close, but even I could admit that she had been more distant than usual over the previous few weeks.

'A little,' I conceded.

'She keeps disappearing and being cagey when I ask her anything.' Tanice rubbed her eyes with the heel of her palm, inadvertently wiping away the last of her mascara. 'At first, I thought maybe she was just having an affair. You know, like Hannah's dad.' Aaliyah snorted incredulously. It sounded unlikely. 'But then ... I logged onto her laptop one time before it had a chance to lock itself and I saw some emails ...' She swallowed, clearly enjoying the attention, the expectant hush in the room. 'There's a fellowship. Next year. At the University of San Carlos ...'

'What?' Chantale asked.

'She's leaving us again,' Tanice explained.

'To go back to Guatemala,' I said, my heart sinking.

It was quiet again then, as we recalled how we'd suffered the first time she left. Aaliyah had been eleven and still remembered the exquisite pain she'd experienced at our mother's departure at the airport. At Marcus's false cheeriness, at my and Tanice's tears. An apocalyptic dread the night before, and the long motherless days and nights after that. Our grandfather came over that night to teach her to make egusi soup. 'You're the eldest daughter,' he said to her in the kitchen, like Zadok anointing King Solomon. Her crown would bestow nothing but duty and expectation.

Aaliyah, more than any of us, remembered what those years had cost. The lines they had carved into our father's brow. That sense we all had that any safety or joy we might manage to find could be sold on a whim by our parents.

'I kind of wish she *was* just having an affair,' I said finally. 'At least that would make more sense.'

'It won't be so bad this time,' Aaliyah said.

'For you,' Tanice scoffed. 'It won't change your life at all.'

Our sister softened slightly. 'And you guys, too. You're older now. You don't need her. Or him.'

'I don't feel old.' Chantale was on the verge of tears. She still needed Dad to check under the bed at night for the *drekavac* – the screaming soul of an unbaptized baby, a creature her Serbian babysitter had warned her about. Chantale was like a child who'd never seen famine, born in the summertime of our parents' marriage, the happy years after Kim returned. 'What are we going to do,' she asked, wobbly, 'without a mother?' I moved to put my arm around her.

'What we've *always* done,' Aaliyah said.

She'd always been proud to be one of four. Proud whenever we went out and a stranger asked our parents, 'Are they *all* yours?' To save on having to sew individual names into hand-me-down school uniforms, our mother had just stitched the label 'The Minton Sisters' into all our clothes. Like we were a band. It had been a mantle Aaliyah was happy to wear. Whenever Tanice and I fought, she'd remind us that friends and boyfriends would come and go, but sisters are forever. Sisters are the only ones who know what it's like to endure your parents, your childhood. Only a sister can understand what you've been through. You might not heal from it, but they can help you to bear it. A sister is a witness, a fellow traveller, a neighbouring star.

'Yeah,' Tanice agreed, gritting her jaw in fresh resolution.

'We look after each other,' Aaliyah said.

Chantale nodded as I said, 'We're all we have.'

BRIAR MINTON – 1 DAY BEFORE

The next morning after the rehearsal dinner, Tanice insisted that she was too sick to go to school. Our parents were still furious with her, and she claimed that Sydney had blocked her on every messaging app. She'd been up all night (I'd heard through the wall) crying.

I was walking alone under the shadowed underpass on the way to school when Axel and a couple of other members of Freya's Group materialized.

'Axel told us.' Beth was the first to speak.

'About your experiences,' Soo-Jin said. I glanced at Axel, who looked a little nervous but nodded encouragingly at me.

'Come on,' he said to them, 'you all saw it, too. Her eyes. Her watch.'

'Axel wants us to invite you to our meetings,' Beth said to me.

'And tonight,' Axel said, 'by sunset, Hero will be visible in the sky. A group of us are going to watch it together at Freya's house.' I knew that she lived just opposite the school in the groundskeeper's cottage.

'The meetings are secret,' said a tall man with dark circles under his eyes, who looked as if he'd been bitten by a snake.

'I think she's ready, Cato,' Axel said.

'We need to be thorough,' Cato said. Then, to me, 'Take out your phone.'

'Why?' I asked. It was Tanice's old Samsung. Somehow, even though I was older than her, I still received her hand-me-downs.

Cato said nothing, just stared at me silently. So, reluctantly, I handed it over.

He took it and nodded as if I'd passed a test. Then he smashed it on the floor. I watched a silver crack lance its screen, and then another as he stamped it with the heel of his foot. It shattered like ice. My memories, my music, my everything. That polycarbonate phone case I'd bought from Camden Market with all my pocket money.

'Hey . . . !' I trailed off.

Cato stared at me dispassionately.

Soo-Jin said the time and place.

By the time I arrived, the session had already started.

'. . . and I keep telling myself that everything will be different after. But maybe I just want it to be?' The voice carried through the old church hall. They were in one of the side rooms reserved for community gatherings, the food bank and AA meetings. 'I've been dreaming about Them a lot lately.'

As I entered the room, I saw that the speaker was Laurie, Beth's brother. He looked like her, blonde and tan and athletic. When they were together, their identical buzz-cuts gave them a kind of epicene strangeness. Laurie had this guileless, puppy-like quality that made you want to believe everything he said. I often wondered if that was the reason the police never kept him for questioning, even though he and Ruby had briefly dated and boyfriends are normally the number one suspects in cases like these.

'Me, too,' said Axel.

The Group was bigger than I'd imagined it would be. Almost fifty people, their creaking chairs arranged in concentric circles. I noticed some similarities in the crowd. About half of them had their heads shaved like Beth and Laurie, and some wore the same muslin shirt and trousers that Freya often wore. Laurie stood on a wooden platform at the front. The air smelled of instant coffee, incense and dust.

I couldn't spot Freya anywhere.

'It's Hero,' Beth said from her seat near the front. 'She's influencing our dreams.'

'Why do they call her Hero?' one man asked.

I was surprised to notice that the Group was a mixture of ages. Around half were teenagers, including a few I recognized from my school, but many were older. There was the man with a ponytail who worked in the local library, there was the woman who taught yoga classes and the couple who ran the organic food stall on Saturdays.

'It's an apt name,' Beth said. 'In the Greek myth, when Hero's lover drowned, she jumped in and died after him. Their romance lasted through the summer and then ended in tragedy. Our Hero will swing by us before spinning out again into the lonely dark. It won't last for long. Like their love.'

Someone in the crowd contributed, 'My roommate said that it – she – could have come from a star in the Andromeda Galaxy.' I would learn that some of them suspected that

Hero was a message launched from the Tau home planet, M31, which orbited AF Andromedae, a massive star over a million times brighter than our sun.

'Astronomers are yet to confirm if that's true,' said Soo-Jin from the back of the room.

'I want it to be, though,' Laurie said. 'I actually received this message from Them in my dreams the other day. They told me that They understand everything. They're on our side and They forgive us.'

As he sat down, it was clear that the Group was moved by his words. A young Black woman in a powder-blue prairie dress started crying quietly.

'Thank you for sharing,' Beth said to Laurie, and then, to the woman, 'Martha? That resonates with you?'

Martha nodded vigorously and then stood. As she did, I recognized her. She was a Jehovah's Witness who had come to our door a year or so ago with her mother (when her mother asked us, 'Do you ever wonder why bad things happen?' my father had just said, 'No.'). She looked a little older now. She wore her natural hair in two big plaits on either side of her head.

'I'm not like many of you,' she said through tears. 'It only happened to me once. When I was very young. But once was enough. When I get up the courage to tell people what happened, they say it sounds traumatic. But it wasn't. When I remember it, all I feel is ...'

'Content,' someone said.

'Yes,' Martha breathed and sat back down shakily.

'Thank you for sharing,' Beth repeated. As she did, a woman with a mohawk and a sleeve of tattoos leapt to her feet and spoke quickly, as if she'd been holding this in for a while.

'You know, it's not like that for everyone, Martha. It's not "peaceful" for everyone.'

'Charlie . . .' There was a note of warning in Beth's voice.

'Well, it's true,' she said. 'I respect your experience, Martha, but also I envy it. I wish I could move through the world as you do, with any *measure* of . . . contentment.' Her face twisted in pain.

I heard Freya's voice then, but from where I stood, I couldn't see her. A couple of other people craned their heads. She appeared like a vision from the other side of the circle.

'What do you need to share?' she asked, moving to the front to put her hand on Charlie's shoulder, who appeared to weaken at her touch.

'I'm struggling again,' she said, 'with anger. I don't understand why it happened to me. Why it keeps happening.'

'None of us can answer that,' said Martha.

'Maybe.' Charlie sounded unconvinced. 'Maybe I just want it to stop now. Or maybe I want to be the person I was before it started.'

The Group was clearly unsettled by her outburst, but Freya took control.

'I used to be angry, too. But now . . . I consider the billions of minds in the world. The millions just in this city. Who am I that They chose me to pour the light of Their consciousness onto mine?' Some quality in her voice seemed to mesmerize the crowd. 'You all know my story. What happened to me.'

Under her breath, Martha said, '*If you glimpse the Tau . . .*'

Others in the crowd followed as if it was a creed. '*. . . you'll be blinded and thank the darkness.*'

Everyone in the room echoed the last words, their voices rising in an eerie reverence.

'*Thank the darkness.*' I felt goosebumps rise up on my back.

Freya lifted her palm as if to check for rain and asked, 'Can you feel Their ancient presence now?'

A couple of people were breathing deeply, nodding. Some had their eyes closed, silent tears pouring down their cheeks. Beth's brow was furrowed. Soo-Jin stared at Freya with a mixture of awe and worry. Laurie's head was raised, and the light from the rose window poured down on him and the rest of the crowd.

There was a long silence, and I shifted uncomfortably. I felt as if I was witnessing some silent, intimate form of communication. I'd later learn that some of the members claimed they could practise 'mind speak', that they could project their thoughts out to Freya. She was nodding, making eye contact, seeming to answer some of their questions in silence.

Finally, Laurie said, as if in answer to an unspoken question, 'It's unlikely that They'll be taking all of us with Them. At least, at the Second Encounter. We will probably be safe, but everyone else ...' His gaze flitted towards the window. The images my father invoked flashed across my mind: rising tides, mushroom clouds, pestilence, famine.

'Obviously,' someone else said, an old woman, 'it won't be corporeally ...'

Cato, who was sitting near the front, nodded. 'I'd be interested to see what kind of substrate they choose to load our consciousness onto ...'

Charlie suggested, 'It'll probably be immortal.'

'Genderless,' Axel guessed.

'Five- or six-dimensional,' offered someone else.

'Like them,' said a couple of people in disconcerting unison.

I saw Soo-Jin nod. For a long time, it surprised me that Soo-Jin was part of the Group. She seemed too rational. Once, after one of her astronomy presentations, someone in our class had playfully asked what her star sign was, and Soo-Jin had looked disgusted at the question. Not just because it displayed a flagrant ignorance of the difference between astrology and astronomy – her pet peeve – but also because, as she declared with great pride, 'I am a child of the Enlightenment ...'

'Our elevated bodies,' Freya said now, 'will see history like a shadow-scarred ravine, all the inhabitants of the Earth like spiralling koi fish we might unsettle with a flick of our wrists.'

Amy Snape, hidden near the back so that I only recognized her nasal voice, asked nervously, 'Um, how will They know? Who should stay and who should be destroyed?'

'Simple,' said Freya.

'They'll choose the fittest of us, right?' asked Cato. 'The ones most likely to survive the Conversion?'

'Or the brightest?' wondered Soo-Jin.

'The truest believers?' Martha asked.

Freya laughed softly, the answer clear to her. 'They'll choose the ones They love.' She opened her arms to the room. 'Are you worthy of love?' There was quiet then. 'It takes a while sometimes. You have to look back over the arc of your life, and only then can you see which way it bends.'

Everyone nodded in agreement.

'When people ask me how it "began", I like to tell them that it happened all at once. For me, belief was like a light switching on in the deepest part of me. One day it all meant nothing, and the next ...' She turned to the doorway then, her hollowed eyes directed at me. 'Briar, They've been calling all along.'

I felt the burn in my face as the Group's attention settled on me. Axel turned in happy surprise that I had accepted his invitation.

'Let's welcome Briar,' he said with a clap.

'Welcome, Briar,' the Group echoed.

Beth appeared beside me then, her hand on my shoulder, directing me to the middle of the circle, where Freya waited. 'We're ready to hear about your experience.'

Standing before them, next to their leader, felt like a recurring nightmare I had, where I was called on to speak to or teach a class, and when I opened my mouth no words came out. My mind reeled. I tallied and renounced every decision that had led me there, before that crowd who regarded me with a mixture of joyful expectation and guarded suspicion.

'I'm ... Briar,' I stuttered. I flailed for words. Should I tell them the truth? *There's this girl in my school who ...* No. I looked at Laurie, back in his seat, his blue eyes warm and encouraging. In his statement to the police, Nico Costa had claimed that Laurie, Ruby's new boyfriend, had been one of the last people to see her alive. I couldn't mess this up. I needed them to trust me. I took a deep breath.

'My experience is a bit like some of yours, actually. Happens all the time. Has been happening since I was a child. It's been getting worse over the past six months ...' I looked up at the fluorescent strip lights above, invoking the sensation. 'I feel it first at the top of my head. Cool blood rushing into my fingertips ...' I took another deep breath; I could almost sense it happening. 'And then, before everything goes dark ... I see Them.'

I hoped that would be enough, but the Group examined me intently. A hundred eyes, staring into my mind. I didn't know then about the story they'd been telling themselves. Of course, they called it a 'prophecy'. Of the Final Messenger, the one the Tau would send before their Second Encounter. All I knew then was their faces, a mix of terror and delight.

Not everything I told them was a lie.

'I used to worry a lot about being alone,' I said. 'And now I believe that ... I never truly have been.'

KIMONA MINTON –
13 HOURS BEFORE

The night that Hero appeared in the sky, Kim spotted our neighbour Gabriel standing in his carefully manicured garden, in a vest and tracksuit bottoms, barbecuing meat. 'Come to join in?' he asked, over the hiss and crackle of beef.

'Sorry,' Kim said, standing on the herb planter, looking over our shared fence. 'I came out to see ...' She nodded up at the sky, where another star had appeared. Hero, hurtling towards us. Slightly brighter than the North Star at Leo's tail. Somehow it felt wrong to watch its approach on her own. 'And then I saw the smoke and ...'

'... smelled the delicious aroma of this filet mignon,' Gabriel said.

Kim was caught a little off guard by her laughter. He was cooking enough for two, and at the smell of it, melting fat and caramelizing tenderloin, Kim realized that she was starving. Over dinner that evening, Aaliyah had announced that she didn't want our dad to come to her wedding. Both Marcus and Kim had been heartbroken, the conversation had fissured into a heated argument and everyone had left the table in tears without finishing their food.

'Come round,' Gabriel said breezily. 'The gate is open.'

'Okay.' Kim smiled, surprised at herself. Gabriel lived in the swanky new-build next door. Kim knew him only a little. They'd first met at the Platinum Jubilee street party, a couple of years before. He was tall and had gorgeous volcano-black eyes, and she'd guessed, at first, that he must be an actor or a model.

For some reason, delivery drivers kept getting our houses mixed up. You can tell a lot about people from their post. He had a subscription to a craft whiskey club and to some luxury watch magazines. Kim thought he was married. She'd seen his wife a couple of times, Michaela, a thin, light-skinned woman with a waist-length weave, taking their little poodle for a walk, returning a pair of leggings to Sweaty Betty or getting a pedicure.

'I was saving this wagyu for a special occasion,' Gabriel explained when he heard her padding into his garden in her slippers, 'and figured ...'

'... this one is as good as any?'

It was a fancy ceramic barbecue. The Green Egg she had envied in catalogues and home showrooms for years. It looked like the first time he had ever used it, pristine utensils still hanging glittering from its side.

'This is a once in a lifetime event.' And she saw that Gabriel had set up a telescope and a deckchair. 'A visitor in our sky.'

Kim glanced back over to our garden, to the telescope I'd left on the patio earlier that week. 'I was supposed to watch it with my daughter, but ...' I'd stormed out, angry at Aaliyah, at my father, at everyone. 'Can I have a look?' Kim asked.

'Sure.'

Kim leaned into the eyepiece of the telescope but saw only the roof of her own house, her own empty bedroom.

'Can you see it?' Gabriel asked.

Kim moved the optical tube around delicately, unsure what she was looking at. Gabriel helped her to find it by putting one hand on her shoulder and the other on the telescope. The warmth of his fingers through her pyjamas made her acutely aware that the last couple of men who had touched her were doctors and radiologists.

'Can you see it now?'

'Oh!' Kim said. In the lens of the telescope, Hero looked like a moon – grey and pock-marked. But the longer she stared, the more unsettled she felt. The craters were too precise, patterned like crop circles, with vast smooth plains that reflected light in an unnatural way.

'Do you feel as if you've waited your whole life to see it?' Gabriel asked.

No, Kim thought. Over the past few months, the planet had been the least of her concerns. 'Maybe it's been waiting for us,' she said.

Gabriel stepped away to put the steaks on plates. He pulled out another deckchair and, sitting beside him, Kim ate quickly, her hands trembling a little with hunger.

She noticed a distracted glaze in Gabriel's eyes as he regarded her. 'What?' she asked.

'Sorry, it's just . . .' He blushed a little. 'You look lovely.'

'Oh.' Kim felt suddenly naked. She hardly ever left the house without makeup, but something about this night and the surprise invite had freed her. She touched her head and realized that her headscarf must have slipped off, exposing her stubbly afro.

It had been two years before she had allowed Marcus to see her without a wig or a headscarf. And she still remembered how self-conscious and exposed she'd felt, frightened that anything he said might stick in her like a thorn forever.

'It's beautiful,' Gabriel said now, as Marcus had. She was sure he was just being kind to her. 'Dark crown.'

She might lose it all soon, she thought sorrowfully, as her mother had, once the chemo started. 'It's full of greys,' she admitted.

'Age is a badge of honour,' Gabriel told her.

She wondered how old he was. Mid-forties, perhaps. A couple of years younger than her?

'Want a drink?' he asked, his eyes flitting up towards his house.

'What have you got?' Kim asked.

'Anything, water, whiskey . . .' He counted them on his fingers. 'Okay, two things.'

Kim laughed again and followed him through the garden and into his house. Up the winding steps that led to his kitchen, which looked like the showroom in a warehouse. Immaculate granite countertops and gleaming designer appliances. The pastel-blue SMEG fridge that Kim owned in her dreams. The kind of order it's only possible to achieve in a house without children.

Some parts of the layout were like a mirror image of her house. Hers, except gorgeous: a gleaming farmhouse sink with brushed brass taps and Carrara marble splashback. Hers, if it was filled with everything she'd ever wanted: a kitchen island with nothing on it.

'How's Michaela doing?' Kim felt embarrassed to ask.

'Just fine, I imagine,' said Gabriel without looking at

her. He reached into a mostly empty pantry and produced a bottle of whiskey.

Behind the dining table, Kim noticed that there was a layer of dust inside the dog bowl. 'Where is she?'

'Living with her aerial yoga instructor,' Gabriel admitted with a slight grimace as he poured two glasses.

'Shit,' Kim said, 'I'm sorry.'

'No, I mean … yeah, it was, but …' He shrugged.

'When?'

'A few months ago now. February. Valentine's Day.'

'I'm sorry,' Kim repeated. She didn't know what else to say.

'Don't be.'

He handed her a drink with a round ball of ice in it. 'Macallan, 18 Year Old Sherry Oak.'

Kim knew nothing about whiskey, so she smiled, nodded approvingly and hoped he wouldn't ask her anything about it.

'To new beginnings.' They clinked glasses.

'I sure hope so,' Gabriel said, taking a sip. It felt good to have a drink. Kim wondered why she hadn't poured herself a gin and tonic as soon as she'd watched Aaliyah and me storm out of the house earlier that evening. Or when Marcus had retreated to his bunker and Chantale and Tanice went to bed in tears.

Gabriel was staring at her. 'What can you taste?' he asked.

'Um …' She sipped again and tried to discern it.

'Honey?' he probed.

Kim took another meditative sip and remained silent.

'Oak … dried figs …'

She ran her tongue along her teeth as if in thought. 'Spices?' she foolishly ventured.

He leaned in, as if fascinated. 'Yeah?'

She took a guess. 'Nutmeg ... clove?'

'Dark chocolate.' He was close to her then. Kim could smell the bergamot in his aftershave, could tell this wasn't his first drink and wondered if something was passing between them, some static of attraction. Up close, his face looked like a statue carved in soapstone. Was she imagining it? She eyed the dark red of his lips, the colour of sunburst cherries.

He leaned in and kissed her, and she let him.

Had she wondered, since the first time she'd met him, what his lips would taste like? How soft his hair might feel in her palms? (Like spun sugar.) In all her life, she hadn't kissed anyone but Marcus. Not that opportunities hadn't presented themselves.

Our parents had met when they were seventeen. They fell into quick, anxious love with each other. They'd been each other's firsts. And now, they knew each other by heart.

Kissing someone new was as strange as looking in the mirror to find a different face. Everything, from the pressure of his tongue to the whiskey and wagyu tang of his breath and his perfect ivory teeth.

She pulled away suddenly, her head spinning.

'Sorry,' she laughed nervously. Gabriel leaned back, some disappointment in his eyes.

'Our body seal' she'd called it. The fact that for over two decades, they'd been with no one else but each other. That they only knew each other's bodies. Sex was just sex with Marcus. And how comfortable she'd always felt with him, completely loved, never ashamed or embarrassed or heartbroken. *What are adventure and variety worth*, she had always asked herself, *when I can have that?*

'Was it ... ?' Self-conscious concern in his tone.

'The whiskey,' Kim said, downing the last of hers.

As Gabriel stood up to pour another one, he asked, 'So, what's keeping you up?'

'Ha!' Kim laughed darkly. 'So many things! My eldest is getting married tomorrow.'

'Wow, congrats!'

'Yeah, it all happened quite quickly.' Aaliyah had only announced her engagement twelve weeks ago. Although Kim had initially been stressed by the prospect of pulling a wedding together so soon, now she believed that it was the perfect time for her. She had hoped that the wedding would offer a bright moment of family togetherness before she had to break the devastating news to everyone about her cancer diagnosis. Before her life halted and she had to defer her fellowship to Guatemala and languish in the house as her mother had, growing thin on the sofa, vomiting in pots.

'I just ...' Kim said, her voice cracking a little at the thought, 'I hope it's the right choice for her. I want her to be happy. I want them all to be happy.'

Gabriel took another sip. 'When Michaela left, my mother said that sometimes you think that marriage is the monument you're building. The one you hoped would defy time. But then it passes, and you realize that marriage was just the scaffolding.'

'She sounds ... wise,' Kim said.

When she'd returned from Guatemala, she'd discovered another woman's bra behind the sofa. Kim had felt so sick to find it, it might as well have been her finger. There were other signs, when she went looking for them. Her Dior lipstick case was gone, there were blonde hairs in the u-bend of the sink in their ensuite. Confronting him, after the girls were asleep, was one of the worst nights of her life.

'Do you believe in soulmates?' Kim asked. Gabriel winced at the word. 'That's how Marcus and I used to describe ourselves.' For a couple of years, they would sleep through their alarms because they'd stayed up all night just talking. He was the only person who could make her laugh. Marcus used to claim that if he saw something without Kim, it would feel like only half an experience; he'd reflexively turn over his shoulder just to say, 'Did you see—?'

Kim asked, 'But are "soulmates" forever?'

Gabriel glittered with promise. 'I don't believe that there is just one person for you,' he said. 'Statistically, most people marry someone who grew up five miles from where they were born.'

'Is that true?' Kim asked. It sounded true. Kim did the maths, tried to calculate the distance from where Marcus grew up (a council house in Enfield, youngest of four brothers who bullied him mercilessly and an alcoholic father) to where she grew up (in a townhouse in Clapham that was too big for just her and her parents).

'Maybe it's not about finding a soulmate,' Gabriel said. 'Maybe it's not about "forever". Maybe it's just about tonight.'

Kim nodded. 'Where's your bathroom?' she asked. Gabriel pointed upstairs, his shoulders slumping a little. Kim headed up. The carpet felt plush and soft as the back of a pet under her feet. In the mirror on the landing, Kim caught an unwelcome vision of her face. Without her hair, she looked like her old, sad self. She'd shaved it all off and worn it short for two years after her mother died. She needed the wigs to act as a shield between herself and the world; she felt vulnerable and exposed without them. But then, it was thrilling to realize that Gabriel still found her beautiful, even in this incarnation.

In the bathroom, for some reason, no water came from the motion-sensitive taps when she leaned down to wash her hands. The lights were flicking ominously.

By the time she came back down the stairs, Kim realized that Gabriel must be rich. Which wasn't a surprise; almost everyone in Clapham was now. Her family were one of the few who had managed to cling on by their teeth, remortgaged to the hilt. Growing up, she'd promised herself that she would move somewhere nicer than this neighbourhood. But now she would do anything she could to stay.

Not a day went by that Kim didn't want to be rich. She imagined it must feel like being warm all the time. Whenever she had a problem, it was easy to imagine how money could solve it. People said that money couldn't buy you happiness, but the sad thing was that it actually could. She'd read that emotional well-being and life satisfaction increased with income up to a certain sum, which was disappointingly obvious.

She'd never thought that Marcus would be rich. She'd married him for love, but she'd come to realize that Gabriel's life, his fridge, his robot hoover, his money and whatever ease it offered would never be hers.

'Did I make all the wrong choices?' she asked as she descended the staircase. 'Did I choose the wrong life?' Gabriel had lit some candles, she noticed. 'You grow up and you think you can do anything, but every choice you make wears away at the grooves, makes it harder to change course.'

'Maybe that's the problem,' Gabriel said. 'Believing that you could do anything. I'm a dentist. My dad and my grand-dad were both dentists.'

'Really?'

'Yeah,' Gabriel said. 'When people ask why, I say, "I like to solve problems. I like working with my hands." When I asked my father the same question, he told me that it was a good job and provided a stable life for his family. I asked my grandfather, and he said, with not a hint of sadness, "It was the only option I was given."' Gabriel shrugged and finished the rest of his drink. 'The problem is thinking that you had all the options. That you could have married anyone, had different children or no children. Happiness is a relatively rare internal state. The suffering comes from thinking that there's more happiness out there. Maybe this is your measure, maybe this is the only groove.'

For a long time, Kim had pondered what it would take to forgive Marcus for the affair. He promised it was over, promised it would never happen again, and seemed genu-inely devastated. But rage would erupt from her randomly. She'd lift a glass and want to break it over his head. She burst into tears once and left a brown handprint of her makeup on the cream rug, and every time she stepped over it, she felt newly furious.

One night, he said, 'Punch me? As hard as you can.' She didn't. 'Do anything to me,' he'd pleaded. 'Do what it will take.'

The next morning, she'd woken us with a breakfast of crepes. We'd been shocked but thrilled – she almost never cooked – and so had Marcus when she'd produced a crepe with cheddar, ham and mushrooms. 'My favourite,' he'd said in quiet relief.

'You can't go back, Kim,' said Gabriel now, breaking her reverie. 'You can't start again.'

'I know that,' Kim said, thinking of the mass of rogue cells blooming in her skull.

'What do you want now?' Gabriel asked.

'I don't want to die,' Kim said. 'I want to have done it all differently. My whole life.'

'Yeah,' he said. 'Me, too.'

She'd stayed out late with some friends after the morning of the crepes and returned to find Marcus bent over the toilet of their ensuite, in his boxers, vomiting. His head on the seat, closed eyes flickering, skin rubbery and wan.

'Oh,' she'd said. He'd looked so sad, so small. 'How do you feel?'

'Wretched,' he'd said. 'I've been up all night being sick. But even before ...' His eyes had glazed a little. 'It felt like something deeper. Sick with something inside me.'

'Good,' she'd replied. 'Now you know how it feels.' He was sick for a couple more hours. At one point, sighting the blood-streaked bile, she'd wondered if she'd gone too far with the mushrooms, miscalculated the dosage compared to his height and weight.

But after the sickness, he'd told her deliriously that he felt a floaty lightness. He lay in bed next to her, cleansed. He held her as a shipwrecked man might cling to a raft. And she said, into the darkness, 'Okay, now I can forgive you.'

BRIAR MINTON – 5 HOURS BEFORE

I feel an ache every time I remember that morning, when I woke up and still didn't understand what was about to happen. It would take me a couple of months before I identified that the unease I was feeling was grief. Memories would occur to me randomly. Stopping at an ice cream van for a cola Calippo the last time I ever walked home from school. The personalized PopSockets I ordered online that never arrived. That I never got far enough in *The Resident* to find out if Austin and Mina ever got together. That, for a while, I could buy a plane ticket to Prague for less than a meal at Pizza Express and I never did.

After the fight at home, I'd stayed out all night – something I'd never done – to watch Hero's approach with Freya and the Group, who had welcomed its ivory light as witches might a solstice. I'd drunk too much Pimm's from the fishbowl they'd brought, danced ecstatically, ran with Beth to hitch up my skirt and pee behind a bush, lay on the grass and told them my dreams.

The next morning, the sound of Axel's phone buzzing woke me. He was asleep, too, his face pressed into the spongy Astroturf of our school's tennis court. As I realized where I was, my head spun in disbelief. I dimly wondered why he had been allowed to keep his mobile when Cato had smashed mine.

'Hello?' he said a couple of times into the phone. 'No, no – switch your Bluetooth off. Wait . . .' It must have cut off because he pulled the phone away from his face and stared at it in confusion.

Reality tumbled back to me. It was Aaliyah's wedding day. 'What time is it?' I still felt helpless without my own phone, which I hadn't yet managed to replace. I had told my mum it had been stolen, but I was still going to be in so much trouble if I was late for the wedding.

'Seven-thirty-ish?' Soo-Jin emerged from Freya's father's cottage – the little groundskeeper's property at the end of the school grounds – and stood on the other side of the chain-link, brushing her teeth with an electric toothbrush.

On the whiteboard on the fridge at home, it said that 7 a.m. was when the makeup artist was expected to start on my face.

I swore. 'I need to get home.' Luckily, it wasn't a long walk. Soo-Jin spat her toothpaste onto the grass.

'Were you guys out here all night?' she asked.

'Must have fallen asleep,' I said. Axel's hand was shaking as he looked at his phone.

'Have you seen this?' he asked.

'What?'

His phone seemed to be on fire with notifications. He tapped one and said, 'Something about Hero changing direction? Only by a couple of degrees, but it seems to have people spooked.'

'Let me see that . . .' Soo-Jin leaned into the chain-link, and he held the screen up to her.

In the sky, Hero looked like a day-lurking moon.

Inside Freya's house, the Group was gathered around the television, where the chyron on BBC News read 'UNIDENTIFIED AERIAL PHENOMENA'. One of the interviewees was identified as Dr Astrid Juma, OBE, General Secretary for the First Contact Committee.

'Our recent observations suggest that Hero is not a natural celestial object . . .'

Martha and Beth were hugging tightly, choking on delighted laughter.

'Its relative motion, its structure and thermal behaviour indicate an engineered object of astonishing complexity. Deliberate design. It is a machine the size of a moon.'

'An *alien* machine?' the host probed.

One member of the group, a young man called Isaac was being sick in the kitchen sink, and the morning light made his skin look jaundiced. Cato was frozen in apprehension.

Beth turned to me. 'Is this how it feels,' she asked, her blue eyes glittering with ecstatic tears, 'when you live to see a prophecy fulfilled?'

'I thought I'd die before . . .' said a grey-haired woman on the bench by the window.

On the TV, Dr Juma said, 'We've only been able to attempt to make contact relatively recently in human history. So it's likely that any civilization we encounter is far more sophisticated than ours.'

'How worried should we be?' the host asked.

'Well, no government or astronomical society has deemed it a threat . . .'

'Yet,' Cato said quietly.

Outside, a dog was barking wildly. Amy was tapping in the Wi-Fi code and then shaking her phone around and asking anyone if they had signal. None of the usual noise from the street outside was reaching us. I imagined a Christmas morning kind of calm, shops failing to open, parents ushering their children indoors. Or maybe chaos, queues for ATMs, panicked shoppers loading megapacks of toilet paper into the boots of their cars. I thought of my father then, of how tense and frantic he had grown over the past few weeks. Was he terrified or thrilled by this news?

'So are there aliens aboard Hero?' the anchor asked.

'Very unlikely,' she said firmly. 'We haven't detected any life forms on Hero. Or any organic matter at all, in fact. The current theory is that it's something like an unmanned space probe, programmed to circle by planets in neighbouring galaxies.'

'Sent by whom?'

'That's a good question,' Dr Juma said.

'What do you think,' the anchor asked. 'Do you really think there's something "out there"?'

Dr Juma smiled. 'I've built my life on that hope.'

MARCUS MINTON – 4 HOURS, 21 MINUTES AND 49 SECONDS BEFORE

The sound of the burglar alarm jolted him from sleep. Marcus leapt out of bed, grabbed the cricket bat from underneath it and felt his pocket for the stiff weight of his hunting knife. Then he made a quick ascent up the hatch ladder and into the garden, where some quality of the light had changed. Shading his eyes, he looked around. Digit darted past, barking at the back garden wall. There was some disturbance in the filthy alley between the houses. A hand, a groan, a pair of pink Dr. Martens.

'Briar?'

I landed hard on the wooden lip of the herb planter, my heel crushing the stems of a few parched basil leaves.

Kim, Tanice and Chantale emerged from the house, marching down the garden like a charm of angry swans. Kim in the lead, looking resplendent in the gold beaded dress she'd had made and shipped over from Nigeria. A woman had arrived early that morning to help her tie her gele, and the stiff fabric fanned gorgeously around her face.

Tanice wore her ivory tulle bridesmaid dress and silver stilettos. Chantale, too, looked lovely with her crown of pink satin roses. In shadows behind them, the makeup artist and the florist lingered by the garden's sliding door. Everyone was frowning at Marcus.

'This?!' Kim huffed. 'On Aaliyah's wedding day?'

'I thought we said no more drills?' Tanice reminded him.

Suddenly, my mother noticed me standing in the mud.

'Where have *you* been?' She stared at me, furious.

'I, uhhh . . . lost track of time and—'

'Have you been drinking?'

'J-just . . .' I stammered.

'Are you *determined* to disgrace us?' Kim hissed. I wasn't sure if she meant me or Dad. We both looked guilty.

'Can someone come in here and turn that off?' Aaliyah shouted from the doorway of the house. She was majestic in her bridal ballgown. I'd seen it before, in those pictures on the landing, seen my mother's dark collarbones under the sheer illusion neckline that was embroidered with delicate blossoms of lavender, baby's breath and forget-me-nots. As my sister stormed barefoot down the garden, waves of mille-feuille organza and lace swirled and crested behind her.

I wondered if the sight of her shunted Marcus back to his own wedding day, twenty-three years ago, to the way Kim's face had glittered under a crown of silver beads and wax orange blossoms.

'You're a terrible bridesmaid!' Aaliyah yelled at me.

'What?' It was hard to hide my hurt.

'You always manage to make everything about you.'

'Oh,' I scoffed, '*I* do? You've always acted like the main character of this family. Everything is orientated towards your next whim. Aaliyah wants to be a tennis star, Aaliyah's on a silent retreat, Aaliyah's getting married to a man she only just met.'

Her eyes narrowed in fury. 'Every mealtime, for *years*, was about you.'

'Hey, hey!' Dad held his hands up. 'Stop this.'

We were all quiet for a moment. The alarm bawled between us, its panicked quality setting my teeth on edge.

'Your dad is right,' Kim said.

'And anyway,' he continued, 'I think it's worth considering, in light of what's going on . . . postponing the wedding.'

Both Kim and Aaliyah turned their anger on him.

'*What?*' My mother sounded horrified.

Marcus gestured up to the sky, where Hero hung, the size of my thumbnail. 'All of this, about the planet and—'

Kim huffed, 'Yes, let's cancel this catastrophically expensive wedding because Mercury is in retrograde.'

'Aren't you listening to the news? Glassford House is fifty miles from here. If anything happens, that's an hour and a half drive, or a full day's walk, to safety.'

'But nothing is going to happen, Marcus. The government, people who know way more about this than we do, aren't worried.'

'They'll say anything to keep the lemmings under control,' Marcus scoffed. 'Can't you see that everything they told us about Hero was a lie?'

'You're being paranoid, as usual,' Kim said.

'That doesn't mean I'm not right!'

Aaliyah hissed at him, 'Well, I hope you enjoy being right alone in your bunker.' Her jaw stiffened. 'You know, it's such a toxically masculine response to build a bunker in the garden instead of confronting the real issue.'

Kim shook her head emphatically, but I could see that Aaliyah was about to dive for the third rail.

'Don't,' I whispered. I'd long worried there was no recovering from this discussion.

Aaliyah announced it as if before a jury. 'Dad killed a man last year, and he'd rather the world *ended* so he never has to deal with it.'

Our father froze, then said in a deadly whisper, 'I didn't kill anyone.'

'Right, right,' Aaliyah mock-laughed. 'It was an "accident".'

'Don't do this now.' Kim closed her eyes as if watching a Ming vase topple to the floor.

'He had diabetes,' said Marcus.

'The coroner said *that's* what killed him,' I added, trying to keep what little peace was left.

'Dad thought he was drunk, he wrote in his report that he was slurring his words.'

'That's how it looked to me.'

I said, 'Diabetic ketoacidosis symptoms include confusion, dizziness—'

'Yeah, but we've all seen the CCTV footage. The way Dad shoved him into the back of the police car. The way he looked when he got to the station, how that man's body flopped out.'

Marcus flinched at the memory. 'He wasn't dead then.'

'Yeah, but he never regained consciousness.'

'And he had other health issues,' I said to Aaliyah, 'that heart thing and—'

'But if Dad had driven him to the hospital and not to the police station? If they hadn't waited ninety precious minutes before calling the ambulance?'

'You don't take a whole medical history before arresting

someone,' Marcus said, morphing back into the policeman he once was. 'Especially if they're making others feel unsafe.'

Aaliyah pointed a recently manicured nail at him. '"A danger to others",' he'd mentioned in the witness report, '"feeling unsafe". I just keep wondering ...'

'It was impossible to know that—'

'... would you have arrested him if he'd been *white*?'

Mum snapped, 'That's enough!'

The alarm's whir sounded like another voice in the fray, *wow-wow, wow-wow* ...

Kim wiped her eyes. I hadn't noticed that she'd been crying. But I could see the effort it took to put a smile back on her face, thought I saw a dozen overworked stagehands quickly rearranging the set in her mind, sweeping away the broken glass, turning the lights up in a way that allowed her to affect a faux cheeriness she thought we needed.

'It's a wedding,' she said. 'I just want ...' She dabbed under her eyes again, careful to avoid disrupting her artfully applied false lashes. 'I just *need* this to be a good day from now on.'

We were all silent a moment. Then finally Aaliyah nodded.

Kim continued, 'Your grandfather will be here soon. He'll take Tanice and Chantale ahead with the flowers. Briar, I know you hate makeup, but maybe Debbie can do *something* with your hair this time? We have to be out of here in one hour, okay, everyone?' She looked around at all of us. 'You all look beautiful. Tanice, Chantale ... Lia especially.'

Aaliyah let her mouth twitch a little, and her expression softened.

'Hard to believe you're getting married soon, when only yesterday – doesn't it feel that way, Marcus? – her head fit in the palm of your hand.' Kim reached out to stroke Aaliyah's hand. 'You were such a bad sleeper, the only thing that worked was driving around. Your dad would take you on these three a.m. jaunts, playing radio static. Maybe you've driven down every lamp-lit street in South London. The two of you.'

'Mum.' Aaliyah smiled forlornly, then turned back inside. 'It doesn't feel like yesterday to me.'

For the rest of the morning, Marcus felt like a ghost haunting his own house.

He had to take the corsages from the bathroom and load them in the back of his father-in-law's car. The Pastor arrived, looking only slightly more kingly than usual, in a flowing agbada exquisitely embroidered with gold thread and the pair of dark aviators he would wear indoors and even at night.

'Now,' he began without any preamble as soon as he slammed shut his Mercedes door, 'what is this nonsense I hear about you and this wedding?'

'Hello, sir,' Marcus said. 'Aaliyah thinks that it will be better for everyone if I sit this one out.' He was devastated but made an attempt to sound casual.

The Pastor shook his head. 'This is not right,' he said, kissing his teeth in contempt. Marcus agreed, but he had tried to win Aaliyah around with no success. She was stubborn, like her mother.

Carmen emerged from the house. 'Oh, hi, Uncle,' she said. 'I'm glad you're here ...'

As they discussed logistics, Marcus slipped away. Back through the house, into the kitchen, where he overheard the glad chatter of his daughters and wife outside.

'Briar,' said my mother, 'you didn't think to shave your legs?'

I was nonchalant, genuinely baffled. 'Why would I?' I never had.

'You look ...' As Tanice regarded me, Marcus saw me brace myself for an insult. I wore a white blazer over my bridesmaid dress. My pink hair was braided back, and I was still wearing my DMs. '... exactly like yourself.'

I thought Kim might argue, tell me to change my shoes at least, but she just smiled, forgiveness in her eyes.

'It takes courage to be exactly anything in this life,' she said, 'especially yourself.'

Within ninety minutes they were all gone, the Pastor first with Tanice and Chantale, then his wife and other daughters with the rest of the women and all their happy noise. With the photographs taken, gifts exchanged, everything packed up or tossed in the boot, all the cars vanished from the driveway, and then the house was hollow as a tomb.

Marcus found himself at the kitchen table, sick with despair, when the sound of a car reversing in the driveway roused him.

Kim emerged breathless through the front door.

'You came back,' he said. She was the person he most wanted to see, still, even after all these years.

'Yes ...' She paused, then remembered her hurry and rifled through one of the bags she'd left on the table. Inside was a jewellery box, and she opened it to pull out a pretty hair clip with pearls and blue gemstones.

'Her borrowed and blue thing,' Kim said, 'and old, I guess.'

'I remember that.'

'Grandma Maeve gave it to me on our wedding day.' Kim smiled in recollection. 'I was almost too scared to wear it after she died. And whenever I do, I remember that speech that she made at our rehearsal dinner. The one about Jacob. How he wrestled an angel all night and wouldn't let go until he got a blessing. And she said—'

'"You only get to keep what you wrestle for,"' Marcus finished, smiling back at her.

'And most times, not even that.'

He reached out for her hand. 'Don't go.'

She squeezed it and said sadly, 'I want the old times back.'

'Doesn't everyone?'

'The two of us. How easy it was. How happy we were that day. Everyone hugging each other.'

'Not everyone. My dad and his ex. My aunt who "cursed" Jennifer.' Marcus and Kim both laughed in recollection at that.

'Yeah! She told me that after they saw each other again, she took her curse back.'

Their laughter faded into quiet. The day had been so happy that everyone forgot whatever grudges they were holding on to. Everyone forgave each other.

'I used to imagine that's what heaven might be like, our wedding day,' Kim said. But then she let go of his hand. There was a silence that stretched, expectant, between them.

'Maybe . . .' She stared earnestly into his eyes. 'Maybe I don't want to wrestle anymore.'

Marcus exhaled in relief. Could he be welcomed back? he wondered. Could he feel it again, the old warmth of her love?

'Neither do I,' he said. No more fighting. A truce.

'No.' Kim grabbed her finger and twisted off her wedding rings. Marcus saw the lighter bands of skin there as she placed them on the dining table. 'I don't want to wrestle for *this* anymore.' Marcus watched in disbelief as she turned and walked away. Out the open front door, to the car that had been idling in the driveway the whole time. Distant, happy exclamation from someone as she got in. The door slammed, and the car drove away.

Marcus jolted into action a little too late. He ran after her, out into the driveway, but the car was already speeding down the street. Leaving the door open, he rushed a few steps after it, before giving up when he realized that the chase was futile.

MARCUS MINTON – 0 HOURS, 0 MINUTES AND 0 SECONDS

My father was in his bunker when it began. He awoke disoriented and tried to sit up against a wave of dizziness. Had he hit his head? When he raised his hand to his throbbing temples, he felt the warm slickness of blood between his fingertips.

Marcus fumbled for a kerosene lantern, and its flickering light illuminated the bunker, which looked like a dollhouse some god had shaken. The neat rows of tin cans that had once lined the shelves were now flung across the floor, dented artichokes and diced tomatoes, cranberry sauce burst open a hysterical purple on the ground. Batteries and duct tape, hand soap and sporks, knives and nails everywhere.

The luminescent needle of the compass he kept on the table was spinning wildly. The bunker itself seemed to be straining in the ground. He could feel something in the air, some subsonic rumbling that made his teeth ache.

It must be some kind of atmospheric disturbance, the

rational part of him concluded. But the part of his mind that was always lurching towards disaster sounded like a clarion.

It took more force than usual to push open the door once he'd climbed up the ladder.

He began to panic as he emerged into the strange light in the garden and heard the sounds in the streets: car alarms, screaming, dogs barking.

There was an alien dread as he walked through the kitchen and into the house, which was in similar disarray. Shattered glass crunched underfoot, the coffee machine, the SodaStream and the toaster all looked as if they'd been wrenched from the walls; plaster and flakes of paint littered the laminated countertops around their plug sockets. At the bottom of the stairs, Kim's graduation picture and the framed scan of baby Chantale lay cracked and broken.

Outside the front door, the streets were utterly devastated. Totalled cars shimmered like dung beetles, smoke blossomed from twisted metal. Lamp posts looked as if they'd been pulled out of the ground, and live wires from electrical pylons snaked across the cracked pavement, throwing sparks. People were screaming from shattered windows or running between buildings. An analogue house alarm was ringing, a hammer trilling manically against a bell. On the next street over, a fire had started, a ruby blizzard of embers tossed up by convection currents, smoke curling erratically into the bright blue sky.

I wonder if his first thought was of us? Of the Pastor, Tanice and Chantale, who were probably already at Glassford House? Or Aaliyah, Kim and me, likely somewhere on the motorway?

Maybe he was just glad to be right.

PART TWO

After

BRIAR MINTON – THE DAY OF

Where were you when it happened? Were you sleeping when the metal frame of your bed began to creak and groan? Or in a doctor's office when the ceiling fixtures warped and the computer screens shattered? Did you see the dome of St Paul's Cathedral crack like an egg? Did you see Tokyo Tower crumple as if in a clenched fist? Were you in Platz der Republik when the vault of the Reichstag splintered?

We were driving across the Hammersmith Bridge, about a twenty-minute ride from our house. I was in the front seat of the car when a sudden wave of intense nausea hit me. I grabbed my stomach and shakily asked Mum to pull over.

Kim didn't answer me, too distracted by Carmen's on-going discussion with Aaliyah. 'Your mum married your dad,' she said, 'and he didn't have any money, right? I'm sure they just knew it would work out eventually ...'

'But they got married in the Nineties, when people just worked hard and got stuff. Now you only get anything if your parents give it to you ...'

'Or your husband,' Carmen teased.

'Mum,' I said louder, 'pull over.'

'We're already late,' snapped Aaliyah from the back seat of the car, where she looked as if she was drowning in tulle.

'Isn't it customary for the bride to be a little bit—' Carmen began cheerily, but I didn't have any patience left.

'Pull over!' I shouted. I could feel it, rising terror, something closing in.

'Briar?'

In some irrational panic, I fumbled for the door, ready to throw myself out of the moving car if she didn't stop.

'Okay, okay!' Mum swerved, pulled onto the pavement and braked so hard that my seatbelt snapped across my chest and Aaliyah gripped the headrest in front of her with a shout of indignation. Other cars beeped their horns.

'What the hell, Briar!' Aaliyah yelled out of the window as I scrambled out.

'Are you okay?' Carmen asked.

I leaned over the bridge, my arms shaking. I could feel a buzzing in my body, a pulling on the back of my jaw, where my permanent retainer was glued.

'Something's happening,' I told them, dizzy with a strange panic. They were still sat in the car and simply looked at each other in worry.

'Can you see that . . . ?' Carmen said. I squinted into the morning sun towards where she was pointing up at a plane which looked as if it was flying way too low. It seemed to judder and tremble in the sky, navigation lights blinking erratically. Something was wrong. Its fluffy vapour contrail sputtered out and disappeared. Had the engines failed? Then the plane jerked suddenly upwards. Realization dawned on me.

'Run!' I shouted at them. The colossal aircraft spiralled like a bird caught in a wind tunnel, pitching and rolling.

I took off, glancing over my shoulder as Carmen and Kim helped Aaliyah, in her massive dress, out of the car.

I was heading towards the south bank of the river when I witnessed the impossible. One by one, cars began to tremble, their metallic bodies shuddering. Then, with a sudden, violent jerk, they were wrenched from the asphalt, rising into the air like marionette dolls. The screech of tearing metal and the shattering of glass echoed around me, along with the distant cries of terrified motorists.

My breath caught in my throat as vehicles of all shapes and sizes – compact cars, family SUVs, massive white camper vans – were lifted from the ground. The force was so powerful that even the heaviest lorries, laden with cargo, were no match. All the vehicles on the bridge levitated, their wheels spinning helplessly in thin air. Some flipped over, while others remained eerily upright as they ascended.

Loose items floated from open windows and sunroofs – mobile phones, keychains, bottlecaps and cables – all suspended in the strange grip. A nearby motorbike, its chrome gleaming dully, wavered before shooting skyward, and its rider tumbled to the ground with a panicked scream.

It was some magician's trick. I felt the blood begin to spin down to my feet at the sight of it. Mum, Carmen and Aaliyah had frozen mid-stride to stare, their bodies darkened under the cool shadow of our family's car, a Vauxhall Zafira that Chantale had affectionately christened 'Zaffy'. They stared in nauseated silence, gazing at its oil-stained underbelly, its rusted cross members and chassis rails. The items inside were hoisted up into the air: pennies and AirPods, an aluminium water bottle, bobby pins and adaptors, something in my mother's clenched fist.

'No!' she said, gripping it hard. It was Aaliyah's hair

clip, the one that she'd rushed back to the house for. Its teeth clawed at her closed fist with enough force to start pulling her feet off the ground. Finally, she surrendered and watched it wheel up into the sky as if caught on a gust of wind, gilt roses and vines, its gems glittering as it disappeared into the maelstrom.

It was like a scene from a dream. The road, which had been a river of rushing metal and noise, was now empty. The vehicles cast their shadows across the tarmac, doors flapping open. A hundred car alarms had been activated simultaneously, and their shrill caterwaul melded with the roar of warping metal and crumbling concrete. I saw a red hatchback pivoting wildly as it ascended, its driver still inside, clinging desperately to the steering wheel. The other people who had managed to escape their vehicles stood frozen on the pavement, watching in horror.

Across the river, I could see scaffolding collapsing like toothpick towers before spinning up into the sky, street signs and bollards, drain covers and manholes popping like corks from champagne bottles, taking bits of pavement with them. In the distance, towards the City, cranes bent their long arms upwards.

'What's happening?!' Carmen shouted. She was on her knees, clutching her belly protectively. She wore a string of pearls that was being yanked upwards, pulling like a noose on her neck. After Aaliyah helped her to rip it free, the pearls scattered like marbles and the chain disappeared.

Stars flickered at the edge of my vision. I clenched my thighs, willing away the blackness threatening to overpower me. I knew we had to run, to find shelter, but I was rooted to the spot, unable to tear my eyes away from the spectacle above.

The sound of a dull wet *thud* jostled us out of our stupor, as further ahead we saw someone drop out of the sky and collide with the tarmac.

Aaliyah made a move to run towards the person, but Kim pulled her back.

'I think ...' As I spoke, I realized that the pull was getting stronger. The metal guardrail along the bridge began to lift, sections of it rising like a snake being charmed from a basket. The sight was both mesmerizing and terrifying.

I thought of my physics A-level class, of iron shavings and copper solenoids. 'It's magnetic!' I shouted at them.

'Briar's right!' Aaliyah raised her voice over the churning of metal and the howl of alarms. 'We need to run!'

We darted back the way we'd come as the historic suspension bridge beneath our feet rumbled. Its massive supports and metal trusses creaked and groaned. Carmen was so heavily pregnant that Aaliyah half carried her away, pulling one of her arms over her shoulder.

As the magnetic force intensified, the entire metal framework of the bridge began to lift off its stone piers. The suspension cables, taut and straining, snapped like guitar strings under the stress. We leapt to safety just as the road behind us buckled and sections of the bridge ascended unevenly.

I don't know how long we ran before 'the prestige'. Every magic trick has it, after the turn. The rabbit back in the hat, the card revealed, the sawed-in-half woman made whole.

The shadow of a hovering car waned as if in a spyglass, and I realized that whatever force had pulled the objects into its grip had set them suddenly free. Gravity remembered its duty, and hundreds of cars, lorries and bikes came down with merciless force. The sound was apocalyptic – twisted steel, shattered glass, blistered concrete. As we dashed across the road, debris rained down, pieces of metal and glass flashing past, cleaving through the air like shrapnel. I felt a sting on my cheek but didn't dare stop to assess the wound.

Next to the river was a park. If we could just get away from the road, we would be safe.

But then, 'Get down!' Aaliyah roared at me. To my left, a car was on fire. I ducked almost too late, just as its engine ignited with a thunderous *WHUMP* that seemed to suck all the oxygen from the air. A dazzling explosion bloomed from the wreckage, bright enough to blind. The impact knocked me off my feet and dashed my bones against a nearby wall.

I opened my eyes to a body full of pain, face and arms wet with blood, burning skin. A powerful gust of hot air from the blast washed over me, searing and intense, as a plume of black smoke rose into the sky. For a moment, I thought the noise had stopped, but as I looked around, I realized with horror that I could no longer hear anything at all. Screeching metal, howling alarms, even my own breath – all of it had disappeared. I opened my mouth to call out for Mum but couldn't hear the words my tongue made. Panic mounted. The air was thick with smoke and the sour tang of burning fuel.

In the pandemonium around me, people were running and screaming, covered in blood or holding loved ones. Drivers and passengers crawled out of wreckage, dazed and injured.

Some were slumped in their cars, heads smashed against steering wheels, or half-flung through windows. Other vehicles were crumpled on the ground like discarded toys, their lifeless occupants still strapped in their seats.

A hand on my shoulder made me scream. I turned around to find Aaliyah. She must have been in the blast radius, too, because her wedding dress was singed and bloodied. There were burns coming up on her arms, and she was limping. Despite her injuries, she helped me shakily to my feet, her ex-athlete's body still strong.

Sound began filtering back to me slowly. I tried to work out what my sister was saying, but it was as though she was speaking under water.

I shook my head to show I couldn't understand her. 'Over there,' I said. I could see the edge of the park through the smoke, its green field a refuge. We stumbled forward, arms round each other, our steps uneven on the littered ground. Mum and Carmen were further back: Kim's headdress had come off, and blood trickled from her rarely seen hair.

'Did you know?' Aaliyah shouted as we ran. Finally, I could hear something.

'What?' I yelled back.

'That this was going to happen?' We slowed as we reached the entrance to the park and stopped to catch our breath, though the air was poisonous, filled with smoke.

'How would I know?' I gasped finally. 'I don't even know what's happening right now.'

Aaliyah frowned. 'But in the car back there ... if we hadn't got out, we'd probably be dead already.'

I'd almost forgotten.

'You acted like you knew what was going to happen.'

'Yeah,' I nodded in recollection, 'I guess ... I had a feeling. Like something was coming.'

In the park, a crowd of dishevelled people were gathered, staring up at the sky.

'Hey, look ...' I said. The blueness of the sky was peeling

open to reveal another world behind it, one with a ghostly light. From where we were, an updraft was gusting away the smoke, and behind it we could see dazzling formations in the sky.

Everyone looked up in fear and wonder. Some people tried to run, covering their eyes. Others were on their knees, tears streaming down their cheeks.

Aaliyah said, 'Do you think it's—'

'It's Hero.' I had read about this phenomenon, but no one had warned us it was going to happen. 'Its presence is disrupting the Earth's magnetic field.' An increased stream of charged particles was colliding with atoms in the Earth's upper atmosphere. A process similar to the Northern Lights.

I thought of Axel and the Group. Of what Freya had said to me on Monday evening: *Have you ever seen an impossible thing?* My head was spinning. What if they were right about everything?

'It's kind of ...' Aaliyah began. It felt almost wrong to say in the wake of all that destruction, all that death. But there were big gashes in the clouds where it looked as if the wounded sky was bleeding rainbows.

'Beautiful,' I admitted.

TANICE MINTON – THE DAY OF

Twenty minutes before the world fell apart, Tanice found the wedding photographer standing in front of the large gilt mirror in the main hall, trying to do up his tie. She'd almost walked into him. He continued to focus, flipping the tie one way and then the other, looking lost.

'Do you need help with that?' Tanice asked.

'Oh,' he exhaled with relief, 'you can do it?' He let his hands fall limply by his sides.

'Yeah.' She put her phone in her bra and reached over to help him. 'In my old school, everyone had to wear one.' She pulled the polyester tie from his collar and flipped it around the right way. 'How have you got this far in life without knowing how to tie a tie?'

He laughed. 'I haven't got very far.'

'My dad taught me something like …' She twisted it around. '"The fox chased the rabbit around the tree once, twice … then it darted under a bush."' She pulled it tight. 'And was eaten anyway.' The photographer raised an eyebrow.

'I added that part,' Tanice said.

He tugged down his collar and regarded himself in the mirror. 'Thanks. I thought I could figure it out myself or at least find a YouTube video, but . . .'

'Yeah,' Tanice nodded at the hard edge of her phone case, sticky with sweat under her neckline, 'mine, too!'

He plucked his camera up off the onyx console table, and they headed out together into the sun.

'I wish they'd warned us that our phones wouldn't work here,' he said. The brightness on the lawn was such a contrast from the gloomy hall that, for a short while, they were blinded. 'I don't mind that much,' he insisted, 'but I need to be told.'

'Yeah, to, like, mentally prepare.'

'Yes,' he chuckled, 'download all my podcasts . . .'

'Warn my loved ones.'

The staff were emerging from the kitchen with canapés and cocktails on polished salvers, serving the guests who had already arrived. Tanice's heart still ached when she saw them. She thought of Sydney. They hadn't spoken since Thursday.

People chatted merrily by the pool or were arranging themselves near the neat rows of chairs. A few were waving their phones around or holding them up to the air.

There was Hugo – the handsomest she'd ever seen him, in a navy tailcoat and top hat – among a laughing group of his friends.

It was only when Tanice eyed one of the canapés – some complicated creamy thing on puff pastry – that she realized how hungry she was.

'What's that?' she asked the waitress. It was impossible to tell, by sight or smell, whether they were sweet or savoury.

'They're vegan,' the waitress said appealingly.

'You know,' said Tanice, 'that does the opposite of sell them to me.'

As the woman walked away, Tanice regarded the guests in their finery. Women in silk dresses and men in linen suits. People she'd never seen before. Their sunhats and fascinators made them look like a muster of peacocks.

'That's how you know this isn't a Nigerian wedding,' she told the photographer, and then explained, 'Mum was an hour and a half late for her wedding – I mean, who isn't?! – and Dad's family still bring it up.' The Minton side were all early, so apparently one side of the church was full and the other was empty. Dad told us that our aunties were still coming in just before the ceremony ended.

On the lawn, rows of elegant white chairs formed an aisle strewn with rose petals. As they headed down it together, the photographer laughed knowingly.

'I've done countless weddings now. Sometimes the start time is just . . . an ambition.'

'Exactly!' Tanice said. 'It's not a military operation.'

The photographer continued, 'It's a cultural thing, punctuality. Across huge swathes of the globe, people don't value it highly, but the English act as if it's an issue of morality.'

'Yeah!' Tanice was grateful to him for putting words to something that had irked her for years. Our grandad always joked, whenever someone asked him when his church service started, 'When everyone arrives!'

That afternoon, Pastor Abiola was standing by the lectern, preaching to a congregation of one, Chantale, who was twisting the heel of her patent leather Mary Jane into the lawn. The Pastor didn't hear them approach. 'Now,' he said, with his usual regal resonance, 'we reach the centre of the centre of the scroll . . . the sixteenth book. The Day of Atonement. "Kippur", the Hebrew word for atonement, means two things ...' Chantale was distracted, gazing up at the sky, frowning.

'Pastor,' said Tanice, shading her eyes from the sun. Our grandad looked up. He stood between two Greek urns heavy with blooms, lilies, white hydrangeas and trailing ivy. 'I think Briar was right. The Book of Leviticus isn't very wedding-y.'

'I must go where the Spirit leads me,' he told her.

'What about a crowd-pleaser?' Tanice suggested.

'"Love is patient, love is kind ..."?' the photographer offered. 'Everyone likes that one.'

'"Love means never having to say you're sorry"?' Tanice added.

'That's not in the Bible,' the Pastor said, unimpressed.

To their left was the string quartet, seated in a temporary bandstand. Through the loudspeakers, the music they were playing – a classical version of Sting's 'Until' – twisted suddenly and discordantly upwards, releasing an electric howl of feedback that made everyone cry out. Then the circuitry seemed to sputter out. The fairy lights hanging from the bougainvillea arch burst like water balloons, flinging glass everywhere. The guests looked around in alarm.

Anything metallic began to rise as if caught in an invisible tide. By the pool, the champagne buckets, serving trays and cutlery lifted off their tables. Silver forks and knives twirled in the sunlight like an airborne school of fish. Tanice felt her phone shift and grabbed it tightly with both hands. It began to levitate, pulling her whole body upwards as she clung.

'Tanice, stop!' Chantale cried. Our sister was a full metre off the ground before she ceded the battle and let her fingers unlock from her phone. She landed awkwardly in her heels and grabbed the arm of the photographer to steady herself. Miserably, she watched as her phone flew upwards along with necklaces, bracelets and cufflinks.

Further away, a vintage Rolls-Royce groaned as it lifted off the driveway, wheels sputtering gravel into the air.

For a minute, it was almost beautiful: an aerial display of glinting silver and glass, writhing below the clouds like confetti, but then, with no warning, everything plummeted back to Earth. Cutlery and phones rained down, cratering tables and spearing the grass. The floral arch collapsed in a heap of twisted metal and scattered blooms. Champagne bottles exploded on the patio, spraying guests with acid torrents of foam.

Tanice heard Hugo shout, 'Everyone, into the house!' At his exclamation, guests ran screaming towards shelter. Tanice's impulse was to grab our youngest sister's hand.

'Come on!' she shouted.

They raced down the aisle, taking care not to trip over falling debris. In the stampede, Tanice was knocked down, her hand losing Chantale's as she fell to the floor, hard, her face hitting the marble tiling of the pool. When she looked up, her mouth was bleeding and Chantale was gone.

'Chantale!' she yelled desperately. Instead, Paris rushed towards her.

'Hurry!'

He helped Tanice to her feet, and together they ran for the doors. Inside the main hall, the chandelier had crashed down hard on the patterned rug. Glass was everywhere, from its shattered bulbs to the imploded windows. The chemical tang of an electrical fire spilled into the atmosphere. Blood whooshed in Tanice's ears, and her eyes swivelled wildly.

People were crying or holding each other, looking scared. One woman was hyperventilating on the floor.

Chantale. Where was Chantale? Tanice shouted her name over and over again, but her face wasn't among the panicked crowd.

Did she make it? Oh God, please, she must have made it.

'It's finally happened,' the photographer declared to the group. Tanice turned to him in confusion. 'The Big One.'

Tanice spotted our grandfather, slumped by the wall.

'Grandad! Have you seen Chantale?' He shook his head. He was sweating. 'Are you okay?' He shook his head again. Between the draping folds of his robe, a shard of glass was buried deep in his thigh. Blood poured from it, black as crude oil. Something had hit his head, and he held a palm up to the tender skin there, his eyes rolling back.

'Tanice?' Hugo was behind her then. He grimaced at the sight of the Pastor, who looked as if he was losing consciousness.

'Take care of him,' Tanice said, getting to her feet. She was worried that he might be trampled.

'Where are you going?' Hugo shouted after her.

'To find Chantale,' she told him, pointing back at the double doors. Before she could run back the way she'd come, though, the photographer grabbed her. Tanice tried to shake herself free, but his grip was tight. 'I think my sister is still out there.'

'If she's out there, she's dead,' he said, matter-of-factly. Tanice looked at him in horror. 'The fallout will kill her and you.'

'Oh.' Tanice shuddered with cold realization. '"The Big One."'

'Exactly,' he said. 'You can't go out there.'

Only Tanice had done drills like this before, and she knew all the ways that a nuclear bomb could kill a person. Our father had explained how, after a nuclear explosion, residual radioactive material propelled into the upper atmosphere eventually fell back to Earth, contaminating the environment.

She told him, 'After a detonation, we have about ten minutes to find shelter before the fallout arrives. Does this house have a basement?'

'The kitchen has a pantry,' Hugo said. 'Though it's not very big.'

The photographer eyed the crowd. There were around ninety people in the atrium.

'I'll find you there,' Tanice said, opening the doors.

'I'm coming. I'm not losing either of you,' Hugo said. 'Aaliyah would never forgive me if anything happened to you.'

'Help the Pastor,' Tanice said, then looked out at the lawn. 'I'm a good runner.'

Outside, the air was so heavy with smoke that Tanice's eyes started streaming and she found herself coughing. The lawn looked as if a bomb had exploded in the middle of it: the grass was blackened and scarred, the few trees that were still standing had had their leaves blown off and the air was thick with ash.

'Chantale!' Tanice ripped a capped sleeve off her dress and held it to her face. 'Chantale!'

Her foot nudged something soft, and she jumped when she discovered that it was Hugo's sister, Eugenia, in her pale pink bridesmaid dress; her head cracked on the patio tiles, blood marbling the pool. Another woman in a blush dress floated face down in the water.

Tanice stumbled past them, dizzy with terror. Further across the lawn was more ruin. Some white folding chairs shattered like matchsticks. Alarms ringing distantly, dead birds everywhere. It was too dark for her to see the sky.

As she looked around, she was reminded of the old dread she had felt when Chantale had been hit by a car two years ago. The horrible crash she'd heard, the dull *thump* of metal colliding with bone. Our sister on the ground. The panicked seconds before we knew she was alive. Tanice had known then what she never had before: how much she loved her. She'd only recognized love as it curdled into terror.

As the smoke drifted, Tanice spotted a bundle of tulle on the grass. Two muddy Mary Janes. She sprinted towards her, zigzagging around debris, and fell to her knees next to our sister.

'Chantale?' Was she dead? Tanice rested two fingers under her chin and felt the warm throb of her pulse. The abyss retreated. She offered up a prayer of thanks and felt everything inside her rejoice.

'Five minutes.' She hadn't heard Paris behind her, but he leaned down then. 'Is she breathing?'

'I think so ...' Paris scooped Chantale up, then jogged back to the house, shouting at Tanice to follow him.

By the time they arrived, the atrium had descended into anarchy. The kind of crowd that made Tanice think of a Tube station at rush hour. The Pastor and Hugo were nowhere to be found, so she assumed that they had escaped to the pantry. Everyone else was trying to shove their way down to the wine cellar for safety, but the photographer was blocking the way.

'There isn't enough room for everyone!' he called out.

'Some of you will have to die up here of radiation poisoning.' But people were shouting over him, pushing. Finally, there was a loud smash and everyone fell silent. 'I said there's not enough fucking room!' He was brandishing a bottle of Bollinger, its broken neck glittering in his fist. The crowd retreated a little.

As they parted, Paris and the photographer made eye contact, and the man gave an almost imperceptible nod. Permission for the three of them to pass through.

As they did, Tanice spotted Hugo's friends, Aaliyah's remaining two bridesmaids, the catering staff and housekeepers with a prickle of shame at her own good fortune. She knew that, out here, the nuclear fallout was likely to kill them quickly – with radiation sickness, vomiting, skin burns, seizures, organ failure – or slowly – cancers, thyroid dysfunction, congenital malformations. She wanted to tell them what she knew, tell them to barricade themselves in the centre of the house and to tape shut the windows or vents or doors. Instead, she silently followed Paris past the photographer and down into the dim cellar. Damp wet air peeled up from the walls. The clicking of Paris's heels on the staircase echoed everywhere. It felt, to Tanice, like a descent into the underworld.

'Ninety seconds!' shouted a man in the dark below.

'We'll be okay down here,' Paris said.

They made it to the bottom of the staircase and into the cellar. The photographer was last through the door, and his leaving must have broken the spell on the crowd, because it sounded as if they all rushed after him.

Turning back to the door, Tanice saw two housekeepers yell at him, '*Proszę! Pomóż nam!*' But the photographer swatted them away with his bottle.

'*Proszę! Proszę! Proszę!*' the second, an old woman, begged.

The photographer slammed the door so hard that he almost trapped their fingers. They were still pounding at it, shouting, though the sound was muffled.

The room was dark, lit only by a torch that someone had placed upturned in the centre. Paris laid Chantale gently down on the floor and put his linen jacket over her.

It was cold. Tanice felt as if her skin was shrinking.

A man, leaning against a wall, was counting down, '... eight, seven, six, five, four, three, two ...'

'Don't,' said a dark-haired woman.

People were still screaming outside. It sounded as if someone was pounding something hard against the door, trying to ram it open.

'They can't,' said one of the musicians, an overweight man in a bowtie. More than ten minutes had passed by; it would be raining radioactive ash outside.

One of the women from the string quartet was crying, 'If the door opens, we could all—'

'No fucking way,' said the photographer. He looked around the room, and his eyes fell on one of the heavy wine racks, almost his height. The fat man helped him to pull it in front of the door. It did the trick.

Tanice looked around. She recognized the string quartet, the photographer, our sister, still passed out on the floor, and Paris. 'Grandad ... ?' she asked him, her voice a hollow tremor.

'I saw Hugo take him and a few others to the pantry. I think he was hoping to do it without drawing too much attention.' Tanice nodded but felt a wrench in her gut. She'd seen the extent of his injuries, and she desperately hoped that Hugo would be able to keep him safe.

The photographer and the musician were breathless, but they turned in triumph to the barricaded door.

'They'll never manage to . . .' the musician said.

The photographer nodded. 'Yeah.'

Tanice listened to the screams outside.

'And after a while,' the first man said, 'they'll . . .'

Tanice felt guilty that she was glad she had made it.

The photographer nodded. Assured. 'Yeah.'

MARCUS MINTON – THE DAY OF

There were a couple of iterations of the plan. In the one we'd practised the most, the Event occurred in the middle of the night. That was the simplest. We'd file down the stairs and congregate in the bunker. Some versions we could only rehearse in our minds. If the Event occurred when we were at school, we were to follow orders but attempt to return home as soon as possible.

Home was the safe place. Home was the fortress.

But Tanice, Chantale and the Pastor were at Glassford House. No cars were working, and the roads were blocked. Marcus calculated that he could get there either on foot – a day's hike – or in half the time by bike.

His mind went next to the car and Kim. She, Aaliyah and I were most likely in one of the worst places to be in the event of this kind of collapse: on a road.

Assessing the danger, he resolved that he would find and rescue us and bring us back home, then set off once more for Chantale and Tanice, who might have been spared from the worst of it out in the countryside in that big house.

Outside the bunker, Digit was running in wild circles,

barking up at the sky. Marcus found that Kim's bike had sustained the least damage, so he spent a short while replacing the chain and hammering some of the bent spokes back into place. Once he'd finished, he strapped his GOOD – *Get Out Of Dodge* – bag onto the panniers. He had a couple of different bags for various scenarios and seasons. This one contained three litres of water in collapsible containers, energy bars and freeze-dried meat, a tarp, a sleeping bag and a comprehensive first aid kit.

Of all the disaster scenarios he had imagined, this was the one he dreaded the most. His family scattered across the city, far from his protection. Marcus batted away the nightmare visions of what might have happened to us and tried to take control of the situation. He plotted the route he thought our car's sat-nav was most likely to have directed Kim. By his calculations, we could be anywhere between Fulham and Kew. He decided to search there first, and he comforted himself with the knowledge that no one could miss the woman in the wedding dress.

All along the street, our neighbours were gathered in horrified groups or trying to repair their cars. Hannah from the flat opposite was sitting on the front step, holding her baby and crying.

'Are you okay?' Marcus asked. She stared back at him, terror in her eyes, rocking. Her face was covered in blood. As Marcus approached, he saw that her eyebrow piercing must have been pulled out. She now had a gash, which bled over her right eye and down her cheek. 'Do you need something for that?'

'I probably have something . . .' her gaze flitted back, 'in the house.'

'Look,' Marcus said, 'if I were you, I'd run all the taps,

fill up every glass and bottle you have with water. Lock your doors. Do you have food?'

'A-a little . . . my last Ocado order was scheduled for—'

'Get as much as you can now, before the looting starts. You'll probably have to use cash.'

'I don't carry cash . . . since the burglary.'

Marcus took a deep breath, his patience wearing thin. 'I have to go.' He took up the bike and began to cycle away. But then, a couple of metres down the road, he sighed, stopped, then turned around. Marcus handed Hannah a rolled cylinder of cash.

'Oh.' She wiped her bloody eyes and took it. 'Thank you. I can pay you back when . . . If you give me your bank details?'

'It's fine.' He jumped back on his bike.

'Do you use Monzo?' Hannah shouted after him.

Marcus sped down the street towards Northcote Road. The Pastor and his wife had bought our family home in the Seventies, when Clapham had been a fairly rough place to live. After our grandma died, Kim never moved out. She married Marcus, and the Pastor chose to take up residence in a flat above Providence House. Kim claimed that her mother used to send her down the hill to buy okra from the outdoor markets while she made soup. But by the time Aaliyah was born the neighborhood had already begun to change. Now, the nickle scent of money was in the air. It seemed to seep from the pores of the bankers outside the artisan bakeries and glisten off the coats of the dogs they walked around the common.

The transformation Marcus saw that morning was more frightening, though. It was almost impossible for him to slalom through the wreckage on the road. Cars, flung into the air, had crashed back to Earth in ruinous heaps. A double-decker bus had crumpled near the curb, its candy-red hull mangled like a Coke can, bodies of passengers sprawled in grotesque stillness. The glass storefront of the GAIL's bakery had blown inwards. Pastries were littered across the floor, and a few staff members huddled together, nervously handing out leftover food to people gathered outside.

Elsewhere, survivors stumbled through the ruin, dazed and bloodied. Parents wailed over the bodies of their children, while others desperately searched for missing loved ones.

Marcus's body grew heavy as he cycled down the road. In all of his preparations, he had never stopped to really think about all the lives that a world-ending Event would cut short. Confronted by the reality of it, he thought of us and picked up his pace.

Near the crossroad, fights were breaking out. Some people were stealing fresh fruit from the Bailey & Sage. Shop assistants in Oliver Bonas were attempting to help survivors, using torn clothing as makeshift bandages. A young man sat sobbing among the upturned mannequins and shattered reed diffusers.

Marcus took a short cut to avoid the main road, turning up the hill opposite the Waitrose. There, he almost crashed into a middle-aged man beating a teenager with the back of a tennis racket.

'Hey!' he shouted to break up the fight, and the boy took advantage of the moment of surprise to wriggle free.

The man growled, 'Fucking—'

He made to lunge for him again, but Marcus yelled, 'Hey, he's just a kid.'

The boy was bleeding heavily. Marcus got off his bike and dropped it carefully on the pavement, moving towards them, hands raised.

'They came out of nowhere.' It was only as he stumbled breathlessly back that Marcus realized the man was injured, too, a dark bruise forming on the side of his head.

'Who?'

The teenager spat blood and saliva on the floor. Peeled out a tooth and staggered backwards. Something glinted in his hand, which he held tightly by his side. Marcus fought the twist in his gut.

'Like a flash mob,' the man gasped. 'A bunch of . . . boy scouts? With knives!'

'Where?'

The man nodded over his shoulder, up the road towards the Asda supermarket.

'They stabbed three security guards. This fucking kid was—'

The boy smiled redly and lifted it up then, a machete, which glimmered in the light.

Marcus was torn between his impulse to reach for one of his own weapons, the closest, a boning knife in the pocket of his cargo trousers, or to try to de-escalate.

The boy walked slowly towards him, his glittering eyes the colour of oxidized copper.

'C-chaos is coming,' he stammered, jittery.

Suddenly, he darted forward, and Marcus recoiled, making a move for his knife. He saw too late that it was a feint. The boy reeled back, grabbed Marcus's bike and in a practised move lifted it up and cycled away.

'You little—!'

Marcus chased after him, sprinting up the road. The

thief weaved in and out of crashed cars, up Lavender Hill, towards the Asda supermarket, where he sped through the car park and pedalled inside.

Marcus slowed his approach as he noticed that all the entrances to the store had been barricaded with pallets and boxes.

In the car park, shopping trolleys were strewn in mangled wrecks, on parked cars or bent around lamp posts, reflecting the afternoon sun in jagged flashes. It was a strangely domestic display on the asphalt: burst cans of beans, scattered crumbs of frozen mince, ripped bags of fresh coriander and Doritos ground to dust. Water and vegetable oil made slick rainbows in the gutter.

Marcus crept up to the one remaining entrance. Unlike the chaotic crowds he had passed on Northcote Road, the people here were being ushered into lines out in the car park. Masked boys with stab vests and motorcycle helmets, holding knives and crossbows, cricket bats and hand-made spears were shouting orders at the terrified shoppers. Marcus thought he recognized the cashier from a couple of days before, the one who had confronted him. She was looking away now, on her knees, begging for them to let her go. Her septum piercing, as Marcus could see, must have been pulled out, as her philtrum, lips and teeth were marbled with blood.

'Hey!' Marcus felt the weight of a palm on his shoulder, as a boy in a Second World War gas mask stopped him from going any further.

'What's going on here?' Marcus demanded.

'We're moving everyone out. You need to leave,' the boy said.

'Wait,' Marcus said. 'Look, one of your ... "comrades"

stole my bike. I want it back. You can keep doing whatever you're doing here, and I'll be on my way.'

'I said move out!' the kid shouted and pushed him again. It wasn't hard but there was a threat of violence behind it. 'Place is ours now!' Marcus assessed the situation; the likelihood of taking this armed boy on, the others hovering nearby. He started backing away.

Marcus realized that this group had stormed the Asda as they might have an unfortified castle. He was almost more impressed than he was horrified by the feat. In a grid-down situation, he'd expected looting and disorder. He'd imagined the strong rising victorious from the anarchy, or the steadfast and the bold eventually restoring order. But he hadn't imagined this. The Asda, set on a hill a little way back from the road, was the perfect location to occupy. A supermarket, filled with months', maybe years' worth of supplies. It was a prime location in the middle of the town, which might draw people from all around to barter for access to food, water and basic supplies.

Marcus wondered how they had done it. This sort of thing would have taken planning and some level of forewarning. Were these boys all in that Discord server that had been warning for weeks of an extinction-level Event? Had they scoped the place ahead of time? 'Like a flash mob,' the man on the street had said, and Marcus imagined what it must have been like in the minutes after the lights went out, as everyone emerged from the store, blinking like deer in the June sun.

Had the boys approached then with their weapons, stationing themselves at key positions? Getting rid of the security guards and intimidating the staff in their bright green uniforms with sudden violent displays?

Behind him, Marcus's attention was caught by a voice he recognized. A couple of metres away, a young man with a ginger mullet was swinging a butcher's cleaver at a man on his knees and telling him to empty his pockets.

'Andrew?' Marcus said. He used to teach him for Cub Scouts. 'Andrew Griggs!'

Andrew looked up, his face hardened as if to fight, but as he approached, he recognized Marcus. 'Hey!' he called, lowering his cleaver to his side.

Marcus hadn't seen Andrew in almost ten years. He remembered teaching him urban foraging on a rainy September afternoon on Clapham Common, how to put up a tent, how to read a map and start a fire. Andrew had been slightly overweight back then, wan, halitotic. He always had a pocketful of polyhedral D&D dice. He liked to do magic tricks when no one was watching.

He must be twenty or twenty-one now. Dressed in black and khaki, he'd smeared his cheeks with warpaint and something that looked alarmingly like blood. He was grinning as if the chaos was a feast he couldn't wait to devour.

Andrew's voice was disarmingly warm. 'Baloo!' It was what the Cub Scouts had nicknamed him, after the sloth bear and strict teacher in *The Jungle Book*.

'Andrew,' Marcus said, still guarded.

'Come to join us?' Andrew grinned and nodded over his shoulder at the store. Through the windows, Marcus could now see that they had illuminated the aisles with storm lanterns. A cave of treasure.

'I need to go,' Marcus said. 'I need to rescue my daughters and wife.'

'Oh ...' Andrew said. 'Shame.'

'Yeah, one of your gang stole my bike.' Marcus indicated

the barricaded doors that he'd seen the boy cycle through. 'If he could just—'

'No one's going in or out at the moment. Those are the orders.'

'From who?'

'I thought you knew.' Andrew examined Marcus with a quizzical face. '@CollapseNow.' He nodded over to a checkpoint, where a dark-haired man was barking orders at a group of boys. Marcus's heart dropped into his stomach.

'He's your leader?' he gasped.

@CollapseNow was the handle of Dennis Crossley, a fellow Cub Scouts leader, who had moved up a couple of years ago to teach the teenage Explorers. During the pandemic, he'd started making YouTube and TikTok videos about how to survive different end-of-the-world scenarios. In the early days of 2020, his content had gone viral.

But Dennis's videos weren't just about how to survive – they were about how to thrive and use anarchy to leverage yourself to a position of more power. Everything, for Dennis, was about power and strength. Marcus had made the mistake, two years ago, of signing up for one of his bushcraft classes. But the sight of the man skinning a hare – the peach-pink fleshiness of its body underneath, the way its leathery hide peeled free of its neck, the warm curl of it between Crossley's thumb and knife – had made Marcus pass out.

Since then, he'd been abruptly demoted in the man's esteem. If they ever crossed paths during hikes or Scout excursions, Dennis would openly mock Marcus, offering to carry his bags or alluding to the way he'd fainted: 'Corset too tight?'

Dennis Crossley was a man eager for the end of the

world. His wife had left him over a decade ago, and he'd owned the camping goods store on St John's Road, which had now been replaced by a laser hair removal clinic. If the Scout leaders ever met in a pub, Marcus might hear him complaining about the relative weakness of the upcoming generation as he nursed a pint. Sometimes he'd say that 'a good war' was 'exactly what they needed'.

Of course Dennis would be in charge of this takeover, Marcus thought to himself that afternoon. He knew the local area intimately and he'd often kept in touch with the boys after they left Scouts, meeting regularly for camping excursions and lessons in archery and bushcraft. It was clear to Marcus then that with the classes and the YouTube tracts, his podcasts and Substack how-to guides, he'd been training a militia.

'Minton!' Dennis shouted as Marcus approached him. 'Matthew Minton.'

He was wearing khaki combat clothing, assault gloves, shinpads and an expensive, lightweight, armoured vest that Marcus had been eyeing online for months.

'It's Marcus.'

'That's what I said.' Dennis looked great. The silver roots of his dyed-black hair did glitter in the sun, but he was bulkier than he had been even a couple of months ago when Marcus had last seen him, raising the flag with his Explorers group on the Common. 'If you're thinking of joining us, you'd better not wet the bed at the sight of blood.'

'One of your minions stole my bike.'

'That's what I'm saying,' said Crossley. 'You need to move fast.'

'I do. I need to rescue my daughters.'

'Daughters?' Crossley had met Chantale a couple of

times. He'd had a brief affair with one of the leaders of her Rainbows group. 'How many do you have?'

'Four,' said Marcus.

'Four!' yelped Crossley – Marcus was used to this reaction. Crossley seemed as if he was thinking of something churlish to say, but finally he nodded. 'Doing your bit to fight population decline.'

'I guess you could say that.' Marcus often had.

'Gotta keep all those daughters safe.'

'Exactly.'

'I wish I could help you. But as you can see,' he gestured around the car park, 'this is a delicate operation. You've got a couple of options. Bug in – hunker down, defend your household, gather resources, ration them. Or bug out – get out of the city, make it on the land. Since you can't stomach skinning a hare, I'm guessing you'll choose the former.'

'I have a plan,' said Marcus defensively. 'A bunker, supplies, a generator.' He cursed himself immediately for saying it. One of the first rules of bugging in was not to let anyone know how prepared you were.

'Good for you.' Crossley's eyes widened with curiosity behind his ballistic goggles.

'But you've got a great set-up here,' Marcus hastily added.

'The ideal set-up,' he agreed. 'I've been thinking of it for a while. Need a good location. Somewhere safe, defensible. From this vantage point, we can see anyone coming from any direction. And obviously, we have everything we need. Food, water, clothing, condoms … Anything else we'll barter for. People will come from far around after the looting has subsided and their taps aren't running. You might, too, and when you do, bring something valuable.'

'Noted. Do you know what's going on?' Marcus asked.

Crossley nodded, self-assured in his knowledge. 'The cars and the buildings are obviously subject to some kind of anti-gravity device.'

'Oh yeah?' said Marcus.

'For sure. Top secret, Deep State stuff.'

'Which state, though?'

'I've been saying for a couple of years that, the rate we're going, China are gonna take over. So that would be my first guess.'

'Yeah?'

'Or some kind of alliance of all our enemies.' He listed a couple of countries and then added, 'Obviously with inside help from Antifa.'

Marcus asked, 'Do you think the military—?'

Crossley scoffed, 'The military? No one's coming for us now, mate.' He was right: without power, with the destruction of transport routes and the lack of functional vehicles, large-scale military coordination had already become nearly impossible.

'Collapse is coming,' he said gleefully, as if he could already see it. In urban areas, gangs and militias would seize control of key locations like food warehouses, fuel depots and water sources. Law enforcement would try but fail to maintain control, leaving a power vacuum. People would form local groups to protect their homes and resources, leading to isolated skirmishes.

More would die in the coming days than during the initial Event. Hospitals would be overwhelmed. There would be a rampant spread of disease because of poor sanitation, contaminated water and overcrowding.

Crossley described it all with relish: without functioning

communication networks or infrastructure, the UK government would effectively collapse. The King might attempt to reach safety in a remote, secure location, but his authority would be completely gone. The country would fragment. There would be no functioning civil administration and no law enforcement beyond local, makeshift groups.

'The Dark Ages,' he said, like a spell he was casting. 'Look at the Mayans. Look at Athens. Look at Rome. Humanity goes through cycles. Couldn't we all feel it? Didn't it feel like the good times were already almost over? "Late-stage capitalism", the high before the fall. Decadence. Hedonism. You could make anything true if you wanted it to be.'

Marcus shifted on his feet as Dennis monologued, trying not to show his impatience.

As the situation stabilized, survivors would revert to a pre-industrial mode of living, relying on basic farming, hunting and scavenging.

'All part of the cycle,' he said.

Marcus let Crossley's words roll off his back. He couldn't think that far ahead yet. He could only think about today. He had to keep searching. He'd return home, get a new bike and save his family.

BRIAR MINTON – THE DAY OF

The sun was low in the sky by the time we returned home. The house was empty. We'd walked for hours, trying to avoid the devastation on the main roads, navigating through the city. At one point, Carmen was in too much pain to walk, so Aaliyah found a dented shopping trolley discarded on the pavement, bundled her in and pushed her home.

I wasn't sure what I'd hoped to find on our return. Our father making beans on the camping stove and grinning? Two bikes were gone, and two of his GOOD bags.

He'd left a note on the whiteboard on the fridge, explaining that if we got back before he returned, he was heading to Glassford House to find the Pastor, Tanice and Chantale. There were a couple of other details about where some of the money was stashed and a reminder to lock the doors and windows.

We felt rootless without him. Anything I might have done that afternoon had evaporated.

Mum sat down heavily at the kitchen table, where I noticed her wedding rings glinted. 'Chantale ...' she sobbed quietly.

'And Tanice,' I snapped, 'your *other* daughter, remember?'

'She'll be okay,' Carmen said, placing a tender hand on Kim. 'They all will be. We'll see them soon.'

Aaliyah leaned over the table and exhaled heavily. 'Help me get this off,' she said, gasping in her ballgown, her hand going to where the boning was digging into her shoulder blades. We all moved quickly to help. Her dress had one hundred and forty pearl buttons that the makeup artist had helped to do up with a special hook.

'Just get some scissors,' Aaliyah said, nodding at the 'miscellaneous stuff' drawer, the one under the cutlery drawer where they were likely to be found, next to batteries and screwdrivers.

'*No!*' Mum shouted.

'It's not as if I'm going to wear it again.'

Carmen produced the scissors, and together they severed and ripped Aaliyah free. She wore a nude strapless bra underneath and matching mini-briefs. I could see on her hips and under her ribs where the bones of the dress had rubbed her skin raw. It could almost stand up on its own in the middle of the kitchen.

'You might have,' Kim said. Then sorrowfully, 'Or I don't know. Your sisters.'

Suddenly, Carmen made a sound, a low groan. I turned to see her clutching her belly.

'What is it?' Mum asked, instantly on guard.

'Braxton,' she winced, 'Hicks.'

'What does that mean?' I asked.

'Not labour, thankfully,' Aaliyah said, then looked at Mum. 'But do you think, just in case . . . ?'

'We should find out where we can see a doctor,' Kim agreed.

'At the petrol station, I heard some people saying that Providence House is a relief centre,' Aaliyah suggested. It made sense. Our grandfather had repurposed the church buildings a couple of times in the past – after a local train derailed, during the pandemic, for the homeless on a particularly cold winter night – to offer help to those who needed it. The people there would know what to do.

'I'll walk up and see if I can find any help,' Mum suggested.

'I don't need help,' Carmen began, but even as she did, she grimaced in pain again. I wasn't sure if I was imagining the skin on her bump growing taut under the sheer silk of her bridesmaid dress. She inhaled through gritted teeth as if she'd just stubbed her toe.

'Shock can trigger these things,' Kim said. 'Cortisol and adrenaline can contribute to the onset of contractions or premature rupture of membranes.'

'I read that lots of women went into early labour following 9/11,' Aaliyah added.

'But ...' Carmen looked terrified. 'It can't happen here. It's supposed to happen in a hospital.'

'It might not happen at all,' I suggested hopefully. 'Isn't it a bit early?'

'Thirty-six weeks,' Carmen said.

'Almost full-term,' my mother explained.

'But they say that first babies are always late!' Carmen was arguing as if fighting for a stay of execution.

'It's okay,' Aaliyah said. 'Mum will go, check out what the medical care situation is there and come right back.'

As they continued discussing the logistics of it, I looked around and realized that Digit hadn't bounded down the stairs to greet me.

'Hey,' I said, looking around, 'do you think Dad would have taken Digit with him?'

'Probably not,' Aaliyah said. 'Why?'

I used to tell people that Digit saved my life. Anorexia nervosa is the psychiatric illness with the highest mortality rate. There are a lot of ways starvation can kill you: electrolyte imbalances, seizures, infections, liver or kidney failure. For me and Axel, it was our hearts.

A couple of weeks before I was admitted to High Tower, I collapsed. I learned later that my heart momentarily stopped due to a dangerous arrhythmia caused by critically low potassium levels.

I woke in the hospital to the sound of Mum crying. Her hand on mine, her shellaced nails sparkling under the hospital's fluorescent lights.

'What can I do,' she asked me, tears peeling trails into her foundation, 'to help you get better?'

It had been Chantale who whispered, 'Ask for a puppy.'

By early evening, I was frantically searching the streets of Clapham with tears in my eyes. I'd scoured the garden and knocked on the doors of all the neighbours, and my voice had grown hoarse from shouting her name in the high-pitched sing-song way I knew Digit responded to. I had some cheese in my hands – her favourite treat – which was growing sticky in the heat. I stopped and quizzed an old man clutching a photograph and a woman cradling a bleeding arm – but they just shook their heads and turned away, too wrapped up in their own tragedies to notice mine.

Auroras made the street glitter like the Tau's home

planet – the flowing green and purple light making shattered glass and dented chrome diamond-bright.

'Digit!' I climbed over the wreckage of a bus, my hands scraping against jagged edges. In the distance, someone was crying, their wail long and guttural, but I didn't stop to help. I pushed on, stumbling through the debris, heart pounding with each step.

I heard a dog bark in a nearby car. A moment of hope. It wasn't mine, though. The owner's hatchback had crashed into a tree. The man looked dead, leaning out of the broken window, limp as a doll, a rill of blood creeping down his widow's peak.

I opened the passenger door, and a little Jack Russell bounded out, yapping.

A couple of the streets were blocked off. A police officer on horseback was riding through the roads with a loudspeaker. *'Attention. Attention. Please remain calm. A curfew is in effect from sunset. Stay indoors. Conserve resources. Listen for updates. Emergency services are working to restore order. Stay safe.'* I didn't know then that that would be the first and last I would see of the police for a while.

The sun was starting to set. I guessed that I had maybe an hour before I would have to return home.

Running back up to the Common, I re-examined all the spots where Digit liked to play; the pond where she chased ducks, the tree with the good sticks. All the places where I'd sat in the grass and Digit had leapt around me or nuzzled into my side, the wildflowers she'd dived in and out of like a dolphin.

Eventually, I sat down on a bench, crying. I could think of nowhere else to look. The thought of losing her was horrible.

I was considering going home and trying again tomorrow
when I saw a flash of black fur darting between brambles.
My chest tightened, and I broke into a run, shouting her
name until my voice cracked.

'Digit! Come here, girl!' The shape disappeared around
the corner, and I followed, skidding on loose gravel. When
I turned the corner, though, she was gone.

The quiet entrance to the school loomed before me. On
the weekends, our school always felt a bit ghostly, like an
abandoned fairground, with the wind carrying the phantom
chatter of hundreds of girls, the whistles of teachers and
the engines of idling cars. Students' bodies, negative space
almost, in the driveway, on the lawn. The term was almost
over, with only two weeks left to go. On Monday, would
anyone return?

The gate itself had been destroyed, so it was a small feat
to climb under it and into the grounds.

I half-expected the groundskeeper, Freya's dad, to
emerge with a trowel and ask what I thought I was doing
on school property. But no one challenged me as I ran
past the swimming pool and the sports hall, the swanky
new Design Technology buildings and the ivy-heavy clock
tower, the grand Victorian main building that had first
captured my imagination on an open day, the centuries-
old stained glass of St Clotilde now shattered into a
million pieces across the lawn. I dashed into the open
field behind the refectory. There, on the other side, were
the ruined tennis courts where I'd woken early that morning. It seemed so long ago now, like I'd lived a lifetime in
between.

I wondered if the Group would still be there. My heart
began to pound.

The grass was soft and undisturbed under my heels as I walked towards the groundskeeper's cottage, catching my breath. There was still no sign of Digit, but I thought I could see shadows in the windows of the cottage. As I approached, I heard music and voices.

I found Freya out in the garden wearing the same linen pyjamas she'd had on that morning. She was leaning over in the grass, blood on her fingers. A crochet blanket was spread over the ground, a mandala print spiralled across it. There was a body underneath.

Freya didn't move at my approach.

'What happened?' I asked.

'It's okay.' She stood. 'It happens gradually, cell by cell.'

The shape of the body looked like a man. Through the gaps in the blanket, I could see the blueish tinge of his skin.

'Entropy only moves one way for us. But for Them …' Freya turned towards the cottage and called, 'It's time.'

A dozen members of the Group came running out, Beth among them. She wore a large sunhat and round sunglasses with little daisies on their frames that had the effect of making her look like an exotic bug.

'You sure you're ready?' Beth took Freya's hand. I wasn't sure if I was imagining the way that Freya's hand trembled. The way she slightly lost balance and Beth had to reach out a hand to steady her. She took a few heavy breaths and seemed to draw strength from deep in herself. Finally, she nodded.

Cato brandished a clear bottle of what smelled like white spirit. He poured it over the crochet blanket, shaking it hard to make sure the spirit leached onto the body as well.

Then everyone stepped back, and he produced a match.

'Rafe,' he said. Freya's father. 'Until we see you again.'

Then a huff of air as the match hit the white spirit, and everyone stood for a long while in silence, beholding the flames. I was a little surprised at how stoic the Group was at Rafe's death, though. As the fire's cinders reflected off their dry eyes, they seemed about as sorrowful as I would be bidding Aaliyah goodbye before a short trip, certain I'd see her again.

I heard Soo-Jin whisper to Laurie, 'We have to get out of the city before it gets too dark.'

'Where are you going?' I asked, and she looked startled to see me behind her.

'You're coming, too?' Laurie smiled at me warmly. He was always so friendly to me. Laurie claimed to be afflicted by several illnesses caused by the Tau. He said he never managed more than a couple of hours of sleep at night because of the nightmares that haunted him, that he woke up in cold sweats or with mysterious fevers, aches and pains. Notably, none of Laurie's ailments seemed to manifest in any visible symptoms other than his clear distress and the fact that he meticulously washed everything his highly restrictive diet allowed him to eat. He wore cotton gloves everywhere and tinted blue glasses to help with the headaches.

'Where?'

'Midacre,' he replied. 'This old pile in Surrey that our uncle owned. It's maybe a day's walk from here.'

'We go every now and then,' Soo-Jin explained.

'And there have been a few encounters there,' Laurie said. It was difficult to tell exactly what that meant, but I didn't ask.

More people were streaming out of the house with

backpacks and bags, sleeping bags and yoga mats. They looked as if they were going to Glastonbury. Teenagers in wellies and bikini bottoms, cowboy hats and dungarees. A woman had put her three cats in a wheelbarrow. There was Axel, waving, all his things in a raffia JD Sports bag. There was Amy with a camping rucksack. All lit by the fire's embers floating over our heads in the waning light. I felt a longing to go with them, as, when I was eleven, I had wanted to leave my family and join the circus.

'But the curfew?' I said.

'If we leave soon,' Laurie replied, 'before the roads are blocked, we should be fine.'

'Why don't you go tomorrow?' I felt strangely abandoned by them. Irrationally betrayed.

'It's probably best to get out of the city,' Laurie said gently, 'now that the Tau are here.'

'You think that's what's happening?' I asked.

'Difficult to tell the exact mechanism of action,' opined Soo-Jin, 'though I have some theories.'

'Yeah?'

She nodded. 'Magnetic levitation? Some anomalous atmospheric condition, a microburst or a powerful updraft, gravity waves ...'

'But why, though?'

'To get our attention, I imagine.'

'But ...' I was thinking about Hammersmith Bridge, ripped to pieces, the hundreds of thousands likely dead across the city. 'I thought you said that the Tau are *good*.'

Soo-Jin hesitated and looked uncomfortable.

'What are you doing here?' Cato cut in sharply. From my vantage point, it looked as if his floppy black hair was on fire.

'I'm . . .' I trailed off. He frightened me a little. 'My dog is missing.'

Freya turned an ear to us.

'What breed?'

'A mix, we think. A black spaniel. We don't know for sure. Her mum abandoned her.' I could feel tears coming again. There were too many ways to describe the cashmere softness of her fur or how happy she always was to see me. 'I don't think I've spent a night without her since . . .'

Mum had brought her home the night I was discharged from High Tower. I still remember how small she looked in her crate. The way I had to wake up in the middle of the night and stand in the garden, in my pyjamas, waiting for her to poo. Initially, I despaired as I came to understand the responsibility of looking after another creature. It seemed intimidating, totalizing. But then I began to realize that the night wakes, the cold, the walks, were all part of transforming me. Love wasn't just a feeling; it was an act performed resentfully or stoically or joyfully every day. How could I not love her after picking up hundreds of biodegradable bags of her poo? Surrendering to it was the love.

'What's her name?' Freya asked.

'Digit,' I said through tears. Digit became the reason I didn't want to be sent back to hospital, the reason I was thankful to be well.

Freya nodded sagely. 'What's her *true* name?' she asked.

I wiped my eyes. 'You mean, the name they gave her at—?'

Freya shook her head. 'Whenever we encounter Them, we hear Their voices in the deepest parts of us. From across time, over light-years of space, because They call us by our true names. The word that first called us into existence. If you know her true name, you can call her, and wherever she is, she'll hear.'

I was too confused to cry then; I just looked at Freya, astounded. 'I . . . I don't know how,' I said. Half the Group was watching, as the other half began walking away.

'I think you do,' Freya said, with a gentle smile. She really believed in me.

'I . . . ' I was sceptical of everything they had told me, but part of me wanted desperately to believe Freya, to call for Digit and for her to appear.

'Just try,' Freya said. I bit my tongue and looked at my feet. Freya placed a cool hand on my chest. I closed my eyes. I felt her other hand on my temple. She instructed me to breathe deeply, to imagine Their deadly home world. To imagine Them reaching out across the stars, calling us by name eons before we were born.

I thought instead about my love for Digit. The way her back felt at my heels when I fell asleep at night. How happy the spring made her. The way she licked my face any time I cried.

Finally, a sound like a bell entered my throat. It was more like a note I sang. And I opened my eyes suddenly as if surprised at myself.

Nothing happened.

'Give it a couple of tries,' Cato said dismissively. 'Come on, everyone, we're going.' Freya turned away.

'They'll probably land soon,' Beth said, 'and come looking for us.'

'You think so?' I asked. She laughed as if it was obvious. I guess, now that the impossible had happened, maybe it was. What else could explain what we'd witnessed that day? What other than alien technology could wreak this kind of damage? I wasn't sure why I was still trying to cling to rational explanations when we'd clearly left the rational world behind.

'Come with us,' Axel said.

The fire was burning out, and they were ready to leave. Isaac and Martha, Laurie and Cato. Charlie, Soo-Jin and Freya. I really wanted to go with them, to be part of something. But I needed to find Digit and get home to my family. I wanted to be there when Dad got home.

'I can't, I'm sorry. Laurie said it's a day's walk,' I said. Axel's face fell, but Beth just looked at me knowingly.

'Here, for when you change your mind.' She dug into her canvas bag and handed me a map with a sticky gold star at the right location. She also handed me some paper cones, which I inspected. Fireworks. 'In case you get lost. Spark them, and we'll keep an eye out for you.'

Axel hugged me. 'I hope you come soon,' he said. He told me that they were planning on doing a recital of *Into the Woods*, and if I came, I could join him as musical director. That offer was more enticing than any other.

'We'll be waiting for you!' he shouted, as they left.

I watched them go as the dark started closing in.

The makeshift pyre they'd burned Freya's father on was still hissing and spitting embers. He smelled of cooking meat. I felt sick and desperately alone.

A sound in the bushes startled me. My heart galloped a little as I remembered that we were post-collapse now. Nothing was safe. My father had warned me about gangs, about people reduced to their basest needs. I started backing away.

Dark eyes in the leaves, a flash of fangs ...

'Hey, who's there?'

She barked once, sharp and desperate, and ran towards me, her body trembling as she leapt into my arms. I sank to my knees, clutching her tight, my tears falling into her fur.
   'Digit!'

TANICE MINTON – THE DAY OF

It didn't take long for Tanice to realize that if they stayed in the wine cellar, they were going to die. After the photographer barricaded them in, they were silent for what felt like almost an hour as the screaming outside abated.

Chantale awoke in a fit of terror and immediately burst into tears when Tanice told her what had happened. She tried to reassure her that everyone was going to be okay, but it was hard to comfort a crying seven-year-old while it seemed like the world was finally, really ending.

'What about Dad and Mum?' Chantale asked. Tanice improvised survival stories as much for herself as for our sister.

'They probably haven't left the house yet,' she guessed. 'They would have had lots of time to get into the bunker and hide.'

'Aaliyah and Briar?' Chantale asked.

'Same for them. In the bunker, just like during our drills.'

They retreated into the cellar's small anteroom, which offered a little privacy. It was a cramped chamber, filled with boxes of unopened bottles, old barrels piled high, a cabinet stocked with wine accessories, corks, a rack of cups, decanters, labels and tags, thermometers and a couple of devices for climate monitoring and humidity control.

'And Grandad and Hugo? Why aren't they down here?' Chantale quizzed, as Tanice helped her take off her dress.

'Paris said there's another safe place in the kitchen's pantry. They're probably there, feasting on canapés.'

'Eugenia?' The image of Hugo's sister's skull, cracked like a chestnut shell on the side of the pool, flashed across Tanice's mind. Trying not to shudder, she dodged the question. 'Why do you care about her all of a sudden?'

She found some blue roll on a shelf and spat on it before carefully beginning to clean the cuts on Chantale's knees from when she had fallen during the blast. Chantale winced in pain.

'Carlotta?' Chantale asked. Her babysitter.

'Doesn't she live in a basement flat?' They'd seen it together once, filled with gaudy photographs of old Popes. 'So yeah, she probably got lucky.'

She moved to dab Chantale's cream satin dress – stained with someone else's blood – dry. Tanice lifted it up, her eyes going immediately to the brown marks, and sighed. It would have to do.

'Mr Barmah?' Chantale asked. She looked so small in her lace-lined vest and floral cotton knickers.

'Who's Mr Barmah?' Tanice asked.

Chantale frowned. Tanice remembered that he was her R.E. teacher.

'I dunno, Chantale, probably fine.'

'And what about—?'

'Stop it!'

Chantale looked as if she was about to cry again, which

Tanice couldn't bear. She wrapped her arms around our youngest sister.

'Look, I'm scared, too,' she admitted. 'But Mum and Dad aren't here, so we're going to have to ...' She said the phrase our Mum often repeated but which she'd always found embarrassing. 'Woman up!'

The main chamber of the wine cellar was the size of our living room at home, filled with floor-to-ceiling racks of wine and barrels with delicate, handwritten labels. As they returned, Chantale clad again in her stained dress, two people were arguing.

'I'm just saying,' said the first violinist, a gaunt man named Jack, 'it's pretty fucking typical.'

Tanice guessed it must be nightfall by the amount of time that had passed by then, though there was no way to tell as all their watches and phones had either stopped working or been snatched away.

'You made it in the end, though,' said Antoinette, the second violinist.

'No thanks to you,' Jack huffed.

The photographer was using the torch to go through all the cupboards and barrels.

'I didn't realize your ankle was stuck,' Antoinette retorted.

Tanice would come to hate the string quartet. Everything she learned about them, she learned against her will. That Yasmeen – the darkly beautiful Iranian cellist – and Antoinette had dated for three years while they attended the Royal College of Music. That Yasmeen thought Antoinette pathetically conventional for finally marrying Jack, her high-school boyfriend. Bartok, the overweight man who had helped pull the wine rack in front of the door and who played the viola, loved Yasmeen, who was disgusted by him. He was also almost a decade older than the rest. He'd been a prodigy once but had famously failed to live up to his potential and now organized wedding concerts and office parties.

'You didn't realize,' Jack said, 'because you were scrabbling around for your violin.'

'I thought—'

'A fucking bomb goes off, and your first thought is—'

'I said I was sorry,' Antoinette mumbled.

The cellar was at least fifteen degrees colder than it was outside. At the sight of her shivering, Paris offered Chantale his silk-lined jacket. Tanice smiled at him gratefully.

'What are you doing?' Tanice asked the photographer, who was counting under his breath.

'Just ... doing an inventory,' he replied without looking at her. 'I think, if we're careful,' he said, 'we could make it two weeks.'

'Careful with what?' she asked. 'The water we don't have?' Tanice repeated her father's rule: 'You die without three minutes of air, three days of water, three weeks of food.'

The photographer looked shocked. 'I thought it was longer.'

'For which one?'

He gestured around as if they'd stumbled upon an oasis. 'Wine has water in it!'

On the other side of the room, the string quartet were still arguing.

'Jack—' Antoinette pleaded.

Yasmeen interjected, 'Jack loves you more than he loves music. And you love the violin more than anyone.'

Bartok plucked a bottle off the wine rack nearest him and squinted, in the meagre light, at its label. '"Leroy Musigny Grand Cru, 2009",' he read. 'How much do you think this is worth?'

Jack pointed at Paris, who was slumped against the far wall. 'Doesn't he know?'

'This cellar is my uncle's, actually . . . and I'm sober now.'

Yasmeen pointed an accusing finger at Bartok. 'Aren't you, too?'

'Yes! But considering the circumstances . . .' He held the wine aloft. 'Come on, we might be here for weeks. We've got time to kill.'

'Is that true?' Antoinette asked plaintively, looking around and inviting anyone to answer. 'Weeks?'

'I don't know,' Paris said. 'I've heard that it's twenty-four hours minimum.'

'Seventy-two,' said Bartok. 'Minimum.'

'Once we go outside, we'll be hit with a dose of radiation,' said the photographer.

'The longer we stay, the lower the dose,' Tanice said.

Antoinette nodded, 'Yes, but . . . *weeks*, though?'

No one said anything, as it dawned on them all that they could be here for the long haul. Finally, Bartok lifted the bottle again.

'Now, let us commence the bidding for this extraordinary offering at—'

'What do you know about wine?' Jack sniffed.

'Bartok thinks he knows the price of everything,' Yasmeen said.

Bartok ignored them and continued. 'Gentlemen and gentlewomen, esteemed collectors and enthusiasts, up for bidding is a true gem of the vinicultural world, a pinnacle of Burgundian winemaking. Who among you will start the bidding?'

'Fifty pounds,' Yasmeen announced.

'An excellent opening offer from my beautiful colleague.' Yasmeen only rolled her eyes in response. 'Come on, we're talking about the illustrious 2009, a year hailed as exceptional in the annals of winemaking. The climatic conditions that spring were optimal, and the timing of the flowering season was nothing short of serendipitous.'

Tanice thought of the most expensive thing she owned.

'Five hundred pounds.' The contracted amount her mum was paying off for her new phone.

'A thousand?' Antoinette ventured.

Bartok smiled at them both, happy someone else was playing along.

'One thousand, five hundred pounds,' Tanice suggested, the cost of the MacBook I'd been begging Dad for.

'Is there a higher bid?'

'Two thousand pounds,' Jack said. A snort of laughter escaped from Paris. Jack turned to him and said, 'Go on, then.'

But Paris didn't want to play.

Tanice thought of the credit card bills she'd seen our father set on fire on the barbecue.

'Ten thousand pounds,' she shouted, then, for good measure, doubled it. 'Twenty!'

Paris couldn't keep quiet any longer. 'So,' he sounded almost exasperated, 'these wines are so rare, they are almost mythical. So few of them are made, and some years . . .'

But Bartok wanted to remain the centre of attention. 'Think!' he urged. 'How much do you owe in student loans? That sort of ballpark.'

Yasmeen hazarded, 'Sixty thousand?'

Paris and Bartok replied at the same time.

'Sold!' shouted Bartok.

'Probably,' shrugged Paris.

'To RCM's sexiest cellist of 2020.' Bartok clapped and handed it to Yasmeen like an Oscar.

She played along by bowing majestically in her black dress and said, 'Oh wow ... I'd like to thank whatever vile way the owners of this estate made their money ...' At this, Paris looked sheepishly at his hands. 'And, um ... my mother, who always told me as a child that wine was a lousy drink.'

Jack laughed. 'Use it to pay off your student loans. Or cover two months of rent in this money pit of a city.'

'Aren't you curious what it tastes like?' asked Antoinette. Her eyes darted to the bottle. 'Does it taste like ... money?'

'What does money taste like?' asked Jack.

Yasmeen regarded the bottle miserably. It was a poor prize after all they'd lost. She said quietly, 'Probably everyone I know in this city is dead now.'

'Probably not ... everyone,' Antoinette said.

Another silence, during which Tanice reminded herself that our family were fine. We knew the drills, we had a bunker, respirators and iodine pills. She thought that we were definitely in a better situation than her and Chantale.

'I'd pay more than that ...' Tanice said. She knew what they would need to survive. In the cellar, they had Burgundy wines and Grand Cru Bordeaux, blue-chip and Napa Valley cult wines, rare spirits and champagne. They had Aaliyah's tiered wedding cake. They had no sanitation system, no beds. But most importantly ... 'I'd pay more than that for water.'

MARCUS MINTON – THE DAY OF

It was a relief to see the armed police officers lined up at the checkpoint near Battersea Bridge; Marcus had been shocked by how few of them he'd spotted during his journey so far. As an ex-policeman, he'd thought they'd be out in force, maintaining order. But he supposed Crossley could be right; with the devastation on the streets, no working vehicles and limited communication, it was probably difficult for them to mobilize. And, Marcus wondered with a pang of guilt, what would he have done if he'd been on shift when the Event happened? Would he have been tempted to abandon his work to save his family? He couldn't blame some of his colleagues if they were doing the same.

By the time he reached the Thames, the sun was setting and the situation was deteriorating. A thin phalanx of officers had barricaded the road on the south bank, but they were barely a match for the surge of panicked civilians trying to push through. People pleaded with them, shouting the names of loved ones they needed to reach on the other side of the river; they wanted to get home; they needed to go to the hospital. The mob yelled and shoved each other as the barked orders of the police were carried up on currents of smoke from local fires.

'Stay back! We can't let anyone through!' an officer shouted, his voice hoarse. His hands shook as he gestured for people to move away, but his pleas fell on deaf ears. A female officer, helmet askew, was struggling to pull a man away from the barricade. He screamed something incoherent as he fought to get past. Around them, the pressure of the crowd was mounting, people pressing forward, trying to force their way through the checkpoint, their faces pale with fear.

'It's not safe!' a woman shouted. Marcus could see that the cast-iron bridge had been decimated by the Event. The destruction was spectacular: whole sections of the bridge had buckled away, torn free of the granite piers, and were half-submerged in the river. The ornate iron panels that had once gleamed on its spandrels were now damming the river at a bend where the relatively slow-moving brown water also churned up against sunk cars and toppled buses, bodies growing bloated in the heat. There were so many dead. Marcus turned away.

He dreaded to think of what might have happened to me, Kim and Aaliyah if we were on a bridge during the Event. It made him sick to imagine our bodies floating in the river like that. He shook the image quickly away. If he couldn't cross here, he would have to try elsewhere. He would swim across if he had to.

But as Marcus regarded the increasing disorder, the enormity of his task – searching the entire city for his wife and daughters – dawned on him. The sheer impossibility of it. Should he just turn back and wait in the bunker and hope for their safe return? He imagined the lonely hours and nights, twisting the crank on his radio, startling at every motion outside. He couldn't bear it. He would rather die out here, searching for them, he realized.

Marcus's attention was roused then by a police dog, a sleek black German Shepherd, barking furiously at him. The animal's eyes were wild, its teeth bared as it strained against the lead held by an officer who was clearly struggling to keep control.

'Heel!' the handler yelled, but the dog ignored him, its attention focused entirely on Marcus. It pulled harder towards him, its deep, guttural snarl triggering Marcus's basic fight-or-flight instinct. He was surprised, as dogs usually warmed to him.

The officer yanked hard on the lead, trying to pull the dog away, but it only howled more ferociously, lunging forward, hackles raised, teeth snapping. The crowd around Marcus recoiled, giving the animal a wide berth, but the commotion only caused them to grow more frantic.

In the fear and confusion, Marcus realized that he had to run, but it was like pushing against a churning tide. The police, now barely holding the barricade, were ordering the crowd to disperse, but no one was listening. It was as if the tension in the air had reached its breaking point. A woman near Marcus was screaming for her children, her voice hoarse, her face purple with bruises. A man pushed past, tripping on the curb, dropping a suitcase on the street with a hard bang. As if in response, somewhere at the front, a gun was fired, and then everyone was screaming, shoving and running in all directions. The dog handler was pulled away by the surge of bodies, and the German Shepherd, barking wildly, was forced back. My father felt the press of people all around him as the scene devolved into chaos. There were no more orders from the police, no more attempts to control the crowd – just noise and confusion as panic surged and the fragile line of order at the checkpoint disintegrated.

Marcus retreated as soon as he could, shouldering back away from the bridge and bolting down a side street, his footsteps echoing off the brick facades of the narrow buildings. His heart pounded in his chest, every muscle fuelled by adrenaline. The air was thick with smoke, but this street was momentarily quiet – a stark contrast to the turmoil he'd just left behind.

He leaned against the cool brick and closed his eyes, gathering his shattered nerves and fighting to recall which route to take. Over the distant shouts of the mob, he couldn't hear the dog barking anymore.

If every bridge and checkpoint was like this, Marcus would have to revise his plan. Maybe his best option would be to try to get to Glassford House, where at least he knew that two of his daughters were. If he was quick, he might make it there by dawn. The change of plan wasn't ideal, but finding where the rest of his family had fled in the chaos seemed close to impossible now. He would just have to hope that we'd manage to make it home safely.

Marcus was still considering the best route to take when the sound of footsteps captured his attention. They emerged from the smoke, masked figures in hazmat suits with biohazard symbols emblazoned on their shoulders. Marcus counted eight of them, rushing at him with a coordinated precision.

'Stop!' one of them shouted, his voice distorted through the respirator.

Dad's initial instinct was to run. He carefully raised his hands in mock-surrender, his eyes wide, before spinning on his heel to bolt the other way. He was almost at the end of the road when two more of them appeared from an alley, cutting off his escape. He was surrounded.

'Wait! Who are you?' Marcus demanded, his voice cracking. But the masked strangers advanced on him quickly, deft and strong despite their cumbersome suits. One lunged forward and grabbed his arm in a vice-like grip. Marcus struggled, yanking it back, but two more of them forced him to the ground. The rough asphalt scraped against his cheek as they pinned him down, his cries muffled by the heavy fabric of their suits pressing against him.

'Get off me!' he shouted, panic rising as he heard the buzz of plastic zip ties, felt them grind together the bones in his wrists. 'What is this? Let me go!'

'Subject secured,' a man said into a small radio attached to his suit. Two of them hauled Marcus to his feet, his arms bound behind him.

'Who are you? Where are you taking me?' he demanded.

But they didn't respond, just propelled him forward, away from the chaos and into a dimly lit side alley. The sounds of the riot faded, replaced by the crunch of their heels on broken glass and the hiss of the respirators in their masks.

Parked in the alley was an absurd-looking wagon unlike any vehicle Marcus had seen before. It was made entirely without metal; the frame and body were constructed from solid, dark-stained wood, reinforced with what looked like dense black polymers and fibreglass. The design was sleek and functional, with smooth surfaces and tight joints that hinted at expert craftsmanship. Large, heavy-duty wheels made from layered wood and composite materials supported its weight. At the front, a horse pawed the cracked ground nervously. Its harness was leather, with no metal buckles or embellishments. The animal's eyes rolled slightly as it sensed the tension in the air.

Together, four of them led Marcus to the back of the wagon, where a door swung open to reveal an interior lined with padding. He resisted, planting his feet firmly on the ground. To go any further, he knew, would divert him from his essential mission. He thought of every warning he'd ever offered me or my sisters about getting into the cars of strangers. He thought about every struggling offender he had ever bundled into the back of a van. He briefly thought about Sydney's father, but then the familiar shutter went down in his mind and his memories went dark.

'Wait!' He bucked and twisted, fighting their grip with all his might, but he was outnumbered. 'You can't do this! I need to find my family!'

One of the figures stepped in front of him, face unreadable behind the tinted visor. 'This is for your own safety,' she said flatly. It took four of them to lift him, kicking and shoving, into the wagon.

The interior was bare except for a bench and restraints – also made without metal – that they sealed around his ankles. 'What's going on?' Marcus pleaded as they locked him inside. But they ignored his cries, moving efficiently to the front of the vehicle. With a flick of the reins, the driver urged the horse forward, and the wagon jolted into motion, its wooden wheels creaking softly as it rolled over the uneven pavement. Marcus imagined the alley behind drifting away, though there were no windows for him to see it.

My father's mind reeled in panic and confusion. Was this a random attack or had he been targeted specifically? His mind raced. They were organized, professional. Government agents? Military? He was alone, restrained and being taken to an unknown destination by faceless figures in a collapsing city.

'Who *are* you people?' he shouted again, banging on the wall with his shoulder.

Someone in the front of the vehicle told him, 'We're the First Contact Committee.'

KIMONA MINTON – THE DAY OF

Kim was shocked by how quickly they'd organized. The main hall in Providence House had been divided into sections: one where they were accepting donations, another where they were distributing essential supplies to people in queues. There was a medical area where casualties were being seen by doctors and volunteers, and little rooms where people with bright yellow lanyards that said 'Prayer Team' were taking mourners.

'So,' said Gladys at the central desk, 'this is not an actual emergency?'

'I mean, it could be,' said Kim.

Gladys raised a sceptical eyebrow. There is a Gladys in every church. She is the officious woman in the vestry, the one who is ready with a brittle smile at the welcome desk in front of the door. She's the over-enthusiastic back-pew-shusher, the woman whose prayers ('May God forgive *some* people for their lack of restraint during the summer fete . . .') double as poorly veiled accusations. Gladys will make sure that the flowers are ordered and everyone is signed up to the meal train, but she'll also remind you that the umbrella you left in the aisle is a fire hazard and corner you by the vegetables at the Co-op and announce pointedly, 'We missed you in church last Sunday.'

'So it is or it isn't?' she asked now.

'Not yet,' Kim said, 'but if you've seen as many labours as I have, you'll know that they can go south very quickly.'

'Women have been having babies for, what ... one, two hundred years?' Kim wasn't sure if this was a joke, so she brushed past it.

'It just might be good to have a doctor on hand.'

'A *real* doctor, you mean?' Gladys said.

Kim flinched at this and said, with restrained annoyance, 'A *medical* doctor.'

Gladys noted something down on her clipboard, ticked some boxes and said finally, 'I'll speak to the volunteers on call. But as you can see, there are *actual* emergencies, not *possible* ones, to attend to here.'

Her eyes returned to her clipboard, but after realizing that Kim hadn't walked away, she gestured to the chairs set up by the organ and said, 'You're welcome to wait.'

'How long will it be?' Kim asked.

Gladys only shrugged. Finally, she raised her eyebrows and glanced over Kim's shoulder. 'Next, please?'

Kim retreated to the empty moulded plastic chair next to a girl with a glittery cowboy hat who was quietly crying. It felt good to sit down. She had walked for what she imagined was almost five hours to get home and then another hour here.

'Here.' Kim handed the girl one of her last tissues.

'Oh,' she said, 'thanks.' She blew her nose. 'Did I hear that you're a doctor?'

'Of public health,' Kim said. The girl blinked at her, unsure about the difference. 'I did a PhD in public health.

"Maternal Health Practices and Outcomes in Indigenous Communities of Guatemala: Bridging Traditional and Modern Obstetric Care."'

'It's just ... I've had this lump in my neck I've been waiting a while to get looked at. I was supposed to have an appointment the day after tomorrow. My friends and I have tickets to see Beyoncé tonight, so I thought, *Well, if it's bad news, at least I'll have something to take my mind off it beforehand*, you know.'

Kim nodded. She actually did know.

'But now, obviously, there's much worse stuff happening, but it would just be good to know for sure.'

'About the concert? Or the appointment? Or your ... neck?'

'I mean ...' Her grey eyes rolled in confusion; possibly she wasn't sure either. 'All – all the things. I paid for the tickets with the company's expense account, and I was hoping that by the end of the month ... But now ... I heard you don't get a refund for, like, "an act of God", but ... What if it's cancer?'

'Cancer's pretty common,' Kim said, as she'd been saying to herself for days. She hadn't been particularly afflicted and she hadn't been judged on a cosmic scale. According to Google, hers was relatively slow-growing.

But the girl looked shocked. 'How can you even say that?'

'About half of people get cancer in their lifetime ...'

Tears started welling in the stranger's eyes again.

'Do you think it could be?'

'Let me see?' Kim said, the same way she would to any one of us when we descended the stairs with a rash or a bruise. Part of being a mum, Kim had always thought, involved becoming a dermatologist, a pharmacist, a counsellor. The girl offered her neck up for Kim to feel. There was a soft lump under the muscle. It moved when she pressed it.

Kim thought quietly for a while and then said, 'My guess would be a parathyroid cyst.'

'So *not* cancer?' A bright note of hopefulness dawned in her voice.

'Well, you'd probably need it biopsied to be sure.'

The word, now, tasted of skin staples and jagged edges. The wound at the base of her own skull. *Oligodendroglioma*, the letter from her GP had read. She was scheduled for an appointment next week with the oncology consultant at St George's Hospital. Was it safe to assume that wasn't happening now? Some part of her wanted to believe that none of it would happen. That the cancer wouldn't spread as her mother's had, increasing the pressure inside her skull. In the final stages, her mother had lost the ability to speak and to move one side of her body. She'd slipped into a coma in the living room and never woke up.

'I think a lot about ...' Kim leaned back in her chair, trying to work out how to phrase it. 'Has anyone ever asked you what you would prefer: to discover that you were dying or that the whole world was ending?'

'No.'

'I think I know, instinctively, what I would prefer,' Kim said.

'Me, too,' the girl nodded solemnly.

'It's something about watching how the story ends. The final chapter.'

'But what if it hurts?' the girl asked.

'At least it won't hurt alone.'

*

After another half hour with no news from Gladys, who seemed to be deliberately avoiding her, my mother decided to return home. She was distinctly aware that if Carmen was actually in labour, they were running out of time.

By the time she rounded the corner to our street, it was dark, and despair rolled over her unbidden. Kim paused, stopping on a low wall to breathe deeply, but instead a sob came out. She couldn't enter the house like this. She had to stay strong for her daughters. *The wrong daughters,* came an intrusive thought she felt ashamed for heeding. Kim's mind kept shunting back to Chantale. *Is she alive? Is she terrified?*

Chantale wasn't hardy like Tanice, there was nothing that couldn't undo her. Chantale was the 'latecomer', as Kim used to think of her. The final passenger. Born fifteen years after Aaliyah.

When they discovered the pregnancy, Kim and Marcus had seriously debated keeping the baby. Their marriage had been strained for a couple of years, and four children seemed like a ridiculous number to have – especially in London. It might have been different for Marcus if it could be guaranteed that the baby was a boy. But four girls? Four girls were as desirable to both of them as four gaudy pieces of costume jewellery. An embarrassment of riches.

But then, Kim had some spotting at six weeks and paid for a scan. The nurse said it was too early to see anything, but then, 'Here's the yolk sac, here's the fetal pole and here's . . .' Whenever Kim was sad, she remembered it, flickering in black and white, the faintest thing: 'A heartbeat.' The nurse wrote something like 'fetal flicker' on the notes, but then, emerging blinking from the dim cave of that ultrasound room and into the daylight, Kim felt strangely powerful. Like a witch who had summoned something from another dimension. She didn't want to be the one to send it back.

The night before the wedding, after Kim had said goodbye to Gabriel, she had returned home to discover Chantale crouched in the utility room, wearing a too-small *Frozen* pyjama vest top and cotton knickers, shovelling a sour-smelling bundle of bedsheets into the washing machine.

At the sound of Kim's footsteps, she'd started and bellowed, '*Intruder!*'

'It's okay,' Kim said, 'it's just me.' But her face fell as she took in the scene; Chantale crouched half-naked in front of the washing machine, terror in her eyes.

'Honey, I thought this wasn't a problem anymore.' Her tone was a mix of pity and disappointment.

'It was just one time!' Chantale yelled, embarrassed.

'Chantale ...' Kim worked hard to keep her voice even, but her daughter ducked past her like a frightened mouse and ran up two flights of stairs. Kim thundered after her. Chantale dashed into her bed, onto the lower bunk, which smelled sharply of urine.

Kim found her curled on her bare mattress, pulling the damp duvet up to her head.

'Where's Briar?' she asked, regarding the empty top bunk. It was almost midnight.

Chantale was crying, 'It didn't happen! It didn't happen!'

Very carefully, as if approaching a fox she might startle, Kim said, 'It's all right that it did.'

'I don't want to go back to Dr Gail.'

Kim couldn't make any promises. The sight of Chantale crying, though, made her own chest tight.

She climbed into bed with her daughter and held her sweaty body in her arms. Chantale sobbed into her mother's chest, and Kim spread her fingers through her soft ringlets.

'Don't go!' Chantale was on the edge of sleep when she jolted awake again.

'I'm not going anywhere,' Kim lied.

Chantale stared at her. Finally, she said, 'Isla's cousin had to have four teeth removed last Thursday.'

'That's terrible,' Kim said.

Chantale nodded in agreement. 'Isla says she looks like a witch now.'

Kim looked up at the wooden slats of the bunk above, where sun-faded *Paw Patrol* stickers curled like dead leaves. Her eyes began to flicker shut as the heavy net of sleep came down.

'I have dreams sometimes,' said Chantale, 'where all my teeth fall out.'

'Um ... don't forget to brush them, then,' Kim said with her eyes closed.

'Sometimes I forget, though,' Chantale admitted.

'It's okay to sometimes forget,' Kim mumbled, breathing in the smell of both of their bodies as she drifted.

'Probably our teeth will fall out anyway, because of all the radiation.'

Kim opened her eyes then, with a familiar surge of rage at her husband. 'Don't worry about that.'

Chantale touched her mouth. 'I don't want anything bad to happen to them.'

'Neither do I.'

Her voice was shaky as she said, 'I love all of them.'

'Me, too,' Kim said. She could see Chantale's panic

rising and tried to hide her own exhaustion and dread at the prospect of it.

'Sweetheart,' she said with the affected calm of a hostage negotiator, 'we have a wedding tomorrow. You need to get some sleep. You don't want your eyes to be puffy in the pictures.'

Chantale nodded.

'What would help you sleep?' Kim asked.

Chantale wiped her eyes quickly and gazed at her mother, her fear turned to hope. She opened and closed her fist, their old sign for milk.

Kim hesitated and then sighed. 'Just tonight,' she whispered.

Chantale smiled and stared with delight down at the caramel half-moon of her mother's breast as it waxed from under the frayed collar of her pyjama top.

CARMEN ATTAH – THE DAY OF

When Carmen had asked her mother if labour had felt anything like menstrual cramps, her mother had laughed.

'How much is a tablet of granite like Mount Sinai? How much is Lake Naivasha like the Pacific?' she said. 'I wanted. To. Die.' Words that had echoed in Carmen's mind whenever she was in pain – when she'd slipped on a patch of black ice and torn her ACL, when Aaliyah had pierced her tongue with a Zippo-scorched needle, when her birth control implant had cracked under her skin: *Do I want to die yet?*

Carmen had never wanted to know how it felt. She had read, with some envy, the tales of Twilight Sleep administered to mid-century mothers who gave birth and completely forgot the pain. Hard to imagine enduring it and then living; much less, enduring it and then, like her mother, going on to have more children.

Whenever she was nervous, Paris would recite the plan to her. They would put a soft catheter into her spine and numb her from the waist down. She wouldn't feel a thing. She'd push when they told her to push, or they would wheel her into theatre and play soft music and pull the baby out, brow-wrinkled and bawling. There were so many modern ways she could choose to buff away the sharp edges of human experience. She would order this birth as if off a menu. She would depart on this voyage and return unchanged. She would climb the mountain without seeing the face of her maker. Man 1: Nature 0. Or '*Woman* 1 ...' as she'd boast to anyone who would listen, to the prenatal yoga instructor who'd promised that laughter was the best medicine, to the hippies in her NCT class who wanted to 'feel everything'.

So when the pain came that afternoon, after the Event, she pushed it back for a while. It was a tide rising in the gloaming. It was another disaster. She wasn't ready. The streets had been crushed to rubble, and she was nowhere near the safe luminescent halls of a hospital. Entonox canisters, pethidine, the anaesthetists who, she'd been told, were mostly beautiful.

It felt the way women had described it, as if her belly was a taut band that had unexpectedly snapped. And the pain, when it came, was something familiar, jagged teeth she'd felt gnaw her insides before, a familiar crush and twist, and then a new thing: suddenly, mercifully, complete relief. Reeling enough to laugh. Except there were tears in her eyes, and Aaliyah was watching.

'Is it happening?' Aaliyah asked, her apprehension clear to see. Carmen felt that if she said it was happening, it would be so.

So she mumbled something plausible. 'Braxton Hicks ...'

But when the pain came again, it almost floored her. She had to bend forward and hold her breath, brace against it.

'That seemed like—' Aaliyah said.

'No!' Carmen said. But under her dress, the backs of her

calves were inexplicably wet. She felt like a vole exposed suddenly, nauseous and terrified. She decided that the best thing to do would be to lock herself in Aaliyah's ensuite, which she did and crouched on the toilet, gritting her teeth and crying from terror.

'I don't think you should . . .' Aaliyah's voice outside was washed away with the pain.

When the tide pulled away again, Carmen found herself on all fours on the floor, breathing heavily. There was something glinting under the canvas laundry basket. Polished metal. She plucked it.

'What is this?'

'What?' Aaliyah's voice came from behind the painted wood. The last time Carmen had seen it, this little bronze cufflink, it had been cushioned in a jewellery box that read, 'Best Man'. The initials PDH were engraved on the green lacquer inlay.

Carmen struggled to pull the door open. 'What is this doing here?' she asked. Aaliyah's eyebrows raised at the sight of the cufflink in her hand.

'Paris was . . .' Aaliyah's mind scrabbled. Carmen had caught her off guard.

'In your bedroom?' Carmen could imagine it vividly, she'd seen him do it a hundred times before: take off his cufflinks and place them on the little glass shelf under the mirror before brushing his teeth. Her suspicions had been right; her husband and her best friend had been sleeping together.

'Mine,' Aaliyah said quietly.

'People don't belong to people,' Carmen snapped.

'We did.'

'You were fifteen.'

The first night that Carmen and Aaliyah had roomed

together at the Montclair Tennis Academy, Carmen had held her wrist up to the energy-saving bulb and let its feeble light sparkle off the diamonds on her new tennis bracelet. A parting gift from her father.

'You've always wanted everything that I've had,' she said now.

A couple of days later, the bracelet had vanished. Aaliyah had suggested that it had slipped off in her sleep.

'You've always *had* everything,' Aaliyah replied.

Before Carmen could respond, she was shunted back into her body by another contraction, this one electric, her nerves crackling with the pain. She felt like an animal being zapped in a cage. Panicked, this whole thing getting away from her. She couldn't have her baby here, in the house of the girl whose trainers she'd once filled with broken glass before a tennis match.

She slammed the door again. Turned the lock.

'Carmen!' Aaliyah shouted.

As soon as she shut it, though, she felt as if she was going to be sick.

'I don't think you should be in there alone.'

Carmen opened her mouth, and vomit launched into the sink, sour-smelling bile which erupted with each breath. She coughed, hearing Aaliyah pound on the door. Frightened suddenly that she'd inhale it and choke alone on the tiled floor.

But Aaliyah knew how to twist a butter knife in the lock and push the door open. She entered in time to help pull Carmen's hair from her face. Carmen tried to shrug her off at first, but she lacked the energy.

Aaliyah hugged her friend as she crouched on the toilet, shaking, marooned on the island between contractions.

'My mum has a book,' Aaliyah said, nodding at a dog-eared copy of *Ina May's Guide to Childbirth* that she had abandoned on the carpet outside. 'Apparently, it's not like the movies. Only twelve per cent of labours begin with the water breaking. Have you lost your mucus plug?' Words Carmen hated to hear alone and together.

'I had an app,' she said. 'You hold the button during a contraction, and then it will tell you if you're in active labour.'

'What do you do in "active labour"?' Aaliyah asked.

'Go to the hospital,' Carmen said and then started to cry. There was obviously no hospital now.

'My mum will be back soon,' Aaliyah said. 'She'll know what to do.'

'How?'

'She's done this herself four times already. She has a PhD in public health. She travelled to Guatemala and watched midwives deliver hundreds of babies. She's not scared of many things.'

Carmen was a little reassured by this.

Another contraction hoisted her up like a toy puppet, and she leaned over the sink and screamed.

Aaliyah watched, wide-eyed, trying to hide her fear. At one point, Carmen was distantly aware that her friend had disappeared. She returned a few minutes later with an egg timer, towels, blankets, things she'd read they might need.

Carmen tried to recall some of the tips she'd learned in her NCT class. *The uterus is the strongest muscle in the human body.* With each contraction, the pain grew worse. It started to feel formidable, mechanical, her body crushed in a vice, her uterus a serrated wheel turning her open.

'That was a minute,' Aaliyah said at the tail-end of one of them. She knelt down so she was at eye-level. 'You can survive anything,' she said, 'for just one minute.'

For the next one, Carmen watched as Aaliyah rotated the egg timer, stared at the pearly gel manicure on her nails. A minute. The seconds crawled past. *I can endure anything for one minute.*

How many minutes until Kimona returned? Ten, maybe. Twenty? Two minutes between contractions. That meant, dividing time up like this, maybe seven more contractions? They counted them together.

Carmen cried through them or clenched her teeth or squatted on the toilet or gripped the cold enamel edge of the sink so hard her fingertips turned white. Or imagined, as Aaliyah instructed her to, the perfect parabola of a served tennis ball. *At the first twinges of pain, watch it rise, observe its terrible velocity, up, up. This is the zenith of the pain now, which is good, because it will only decrease from here. Gravity does its familiar work, here comes the ground. You can endure anything for just one minute.*

Except that seven contractions went by, and our mother was still not there.

'Where *is* she?'

Aaliyah looked out of the window, unable to hide her fear and uncertainty. She looked like she had that time at school when they stole a boat and ran out of fuel in the middle of a lake.

'I don't know,' she admitted. But then remembered her role. 'Women have been doing this for centuries.'

'Yeah,' Carmen said. Without doctors and hospitals. Without the wonderful needle and the perfect numbness it promised to deliver into her spinal cord. 'But ... ' Carmen didn't want to remember, 'didn't lots of them *die?*'

Aaliyah didn't know what to say to that.

She disappeared for three frightening contractions and returned with a big green water butt that she emptied into the porcelain tub.

Once it was full, she took off her clothes – stood in her nude bridal underwear – helped to pull off Carmen's tulle dress, and they both climbed in. The contractions were coming back-to-back now, sweeping Carmen up, tossing her down. Her mother had told her that her mind would eventually wipe the pain away. That she would recall only the time in between contractions. Remember Aaliyah's honey eyes, her quiet vigil. The sweat on her friend's upper lip. She would remember leaning over the tub, swaying in Aaliyah's arms as if to a first dance, their story, a love story. The *fleur-de-lis* pattern on the tiles, the way that her eye followed them, the way that tracing their monochrome motifs made them luminously beautiful to her. 'I can never leave,' she told Aaliyah. She had come to rely on them; her attention had transformed them; they had become sacred, almost, to her.

When night descended, Carmen wanted to die.

'No,' Aaliyah said, tears crusted in mineral streaks down her face. 'She's almost here.'

'Who?'

'My mum. I think I can see her?' Aaliyah nodded at the darkening window.

It seemed that she had been invoked so long ago by then that our mother was almost a legendary figure. The Oracle of Delphi. Morgan le Fay.

'I think I need to push,' Carmen said.

'Um ...' Aaliyah craned her neck to see if it *was* her

mother outside the window. It seemed absurd to tell Carmen to wait.

With the next contraction, she gave in to the thunder in her body and pushed.

Aaliyah reached down. *At ten centimetres, the cervix is as wide as a grapefruit.*

'I can feel something!' she said, elation that curdled suddenly into terror.

'Her head?' Carmen was hopeful. *This will be the worst bit, but then it will be over. I'm probably going to survive it.*

'No.' The blood had drained from Aaliyah's face. 'I think it's a foot.'

BRIAR MINTON – THE NIGHT OF

Kim told me she'd had a dream once about heaven. She'd described it as a kind of weightlessness, the kind which comes with transcendence. What else in this life feels that way? Leaving your daughters, I always imagined.

She told me that, until she did it, she had always wondered how a person could leave their children. Wouldn't the guilt poison them, turn every good thing into ash? But then she was offered a prestigious scholarship to study for a PhD in public health. Writing her thesis required extensive fieldwork in Guatemala: in Chichicastenango, Cobán and Nebaj, among other places. Interviews with *comadronas*, traditional birth attendants, healthcare providers and pregnant women.

Apparently, she'd agonized over the choice to leave, but I was never sure how true that was. Aaliyah was eleven, I was six years old. Tanice had only just started pre-school. I still don't know how Kim and Marcus finally agreed to it. I've heard a couple of different stories. That it was only supposed to be nine months initially, but then multiple exigencies of fieldwork delayed her return by three months, then six, then twelve, until in total she'd spent four years out there. And when she returned, Tanice and I barely knew our own mother.

She'd been studying for a doctorate in public health at LSE when she'd got pregnant with me and was so sick that she'd had to drop out. This had been her chance to start again. To live the life that she wanted. I never understood why the life that she wanted was so far away from us. But I often imagined that getting off the plane at Mundo Maya airport, where no one knew she was a mother, had felt like waking up as a newly hatched chick. Maybe it had been startlingly easy to box everything up – *can you use coconut oil for oral thrush? What's the right shampoo for 3C baby hair? If she wakes from her nap at 5.30, will she go down to sleep at 7?* – and seal it in some vault in her mind. Apparently, she never mentioned us to her colleagues or the women she worked with. Maybe the hard thing had been the Skype calls home. Maybe the hardest thing had been coming back. Had she felt, on her return, like a spaceship capsule burning up on re-entry, subject to the old forgotten gravity?

For the years she was gone, a mother was a good dream to me. The god-like figure the orphan Annie imagines when she looks out of the window. Marmee in *Little Women*, her daughters like grateful ducklings. The elegant foot around the corner of the door in *The Cat in the Hat*. She didn't really exist outside the brief windows of time when we spoke. I never thought about the nights she spent on brightly woven rugs in adobe houses, listening to the cries of women in labour and watching the ritual prayers of a *comadrona*. Or the day she rushed a patient to the community clinic on the back of a motorcycle, arriving just in time for her to deliver her son on the lino floor. The time she travelled four hours over bumpy dirt roads to reach a house where a baby had just been born; how she'd climbed the steps to find an old midwife wrapping the tiny bawling girl in her vividly coloured rebozo and wiping vernix from her eyes with wizened fingers.

I had never cared or thought about what her life had been like without us, until that night.

After I found Digit, I returned home to the sound of Aaliyah thundering down the stairs. She didn't look happy to see me.

'Oh ... we thought you were Mum.' She was crying as she led me through the house to her bedroom, spattered with blood and vomit, sweat sticking her once perfectly tonged curls to her temples. 'Where is she?'

It was swelteringly hot. The room smelled of sweat and iron. With the candles and kerosene lanterns dotted around, Aaliyah looked as if I'd caught her in the middle of a seance. 'I thought she was here ...' I looked feebly over Aaliyah's shoulder, taking in the sight of Carmen groaning in a tub. She was naked, and her eyes were squeezed shut. The dome of her belly crested like a volcanic island in the blood-marbled water. She looked as if every cell in her body had been wrung out.

'The baby is breech,' Aaliyah whispered, though Carmen didn't seem aware of our presence.

'Is that bad?' I asked dumbly.

'Of course!' Aaliyah hissed. I was crying, too, already embarrassed by my tears. I'd sincerely hoped that I would live and die and never see a baby being born.

'I mean, why ... why is that bad?'

Aaliyah opened her mouth, but I could tell she wasn't

completely sure. The birth book on the landing strongly advised a C-section in the case of breech births to avoid the risks to the mother and baby – umbilical cord prolapse and head entrapment. I only know this now.

'Where the fuck is Mum?!'

This was her speciality. It wasn't just that she'd witnessed hundreds of births, but she'd experienced it four times herself. We had a tradition in our family – possibly because we were a houseful of women – that at every birthday, Kim would tell the tale of each of our births. I could recite them all, too. I knew about the days our mother had laboured with Aaliyah. The way that, in the taxi home, the driver had asked our horror-stricken Dad, 'Are you sure you're going to be okay?' I'd heard about how my birth had spiralled away from her, ended in an unwanted emergency C-section; and then a routine one with Tanice. Chantale had been born on our kitchen floor – fast, terrible, then triumphant – and Dad had been the one to catch her. Mum had lost an AirPod in the process, and Dad had laughingly said, 'I guess that's the price we pay,' instead of actually looking for it.

I loved the birth stories and still do. A birth story is the Platonic ideal of a story. I love their classical arc. The way they begin in the middle of the night or in the bathroom during an international conference, with a promise or with a 'feeling'. I love the ones that end victorious, the way they exact a profound change on the parents and the baby and the universe.

It was impossible to see, though, how this one wouldn't end badly.

Fifteen minutes after I returned home, Digit started barking at the sound of footsteps on the gravel.

I dashed downstairs. I had never been more relieved to see Kim.

She knew what was happening almost at once and took in the scene with no explanation. Our mother instructed us with all the seriousness of a general. She told me to get some newspaper (I hadn't seen a newspaper since I was a child, so I settled for printer paper) and a bag for the placenta.

I knew that for all the births she had witnessed and recorded, she'd never performed one herself. Never reached her fingers to check if a cervix was effaced or dilated, only ever placed her palm on the hot drumskin of a woman's belly to find a heartbeat, a foot. Of the breech births she'd seen, all but one had ended tragically. She'd written in her thesis and repeated in her PhD viva and to anyone who had asked her that, 'the indigenous population disproportionately represent more than fifty per cent of all maternal deaths.' A few of which she had seen. Mothers she had carried, eyelids she had pushed closed, quiet infants she had cradled.

That evening, she tried a couple of manoeuvres she had only read about: the Løvset, the Mauriceau–Smellie–Veit. She instructed Aaliyah to help hold Carmen upright so that gravity could work with her. She sent me downstairs to gather more supplies. Rubbing alcohol, drinking water, whatever ice hadn't turned to slush in the toppled fridge-freezer.

When Carmen was too exhausted to keep pushing, Mum said, 'We're almost there, just a couple more and ...'

'*I can't!*' Carmen wailed. She was in more pain than I'd ever seen a person. They repositioned. She leaned forward over the towel rail, and I crouched on the bathroom floor, the hem of my white dress soaked pale pink in diluted blood. Feebly, 'I can't do this.'

'I had to have an induction with Aaliyah,' Kim said. 'Everything went wrong, I lost litres of blood, I tore, got an infection . . . It was nothing I'd planned, nothing I'd visualized in birth class.'

Once she had told me that as she arrived on the ward before her induction, listening to the groans of the women behind the synthetic curtains, a thought had occurred to her, a bright pinprick of light: *I could just go home.* A good idea, call it off. But then, the dismal realization. It was going to happen wherever she went. She might go home and barricade herself in, creep under the covers, take a plane to Flores or bury herself in a hole in the ground, but it was coming for her. 'A near-birth experience,' she'd joke about it later. 'Are you brave for not running away when you *can't* run away?'

Now Kim locked her eyes with Carmen's. 'Sometimes the only way out is *through.*'

The baby's head was stuck, but her body was out, pale and floppy like one of Chantale's old dolls.

'It's okay.' Mum sensed my worry. She pointed out the umbilical cord, which was still pulsing, the baby's lifeline. Though terror gnawed at me, I marvelled at my mother's calm. There was no one we needed more. Even Carmen appeared to discover some new reserve of strength under Kim's cool gaze. Suddenly, she wasn't just a mother to me. The French word for midwife translates to 'wise woman', and, for the first time, I came to a grudging new respect for what that wisdom had cost to acquire.

'Carmen,' she said, 'I'm going to try something called a shoulder press.' She had only ever seen this performed in candlelit *casas de parteras.*

Kim leaned down and stared at the baby's silver chest, delicate bones, long clavicle that could snap like a twig.

She reached out and, with a surge of effort, shoved. Her hands must have felt the resistance, then the glorious pop of release as the baby's head slipped free from the birth canal and dropped into Kim's arms. She wrapped her in a towel.

Carmen collapsed on the tiled floor.

A long silence in the room.

'Is she . . .'

The baby's chest suddenly quivered. I watched as Mum wiped away the mucus from her face. She started crying, a high-pitched mewling sound, and we all breathed out in relief.

'You saved us,' Carmen said weakly, staring at Mum in awe. I stared at her, too, as if beholding her for the first time. Amazed and proud.

'You did it!' Aaliyah kissed her friend's sweaty forehead. Mum offered her the baby, but Carmen was shaking too much to hold her.

'Can I?' I asked my mother, and she let me. I stared at the creature we'd welcomed into the world. Wild to think that Carmen's body had knitted together her bones, had spun her neurons like gold from straw. Did all babies move in this alien way? Did they all have that same ancient wisdom in their eyes? Had they all travelled light-years to visit us from their world before they made up their minds whether or not to stay?

We named her Hero.

MARCUS MINTON – THE NIGHT OF

In the headquarters of the First Contact Committee, it was as if the Event had never happened. It was a bunker deep underground, a shadowed rabbit warren of cells and conference rooms. Labs and locked doors. Two agents in hazmat suits marched Marcus through it, and when he asked how they still had power, how those LED screens were still running, how the scanners on the doors were working, one of them said, 'It's mu-metal alloy.'

'What?' Marcus had never heard of it.

'Tonnes of the stuff,' said the second officer, 'lining all the walls. It shields this place from EMPs and magnetic field attacks.'

'So ... you knew this was going to happen?' Marcus asked. 'You prepared for this?'

'It's our job to anticipate events like this.'

They led him to a padded cubicle where he was told to strip off his clothes and place them in a lead-lined box, which disappeared through a hole in the wall. They hosed him down.

Then they gave him papery white overalls to wear and

transported him to a lab where scientists in suits snipped locks of his hair, swabbed the inside of his mouth and X-rayed his skull.

After all of that, the officers ushered him into a room with a smooth oak interview table, where he sat alone for what felt like half an hour. The soft hum of air circulation was the only sound. Marcus rubbed his wrists where the restraints had been, his mind racing with questions. There were two cameras pointed at the chair he was in, projecting a closed-circuit recording of him onto a screen on the far wall. It was disconcerting to see his head from those two angles. He recognized, for the first time, that he'd gone grey in a peculiar pattern. It looked as if a witch had pressed her hand on the side of his head and turned his mousy hair silver wherever her fingers had touched.

'Do I need a lawyer?' was the first thing Marcus said as a woman in white overalls entered.

'You're not arrested,' she replied.

'So I can go?'

She only smiled. Marcus glanced up as two armoured guards followed her in, flanking the door.

'My name is Dr Sengupta,' she said. 'And you are . . .' She lifted up a tablet computer. 'Marcus Keith Minton, is that right? 27/11/1980? Of 14 Albert Road . . .'

'Where am I?' Marcus asked.

'This is the headquarters of the First Contact Committee.'

'And what exactly is that?'

'We're a branch of the Security Service,' explained Dr Sengupta.

'Like MI5?'

She nodded.

Marcus prickled with dread. The last time he'd found

himself in a set-up like this had been during his interviews
for the Independent Office for Police Conduct, last year,
when that incident happened at work. He wondered what
he was being accused of now.

'Look, I don't know what any of this is about,' he said. 'I
didn't have anything to do with this attack. I'm just looking
for my daughters. They're about a day's walk away, and if
I don't get to them soon ...' It didn't bear thinking about.
'I'll tell you anything you want if you let me go so I can
help them.'

Dr Sengupta's right eyebrow twitched slightly. 'You called
this an "attack"?'

'I mean ... you probably know more than I do, right?
Terrorist? Nuclear? Solar? What ... what do you think
it was?'

'You may have heard about a novel celestial body that
astronomers have been observing recently, designated as
Hero.'

'Of course,' Marcus said.

'Yesterday, Hero emitted a powerful magnetic field, a
"pulse" of between ten and thirty teslas, lasting seventy-
four seconds.'

'Oh.' Marcus nodded. 'Magnets.'

'That's right. For context, the Earth's magnetic field is
fifty microteslas. That's a five with five zeros before it.'

'So that's ...' He tried to do the maths.

'About half a million times more powerful than the
magnetic field of the Earth. Which explains the devastating
consequences.' The doctor waited for him to catch up.

'So this is likely ...' He didn't want to say it.

'Its capabilities far exceed anything humanity can produce with present-day technology.'

Marcus sat silently for a while. His head was spinning. 'First contact,' he whispered finally.

'It seems we have made it,' Dr Sengupta said. Of all the end of the world scenarios Marcus had imagined, this one was low on the list.

'But ... what do I have to do with any of this? Why am I here?'

'Our field agents flagged you. Our sensors have detected trace amounts of a xenobiological substance on your person.'

'Xeno—?'

She sighed and read off her tablet: '"The substance consists of nanoscale particles that appear to self-replicate. Unlike any known biological organism, this substance does not rely on DNA or RNA for replication. Spectroscopic analysis reveals that the substance produces both enantiomers of certain organic compounds – specifically, amino acids and sugars."'

She looked up and put down her tablet.

'This is an amino acid.' She held up her left hand in demonstration. 'Biology could produce this kind.' She waved the fingers of her left hand. 'Or this kind.' She lifted her right hand and did the same. 'In the lab, we can make equal mixtures of both. But in nature, if it's an amnio acid, it's mainly this kind.' She put her right hand down and waved her left again. 'On Earth, anyway.'

'So this substance ...' Marcus scratched his head.

'The presence of this mixture of left- and right-handed amino acids suggests that the substance may not have originated from any known biological process on Earth.'

Marcus felt as if she was trying hard not to say the word.

'Aliens?'

She looked grave, like a doctor delivering a fatal diagnosis.

'And you found this "substance" on *me*?' Marcus felt alarmed now, a little sickened.

'On the soles of your shoes, and some trace amounts on your jacket and in your hair. We've decontaminated you and your belongings.'

'What will it do to me?' He thought about the towns-people inhaling radioactive isotopes in the wake of the Chernobyl disaster. He thought about Chernobyl often.

'Preliminary assays show no immediate cytotoxic effects at low concentrations.'

'Not immediately,' said Marcus, not reassured. 'But ... eventually?'

'The lab is conducting more research as we speak. However, the long-term impact on cellular function and gene expression is unknown.'

'And the short-term impact?' Marcus probed.

'In vitro studies using human endothelial cell models of the blood–brain barrier demonstrate that the substance can cross it.'

'I don't know if that's good news or bad news.'

'It normally isn't good.'

'Can we get rid of it?'

'Current findings demonstrate that high temperatures denature it.'

'So, fire? What else?'

'Hydrogen peroxide and certain classes of azoles.'

'Where did it come from?' Marcus asked, retracing the steps in his mind, the journey from his bunker to Asda to Battersea Bridge.

'That's what we're here to establish. We'll need to retrace your steps through the city.'

This sounded like a process that would take a while. 'Has anyone else been exposed you can do that with? I need to get out of here soon. I need to find my family. If I'm not arrested and I'm not in immediate danger, please let me go.'

'We're gathering reports of a few other cases, but as you can imagine, our efforts and capabilities have been severely compromised by the magnetic disturbances. Your cooperation could help us collect vital information from the field.'

'What do you want me to do? I've given you as much as I can.'

'You can start by showing us where you've been today.' A couple of taps of her tablet allowed the doctor to project a map of London onto the oak table.

It took a moment for Marcus to realize what he was looking at, the Thames a silver boa slithering through jagged grey teeth, roads and estates, teal patches of parklands and common. There, he found his house circled in red.

They asked him to point out where he'd been. He showed them the route he'd taken through Clapham and Battersea until he'd reached the bridge. Then he showed them where he needed to go next.

'Radclive in Buckinghamshire? We have some field agents being dispatched to a relief centre near there. If you help us, we can authorize your inclusion in a field team.' Marcus's chest expanded in relief. 'But we need you to think carefully,' said Dr Sengupta. 'Even the smallest detail could be important. Did you touch anything unusual? Debris, plants, animals behaving strangely?'

'Everything is strange. I mean ... nothing particular stands out.' Then he remembered and mentioned the dog that had barked wildly at him at the checkpoint near the bridge. The doctor nodded, unimpressed. 'Yes, that was one of ours.'

An alarm rang distantly, and Dr Sengupta's eyes floated away. She looked as if she would have to wrap the interview up. 'Thank you for your cooperation, Mr Minton.'

'Wait,' he said, as she moved to stand. 'What does it want?'

'It?' she asked, raising her eyebrow.

'Hero,' said Marcus. The name seemed almost menacing to him now.

'We don't know the purpose behind Hero's actions – or if there is even intent. It could be an automated process, a malfunction or something else entirely.'

'Where did it come from?'

'We haven't yet been able to verify its origins.'

'And now I've answered your questions,' Marcus said, 'I'm free to leave?'

Dr Sengupta smiled tightly. 'Certainly, Mr Minton. Once the forty-eight-hour quarantine period is up.'

'What?' She hadn't mentioned this before. In forty-eight hours, the streets could have descended into complete chaos. 'Please! My daughters might not have that long.'

Her smile didn't falter. 'We all have a job to do, Mr Minton.'

As the armed guards dragged him away, he was screaming our names.

TANICE MINTON – 1 DAY AFTER

The only good thing about fruitcake was that it could last forever. Tanice had protested at the cake tasting, had lobbied for chocolate or red velvet, had insulted Aaliyah for her traditionalism, her lack of imagination, but in a couple of days, a lemon cake might be furred with mould and a chocolate cake might have collapsed. The fruitcake, though, would probably last longer than they would.

During the night, Tanice had found a whiskey tumbler in the little portable bar in the adjoining room. She pressed it into the cake, cutting a round little ball into a slick tier of royal icing. Chantale peeled off a sugar paste apple blossom and then bit into a gum peony.

Tanice had always hated fruitcake, despised its sour heaviness, the slimy rind of candied fruit in every layer. The way it made her think of school or charity bake sales, or her grandfather, who'd once spat a mince pie into his monogrammed napkin and asked why everything the English ate for Christmas tasted like rotten fruit.

She was grateful for it now, though, for the way it

soothed the snarling of her stomach and sent a pleasant rush of sugar to her head.

By the next day, they were all suffering, in various stages of dehydration. Tanice was the first to wake and staggered over to the anteroom, sat on the foul-smelling barrel they were using as a chamber pot and let out a thin, painful stream of pee.

She thought of home again, of her father's vast drums of water. Thought of the wedding at Cana, illustrated in one of her grandfather's Bibles. What a reverse miracle it would be to turn all this wine into water.

Then another thought, bright and disruptive, soared through her mind like a comet. She wiped quickly and returned to the neighbouring room, where the photographer was asleep by the door as if keeping guard.

'Hey,' Tanice said to him, 'I didn't see the cloud.'

He woke reluctantly, groaning and rubbing his eyes.

'I didn't see the cloud,' Tanice repeated urgently.

'What?' the photographer asked, voice like sandpaper. He was clutching a bottle of Mouton Rothschild.

'The mushroom cloud,' Tanice said. 'Like in the movies.'

The photographer seemed initially confused but finally said, 'We weren't close enough.'

'But wouldn't it—?'

From across the room, Bartok darted a furious look at her. 'What do *you* know about this stuff?' he asked aggressively.

'Enough,' Tanice argued. Our father had shown us so many YouTube videos that she could deliver a lecture on Chernobyl or Fukushima. In her nightmares, sometimes her hair fell out in clumps and her blackened skin peeled off in sheets.

'Maybe it was a small bomb,' the photographer said. 'They come in different sizes.'

Antoinette, roused by the sound of them, said, 'We all saw the explosion, though.'

'And the ... casualties,' Yasmeen added.

'But not all explosions are nuclear,' Paris noted, 'and I mean ... floating serving trays? That's not like anything I've heard of before.'

'Yeah.' Tanice appreciated his support. 'What if it was just, like, a normal bomb?'

'Or something else entirely,' Paris suggested.

'Like what?' the photographer asked.

'I dunno,' Paris guessed, 'some atmospheric disturbance? An industrial accident?' The more they discussed it, the more convinced Tanice became that this must be true. 'Who would bomb a wedding?'

Yasmeen said, 'That's a good point. Who would nuke Buckinghamshire? It would be one thing if it was *London*, but ...'

'Maybe they missed,' Bartok said.

The photographer shook off their protests. 'It could be any number of people,' he said, counting on his fingers. 'The Russians, the North Koreans, the Chinese. It could be all-out war up there. Retaliation, nuclear winter. What do you want to do, check?'

'Maybe ...' whispered Tanice.

'We said we'd leave it seventy-two hours,' Paris reminded them. It had only been a day so far.

'We said a week,' Bartok protested.

'We'll all be dead in a week!'

'We'll be dead from cancer if we go up there,' the photographer argued. 'Do you know what radiation does to every cell in your body? Organ failure, hallucinations, burns, massive internal bleeding ...'

'We could lose all our teeth!' added Chantale, her voice hollow with terror.

'It's probably one of the worst ways to die,' Antoinette conceded.

'We can't stay in here, though,' said Paris. 'There's no water. It's obviously untenable.'

They paused and stared at each other. Then Paris made a move for the wine rack in front of the door. It would probably take two people to shift it out of the way, but the photographer leapt to stop him.

'If you open that door,' said Bartok, 'you'll poison us all.'

'Could be in a couple of days,' said the photographer, 'when we shit our intestines out. Or in months when our skin rots and we die of leukaemia.'

Antoinette and Chantale started crying. The tension in the room felt palpable.

'I don't want to die,' Jack said, sat on a crate at the far end of the room, twisting and untwisting his bowtie in his fist.

'None of us want to *die*,' Yasmeen said.

'I think we should stay here a bit longer,' Jack sided with the photographer, 'just in case.'

'How about I go out and check?' Paris made another motion towards the door, grabbing on to the wine rack.

'Me, too,' said Tanice, who ran over to help him. It was heavy, but they could move it together.

'Not you!' Chantale protested through tears.

'Don't you dare!' The photographer lunged for Paris and pushed him, making him stumble away. 'As soon as you open that door, radioactive dust will fly in and kill us all.'

Paris regained his balance quickly, his brow knitted in fury. 'You can't hold us prisoner in here.'

'Do not open that door ...' the photographer warned, but Paris ignored him.

'You take that side,' he said to Tanice, who grabbed on to the lower shelf of the wine rack and felt its weight shift as Paris pushed it towards her.

'If you open that door, I'll ...'

'What?' Paris scoffed. But Tanice saw the photographer come up from behind, grab Paris by the shoulders, scrunching the man's cream dress shirt in his grimy fists and tackling him to the ground.

'Hey!' Paris shouted, half in surprise at his strength. The photographer had a crazed, determined look in his eyes. He held Paris down and put a knee on his chest.

'Get off him!' Tanice shouted.

Paris spat in his face. The photographer roared with rage, then buried an elbow in the hollow of his neck.

'What if he's right?' asked Yasmeen. 'And there really is no radiation?'

'What if he's wrong?' asked Antoinette. 'He could compromise the safety of everyone.'

'I'm just ... trying ...' Paris wheezed, as his fingers clawed in vain at the other man's arm.

The photographer pushed down harder, choking him. '*I'm* trying to survive,' he said.

'Don't!' Antoinette cried.

Tanice pounced on the photographer, wrapped her arms around him and felt the hard wall of muscles in his side.

'Stop it!' she shouted, trying to grab one of his arms. 'He can't breathe!'

Bartok reached for Tanice, though, and pulled her back,

holding her tightly as she kicked and fought. His whole hand fitted around her arm, and he locked on to her like a sweaty vice.

'You're going to kill him!' Yasmeen's cries rose frantically.

Jack stood frozen, mouth open, eyes wide with disbelief. He raised his hands feebly as if to intervene, then stepped back, shrinking into the shadows.

'He was going to kill us all!' Bartok yelled, struggling to restrain Tanice's violent thrashing.

She strained desperately, muscles burning, but eventually went still and cold as she realized, to her horror, that the photographer really was going to do it. Paris's eyes were wide with disbelief and fear, his struggles weakening as the colour drained from his face and his lips began to turn purple. The photographer gritted his teeth, unblinking, determined, vengeful. 'You think you can have everything,' he said in a savage whisper.

It took longer than Tanice could bear for Paris to die. But eventually, with some wet gurgles, his ashen hand dropped limply to his side.

In her sleep that night, Tanice would dream about his hand. The way he splayed his fingers before it looked as if all the bones dissolved within them.

She'd dream of Chantale and Antoinette's screams, Jack's cowardly silence and the way they left Paris's grey body in the middle of the room for a couple of hours before Tanice tore the petticoat of her dress and put it over his face and then she and Yasmeen dragged him into the anteroom.

BRIAR MINTON – 1 DAY AFTER

The sunlight streaming through the curtains woke me. I'd fallen asleep on the living room sofa, and for a short, peaceful while, I'd forgotten everything. The disaster, the wedding that wasn't, why the bathroom was covered in blood.

'How rare do you like your steak?' Aaliyah's voice rose from the kitchen. I rubbed my eyes. Looking down, I found that I had put on last year's Christmas pyjamas, cotton sateen spangled with illustrated stars.

'Fossil-grey and well done as a flat tyre.'

I entered to find them at the kitchen table. Carmen was clutching a brushed steel steak knife in a tight fist and leaning over a bowl. I couldn't see its contents from the doorway.

Aaliyah stood over her. Neither of them looked as if they had slept much. 'We could have cooked it,' my sister said.

'I know,' said Carmen. 'It's just, the nutrients and stuff ...'

The kitchen was a strange assortment of yesterday morning's debris – the chaos of the bridesmaids. Half-open makeup cases, balloons, piles of candy-coloured gift boxes.

Cards. Cardigans and shoes, discarded clothes. Someone had attempted breakfast, and sourdough bread was still scattered on the cutting board.

Carmen's skin was grey, and she looked as if she was about to be sick. The salad bowl in front of her was full of blood.

She started, mid-mouthful, as I came further into the kitchen, then closed her eyes, held her breath and chewed.

Aaliyah noticed my expression. 'Most mammals do it,' she said, as if to ward off any defiance from me.

Carmen nodded. Swallowed. Took another careful bite.

Her placenta was about the size of a dinner plate. Spongy and puce. Sinuous veins and arteries sprawled and bubbled across its translucent surface. It looked deeply alive, as if it would startle if I touched it.

'Maybe put it in a smoothie?' Aaliyah suggested, but stopped herself when she remembered, as I did, that we didn't have electricity to use the blender anymore.

'I was going to get it dried and ground into capsules,' Carmen said. 'There's a lady I saw on Etsy who does it ...' She held her nose with her fingers and took another bite.

'Add some seasoning? Pepper, beef stock ...'

Carmen bolted up suddenly, puffing out her cheeks and spat it out into the sink. Afterwards, she reached with trembling fingers for the tap, but when she pulled it, of course, nothing came out.

'Sriracha?' Aaliyah continued. 'Hussain duck sauce?'

In spite of herself, Carmen's lips barked open in a laugh. She spattered saliva and sinew across the steel basin.

'What did you just say?' I snorted.

Aaliyah looked at us both blankly, not sure what we were laughing about.

'What?'

'It still hurts,' Carmen gripped her belly and winced, 'to laugh.'

'*Hussain* duck sauce?' I teased. But my laughter petered out as I caught sight of the placenta again.

'It's supposed to be good for, like, postpartum depression, milk supply. Strength,' Carmen explained.

I nodded, unsure. 'Is that evidence-backed?'

'It makes a kind of . . . intuitive sense,' Aaliyah said.

'Does it?'

'I just want to give Hero everything I can.' Carmen leaned over the sink, breathing heavily. 'And myself. I'm still so tired. Like, bone-deep . . .'

As if hearing her name, the baby started crying. Kim had been sleeping in her bed with her. She came down the stairs, and Carmen rushed out to meet her.

I heard their voices out in the hall. 'Someone's hungry,' Kim said.

Carmen laughed nervously. 'I still don't think she's getting anything.'

'It takes a little while for milk to come in. And her little belly is the size of a thimble at the moment.'

Aaliyah listened for the sound of their footsteps vanishing upstairs before she allowed herself to slump into a kitchen chair. 'I slept about two hours last night,' she said. This was probably not how she had imagined her wedding night. She and Hugo had planned to charter a flight to the Maldives. Did she live in a split world, where she could almost see that reality? Those sun-seeking honeymooners, their marriage a few hours old. Not marred by death, separated by disaster.

'I'm sick with worry,' Aaliyah said. 'I keep thinking about Hugo and Grandad, everyone . . .'

'Me, too,' I said. 'It's only been a day, though. It's a long walk from Glassford House, and probably loads of the roads are closed.' It could be a week, I thought, until we heard any news about them. 'They'll be safe there, anyway. They're probably feasting on, what was it you ordered ...?'

'Lobster bisque with cognac cream,' Aaliyah said longingly. 'Quail's egg tartlets with truffle mayonnaise.' I imagined Grandad, Hugo, Chantale and Tanice in the pantry, digging into the feast with serving spoons.

Aaliyah looked at the Nespresso machine. 'And how are we going to make it,' she sighed heavily, rubbing her eyes, 'without any coffee?'

'We don't need electricity for coffee,' I told her.

It took me a while to find everything, to set the rocket stove back in its usual position on the patio, to locate the dented steel kettle which had been tossed by the magnetic storm into the corner of the kitchen.

I filled it with water from one of the storage containers we'd brought from the shed, carefully fed a few dry twigs into the stove's cylindrical opening – as I had occasionally watched my father do – and then listened for the satisfying crackle as the flames took hold. As the water in the kettle began to hiss, I returned to the kitchen for coffee beans. Opening the cupboard doors, though, I realized how hungry I was. I did a quick inventory of what we had, took some eggs, bagels and butter that hadn't turned sour yet, found the cast iron griddle and witnessed the quotidian magic of the eggs turning white and solid.

I ground the beans and dug through the cupboard for the French press. Thankfully, there was some UHT milk in the bunker. I brought the coffee through to Aaliyah, who thanked me with more sincerity than I'd ever heard from her.

'I thought you gave up on coffee, anyway,' I said as I watched her close her eyes in rapture at the taste of it.

'I thought I had to. Trying to get to the bottom of the IBS thing. But you know the thing about not drinking coffee, you wake up in the morning and you have to *wait* to feel better.' She took another loving drink. 'When I have a coffee, I feel as if the sun has risen in my brain.'

I popped open the sweating can of Dr Pepper I'd taken from the humid fridge. I had never been a fan of coffee. 'That's how these make me feel,' I said.

'And the other thing,' Aaliyah continued, 'when you don't drink coffee, you don't get that moment when someone asks, "Would you like a coffee?" And you go, "Ah! A coffee—"'

I said it with her, in affectionate imitation, '"—would be *wonderful*."'

We both laughed, and I felt a lightness settle dizzyingly in my chest. I heard the eggs crackling outside and went to check on them. When I returned to the kitchen, though, Aaliyah was gone and my mother was there, searching under the sink.

'What are you looking for?'

'I thought we had—' Mum hit her head coming out of the cupboard and swore quietly to herself.

'What?'

'Some baby bottles, from when Chantale was small.' I tried to remember when I'd last seen Chantale with a bottle.

'Well, there was that collection we had a couple of Christmases ago for the baby bank ...'

'I thought we kept a few ...' She sounded absent-minded.

'Isn't baby milk the one thing we don't have to worry about? Seeing as it's free?'

'Just thinking ahead,' Kim said. 'In case. Carmen is having a bit of trouble.'

I could hear the baby howling distantly. Was this the new way? Half the time, day or night, would there always be a baby crying somewhere?

'You made breakfast!' Kim cast her eye across the table. 'Oh, I hate runny eggs.'

I always hated how quick she was with criticism. How physically painful she seemed to find it to deliver praise and not temper it in some way.

'You don't have to eat them,' I said sulkily. Kim shrugged.

'I'm too worried to eat, anyway.'

I was worried, too. Only two days ago, we'd all had breakfast together. Dad had made buckwheat pancakes, and Tanice had played a song her friend had written over her Bluetooth speakers. Chantale had been practising for her vocab test with the fridge magnets. The word 'steadfast' was still spelled out in primary-coloured plastic.

I tried to reassure myself as I had done with Aaliyah, reminding myself how far away Glassford House was. That if anyone could find them, Dad would. My sisters would be here at the table in a couple of days, sharing canned sausages and beans. I felt some peace at the thought of it.

I blurted out, 'I'm glad you can't go now.'

Kim looked at me, her eyes searching my face to discern exactly what I meant.

'To Guatemala,' I said.

'It was – is – a prestigious fellowship,' she replied finally. Kim was stuck here indefinitely. I'd had dreams where this happened. Dreams where I locked my mother in the house. Dreams where she was sick and couldn't leave. Another gas cloud erupted over Iceland, grounding all the planes forever. Digit ate her passport. Or the best one: she just decided to stay.

'Training midwives. Implementing our findings about maternal mortality. Saving babies, saving mothers.' She made the pitch to me professionally as if I were a potential donor. The truth was that I'd never cared about the work she did until I had witnessed her save Carmen's life, the life of her baby. But I still needed my mother.

'You have a job to do here,' I said.

'Briar, next year you'll be in university! And Nicey soon after—'

'We *hope*.'

'And—'

'Chantale?'

'I'd take her with me, of course.' It was the 'of course' that made me furious. I felt the old anger rise within me like a wave.

'You didn't take any of us with you. Last time.'

'Well, you were ...' Kim flailed for an answer. '... younger, and Chantale's ...'

'Your favourite.'

'Yes— *no*!'

I stared at her with gritted teeth.

'Is that what you *want* me to say, Briar?' Kim asked. I stood in silence, aware that we were on a precipice we had never reached before. 'Do you *want* me to say that Chantale is easy to love? She *makes* it easy. She clings to me like a limpet. She believes me. She doesn't hold a mirror up to everything that's wrong with me. If she ever falls down, she calls for me reflexively! Chantale lets me be the mother I want to be. She doesn't twist me into something else. She's not angry with me all the time.'

'You haven't given her anything to be angry about yet!' I yelled then. 'You go away again, come back, see how easy she makes life for you. Or take her away from the things she loves: sleepovers with her friends, her sisters and Dad. See how easy she makes it then.'

I saw then what I had always known. Kim could only be a good mother to young children. She was a good mother when her children could reflect her. When motherhood was to-do lists and schedules and birthday parties and drop-offs. No hard emotional labour, no doubt.

'Why can't you just go later? In a couple of years?'

'I might not have this opportunity in a couple of years, and . . .' She touched the back of her head. 'Now might be the only time I *can* go.'

'What about Dad?' I asked after a pause. 'Does he know?'

'Not yet,' she admitted.

'Were you just going to leave him?'

She struggled to say something. 'It's a good job.'

'But you have a good job here.'

'Well, the clinic here is—'

'I mean *us*!' I shouted. 'Being our mother!'

She was quiet for a moment.

'So that's it,' Kim said. 'Am I just your mother forever now? When do I get to stop?'

They were distracted in the garden when I decided to leave – burying Carmen's placenta in the dirt. 'I thought we were Christians,' Aaliyah muttered as she dug. Mum sang a song in halting Spanish, and Carmen lit a candle.

'It's Hero's companion. It came into this world with her. Looked after her for nine months.'

I left them to it and ran up the stairs. It was hard to know what to pack. Summer clothes, jumpers? I didn't even know what the weather would be like tomorrow, which was more disconcerting than I would have imagined. Waterproofs, wellies? Only what I could fit in the big camping rucksack that I'd been instructed to keep at the foot of my bed for years now.

'One day, you might have five minutes to leave this house and never come back,' our father often prophetically repeated to us. 'Think now about what you'd take.'

My saxophone? It was stupid, but I couldn't bear to part with it. I'd played it almost every day for eleven years. Sheet music for *Into the Woods* was inside the case, which used to feel so heavy to me. When I was younger, it had been like hauling around my own coffin.

Kim's voice floated up to my room as she sang. '"Before I formed you in the womb, I knew you; before you were born, I set you apart ..."'

It gave me a thrill to imagine how she'd react to my departure. I pictured her entering the house, the casual way she usually called my name, her surprise at my silence. She'd discover that Digit had vanished and think I'd gone out to walk her. By nightfall, a dread would settle over her like a chill. She'd find my GOOD bag gone, my boots, all the Dr Pepper from the fridge.

Kim would finally know how it felt to be abandoned.

TANICE MINTON – 2 DAYS AFTER

From then on, Tanice kept a shard of glass from a broken wine bottle in her pocket and thought often about when to use it. By then, she'd convinced herself that there had been no bomb, that the enemies to defeat were the photographer and Bartok. If they were gone, she would need help moving the cabinet from the door, and then she could save her sister and find her grandad.

Everyone was fading by the next day. Severe dehydration had set in. Tanice could feel her tongue swell and crack. Swallowing was becoming difficult. She had awoken several times in the night with leg cramps twisting her calf in a vice.

Chantale seemed to be weakening the fastest. By Monday morning, Tanice had to shake her hard to wake her. Her pulse felt shallow and fast.

They had to get out, Tanice thought, today or tomorrow, before they all died here. But Bartok and the photographer spent most of the day slumped against the wine rack in front of the door. They seemed to have discovered the hard way that wine only made them sicker faster, but they still took a couple of sips to numb the pain in their heads and guts, to swill around their parched mouths. It made them irritable and erratic. How long until they gave in and let everyone out? Or would they commit to keeping the group imprisoned, dooming everyone to a preventable death?

As the hours passed, Tanice thought miserably of her family. If Paris had been right and there was no nuclear bomb, then our parents could be completely fine and looking for her. Or maybe Bartok was right, and a war had started. Her imagination flitted between the two extremes.

She tried to guess where Sydney might have been when the Event happened. Asleep after a long shift, when his phone pinged with a news alert? Or jogging around Battersea Park when he saw the impossible, every metal structure rising into the sky? She hoped he was looking for her. She doubted it, though.

'I keep thinking of all the things I'll never do,' Antoinette said quietly. Everyone's eyes drifted to her. But Tanice glanced at the anteroom. Chantale had limped over to the bathroom, but she'd been gone a long time. Tanice hoped she was okay.

'Run the London Marathon?' Yasmeen hazarded.

'Play the Last Night of the Proms?' Bartok croaked.

'Start a family.' Antoinette started crying.

Yasmeen looked between her and Jack in confusion. 'I'm sorry. I didn't know that you and Jack were . . .'

'Trying,' she sighed. 'And failing.' Jack shifted uncomfortably.

'I always hated that phrase,' Yasmeen said.

'Me too,' Antoinette admitted.

'It makes it sound as if it's all a matter of determination and strategy. Like, if it doesn't work, it's your fault.'

'Whose fault *is it*?' Bartok asked mischievously. A tense

silence extended between them. 'I think I've guessed,' he slurred, waggling his brows at Jack.

'Oh yeah?' Jack stood, his jaw gritted.

'I always figured that you would be ...' Bartok grinned, laughing drunkenly, slightly hysterical, '... firing blanks.'

Jack clenched the bottle of Grand Cru in his hand, his knuckles tight. 'You know,' he said, 'it doesn't make you tough, that impulse you have to say the most spiteful thing.'

Bartok, surprised by Jack's tone, tried to inject some false levity. 'Come on, it was—'

'No. There are things I could say, too.' Jack was like a dog Bartok had kicked, and now the man was surprised he was making a move to bite him. 'You think we all admire you because you were thirteen when you graduated from the Conservatoire. But really, we pity you. You're like a cautionary tale. Still playing weddings and freelancing at cocktail parties ... A ghost story about wasted ambition.'

'Hey.' Tanice felt her head spin as she stood, as if her brain was floating in a fishbowl. She was glad that Chantale was in the other room. 'Stop this.'

Jack and Bartok ignored her, though.

Jack said, 'And everyone knows how much you want to fuck Yasmeen. And that even if you were literally the last person on Earth, she never would.'

Bartok's eyes darted involuntarily to Yasmeen's as if for confirmation. She looked away. So Bartok turned his rage on Jack and shoved him in the chest. Bartok weighed twice as much as the other man, and although Jack was braced for the blow, he lost his balance quickly.

On the floor, Jack scrabbled for the bottle of Grand Cru and brandished it.

'Why don't you just do it?' Bartok teased. Jack pulled himself upright, only for Bartok to push him again. 'Why don't you just fucking do it!'

Jack made a great swing for Bartok's head. The man ducked with the agility of a boxer, but the bottle exploded like a watermelon on the wall, spraying wine and glass everywhere.

Tanice darted out of their way, tripping over shattered glass as she ran. Her foot nudged Antoinette's thigh as she pulled open the door to the anteroom and then slammed it shut.

The smell in there was overpowering. Urine and faeces and bile, sloshing around in barrels. It was all she could do not to retch. Tanice fought the clenching in her gut and reminded herself to breathe through her mouth.

As her eyes adjusted to the dark, she found Chantale crouched behind a dehumidifier, kneeling on the floor in front of Paris's cold body. She was arranging her flower hairclips in his hair.

'Stop that!' Tanice said in reflexive horror.

Chantale turned calmly to her sister. 'It's not as scary as I thought.'

'What?' Tanice gasped. Half listening to the grunts and shouts of the fighting men outside, she wondered if they would end up with more dead bodies to store. If one by one they would all be picked off by violence and stupidity.

'I thought it would be the end of everything,' Chantale told her.

The sight of Paris made Tanice feel weak. Now that he was gone, she felt acutely aware of how vulnerable she and her sister were. Paris had always been kind to her, if distantly, and she would forever be grateful to him for trying to save them both when the worst happened. And she'd always regret not being able to save him in turn.

Tanice had seen Aaliyah sneak off with him in the months running up to the wedding. Jump quickly in the back of his car when she thought no one was home. She had caught him once, on the tennis court, with his hand in her sister's Lycra skort. She'd known it was wrong, but she didn't want to get involved in Aaliyah's personal life. Paris had been Aaliyah's first love, Tanice knew. He also happened to be Hugo's younger cousin. He was handsome, with a smattering of dark freckles on his cheekbones and tattoos her sister said she knew by heart. With his shirt unbuttoned now, Tanice glimpsed the one on his ribcage that (she'd overheard him boast) a monk had drawn with a bamboo rod during one of his gap years in Southeast Asia.

Sunk now, in slow decay. Paris would never again say, 'Hey, sport' to her and smile.

Tanice had never felt worse in her life. 'I don't want to die, though!' she cried. It was coming for her. Tonight or tomorrow, from dehydration. Or at the spiteful hands of the photographer or at the sharp end of a flung bottle of blue-chip wine.

'It's okay, it's okay.' Chantale came over to comfort her. 'This is the worst thing.' Her little sister held her as she sobbed dry tears. 'The bomb. The radiation,' Chantale said. 'Probably everyone we love is dead.' A fresh sob escaped Tanice's lips at the notion. 'And all the animals in London Zoo,' Chantale told her. 'It's a relief, though. We don't have to be scared of it happening now that it's happened.'

Tanice nodded, and they sat for a long while in the gloom.

After a while, the noise outside died down.

Her thoughts drifted, as they did every couple of minutes

now, to how thirsty she was. And she remembered suddenly the previous summer, and the hosepipe ban. How their father had used water from the dehumidifiers to water the plants.

'Hey.' Tanice looked up at the defunct one at the end of the room, covered in dust although it was still plugged into the wall. It must have been running before the mains cut out. She wriggled out of her younger sister's embrace and fumbled around, her fingers trembling, for an opening near the back. When she found it, she dropped to her knees in worshipful tears.

'What is it?' Chantale asked. Tanice lifted the mildew-spotted lid of the back chamber to show her the tank.

'Water!'

BRIAR MINTON – 2 DAYS AFTER

In the middle of the night, I woke to the sound of my tent being zipped open from the outside. My heart started pounding as I remembered immediately how vulnerable I was, sleeping alone in the woods. I sat up and rubbed my eyes, looked again to find that the metal teeth of the tent's zipper were still clenched tight. Digit, curled up by my feet, gave a low, sleepy growl but didn't stir further.

I had walked for most of the previous day, trying to find Freya's Group. I'd hoped to make it to the spot marked on the map by sunset, but I found myself lost in the woods by the time it was too dark to keep looking. So I had pitched my tent, eaten a Pot Noodle that I cooked with water from a flask I'd taken from the kitchen and tried to get some sleep – before being woken by that vivid dream, the sense that someone was coming for me.

Luckily, it was summer, and the sun would rise by 5 a.m. I just had to try to rest until then. Silence again, save for the rustle of leaves. My imagination kept conjuring creatures in the darkness. I tried counting to get back to sleep, waiting for my heart rate to slow back down.

I was just drifting back off when I was certain I heard footsteps and breathing outside. I thought of everything I'd been taught to be afraid of in the woods.

Sleep wasn't coming now. I had to check. I moved carefully, climbing out of my tent. Digit followed close behind, her paws padding silently on the damp earth as I assessed the darkness. It was maybe 3 a.m., and the moon cast a thin glow over the clearing. Mist swirled between the trees.

I was just about to give up and return to my tent, when I saw something. A figure in the trees, approaching.

'Briar?'

My heart was a thunderclap. I squinted into the gloom at the speaker. I recognized her voice.

'Ruby?'

Was she hiding out here in the forest? The notion made my head spin. I thought I saw the beads in her box braids glitter in the moonlight. She stopped suddenly, tilted her head to one side. Goosebumps rose on my arms.

'Run,' she whispered. And then she did, her form disappearing into the mist. I didn't stop to think, just chased after her, damp leaves clutching at my ankles as I sprinted. Digit bounded ahead, her black coat blending into the shadows. My gaze darted forward, Hero's light making scattered patterns on the forest floor. Up ahead, the trees were less dense. Ruby's silhouette vanished once more.

As I chased after her, I felt the ground slope and grow soft under my feet. Pre-dawn light filtering through. A sound like rain. No, running water. A river.

I felt a wave of relief at the sight of it. The landmark would help me to get my bearings when the sun rose; I could use it to find Midacre on the map.

The heels of my boots sank into the sticky mud at the

river's edge. I stumbled and caught myself before I toppled into the water. Digit barked as she circled back to me, wagging her tail nervously. Further down the bank was a wooden bridge. It looked rickety and ancient, swaying in the wind, its ropes frayed by weather and time. On the other side, barely visible in the dawning light, I thought I saw Ruby in the same hoodie she was wearing in that final photo of her, that electric green one which read 'FRANKIE SAYS PANIC'. I faltered in disbelief at the vision and rubbed my eyes.

How could it be that she was here?

'Ruby!' As I ran towards the bridge, she seemed to melt into the darkness. I bolted on to it but then stopped dead as the boards groaned loudly beneath my feet. Breathing heavily, I took careful, uneven steps as the wind picked up. Digit stayed behind me on the riverbank, whining and pacing.

'Run!' Ruby shouted again. As I looked up, my foot slipped, and the world tilted suddenly, violently. The old wood snapped beneath my heels. My leg speared through the gap, and the bridge jerked sideways. I fought to steady myself, my fingers clawing at the ropes, but I felt the wood crumble beneath me.

I fell, a rush of cold air seized me and then my stomach slapped the water below. I fought against the current, my limbs flailing. I had never been a strong swimmer, and each stroke seemed to push me down instead of forward. Panic surged through my chest, my thoughts splintered in terror – *I might drown here*, I realized, the current far too strong, my strength slipping away. Above me, I heard Digit barking frantically, her voice almost washed away by the river's roar.

At the last desperate moment, my hands brushed against something solid – an overhanging willow tree, its roots jutting out into the water. I flailed, my fingers catching the rough bark, and clung to it with everything I had. Slowly, painfully, I dragged myself up onto the muddy shore. I lay there for a moment, gasping for air, my limbs trembling, my heart pounding in my ears. Digit came to my side, licking my face as if trying to wake me.

'Digit,' I croaked, gripping her damp fur. She nudged me with her nose, and her tail wagged furiously now that I was safe.

But then I heard it again – a rustle of movement, the soft crunch of footsteps. Ruby, returning to me? I looked up, my vision still blurred.

I was sure I was dreaming then. It was the wolf from *Into the Woods*; his eyes were dark glass marbles, and his face was covered in red fur. His teeth glistened in the pre-dawn glow. But then, a laugh.

'Cato?' I said. A smile from under his whiskers. Digit growled, stepping protectively in front of me.

As Cato extended a hand towards me, my heart leapt. The Group had come to rescue me.

Instead of helping me up, though, Cato dived for my pink hair. His fingers curled into it, his grip sudden and vicious. He shoved me back into the water, face first.

My mouth filled with the river, and my vision went black at the edges. My arms thrashed, dark panic rising as Cato held me down. I bucked and writhed to push him off. I tried to scream, but water only invaded me further, setting my throat on fire where air should be.

I felt my nails on his skin in the mud. I kicked wildly, but he held still as my strength began to wane. Digit barked and snapped at him, but she had never been an aggressive dog. She didn't know what to do.

It's hard to know how long it was before the world began to slip away and the murky dark of near-death washed in like a tide.

I saw it then, an alien sky, vast and black, diamonds condensing from methane clouds in sparkling waves. Below it, cities were carved deep into the planet in elaborate networks. Transparent panes bored into the ground, a system of mirrors and vaults, canals and tunnels. The Tau were born blind, but even after they had engineered eyes, they mostly kept them closed. They focused instead on their inner eye. They pushed the tendrils of their sentience out towards each other. They shared each other's dreams. They knew perfect love.

Who can fathom the mind of the Tau?

I would spend the rest of my life trying to describe it. Can you imagine the mind of a glacier, placid, crystalline, unceasing? A mind that quietly watched the birth of a thousand nebulae. Saw civilizations bubble up and burn out. Flung starships at supernovae. Spread across the galaxy, hungry just to behold it. Surveyed the vastness of space and identified our minor planet, discerned the petty cares of humans and beheld them with immortal tenderness.

I felt what I hadn't realized I'd been seeking. Eternal love. I had wanted to know that my life mattered, that I was being regarded with care. I had hoped that my efforts and achievements were meaningful, rather than useless bulwarks against death.

When I opened my eyes, I was crying. Lying on the riverbank, covered in mud. Faces were emerging from the trees as the sun lifted its countenance on us.

The warmth of the vision dissolved, replaced by a rush of

dread. My breath caught in my throat, and suddenly I was vomiting up water and bile.

'It's okay.' Cato pulled off his mask and reached out for me, but I flinched, half expecting him to pin me down again.

'I told you!' Beth punched the air in triumph. 'I told you we were right about her.'

'It doesn't happen to everyone,' Amy said, walking carefully along the bank and trying to avoid slipping on the silty earth.

I curled forward, arms wrapped around myself. I was shivering uncontrollably, too weak to rise. Every time I blinked, there seemed to be more people from the Group emerging from the trees.

'Did they have a message for us, Briar?' Martha asked gently.

'Are they coming for us soon?' Isaac added, breathless with hope.

'What—' I managed to gurgle at Cato, as my senses returned. I felt furious at him. 'Why did you do that?'

'Did you meet them, in the dark?' Cato's mask was half-sunk in the mud, and I examined his depthless eyes in alarm.

Finally, I nodded.

'You can thank me later, then,' he said.

'You found us!' Axel was beside me, bending down, his arms warm and certain. He hugged me tightly, not caring that his lime shirt was getting smeared with mud.

'More like *you* found *me*.' But even his familiar face wasn't reassuring. Some part of me wanted to run. Was counting the hours it would take for me to get back home. When I tried to stand, my knees buckled, but Axel caught me.

'I like your shoes,' he said, grinning at my muddy pink DMs. Then he wrapped his arms around me and kissed me on each cheek. Digit barked sharply, not understanding the sudden intimacy.

There were more hugs after that, a flurry of arms. I was moved from person to person as they all said, 'Welcome, Briar.'

'We're so happy you're here.'

'You were chosen.'

'You are loved.'

That last one made a hitch catch in my throat. I felt disarmed by their affection. Their shift in energy from the wary suspicion they'd viewed me with only a couple of days ago to this.

I thought I'd come here to investigate Ruby's disappearance. But after the impossible things I'd seen, the morning of the wedding and then in the water, I felt unmoored and undone.

The Tau had said it, too: *You are loved*.

Was that actually all I'd ever wanted?

Finally, the crowd parted, and I saw Freya in a beam of early morning sunlight. She raised her arms, and the others grew quiet.

'We must test our prophets,' she said.

I blinked, shell-shocked, my body still aching. Then I realized, with an unexpected thrill of delight, that I must have passed.

MARCUS MINTON – 3 DAYS AFTER

Seeing the astronaut made him feel old. Her reflection in the window reminded him that it had been thirteen years since that bright morning when he'd stood with Aaliyah, Tanice and me at the rocket launch. Tanice had been three then, and he'd hoisted her up on his shoulders. Aaliyah had painted her face with red, white and blue stars. She'd worn a Union Jack crop top that Marcus had insisted she cover with a yellow trench coat. I'd waved around a model of the rocket ship I had made with toilet roll and plastered with collectable stickers.

The last time he'd seen her face, it had been a quarter of a mile away, projected on a screen. With her hair in cornrows under her skull cap, she'd looked even younger than her eighteen years, and he'd felt a pang for her as she waved goodbye. The naïve excitement in her eyes had reminded him of his mother, who'd eloped with his father on her eighteenth birthday. Even after she finally left him, she still had their wedding photo on her nightstand. Her eyes had been filled with the same guileless delight.

''Scuse me.' Marcus leaned forward in his seat. They were

making slow progress in the First Contact Committee's strange horse-drawn wagon, trying to get to the relief centre via deserted or half-clear roads. He could only see a patch of the astronaut's face over her mask, in the square of mirror. He recognized those famous eyes, though. 'You're ... ?'

She nodded curtly. She was tired of being reminded of who she was.

It had been two days until they'd finally cleared him to leave his cell in the Committee's underground headquarters. He'd been furious, demanding to be released the whole time, though he'd been well fed and the scientists had explained that they would have preferred to keep him under observation for longer.

Marcus was grateful that they were driving him to the relief centre on the edge of the city, though. If Chantale and Tanice weren't already there, by his estimations Glassford House was only a couple of hours' walk away. Maybe they'd be fine. They were smart, well-practised. The Pastor would look after them, and they had all that food left from the wedding ... but an unbidden alternative image of them, crushed under rubble and already dead, haunted his mind.

Marcus tried to dismiss the thought.

He caught the astronaut's eye in the mirror again.

He did the maths. She must only be about thirty now. Still young. Though, as he liked to tease his daughters, he'd had three children by thirty. He'd already realized by then that life, which had once seemed like a wide-open vista, lavish with possibilities, was actually a ghost train, bound where everyone was heading, on only one track.

Did her eyes look as if relativity had played a trick on her? As if she'd lived a thousand years in that freezing spaceship before the end?

What had he always wanted to say to her?

He looked out at the city, at the damage Hero had wrought. The kind of destruction that might take a generation to recover from, and maybe more. Thought about what she had said on the radio, about how she'd devoted her life to the notion of extraterrestrial intelligence.

Marcus asked, 'Is it worse to be endangered or alone?'

Astrid answered immediately, 'Alone.'

The relief centre was a hastily repurposed sports hall on the outskirts of the city. The building loomed ahead, its brickwork bearing the marks of recent chaos – cracked windows patched with boards, doors propped open with debris to accommodate the constant flow of people.

Marcus stepped out of the vehicle, his eyes scanning the area with a mix of hope and dread. The air was heavy with the scent of smoke, sweat and the faint odour of antiseptic. Makeshift tents sprawled across the adjacent field, their vinyl flysheets fluttering in the breeze.

As he approached the entrance, the murmur of voices grew louder – crying children, anxious conversations, the distant wail of sirens. Volunteers in brightly coloured vests moved through the crowd, among them, a couple of medics and one police officer.

Inside the massive hall, a sea of cots and blankets was strewn across the parquet floor. A bulletin board pitched near the entrance was covered with handwritten notes and photographs – a makeshift message centre for people seeking loved ones.

Near the doorway, an argument had erupted between two men over the dwindling supply of bottled water. A volunteer made a vain attempt at mediation, but the tension was palpable. The haunted refugees nearby watched warily, some inching away to avoid being drawn into the conflict.

Marcus made his way to the reception desk, where a harried-looking woman was trying to answer multiple questions at once from the small crowd gathered around her. Her eyes met his briefly as he stepped forward.

'Excuse me,' he began, his voice strained. 'I'm looking for my daughters: Chantale and Tanice Minton. They're seven and sixteen.'

The woman glanced down at a battered notebook. 'Names again?'

'Chantale and Tanice.'

She flipped through pages filled with lists of names; as she did, he noticed that his breath had stopped and his eyes were scanning the pages, too. After what felt like a long while, she said, 'I'm sorry, they're not on here. But not everyone has been processed yet. You might want to check the waiting area or the medical tents. Or ...' She hesitated, seeming to choose her next words carefully. 'Earlier today, rescue teams brought in several people from Aylesbury and High Wycombe. I think there were a couple of children among them, maybe girls in that age group.'

Hope surged through him. 'They might have made it to Wycombe.'

She bit her lip. 'Well ... it's the tent at the far end of the field. You won't miss it.'

'Thank you.' He turned away, about to run there, when she called him back.

'Wait! It's just the people they're bringing now for identification, they're all ...' He could see in her eyes that she'd delivered this news many times. 'Dead.'

The world seemed to tilt around him. *It's not them, then*, Marcus told himself.

He nodded, unable to speak. He'd search everywhere else first. The knot in his stomach tightened as he moved deeper into the hall.

Marcus weaved through the rows of cots, examining each face. Occasionally, a flicker of hope would ignite when he caught a glimpse of dark hair or heard a familiar laugh, only for it to be extinguished when he realized that it wasn't his daughters.

'Chantale! Nicey!' he called out, his voice echoing slightly in the vast space. Heads turned, though none belonged to them.

As he reached the back of the hall, a familiar voice called his name. 'Marcus!'

Marcus turned to find Pastor Abiola sitting on a camp bed and waving at him. His tall frame was unmistakable even in the dim light. As he approached, his father-in-law's eyes reflected a depth of sorrow that Marcus had never seen before.

'Pastor!' Marcus breathed, relief and apprehension washing over him.

'Thank God for answered prayers,' the man said as he got up off the creaking camp bed and wrapped Marcus in a sturdy embrace. He still smelled of his fancy cologne, the must of his garments, shipped as they had been from Nigeria, and under it, the odour of an unwashed body.

'Some, at least,' he continued, stepping back.

'You're okay?'

'On the mend.' He sat back down carefully, and as he did, Marcus saw where his robe had been cut open, the brown stains of long-dried blood. 'A flesh wound.'

'You haven't seen . . . ?'

'I was hoping that *you* might have,' the older man said with a sigh.

Anger seeped into Marcus's voice. 'I wasn't there. *You* were supposed to look after them.'

'I know ... but it happened so fast.' Marcus noticed another gummy wound above his right brow. 'When I woke, they were gone.'

'What do you mean, "gone"?'

The Pastor shook his head sadly and explained how he had been injured, had suffered a severe concussion, and Hugo had helped him into the pantry. The two men had recovered there for a while before another group of wedding guests found them and explained that everyone had left for the nearest relief centre. Hugo and the Pastor had made their way here, assuming they would be reunited with Chantale and Tanice.

'When we didn't find them,' the man explained, 'Hugo suggested that I wait here for news while he ventured out to search the city for Aaliyah and the others. I'd assumed Tanice and Chantale would have turned up here by now. I didn't know if what happened to us at the wedding was an isolated event, you see. I thought that if I came here, I might find a way to contact you or Kim ...' He shook his head again, tears welling in his eyes. He'd spent the past few days going over and over his mistakes in his mind.

After sharing the rest of their stories, Marcus and the Pastor decided to search together. They made their way around the entire complex, covering the bunks and the encampments, the medical tents, the food queues. Finally, they approached the rescue tent at the end of the field.

'Just to rule it out,' Marcus said, and the Pastor nodded, his gaze steady but filled with worry.

There was a volunteer on a camping chair at the entrance.

Marcus told her who they were looking for, and her face dropped in sympathy. 'It only needs to be one of you who does it,' she said gently.

'I can go,' the Pastor offered. But Marcus knew it had to be him.

'I need to do it,' he said.

He walked, in silence, into the tent. 'He's here to try and identify a couple of people,' the volunteer said sombrely to a woman in a battered-looking paramedic's uniform.

She nodded, pushing open a curtain. 'Take all the time you need.'

Inside, there were rows of bodies covered in sheets. Marcus counted twenty. A smell of death lingered in the hot air, and flies were already buzzing around. He desperately didn't want his daughters to be here.

The woman pointed to the two figures in one of the corners, each covered with a white sheet. Marcus hesitated, his heart pounding.

A couple of years ago, the Pastor had spoken at the funeral of one of Marcus's colleagues from the Met. A young man at the beginning of his career, who had unexpectedly died of an overdose. 'It goes against nature,' the man's mother had told Marcus, 'to bury your child.' She hadn't wanted to come to the interment, hadn't wanted to see the wound in the earth made for his coffin, the final view of him being lowered into the ground.

The Pastor had delivered a moving speech, though. He'd spoken of Job, a wealthy, faithful man who had lost everything: his property, his children, his health. The Pastor had spoken of the stoical way that Job had accepted the news of the death of his children, the way he had offered praises to the Lord when anyone else would have hurled curses. Impossible for Marcus to imagine doing anything but shaking his fist up at heaven and grinding his face into the dirt if he ever lost anything as dear to him as a daughter.

He stepped forward, his legs like lead. With trembling hands, he reached for the edge of the first sheet.

But even as he touched it, he realized, with disgusted relief, that it was someone else's daughter. Seventeen, maybe, her hair in two French plaits. A nose ring torn out, a gash on her neck and dried blood on her GAP hoodie.

He moved to the second gurney, a glimmer of hope flickering in his chest. Repeating the motion, he lifted the sheet. The girl beneath had features similar to Tanice's – the same dark skin and tight afro – but he knew instantly that it wasn't her.

'I'm sorry,' the woman said. It was only then that he realized he was crying.

Marcus covered the girl's face gently, his hands shaking. 'What a good world it would be,' Aaliyah had once said, 'if everyone loved other people's children like their own.' Except, Marcus had always feared, it defied his nature. Maybe he loved his own children more than a thousand of anyone else's. The thought filled him with a sticky disappointment at himself that he quickly shook away.

He was in shock. 'It's not them,' he whispered.

Back outside, the Pastor hugged him as he cried. 'It's not my girls.'

'We live in a vale of tears,' his father-in-law said. 'I'm glad for us, though it's tragic for their families.'

Marcus wiped his eyes with the back of his hand. He couldn't fall apart now.

'I need to find them.'

'We'll keep looking,' the Pastor assured him. 'There are

other centres, other places they might be. We'll go back to Glassford House, start there.'

'If we set out now, I think we can make it before nightfall,' Marcus said. But our grandfather looked tired. Marcus dimly wondered if the man would be able to walk, considering his injuries. But as always, the Pastor wasn't thinking about himself.

'Well, let's find you something to eat first. You need your strength.'

'I don't think I can,' Dad replied, but allowed himself to be led back towards the main hall.

As they walked, the Pastor spoke softly. 'This crisis has tested all of us, but we must hold on to hope. Tanice and Chantale are strong and resourceful. Like their father.'

'Tanice is,' Marcus said. He'd always worried that being the youngest had handicapped Chantale. She'd been spoiled, by all of us.

'We'll find them.'

Marcus nodded absently as they re-entered the bustling hall, where the atmosphere had grown more tense. A scuffle had broken out, voices raised in anger and frustration. Volunteers rushed to intervene.

'The longer this goes on, the harder it becomes to maintain order,' Pastor Abiola observed quietly. 'People are scared.'

'What's the government doing?' asked Marcus, 'There must be some plan.'

The Pastor shook his head. 'Communication is fragmented. There are rumours of a Post-Collapse Task Force forming, but so far, it seems we've been abandoned.'

There was a loud crash, and they turned to see a stack of crates toppled over near the food storage area. The noise

startled everyone, quieting the din. A teenage boy in tat-
tered clothes emerged from the clutter, his eyes wide with
fear. In his hands, he held a bag of crisps, some cans and
bread. A stern-looking volunteer grabbed his arm.

'You can't just take what you want!' he admonished.

'We're hungry!' the boy pleaded, his voice shaking.

The scene drew the attention of those nearby, whispers
spreading as people took sides. Someone shouted, 'We're all
hungry!', while others grumbled about fairness.

The situation was deteriorating rapidly. As Marcus and
the Pastor made their way back towards the exit, the surge
of people made movement difficult.

A fight broke out, two men grappling over a fuel canister. Others circled around them, some trying to intervene,
others egging them on.

We need to get out of here, Marcus thought. He'd once
heard that society was only nine missed meals away from
anarchy.

'Enough!' a stern voice bellowed, echoing off the rafters, momentarily silencing those nearby. The Pastor had
somehow stood up on a camp chair while Marcus was distracted. Despite his injuries and his age, he commanded his
old authority. 'This isn't helping anyone. We need to work
together if we're going to get through this. Fighting over
scraps will only make things worse.'

A few people muttered under their breath, but most were
gazing up at Pastor Abiola, listening intently.

'"*The end of all things is near. Therefore ... love each
other deeply*,"' the Pastor said into the quiet. 'This is the
opposite of our instinct. No hiding ourselves away, nor
fortifying our walls and creating divisions. The end is a
time to throw *open* our doors. "*Offer hospitality to one*

another without grumbling." Be pillars of strength in your community.'

It had been a long time since Marcus had heard a sermon from his father-in-law. He had never believed in anything except for what he could see. He was grateful now, though, for the Pastor's level-headed presence, for his ability to command a crowd, even in the worst of scenarios.

'What haven't we witnessed?' Pastor Abiola asked. 'Civil unrest, natural catastrophes, wildfires, pestilence and plagues. Which of these have we managed to endure by ourselves? If we are to survive this, we will only do it together.'

TANICE MINTON – 3 DAYS AFTER

Marcus had told us that the average man is twice as strong in his upper body as the average woman. That, considering the relative dimensions of the female neck and skull, almost all men could kill almost all women with their bare hands. It was a fact that rang with a clarion quality in Tanice's head every time she walked down the street at night or heard footsteps behind her in an alleyway.

Or now, as the photographer drunkenly guarded the door. If they were going to make it out alive, they were going to have to kill him.

It was the third day in the cellar. The stolen sips of water from the dehumidifier that she and Chantale had been living off had run out, and the photographer was still adamant that no one could leave.

Tanice had been gaming the strategy in her head. She kept running the edge of her thumb over the shard of glass she'd saved and thinking. It would have to be the photographer first. But then, she couldn't move that cabinet in front of the door on her own. One of the string quartet would have to help her.

She would have to do it today. Because tomorrow she might be too weak.

'Is it the worst thing I've ever done?' Antoinette asked that day. 'Leaving those people out there?'

'I can think of worse things,' Jack said. Their voices sounded like sandpaper, and they were slumped like drunks at the edge of the room.

'Oh yeah?' she drawled. 'Like what?'

'What is this, confession?'

'Not a bad time for it,' rasped Yasmeen without opening her eyes.

'What?' Antoinette wouldn't let it go. 'What have you done that's worse than leaving over a hundred people to die?'

'Okay ... when you put it that way,' Jack conceded.

'I wish you wouldn't,' said Tanice. 'Put it that way.'

'I'm just saying,' Jack said, 'everyone does things they aren't proud of. Haven't you?'

Antoinette shrugged. 'I *try* to be a good person.'

'None of that shit,' said Bartok. 'Doesn't everyone?'

'Do you think the Nazis thought they were bad?' mused Yasmeen.

'Why do you always bring the Nazis into everything?' Antoinette asked.

Tanice could think of a couple of terrible things she'd done. Things she'd stolen, people she'd lied to. She thought of Sydney.

Then her mind drifted to the argument she'd had with Chantale two years ago, when she had cut one of Tanice's favourite dresses up with a pair of kitchen scissors. Tanice had been furious, had told her sister that she hoped she'd get what she deserved and, for a while, she had meant it. She had watched Chantale playing with her remote-controlled car in the front garden and really wished harm would come to her. Had she left the gate open? Her mind wouldn't let her remember it. Chantale must have lost control of her toy and chased after it into the road. Tanice had been watching TV when she heard the squeal of brakes and the shouts of onlookers. For half a second, she'd been satisfied.

'Hey,' Tanice said now, 'did you hear that?'

Watching her mother crying in the hospital's hall, Tanice had thought, *Whoever hates his brother is a murderer*, and felt sick with conviction.

'What?' The photographer rolled his bloodshot eyes towards her.

She had hoped it would happen.

'It sounded like . . .' Tanice pulled herself up. 'Footsteps.'

'Where?' he asked.

Tanice stood shakily. 'I thought—' She stumbled to the shelving unit blocking the entrance. As she approached, the photographer raised his arms feebly.

'I heard them, too,' Yasmeen said.

'They won't—' the photographer began.

'Hello?' Tanice shouted at the door.

She thought she heard a man's voice.

Yasmeen stumbled to her feet and grabbed one edge of the wine rack. It was too heavy, and she was too weak.

'Hey!' The photographer got up and pushed her away, hard enough to make her lose her balance.

'Please!' she shouted on the floor.

'There's no way—' he began.

'We're going to die in here!' Yasmeen cried.

'They're *already* dead out there.'

'Then let me join them,' she pleaded.

There was a muffled shout from outside again.

Yasmeen scrambled to her feet, but the photographer shoved her against the wine rack, causing her skull to crash against it with a force that made Tanice wince. 'Don't you fucking dare,' he hissed at her.

Of course, thought Tanice, *he'll never let us go.* And then a cool resolve settled over her. She turned to Chantale and whispered, 'Close your eyes.'

All she had was this second of surprise while his back was turned.

Tanice rushed at him, pulling the glass from between the folds of her skirt. He turned at the sound of her approach and made a move to stop her.

Too slow. She managed to push her makeshift blade just under his ribs and thrust up, hard. She would never forget the sound he made as she did it. She'd think every day for the rest of her life about his arctic eyes, the violet bow of his lips as his mouth fell open as if at the revelation of a magic trick. 'Oh.' She'd tell herself that she'd had to do it to save her sister, to save them all. But she'd think often about the state of her soul in quiet moments: *I'm the kind of person who can kill a person.*

Jack leapt into action, helping Yasmeen to move the heavy rack. Antoinette was trying to shout to the rumble of the voices outside, the pounding on the door. 'We're in here!' she screamed, her voice a rasp. 'In here!' Bartok just sat, staring dumbly at the photographer's body, slumped on the floor.

The pounding got louder, someone ramming their whole body into the door, rattling its hinges.

Tanice dimly recognized the voice but told herself to stop dreaming. Really, it could be anyone; one of the wedding guests who'd survived the initial blast or anyone who had come across Glassford House in search of things to loot.

She grabbed a side of the cabinet to help, and with one final haul, they managed to pull it aside – though, in their effort, they toppled another shelf and sent bottles flying like bowling pins, crashing to the floor, sending splinters of glass and wine into the air with ballistic force. Everyone screamed. Tanice reflexively covered her eyes. The photographer's blood was like honey on her fingers, which might always smell of him.

'Tanice?'

She saw, then, that she would live. Though it would take years for her to tell me about any of it. She'd begin the story with, 'What's the worst thing you've ever done?'

'Chantale?'

'Can I open my eyes now?'

He was unscathed. He was massively tall. She had never been so happy to see him.

Tanice whispered, 'Dad?'

BRIAR MINTON – 5 DAYS AFTER

If this had all happened in the Before Times, you might have heard of them. If you had a strong stomach or a morbid disposition, you might have sought out some of the final photographs of them in Midacre. You might have seen Beth and Laurie, Freya, Martha and me with our hair shaved off. Freya's blood-spattered nightdress. The pink Dr. Martens that Axel stole from me.

I can imagine what pop psychologists might have written, the think pieces and essays. Every now and then, some true crime podcaster or cult-obsessed documentary filmmaker might DM me and ask to talk about that summer.

I try to. Even now. I have so many questions about what happened and what their final hours might have looked like. If what they did was inevitable.

When people ask why I stayed so long, I never tell them that I was happy. It's hard to explain that, even now, there are things I still miss about that place. Midacre was a beautiful crumbling mansion that belonged to Beth and Laurie's uncle, an eccentric Buddhist earl who had given away all of his money and then mysteriously disappeared.

When I'd asked who the house actually belonged to, Beth had mumbled something about probate and 'the Trust'. But it was clear that the Group had taken it over. The only member of staff on the once active estate seemed to be the elderly former house manager with a stutter, who lived in one of the staff cottages at the end of the drive and mostly kept himself to himself. He didn't even seem to notice that the world had ended.

Is it crazy that I miss it sometimes? That if I could go back to one week of my life, it would be that one?

The Group believed that the Tau were coming to usher in the new utopian age any minute and, until then, all we had to do was wait in happy anticipation. I felt as rich as an empress that summer, only with time. The days seemed interminable, the way they had felt early in my childhood or during that unseasonably hot spring of the first lockdown, when school was cancelled and all obligations went up in smoke.

I kind of liked that I was never alone. I'd wake up in the library with other girls dozing on blankets and then head out into the orangery, where the Group would be peeling fruit or chopping vegetables and singing. People were always singing.

Axel and I managed to gather a passionate troop for re-hearsals of *Into the Woods*. He'd made good on his promise to appoint me musical director. Laurie helped Amy wheel the old grand piano onto the porch, I brought out my sax and we spent many happy hours rehearsing.

I taught Isaac how to swim in the lake. I became friends with Soo-Jin when we stayed up late stargazing; she had an almost encyclopaedic knowledge of all the planets and galaxies and the distances between them. I enjoyed picnics with Beth and Laurie, drinking Pimm's and indulging in languorous conversations about the nature of the Tau. I taught Martha everything I'd learned foraging with my father. She was thrilled to discover how many things in the forest were edible. One afternoon, she shouted in delight at the sight of berries, but I warned her against eating them. 'Belladonna,' I said, scooping up her handful of dark berries. 'Deadly nightshade. These can kill in hours.' She gasped and looked down at her Tupperware box, where they were piled like marbles.

'And I almost baked them into a pie.'

In the evenings, we gathered by the campfire for dinner, listening to Cato reciting the 'Tracts'. These were teachings from the Tau, communicated through our dreams and near-death experiences, that he felt compelled to record and share. I never stopped being wary of Cato after he tried to drown me. But it was he who sought to distil our beliefs into a religion. Into divine tenets and a creed. And to give us a name: the Order of the Tau. Or Tauans, as some also said.

Every night that we gathered, Hero waxed in the sky. By the middle of the week, it was twice the size of the moon and as bright as the pendulum of a grandfather clock. The Group began to divide in their opinion of it. Half of them believed that Hero was a messenger, sent to make the world take notice before the Tau arrived. And when They did, They would restore all that we had lost, revive our dead, rebuild our bridges, raise a dazzling new city from the ruins. A minority began to wonder if Hero was a judgement. Were the Tau intentionally biding Their time, waiting for the strongest human survivors to emerge before anointing them as kings?

I desperately wanted to believe that the Tau were coming

to save us, but with every passing day, my newly discovered faith wavered.

By Wednesday, members of the Group were clamouring for a sign. Why had the Tau fallen silent? Why weren't They revealing when They were coming?

Some people had tattooed the symbol of the Tau on their arms with stick and poke kits they'd brought from home, while others carved it into trees. Members began experimenting with different cleansing rituals. We were encouraged to fast for two days, and on the second evening, we feasted on bushmeat that Cato, Isaac and a couple of others had slaughtered for us. We ate it raw.

Most of us shaved off our hair – we were told it would improve the 'fidelity' of Their transmissions. Beth did mine. When I woke up the next morning and ran my hands over the patchy stubble on my scalp, I burst into tears. 'It's okay,' Martha said as she climbed under the covers to comfort me. 'This suffering will be over soon.'

That was the first morning I began to miss home. Although Digit's company was a consolation, I kept worrying about my sisters and wondering what my parents would say when they saw me with a shaved head.

When people ask why I stayed so long, I tell them about Ruby. I tell them that I was committed to uncovering the truth about what had happened to her. On my second day in Midacre, I discovered an empty prescription box for Omeprazole in her name, Ruby Barker, in the guest bathroom trash. The sight of it made my stomach roil. It confirmed to me that she'd visited Midacre before.

I searched the house surreptitiously for more signs of her. But the only other clue I was able to uncover was something the stuttery former house manager said about 'trespassers' on the property. Two men he'd told to leave, one around Ruby's age. *Nico Costa?* I wondered. Apparently, he had been camping the weekend she'd disappeared, and isn't it always the ex-boyfriend?

That night, Laurie tapped my shoulder and asked, 'What's this?' By bonfire light, I saw that he was holding Ruby's prescription box. I reached reflexively into my pocket, where I'd been storing it, and found nothing. It must have fallen out, I supposed.

'I found it in the guest bathroom,' I said, feeling a little embarrassed.

'And you thought you'd hang on to it?' Laurie looked more serious than I'd seen him before.

'I, uh . . .' I cursed myself for not thinking of an excuse.

'Did you even *know* Ruby?'

I felt a little cornered by that question.

'A-a little,' I stammered. We'd actually only spoken once.

'Because I did,' Laurie said, his voice cracking a little. 'I *loved* her.' He squeezed the pill packet in his gloved fist until it started to crumple.

'Did you see . . . ?' I asked carefully. 'What happened to her?'

Laurie recovered himself, letting his gaze dart quickly away to the fire. 'Course,' he said.

'And it's true? She—'

'Disappeared,' he confirmed. 'Transcended.' He took a deep breath. 'The Tau chose her.'

'Why, though?' I pressed.

'How do I know?!' Laurie snapped. 'All I know is that she's the luckiest of us.'

I kept flitting between doubt and belief. You must remember what the atmosphere was like just after the Event. Like

we'd peeled a layer of skin off anything we thought we believed in. Like the world was stranger and more dangerous
than we ever knew.

'Hey, Briar?' Axel, Martha and Soo-Jin were singing near
the fire, and they turned from its light to beckon me, with
hoots of laughter, to join in. I could feel Laurie watching me
walk away. Martha threw an arm around my shoulders and
started up on the chorus of 'America' from *West Side Story*.

I feel ashamed to admit it now, but that's one of the reasons I stayed. How could I doubt everything they believed
after I'd seen cars fly into the air and the Tau had spoken
to me in the river?

In the Group, it had been exhilarating to meet people
who really believed in something. And like my father's, it
seemed that their belief had been vindicated.

For me, it was thrilling; it was what I hadn't realized I'd
been hoping for. The world was magic, and in the vastness
of the universe I was regarded and cared for. And not just
by the Tau – for the first time in my life, I thought that I had
real friends. That I belonged.

I woke bleeding, with a lightning bolt blistering my spine.
When I rolled over, I saw that my bedsheets were sticky. I
cursed under my breath, got quickly to my feet to assess the
damage. My period didn't normally catch me by surprise,
but, post-collapse, it had been difficult to tell the days apart.

That morning, the sun was just rising behind the mul-
lioned window of the library and, in the bay below it,
Martha was sleeping like a cat. Amy was next to her, in a
night dress patterned with Black and White Santas. Digit
lifted her head lazily.

I took off my stained nightdress and peeled off my pants,

then bundled them up with the paisley throw and thin duvet I'd been lying on. I changed quickly into new clothes, lime-green dungarees and a black vest. There was no washing machine, I remembered with despair. I would have to figure out how everyone was washing their clothes.

I couldn't find my shoes, so I headed out barefoot, quietly promising Digit I would be back soon.

The library was in the annex of the house. Heading into the main building, the halls were quiet and the light slanted in. Midacre was a strange mix of beauty and dereliction. I took a left, which lead me through a Rococo ballroom. Gold leaf flaking everywhere. Glass mirror oxidized black, ferns pushing through the floorboards. Axel had told me that lots of houses in the area were abandoned like this. Once grand mansions, dissolving like Cleopatra's pearl in a glass of vinegar.

In other rooms, people were sleeping: on mattresses laid out in the middle of floors, on blankets and cushions piled in the claw-footed bathtubs. Signs of habitation were everywhere; polka dot underwear hung from a makeshift washing line, a half-finished canvas portrait was propped up in the hall next to a guitar.

I didn't want to wake anyone, so I moved carefully, searching for an empty bathtub I might be able to soak my sheets in.

In the massive entryway, I was startled by a whoosh of flapping. A shower of dust. Pigeons in the domed ceiling, batting like moths against it. The air smelled of rot, and there were black poppies of mildew everywhere. Half-decayed skeletons of mice were littered under a footman's chair.

Footsteps creaked on the floorboards behind me, and I turned with a noise of surprise to see Edith, one of the older group members, in a faded velvet dressing gown.

'Looking for something?' she asked. Edith claimed that Freya had healed her chronic pain.

'Is there ... a bathtub anywhere I can ...' I glanced at the bundle of laundry I was carrying.

'We're washing our clothes in the river,' Edith said. Then, 'I think there's a tub upstairs.'

Like everything else in the house, the stairs were falling apart. I took them carefully, dodging the rotting boards, and reached the second floor, where the roof looked as if it was one gust of wind away from collapse. Water streamed from a crack in the ceiling and, at the end of the corridor, an empty oak cabinet made a moist bed for mushrooms. Ivy had broken through a window and spidered along the carpet. It was as if nature was digesting the house.

Edith was right, though, there was a bathroom along the hall, with shattered tiles and someone's makeup strewn along the windowsill.

I bundled my laundry into the tub and resolved to get some water from the river and bring it back to wash my clothes here in privacy.

As I turned to leave, the door on the other side of the bathroom opened.

'Hello?'

It was Beth, wearing a camisole and lace-trimmed pants. She had the thighs of a Barbie doll.

'Briar, what are ... ?'

I looked in alarm at the bloodied sheets I'd left in the bathtub. 'Sorry, I ... I didn't realize anyone would be here.'

Beth took in the entire scene calmly. She pointed to the sheets.

'Don't worry about it. Do you need some tampons?'

'Please.'

Beth indicated for me to follow her into the adjoining room. It was a nursery. Or once had been, with a moulting rocking horse and a music box. A dust-caked mobile of hanging doves caught the light. There were two junior beds in the middle of the room, pink and blue.

'It used to be ours, when we came to visit,' Beth explained.

'How long ago was that?' I asked.

Beth shrugged. 'I'm not sure, I was really young. I don't have a lot of memories of it. Little things. Grandad's eightieth and a thousand balloons in garlands on the lawn. Uncle Igg at the piano . . . The last time we were here, though, was the first time I saw Them.'

Beth told me the story. The family had gathered on Boxing Day for a lunch: roast chicken with pine nut stuffing. She'd suffered an almost fatal allergic reaction and had stopped breathing at the dinner table. She'd been saved, apparently, by their uncle, who had plunged his old EpiPen into her thigh at the critical moment.

'Laurie can hardly talk about it without crying,' Beth confided. 'He says that I was blue.' She shuddered. 'All I remember, though, was that They were calling my name.'

'Bethany?' I asked.

'No, my true name. When you know the name of something, you can change its nature. You can turn water into ash. Oxygen into ice. You can turn a coward into a hero.'

'How old were you?'

I hadn't noticed Soo-Jin, who had been dozing under a pile of clothes. She roused and stretched her back like a cat.

'Six,' Beth said. 'It only happened to me once.' She sounded a little mournful then. 'I don't even dream of Them. I always said that once was enough, but . . .'

Suddenly, her behaviour made sense. Beth was one of

the most obsessive of the Group: the first to shave her hair, the person who fasted for the longest. I had even watched her ingest small quantities of psychedelics. Clearly, she was longing to contact Them again.

I glanced around the room; on the dresser, it looked as if Beth had set up an altar. She'd drawn the symbol of the Tau in lipstick on the mirror. Strewn across the table in front of it were crystals and feathers, stones and candles, a wishbone and a silver bowl of salt.

'What are you doing?' I asked Soo-Jin, who had got up and moved to her telescope, mounted near the open window. She was surrounded by sketches and books on astronomy.

'She's trying to plot the movement of Hero,' Beth said, as if it was a fool's errand.

'Just trying to figure out where it came from,' said Soo-Jin.

Beth fumbled through her dressing table then and offered me a paper box.

'Thanks,' I said.

'You can take them all,' Beth shrugged. 'I hardly get my period these days.' I did and retreated to the bathroom.

Sitting on the edge of the bathtub, I noticed a dark crack through the mirror. It looked as if someone had tossed something heavy against it. I hated the sight of my reflection. My pock-marked skin and pink eyebrows. With no hair, I hadn't achieved the androgynous, edgy cool of some members of the Group. I looked like a cancer patient.

When I was finished, my eyes alighted on a number of Polaroid pictures scattered on the windowsill. Cato was in one of them, a red moon above his head. The lunar eclipse. He wore a laurel crown and was smiling. Other pictures showed a statue of a god with a cracked skull, people from the Group lounging around it. In one, Martha was emerging from the river. In another, Ruby.

I gasped when I saw her. She looked the same as she had when she appeared to me in the woods, in that green hoodie. It was slightly rumpled, so the only word I could read was 'PANIC'. I examined her expression. Her mouth was set in a hard line, and her brows were raised, as if she was frightened of the person behind the camera.

'You okay in there?' Beth's voice.

'Yes,' I said, almost too quickly. 'I don't normally use ... I forgot to pack my Mooncup.'

Beth pushed open the door and eyed me for a moment. Her eyes fell to the windowsill, the pictures. She took the one I was holding and examined it, too, as if for the first time.

'When were these taken?' I asked. My voice faltered a little. Beth's placid smile never left her face.

'I can barely remember,' she said dreamily. 'I must have left them here to develop ...' I didn't answer. My heart was pounding. I knew the answer. Knew that they had clearly been taken the night of the lunar eclipse, which was the same weekend that Ruby had disappeared. Had she spent her final hours at Midacre?

'You know,' Beth said, her thumb rolling across the bottom of the image, 'she wasn't a well girl.' I could see Soo-Jin listening from the nursery.

'Oh yeah?' I wondered if it was true. I had to remind myself that I really hadn't known Ruby at all.

'Yes. A laundry list of medications and diagnoses. Antipsychotics.' Beth sighed. 'It's a shame, really. I know Freya tried to ...' She trailed off.

Her eyes bored into me, waiting for a response.

'But now she's with Them,' I whispered, as I had heard others in the Group say about the dead. Beth nodded approvingly.

'I hope we'll all be so lucky.'

Outside, someone started playing the drums, the sign to gather for breakfast. Soo-Jin offered to fetch water with me from the river.

We circled around the estate to a bend in the river where a little stone temple was carved into the rock. It was impossible to reach from where we were, but at certain times of day, the sun illuminated a bronze figure on the other side of the water. A deity with a crown of five skulls and a garland of severed heads.

'I always wonder why he chose that one,' Soo-Jin said, following my gaze. 'Beth and Laurie's uncle.'

'Who is it?' I asked.

'In some traditions, he's a protector of the Dharma; in others, he and his wife have the power to dissolve time and space into themselves and exist as the void at the dissolution of the universe.'

We had a good view of the estate behind us. The early risers, the meditators and yoga practitioners, emerged from the orangery to greet those who had been awoken by the drums.

The water was loud here, and Soo-Jin gave me a look, before leaning towards me. 'Do you believe that people can just *disappear*?'

I was caught off guard by the question. My immediate impulse was to ask, 'Do you?'

'I didn't ...' she admitted.

'But how can we question anything anymore?' I said.

'Didn't you see cars fly? Aren't we living outside of any of our old beliefs? Isn't this the season of the impossible? Do you believe in alien satellites sending us dreams?' I trailed off as I realized I sounded like Beth.

Soo-Jin reached into the pocket of her trousers and pulled out a brass pendant with the phases of the moon on it. The one Ruby had been wearing in that final Instagram picture where she'd said, 'Are you ready?'

'This is hers,' she said, handing it to me.

'Ruby's?' I held the chunky necklace in my hand.

'I gave it to her for her birthday last year.' Soo-Jin sounded like she might start crying. I looked at it, the little crumbs of dirt buried at the moon's raised crescent.

'I found it in the woods down there,' she continued, pointing. 'Yesterday. Half-stamped in the mud.'

'So ... ?' I felt stupid for asking.

'So I think she disappeared *here*, on the night of the eclipse last year. And—' Her fingers flitted to her pocket, a phantom gesture I was used to. She was looking for her phone but then remembered everything again. 'The Group keeps saying that she transcended – that they *saw* her, but ...' Her breath hitched.

'Where were you?'

'I had mock exams. My parents wouldn't let me come.' She shook her head, heavy with regret. 'I think something happened to her here.'

I believed that, too, but I tried to play devil's advocate. 'Or the clasp came undone, and her necklace just fell off ... It must happen all the time.'

Soo-Jin shook her head. She said that when the Group returned from Midacre in December, they'd seemed differ-ent somehow. Axel had started losing weight again. Beth and Laurie had shaved off their hair. Cato had a scratch on his face that he'd said was from a cat. Ruby didn't answer her phone. Soo-Jin had thought that she'd been angry with her at first, that she'd felt let down because she hadn't come. When Ruby's disappearance became public, Soo-Jin had asked the Group what had happened, but everyone had the same story: that on the night of the eclipse, they had watched Ruby disappear.

Although the police had questioned a few of the members, they'd stuck to their story. The officer had decided to release them with 'no further action'. Presumably because, implausible as their tale was, there was no evidence of wrongdoing.

Soo-Jin finally revealed to me that she'd decided to stay in the Group to try to uncover what had happened to her friend.

A cloud passed over the sun then, and the woods were temporarily darkened. Soo-Jin looked around carefully.

'I think someone in the Group did something to her.'

'But why?'

'She was writing about them for my zine. Said she'd found some evidence about Freya.'

'What?'

'Some evidence about the years she disappeared.'

Soo-Jin took a deep breath. Speaking to her made me feel dizzy. I didn't want to believe that my new friends were lying to me, but all the signs made me doubt them even more. The reasons I had joined in the first place were becoming murkier the longer I spent with them.

She sighed, a pillar of her own belief crumbling. 'I thought you knew something.'

'Why?'

'I thought . . . I thought that was why you were here. Why you'd joined us all of a sudden. I thought you had a lead.'

We were allies, I realized, and she did, too.

'We're looking for the same thing.'

'Well, we need to find the truth soon,' Soo-Jin reminded me. We watched as the Group started dispersing after breakfast. 'Because if someone killed Ruby, they're living with us now.'

AALIYAH MINTON – 5 DAYS AFTER

It was only when Aaliyah looked back that she noticed the signs. How tired was a woman supposed to be a couple of days after childbirth?

She made tabs in all the baby books we owned. She wrote down anything that could turn out to be helpful and clung to the words as if they were doctrine: *'Sleep when the baby sleeps.' 'Wake, feed, play.' 'After a breech birth, your baby may rest with its legs in a "frog-like" position for a few days.'*

When Kim discovered that I'd run away, she slipped into an almost catatonic despair for a couple of days – rising late, crying often, leaving Aaliyah and Carmen to look after Hero alone.

Aaliyah felt like a guileless serf under a capricious new lord. At any time, she could be wrenched from sleep by a sound like a siren. Urgent, desperate bawling. The baby in a box by her vanity table, the baby in weeping Carmen's arms. The hours meant nothing. The night was a river to ford, and in the middle of it Aaliyah would feel the most helpless. She'd flip through the notebook so she wouldn't forget: *2 a.m., breastfed, right breast – 2.30 a.m., BF, L breast – 3–5 a.m., colic? – Still no milk?*

By dawn, the sleep deprivation would wipe all things clean from her head.

It took three days for Carmen's milk to come in, which Kim promised was normal. Though it didn't feel that way. Three days during which the baby did nothing but howl. Aaliyah would gaze into Hero's scrunched face, at her puce maw, and curse the sequence of events that had brought this child that she hadn't asked for into her life.

Aaliyah had always wanted everything that Carmen had. By the time they'd first met, Carmen had already been making a name for herself on the junior tennis circuit. She was a polished, disciplined and strategic player. Her game was textbook-perfect, honed through years of professional coaching. In contrast, Aaliyah had been described by scouts as scrappy, unpredictable and highly instinctive.

The first match they'd competed in together, Carmen had beaten her easily. It had been one of the first that Aaliyah had played after winning a scholarship to Montclair Tennis Academy, and the humiliating loss had only intensified her crippling imposter syndrome.

Carmen found her, an hour after the game, crying in a bathroom stall. She must have identified her shoes, Aaliyah guessed, because she said, 'You'll have to grow a thicker skin than that.' Aaliyah hadn't said anything, just stared up at the pattern on the ceiling tiles, waiting for Carmen to leave. She didn't. 'Your serve is weak. You made more unforced errors than me, and your risky shot choices didn't always pay off – obviously.'

Aaliyah opened the stall door to find Carmen staring

at the mirror. She was small and had a face that was more striking than beautiful. They would often be compared to each other, likely because they were two of the only mixed-race girls in their year group.

Aaliyah washed her hands, taking care not to look at Carmen. Then splashed water on her face and headed out.

'Wait!' Carmen bounded towards her, moving so quickly that Aaliyah flinched. Carmen grabbed her skirt and tugged it. It was only as the stretchy material shifted that Aaliyah realized it had been stuck in her knickers. She'd almost left the room with half of her bottom showing.

'Thanks,' she said, and Carmen smiled.

They became friends after that, but it was a fraught relationship. Although they roomed together for a year, they might have been closer if they weren't always competing with each other, both on and off the court. For Carmen's fifteenth birthday party, her father had flown her and some friends to one of his properties in the south of France. Looking around Carmen's palatial home, Aaliyah had resolved never to invite the girl to hers.

In the weeks leading up to the Junior Orange Bowl when she was sixteen, Aaliyah watched Carmen carefully in training. She began to notice that her rival wasn't invincible. Her brilliance lay in her precision, but she wasn't adaptable at all. If a player threw something unpredictable at her, Carmen floundered.

By the time the finals arrived, Aaliyah was ready. Carmen opened strong, but Aaliyah refused to engage in endless rallies; she shortened points, rushing the net and hitting sharp angles that forced Carmen to sprint. Carmen, clearly frustrated, started making mistakes. Aaliyah's adaptability kept her one step ahead.

In the final set, as the crowd held its breath, Aaliyah held her nerve, closing out the match with a perfectly placed drop shot. The applause was deafening, but it was the shock on Carmen's face that had been delicious to see.

Later, in the locker room, Aaliyah had still been thrilled by the victory when Paris, the twenty-one-year-old assistant coach, had entered. Paris always had an easy smile and a sharp eye for talent. Aaliyah had guessed that Carmen had a crush on him, because he'd offered her a sandwich when she'd complained of dizziness after a match and she'd kept it for two months, letting it fur over with mould on her bedside table.

Now he said, 'That was gutsy,' and before Aaliyah could respond, he'd leaned in and kissed her. It sent a thrill through her. When he pulled back, he said, 'You've got something special. Maybe I can help you take it further?' He'd offered to be her coach. And Aaliyah had nodded, barely able to breathe. For the first time, she felt she had something Carmen didn't.

That December, when our father came to pick Aaliyah up for the Christmas holidays, Carmen was still in the dormitory. She had looked small and lost, sitting next to Aaliyah's stripped bed.

'What are your plans for Christmas, Carmen?' Marcus had asked casually.

Carmen had just shrugged.

'Where are your parents?' he'd asked.

Carmen looked away then and mumbled something about a conference, the LA house. 'I'll be fine here.' She gestured around the half-empty room.

'Oh no, you can't stay here alone!' Marcus had said. 'Come with us!' Carmen had lit up at the offer. Aaliyah froze, mortified. Carmen's eyes darted to her, as if waiting

for permission. Our father had turned to Aaliyah with a
smile, oblivious to the tension in the room. 'The more, the
merrier, right?' My sister could only muster a tight smile.

Her adolescent shame at Carmen recognizing the relative
squalor in which our family lived struck Aaliyah as ironic
now that Carmen was living with them indefinitely.

By day three, Carmen seemed to have a fever, and
Aaliyah announced that she was going to the store to buy
some formula. 'It's too dangerous,' Kim said firmly, her
eyes darting to my parents' bed, where Carmen had drifted
into a fitful sleep. Hero had been up all night bawling, and
Aaliyah's nerves were frayed.

'She needs milk,' she told our mother.

'She's getting a little from Carmen. Babies often lose
some weight in the first few days.'

Kim had said this before, but Aaliyah wondered if a
full belly would help the baby to sleep. Along with the rest
of them.

Aaliyah took some of the cash from the safe in the
bunker.

'I'll go,' Kim offered, catching Aaliyah by the arm as she
reached for the door.

'You'll be more helpful to Carmen here,' Aaliyah said.
But Kim's lip quivered.

'What if you don't come back?' she whispered. 'It's dangerous out there. I can't lose all of my daughters.'

Her words made Aaliyah's heart sink as well. She'd been
sure that one of us would have returned home by then.
Every time she heard a noise near the door, her spirits would
soar, but then disappointment and worry would wash over
her once more. With every day that passed, she felt worse.

'We can't do anything to bring them back safely,' Aaliyah said, grabbing her mother's arm as more tears spilled down her cheeks. 'But we – *I* – can help Hero and Carmen *right now.*' Kim nodded, wiping her eyes.

'Be careful!' she shouted as Aaliyah left. Then, more quietly, 'I couldn't bear it otherwise.'

Aaliyah walked there quickly through Clapham's side streets, keeping her head down. The windows of shops were smashed in and graffiti scrawled angry messages on brick walls. At a distance, she thought she heard gunshots.

Aaliyah had heard from a neighbour that a local gang had taken over the Asda supermarket and were willing to trade with people. Her nerves prickled at the thought of confronting them as she approached the entrance. But the baby needed formula.

Before the crisis, supermarkets had always soothed her. They were floodlit reminders of how far humanity had come from hunting and gathering. Her favourite thing had been to browse the shelves of organic food stores, marvelling at the glistening cornucopia of fruits and veg. Now, the place was closer to a war zone than a supermarket, patrolled by armed thugs.

Outside, broken trolleys and torn posters littered the forecourt. Standing in front of the entrance was Andrew Griggs – a boy Aaliyah recognized distantly. Our father had invited him home for dinner after the Scouts a handful of times. She'd always found him a little off-putting and socially awkward, but never outright menacing. Now, though, he wore a makeshift armband and carried a butcher's cleaver. His greasy ginger mullet was plastered to his neck.

When she asked him for baby formula, a cruel glint sparkled in his eyes. 'Well, looky here, famous little Lia Minton!'

She wasn't sure where that moniker came from, considering she was almost his height and at least two years older.

'How much?' she asked, keeping her focus on her objective.

'A hundred,' he said.

'Pounds?' she scoffed, incredulous. She'd only brought fifty.

'No, *pesos*. Of course fucking pounds.'

'That's crazy,' Aaliyah said, though she had no idea how much formula had cost in the Before Times.

'Call it post-collapse inflation,' he chuckled.

'I don't have that much,' Aaliyah said.

Andrew eyed her speculatively. 'What do you have?'

'Fifty.' Then she cursed herself for telling the truth.

He held out his hand, and she pressed the plastic banknotes into his palm. He turned to a companion near the door – a tattooed blonde boy, who asked, 'What does she want?'

'Baby formula,' Andrew said. Aaliyah watched as he pocketed the fifty. 'What else do you have?' he asked, and his eyes went to the three-carat diamond on her finger. Aaliyah clenched her fist and angled her hand away. 'How about a kiss?'

Aaliyah's stomach twisted. 'What?' When she looked up again, his blonde friend had vanished.

'I said a kiss,' Andrew repeated, leaning in, his breath foul. Rage set fire to her belly, but she swallowed it down and reminded herself: *Formula for Hero. Sleep for us all. Just get this over with.* She moved in and pressed her lips briefly against his, fighting the surge of disgust.

Andrew forced her mouth open and thrust his grey tongue into her throat. He gripped her waist and fumbled for her bra. Something inside her snapped. Aaliyah bit down until she tasted iron. Andrew howled and wrenched away, clutching his mouth.

'Bitch!' he spat, blood trickling down his chin.

At his shout, the blonde boy emerged running. 'Hey!' He dropped the tub of formula and rushed to his friend's aid. 'What happened?' he asked.

Aaliyah watched the tub roll across the ground.

'She did it!' Andrew came at her with his knife, spitting blood, his eyes blazing. But Aaliyah was quick, diving for the formula, scraping her knees in the attempt. The blade of Andrew's cleaver sliced the air near her cheek, but she scrambled out of his way, leapt over the low wall and dashed across the parking lot.

Andrew's curses echoed behind her as she ran between smashed cars and piles of debris. Only when she'd put several streets between them did she stop to catch her breath, tears burning at the corners of her eyes, the taste of his blood in her mouth.

Clutching the formula to her chest, Aaliyah returned home a victor. Kim retreated to the rocket stove and carefully prepared Hero's bottle using boiled water. Then Lia crept back into the lamplit bedroom, testing the temperature on the back of her wrist. Carmen was writhing in pain as she held her child, and Hero's tiny face was pinched with hunger. Aaliyah took the baby into her arms, and within minutes, Hero was feeding. She was moved by the unblinking way the baby stared into her eyes as she fed.

'She looks like an old soul,' Aaliyah teased. 'Like she's been here before.'

Carmen tried to smile.

*

Carmen had been a favourite to win the Junior Wimbledon title. By sixteen, she was the top player in their year and was on track to be the next great star. Aaliyah envied the ease with which success seemed to follow her.

They were set to face each other in the semi-finals when the rumours started. Whispers in the locker room turned into headlines – accusations that Carmen had been using performance-enhancing drugs. It reached the media attending the tournament and created a real scandal. The stress of the ordeal was too much for Carmen. Before she was proven innocent, she'd dropped out and returned home, disappearing from Aaliyah's life as suddenly as she'd dominated it.

Aaliyah won the semi-final by default and then fought her way to victory in the next round, finishing that year in the top ten of the International Tennis Federation's junior rankings. The triumph marked a turning point. Aaliyah was glory-bound, set to make history; on the court, she was ecstatic, but then she'd return to sterile hotel rooms and cry because she was so lonely.

At twenty, Aaliyah reached the third round of Wimbledon, causing a stir by defeating a top twenty seed. The tennis world took notice, but her personal life was a mess. She'd switched coaches by then, but her on-again, off-again relationship with Paris was taking its toll. He'd shower her with affection, then vanish without warning, leaving her reeling and heartbroken each time.

The year before the Event, Aaliyah reached the fourth round of the Australian Open and the semi-finals of the French Open. She had been set to sign lucrative endorsement deals with major sports brands when, in December, Paris gusted back into her life. He invited her on a romantic skiing holiday in the Italian Dolomites, telling her that she needed to relax before the intense demands of the season. Against her better judgement, Aaliyah agreed.

It had been on that trip that she had shattered her wrist. She'd come round from surgery calling his name, her head still cloudy with opiates, but Paris was nowhere to be found.

In January, Carmen had reached out – for the first time in six years – to invite Aaliyah to her engagement party. Aaliyah had gone with her arm still in a cast, excited at the chance to make up with her old friend.

The party had been every bit as grand as Aaliyah had expected, at an exclusive Georgian townhouse in Mayfair that gleamed with understated elegance. Aaliyah was nervous, scanning the crowd for anyone she knew. It was a relief to spot Paris at the bar, looking elegant in a green velvet smoking jacket.

'You're here,' he said. Her stomach tightened. She'd imagined this moment many times – what she'd say to him after he'd left her in Bolzano hospital, alone and confused.

'Yeah,' she replied, 'Carmen invited me.'

He hesitated, guilt flickering across his face. 'How's the ...?' He pointed to her sling.

'Lia!' A shout of delight from across the room. Carmen was radiant, gliding towards them in an empire-line dress, flushed with a healthy glow. Her pixie-like face had lost some of its buccal fat, making her look elegant and demure.

'Aaliyah!' Carmen reached out and clasped her free hand. 'It's so good to see you.' For a moment, Aaliyah forgot her tension. She felt a rush of relief at seeing Carmen so well, so happy.

'You, too,' she said, and she meant it. 'I've been following your work at the foundation. You're doing incredible things.'

Carmen's face lit up. 'Thank you. It's been a whirlwind, but I'm loving it.'

Aaliyah opened her mouth to say more when Carmen slipped her hand into Paris's arm, and her onyx engagement ring sparkled in the chandelier light.

Aaliyah's words caught in her throat. Her mind spun, struggling to piece together what was happening.

'You're—' she stammered, her voice cracking. 'You two?'

Carmen beamed, squeezing Paris's arm. 'Yes,' she said. 'It's still so new, but we're so happy.'

Aaliyah forced a brittle smile. 'Congratulations,' she said, though her voice barely sounded like her own. 'When's the big day?'

When Carmen said the date, Aaliyah did the quick maths; it was less than twelve weeks away. 'Why so soon?' she asked. Carmen blushed and placed a hand on her belly.

Aaliyah had felt the world tilt then. A boiling lava of fury rushed through her veins. Carmen had not invited her to this party to reconcile. She had invited her here to gloat. It wasn't tennis anymore, but Aaliyah felt sure that, to Carmen, their lives were still just a game. And once again, she'd won.

Aaliyah's initial hopefulness that her family would soon be reunited, that she would see Hugo again, seemed laughably naïve by day four. What if something really bad had happened? She thought of her sisters, her father and grandfather, her fiancé. Recalled the bodies she'd seen people burning out in the streets. Anything could have happened to them – it was harder and harder not to consider – any awful thing.

And something terrible was happening to Carmen,

Aaliyah finally realized. By Wednesday, her fever was so high that she woke delirious, shivering and clutching her abdomen, trying to breathe through the fierce pain.

Gabriel, who had come over to check on them, took one look at Carmen's greyish pallor and told Aaliyah that they needed to go to the hospital. Now.

It took them nearly an hour to walk there. Kim helped Aaliyah load Carmen into the battered shopping trolley they'd kept in the driveway, and together they pushed her to St George's Hospital. The journey was harrowing; the road was littered with rubbish, and every bump or jolt elicited a moan from Carmen. As they went, Aaliyah cursed herself for waiting so long to get help.

Kim walked ahead, trying to clear a path for them as best she could. 'Just hold on,' she kept whispering. 'We're almost there.'

On the way, Carmen said to Aaliyah, 'Do you remember ... that Christmas I stayed at yours?' Of course, Aaliyah had never forgotten how polite Carmen had been – about their house, about having to spend a week on a blow-up mattress on the grimy floor of Aaliyah's room. About the interminable Night Watch service at Providence House.

She'd been like a princess visiting a foreign country, diplomatically sampling all the local dishes. She'd sung along to the carols and complimented Kim's mulled wine and Marcus's Christmas feast. She'd won the game of charades, obviously. She'd been so touched to receive presents – an unwanted dress-up doll kit from Tanice and Chanel nail varnish from Mum – that she'd burst into surprised tears.

'I always felt so jealous of you ...' She paused, fighting for breath. 'Of your family.'

'Really?' This was news to Aaliyah, who had been angry with our father for weeks after for his impromptu invite.

Carmen winced as they rolled over another bump. 'If I don't make it—'

'Don't say that!' Until that moment, the possibility hadn't quite occurred to Aaliyah.

Carmen's eyelids fluttered, and for a moment, it seemed as if she might slip away then and there. But she forced her gaze back to Aaliyah, desperation lighting her feverish eyes. 'If anything happens to me, promise me you'll raise Hero.'

A cold knot of dread hardened in Aaliyah's stomach. She had never wanted a child. She'd had nightmares where she woke up pregnant. In those dreams, her body was a cage. Kim had told us that she had burned everything she loved on the pyre of motherhood: hair, sleep, skin, teeth, money. Aaliyah had spied that jagged keloid C-section scar, the tiger-stripe stretch marks. Kim's hair had fallen out in great fistfuls after Chantale was born and never properly grew back. 'Have a child, lose a tooth,' she'd warned us all darkly. She'd lost four.

'Carmen, no.'

'Please!' Carmen pleaded. 'You can show her what a ... real family is like.'

Aaliyah's vision blurred with tears. Her throat felt tight, and the words stuck. How could she say no to that? She took a shaky breath and replied, 'Okay, but ... you'll just have to never die, then.' Carmen's breathing hitched, but there was relief in her eyes.

When they finally reached the hospital, they discovered it a shell of what it had been. Most of the windows were boarded up, and people in ragged clothes milled around the entrance, begging for medication or news. Inside, the corridors were dimly lit by a flickering back-up generator that sputtered on and off without warning.

Beds and stretchers lined the halls, patients packed in so tightly that staff had to thread their way through the crowd. A nurse in a stained uniform guided them to a corner of what had once been the triage area. The walls were scorched from an electrical fire, the smell of burnt plastic still heavy in the air.

After an excruciatingly long wait for an examination, a doctor eventually told them her grim conclusion: 'Sepsis.'

'What does that mean?' Aaliyah asked, clutching a sleeping Hero to her chest.

'Likely an infection of the uterus – probably postpartum endometritis. It's overwhelming her system.'

'What can you do about it?' Aaliyah felt something icy coil in her stomach. She looked at our mum's reaction for guidance.

'They used to call it "childbed fever",' Kim said softly. Her voice trembled as she spoke. 'But that was before antibiotics.'

'We'll do what we can,' the doctor murmured. Aaliyah could hear the defeat in her words. 'We have some medication – enough for an IV drip. But without a functional intensive care unit, with no ventilators and no dialysis machines . . .' She gestured weakly around them. 'This woman needs organ support. Things we just can't provide anymore.'

Aaliyah's eyes brimmed with tears. She leaned over Carmen. Brushing her friend's damp face made her remember being fifteen and nursing her through her first hangover.

'I'm so sorry,' Aaliyah whispered, throat tight. 'We should have come sooner . . . we should have done more.'

'It's not your fault,' the doctor offered gently, but the

weight of Aaliyah's guilt was already crushing. Kim reached out and took her daughter's hand. Neither spoke.

They watched as the nurse set up the IV line for pain relief, hooking it to a stand that threatened to topple. Kim wrapped one arm around Aaliyah's shoulders. Together, they watched Carmen's chest rise and fall in diminishing increments. By midnight, she woke and asked to hold Hero. Aaliyah helped place the baby on a pillow in the crook of Carmen's arm. Carmen looked as if she was trying to memorize every detail of her daughter's face. Her lips, the perfect auricles of her ears.

Each second was a heartbreak. Aaliyah wished she could turn back time or conjure the electricity to power the life-support machines lying dormant in the next room. But all she could do was hold on to her friend's hand, hoping against hope that she would rally.

Carmen probably knew she was dying long before Aaliyah did. Aaliyah didn't believe it was happening until the moment her eyes fluttered shut. And even after that, some hopeful part of her believed that somehow medicine could still come to their aid.

Later that night, Kim would tell Aaliyah the old rhyme about childbed fever: *Well on Monday, taken ill on Tuesday, worse on Wednesday, dying on Thursday, dead on Friday, buried on Saturday.*

Aaliyah had always been somewhat indifferent to her own life. 'Not in a depressed way,' she would say, but she'd always been fine taking risks. During Marcus's drills, she'd joke that she'd be fine not making it through the end of the world because, 'I'm not sure I want to make it if there won't be any Wi-Fi.'

After Carmen died, she felt differently.

In the morning, Hero's cries woke her, and a nurse asked, 'Whose baby is that?'

Aaliyah looked down at the baby's little face and thought, with some resignation, *Oh … I have to live now.*

Of course Carmen would leave her the one thing she had never wanted.

'Excuse me, who is that baby's mother?'

Aaliyah said, 'I am.'

BRIAR MINTON – 6 DAYS AFTER

The raid was Isaac's idea. We had been running out of food for a couple of days by then – although the fasting had made it last longer. The Group had only brought about a week's worth of supplies because they'd been sure that soon the Tau would materialize.

The arrival of the Tau was the event horizon. Everyone entertained different ideas about what it would mean. Beth and Martha believed that They would begin Their benevolent reign, sharing Their resources and wisdom, ushering in a platinum age of human harmony and flourishing. Freya suggested that They would transport us to a different plane of existence where we'd dwell as immortal spirits. Cato hoped the Tau intended to judge the unworthy and to upload our minds onto new indestructible hardware that would guarantee immortality.

Whichever way, when the Tau arrived, we probably wouldn't need food. But we couldn't starve while waiting for Them. Martha and Charlie had ventured into the woods on a scavenger hunt and had returned with baskets full of berries, which we had devoured excitedly, but, of course, there weren't enough calories to sustain us even into the night. There had been some talk of hunting for animals. Cato and Laurie had led a party out, but they'd returned with only a couple of pheasants and a sickly rabbit. Some people claimed they'd spotted deer, but the hunting party hadn't been able to locate any.

Isaac suggested that we scour some of the neighbouring houses. He had a real anarchist streak. He claimed he'd seen the Tau for the first time during a drug overdose, and They told him: *History belongs to those who seize it*. He'd spent most of his childhood in care and then a lot of his adulthood on the streets, in squats or on other people's sofas. He was always commenting on the vastness of Midacre, disgusted that such a place had been allowed to fall into ruin. He liked to remind us that, pre-collapse, the richest one per cent of the world's population had owned nearly fifty per cent of global wealth. Perhaps the Event would be part of resetting the economic scales, he said. I wasn't so sure. I imagined that the billionaires of the world were, even then, watching reruns of old movies on their private islands, waiting to emerge as kings.

'You know what they say,' Isaac reminded us. 'It's easier to imagine the end of the world than the end of capitalism.'

Laurie and Beth explained that most of the surrounding houses were vacant second homes or Airbnbs. Isaac had found some maps and surveys of the local area in the library. For the mission, he selected the usual hunting party – Cato, himself, Laurie and three other boys – as well as Soo-Jin and me. I had proven myself useful when it came to foraging, and Soo-Jin was the best at reading maps.

We left before noon and headed through the estate

towards the river, leaving Digit lounging on the patio with Axel. We crossed the dilapidated bridge, though, in the daylight, it was easier to do without tripping. The region was dense with oak, beech and pine. But from certain vantage points, through the trees, we could see rolling hills with fields of crops. Soo-Jin marked them on the map to return to.

By late afternoon, we came across a golf course. We climbed over the fence and dashed across the lush grass. The first building we encountered was a caddy shack. Most of the golf equipment in it looked as if it had been destroyed, though Isaac found a couple of useful wrenches and screwdrivers. The refreshment stand had been emptied by looters, and the clubhouse, too. We spent about forty minutes scouring the place; Jacob mourned over the empty bar, the food already spoiled or stolen from the freezers. Bottled water, soft drinks and snacks, all gone.

Laurie emerged from the shop with a grin, a tartan hat placed jauntily on his head. He swung a club in a way that suggested to me that he had never played golf. 'They left the best stuff!' he said, the setting sun casting a slanting light off his broad shoulders.

'Come on,' Ishaan said. I could see her calculating how far we'd have to walk to make it home and how humiliating it would be to return empty-handed. 'It's getting late.'

Cato knocked the cap off Laurie's head.

'She's right,' he said. 'We need to keep moving.'

The sun was sinking lower, and by the time we emerged onto the road, the air was heavy and cool.

Further along the road was the local village, nothing more than a smattering of houses huddled beside the country lane. There we found a couple of shops looted and abandoned: a farm stall and a convenience store where it looked as if the owner might have put up a fight. Through the shattered window I glimpsed empty shelves, and flies buzzed around a body.

Outside, Soo-Jin broke down, collapsing on the road, real panic in her eyes. 'What are we going to do?' she asked as the gravity of our situation suddenly dawned on her.

'We'll find something,' I promised. 'At least we have water.' We had been filtering it from the river. 'And look, there's so much we haven't explored yet.' I pointed to the map, where we'd circled places of interest. 'That allotment.' It was another hour or two's walk away, but we hoped that it might have some untended vegetable patches. 'And that farm.' In the other direction. We thought that there might be some livestock, some farmers we could barter with. In the long term, I had suggested that we consider growing some of our own produce, but no one was thinking past the end of the summer at that point. They were all so convinced that the Tau were coming to take us away.

We'd begun to circle back when we came across an old hunting lodge. By then, the sun had set and the land stretched into shadow, a jumble of wild thickets where the call of an owl or the bark of foxes could be heard.

The lodge itself seemed to emerge from the mist, a small rustic building with a weathered stone facade and a chimney rising from one side.

Laurie's flashlight flickered off a leaded-glass window, and through it we spied a fireplace, hunting trophies mounted on the walls, taxidermy heads and deer antlers.

We walked all around to assess if anyone was inside. Soo-Jin even rapped noisily on the heavy oak door. There was no answer.

'A holiday home,' she guessed. Though it looked more lived-in than that.

We stepped back as Cato launched a rock at the window. The sound seemed impossibly loud in the darkness. We all flinched and looked around.

Inside, the parquet floors creaked underfoot. The main hall smelled of aged leather and woodsmoke. Laurie dived into one of the overstuffed armchairs by the fireplace and blew the dust off a Robert Harris novel he lifted off the side table. The way he moved through the world astounded me. It was as if he owned it.

'I wouldn't mind some of these books,' Soo-Jin said, examining the packed shelves.

'I couldn't eat more than one,' I teased.

We headed through a narrow doorway and into the kitchen. It had a kind of provincial charm. There was a chipped dining table surrounded by mismatched chairs, a cast-iron stove and a large cabinet displaying an assortment of tarnished silverware and collectable crockery sets commemorating a century's worth of Jubilees.

Cato let out a yelp of delight, and we all followed after him to find that he'd discovered the pantry in the back. It was a small, windowless room with floor-to-ceiling shelves that sagged under the weight of their contents. Earthenware crocks were scattered along them, filled with pickles and brined meats. The middle shelves heaved with tins of biscuits, boxes of tea and tightly packed bags of flour and sugar. A few bottles of whiskey and sherry were tucked in one corner alongside a stoneware jug of cider.

'Loganberry jam,' Laurie read, reaching for a dust-caked jar, and squinting to read its handwritten label.

'We've hit the jackpot!' Cato laughed. Soo-Jin was

trembling with delight. I breathed a sigh of relief. The well-stocked shelves reminded me of my dad's supplies back home, and for a moment I felt a twinge of guilt as I wondered if my family were okay.

'We'll take some and then bring the others back,' said Laurie. 'We'll need more of us to carry it all.'

On the lower shelves were wooden crates of potatoes and onions. Garlic bulbs tumbled from a woven basket. Dried herbs hung from the ceiling tied in bundles – rosemary, thyme and bay leaves, their pungent scents filling in the air.

Cato wasted no time, already filling his rucksack. 'First things first,' he said, examining a jar of fat.

'Does that say "rabbit"?' Soo-Jin asked, wrinkling her nose.

Jacob stuck his finger into a ceramic pot of duck confit and licked it with relish.

I couldn't help myself. I reached for a packet of Jaffa Cakes and ate one, delighting in the sensation of chocolate snapping between my teeth, soft sponge and orange-flavoured jam. The sugar, which I hadn't tasted in a couple of days, rushed to my head.

Suddenly Soo-Jin grabbed my arm.

'What's that?' she gasped.

Cato was struggling to zip up his rucksack. Isaac was stuffing venison sausages into his pockets. Tins clattered as the others cleared the shelves.

'*Shhhh!*' she hissed at them. And in the sudden silence, I heard it, too. A faint creak outside. Laurie's eyes narrowed, his flashlight beam wavering.

I felt the hairs on my arms rise. We weren't alone. Soo-Jin, Laurie and I exchanged glances. Isaac's breath was suddenly shallow. The grin wilted from Cato's lips.

A muffled thud echoed from somewhere in the house, and then the unmistakable sound of footsteps – heavy, deliberate, getting closer. Panic gripped me. We moved, slow and careful, inching away from the door. Laurie motioned for us to hide, and we scrambled, pushing ourselves up against the shelves.

The door next to me flew open, and a beam of a flashlight swept across the room. It found Isaac first – his ashen face, eyes round in terror. Then Cato, who was next to him but ready with a ceramic jar of rarebit that he tossed at the intruder's head.

A howl of pain and fury. 'Run!' Cato ordered. And we had to.

I leapt over the dining table and pushed myself towards the nearest window, my fingers scrabbling at the frame, but it wouldn't budge. I yanked harder, feeling the cold sweat on my palms. It was stuck. I reached into my pocket, my hand closing around a jar of Biscoff spread I'd grabbed, and without thinking, I smashed it against the window. The glass shattered. Sticky, sweet cookie butter splattered onto my wrist. I could hear Laurie shouting something behind me. I cleared away the jagged edges, feeling them bite into my hands, and pulled myself through.

I hit the ground running, fighting to ignore the pain. We scattered into the trees, branches slapping at our faces, the earth uneven beneath our feet. I could hear Soo-Jin behind me, her breath sharp and panicked.

The crack of the rifle was louder than I'd imagined it would be. I screamed, my heart seizing.

I pressed my back against the trunk of a tree, my breath locked in my throat, afraid that if I let it out, the hunter would find me next. I watched as the man moved through the underbrush, his silhouette hulking, fixing his gaze on the swelling darkness between the trees.

The beam of his flashlight moved closer, the light flickering off the bark inches from my face. I held my breath, every muscle in my body tensed to the point of pain. The urge to run was almost unbearable. I did what I often did when I was terrified – recited a line from *A Midsummer Night's Dream* to myself, let its familiar edges tug at my mind: *If we shadows have offended, think but this, and all is mended.* It worked at the dentist's office and at the hospital. It was something for my mind to grip on to before the anaesthetist got hold of my veins and untethered my consciousness like a balloon.

The moment passed. The man turned away, his footsteps receding. I exhaled shakily, tears stinging my eyes.

I waited for silence before I ran again. The forest seemed to come alive around me, every rustle a warning. My ankle caught on a root, and a branch cracked loudly beneath me. I stumbled, falling so hard that all the air was knocked from me. The flashlight beam swung back, catching the movement. My heart stopped, my whole body going cold.

He was running towards me then, his rifle raised. I stumbled to my feet and bolted deeper into the forest. Branches clawed at my face, thorns caught on my dungarees. I could hear him crashing after me, and the click of his rifle as he readied it.

Then I spotted a low tree branch, thick and sturdy, just above my head. Without thinking, I leapt, grabbing it with both hands, my muscles straining as I pulled myself up higher, pressing my body flat against the trunk. The beam of light swept beneath me. The man fired his gun, and I heard a scream.

He stopped. He'd heard it, too. I thought he would look up and find me, but instead his torch illuminated Soo-Jin, lying in the underbrush.

I tried to keep quiet as he pulled at her dark hair. She had tears in her eyes, reflecting Hero's ivory light. I could see a dark hole in her chest.

'Fucking kids.' He let her go and sighed heavily. Maybe disappointed that his assailants weren't fiercer.

The torch disappeared. I listened for the sound of his footsteps as they crunched away through the forest.

Through Soo-Jin's cries of pain, I could hear a whistling in her chest.

I was about to scramble down when I heard more motion in the forest. Cato. He crouched down next to her.

'Punctured lung,' he said to her after a quiet examination. 'There are bubbles in the blood.'

Soo-Jin was gasping and crying. I couldn't quite see her face from where I was hiding.

Cato asked, 'Should we do this the easy way …?'

I didn't hear anything but bit my lip, my vision blurring with tears.

'Thought so,' Cato said.

I don't know how he did it. But in a minute, there was silence.

AALIYAH MINTON – 6 DAYS AFTER

A pounding at the door jolted Aaliyah awake with a start. As far as she could tell from the depth of the darkness, it was the middle of the night. Hero stirred and started whimpering.

For a hopeful minute, Aaliyah's mind went to her sisters. She imagined me at the front door with my camping bag, home, mercifully safe. She imagined Dad and Grandad, Tanice and Chantale. Paris. Hugo, alive and well, relieved to find her. Aaliyah pulled her dressing gown tighter and ran downstairs, following the noise. Voices, shouts of men, hard pounding at the door.

'We know you're in there!' someone shouted.

'Open the fucking door before we break it down.'

They'd have to push hard, Aaliyah thought. The front door had been warped a little during the Event, and it now took a strong shove to knock it into place. Plus the padlocks Marcus had installed – Aaliyah was glad she had remembered to bolt a couple of them.

'Who is it?' she asked.

'Is Minton there? Marcus?'

If she said no, would they leave them alone? Behind her, Aaliyah heard her mother's slippers creak on the staircase. Hero was in her arms. Aaliyah put a finger to her lips and crept around to the bay window that looked out into the driveway. She tugged on the corner of the curtains.

She jumped when she saw a face staring back at her. Eye-level. A man with a black eye and blood spatters across his chin. Red hair stuck to his forehead.

'Andrew?'

Andrew Griggs pounded his fist against the window. Aaliyah could see that there were about a dozen boys by the front door. Two were holding a slumped man between them.

'Open up,' Andrew said. Aaliyah just stared. There was nothing she wanted to do less.

Andrew leaned back, nodding in silent acknowledgement. Then he lifted his arms. Aaliyah saw the cricket bat flash in the moonlight and leapt out of the way just in time. Glass exploded onto the carpet. Swampy night air rushed in. The shouts from outside grew louder, the noise merging with the mechanical howl of our father's analogue burglar alarm: a steel hammer hitting a bell over and over. The sound always gave her heart palpitations. Hero immediately started screaming.

'Over here!' Andrew shouted and then climbed inside like a black spider, his metal-capped boots grinding window glass to dust in the carpet.

They stormed in with bats, arrows and knives, smelling of sweat and blood. They looked as if they'd just been in a fight that they'd badly lost.

Andrew grabbed Aaliyah by the shoulder. 'Did we wake you, princess?'

All the muscles in her body stiffened. Before she could react, Andrew stepped closer, and Aaliyah saw something flash in the darkness. A blade. The next thing she knew, he was holding it to her jugular.

'Open the door,' Andrew leaned in to whisper, his breath acrid. 'Now.'

Aaliyah stood frozen, every part of her resisting the command, but Andrew nudged the blade harder so that her vein pulsed against it.

'No!' Kim was in the doorway. Aaliyah could only hear her voice, but she could imagine her mother taking the scene in with horror.

'I'll do it,' she said, rushing for the front door.

'This isn't over,' Andrew promised Aaliyah. By the time she had stumbled out into the hall, the front door was open and more rowdy men poured in.

Aaliyah saw that a couple of them were holding the body of an unconscious man. They made a beeline for the kitchen. She watched with our mother from the shadowed hall as one of the men swept everything off the table, shattering glasses and plates on the tiles, the tub of formula flying off last, spilling all its sacred contents onto the ground.

'No,' Aaliyah said in a hollow whisper.

'Which one of yous is a doctor?' said one of the young men. Aaliyah's eyes flitted imperceptibly to her mother, but neither of them said anything for a moment.

Finally, raising her voice over the alarm and the crying baby, Kim said, 'There's a hospital just—'

'It's too far,' Andrew said.

'And it's a shambles,' said another.

'We need help now.'

They laid Dennis Crossley out on the table. It wasn't easy to see at first, but blood was pulsing from a wound in his gut. 'What happened?' Kim asked.

'Insurgents,' said Andrew. 'Some false moves ...'

I hope he dies, Aaliyah thought, looking at Crossley writhing on the table.

'You said she was a doctor!' shouted a man with a mohawk.

'Look—' Kim said.

'Kim? Is ... is everything okay?' Aaliyah turned to find their dark-eyed neighbour in the hall in a hastily buttoned shirt and checkered briefs.

'Gabriel?'

'I heard the alarm and thought I'd ...' As his eyes grew accustomed to the dark, he took in the scene.

'We need a doctor!' shouted a young man with a crossbow.

'She's not a doctor!' Aaliyah shouted back.

'Someone turn that fucking thing off!' Andrew pointed to where he thought the alarm was coming from.

'And the fucking baby!' shouted Mohawk. Hero was blue in the face now, bawling.

Andrew stormed into the hall, leapt up onto the rickety console table and smashed the alarm, denting and then destroying the hammer and bell. He took a couple more shots at the wall, knocking a chalky flurry of plaster into the air, leaving a wound in the panelling.

Aaliyah felt as if her ears might pop in the sudden quiet. A pressure released in the middle of her skull.

Crossley groaned.

'If he dies ...' said Crossbow, menace in his voice.

'Look,' Gabriel said, 'I'm a dentist. She's a public health

specialist. Neither of us are trained in emergency medicine. We don't know how to treat stab wounds.'

'But you know something, though,' said Mohawk, circling towards him.

'*Minton*,' Crossley moaned.

Andrew pointed at Aaliyah. 'He said that your dad had a whole set-up ... a bunker, food, water, a generator.'

Gabriel eyed Kim quizzically. Aaliyah frowned, wondering why on Earth Marcus would tell anyone about the bunker. We'd always been sworn to secrecy.

'You look at him,' said Mohawk, pressing a blade into Gabriel's back. The man's eyes widened, and he raised his hands.

'Wait, don't ...'

He pushed the knife harder into Gabriel's back and hissed something in his ear.

'If we help you,' Kim asked, 'you'll leave?'

There was a long pause. Finally, Andrew said, 'Sure.'

Mohawk lowered the weapon and gestured at the table. Gabriel stepped over to Crossley and examined his wound.

'You need to be applying pressure to it,' Kim said. 'If you want to stop the bleeding.'

Two of the men looked at her. She handed Aaliyah the baby, gave the boys some clean dishcloths and instructed them in how to do it. She told one of the others to get some sofa cushions to elevate his legs.

Aaliyah was shocked that Kim was letting them put their muddy boots on her beloved William Morris-print soft furnishings. She rocked Hero back and forth, patted her back, felt the baby begin to calm down.

'My knowledge of anatomy is pretty basic below the

shoulders, Kim,' Gabriel said shakily. He kept darting his eyes towards the man who had held the knife to his back.

Aaliyah could see that something had occurred to our mother. 'There's a relief centre near Balham,' she said, 'in a church. I've been there before. It's a bit of a walk. But if we stabilize him and pack up his wounds, you should be able to get him there. The doctors there will be able to help you better.'

The men exchanged glances, communicating silently.

'Okay,' said Andrew.

'We're going to slow the bleeding and stabilize the patient,' Kim said.

'Can you stitch him up?' Mohawk asked.

'I can suture his skin, but I don't have the expertise to deal with an internal wound. We stitch him up now, it doesn't change anything if he dies in a couple of days of internal bleeding or an infection or shock.'

Kim rifled around for some hand sanitizer and more towels.

'We're going to need sterile gauze,' she told Aaliyah, 'antiseptic solution, non-adhesive dressings, medical tape, gloves and scissors. It should all be in the first aid kit.' Aaliyah knew that the kit was in the bunker. 'Can you go get it?'

She nodded. Hero seemed to have fallen back asleep in the warmth of her arms. Aaliyah knew that the relative calm wouldn't last very long. Soon she would be hungry, and once again, they'd have nothing to feed her. She looked sorrowfully at the snowy drifts of formula on the edge of the dining table. The footprints in it on the floor.

Outside, the air smelled ripe, of mounting sewage and rubbish set to rot in the June summer. An owl hooted. Something on the ground behind her snapped, and she realized she was being followed.

It was Andrew.

With little other option, she kept walking and pressed the code for the bunker, trying hard to cover it from his prying eyes. The pin was 0706, our parents' anniversary.

It was an awkward climb down the ladder, one-handed, holding the baby. The motion-sensitive lights clinked on as she descended. Aaliyah searched through the medicine shelf for the first aid kit and the items her mum had listed. As she looked, though, she heard a noise above her. An intake of breath. Boots on the ladder.

Something about him here, in this space that was supposed to be safe, was sickening to her.

'Oh, wow!' Andrew let out a whistle of delight at the sight of it. 'He wasn't lying. This is a work of fucking art.'

He marvelled at it all. The bunker was about five hundred square feet, maybe the size of their living room and kitchen combined, with two adjoining chambers. The sleeping areas, where there were three bunk beds, and the living areas were mainly filled with shelving units and storage boxes. To one side was a composting toilet and bucket, surrounded by a curtain.

Although, for the months he'd been building it, Aaliyah had regarded the bunker with alarm and disgust, Hugo had been more relaxed about it, reminding her that his parents' estate in Switzerland came with a nuclear shelter.

Andrew opened a packet of biltong that he found in a plastic storage box and ate it hungrily.

They were alone. Aaliyah imagined cracking a tin of mashed potatoes on his skull but then shook away the thought, remembering the knife at her throat. *Follow the plan. Maybe they'll be gone soon.*

'We need to get this stuff back,' Aaliyah said. 'For your dad.'

'Oh, he's not my dad,' Andrew corrected her.

'He isn't?' Aaliyah wasn't sure why she'd made that assumption.

'Mr C? No. My dad's just some twat who left my mum when she was pregnant. My stepdad was the real bastard, though.' He pulled back a sleeve to reveal thick little burns on his forearm. Cigarettes, Aaliyah guessed. 'But Mr C . . .' He swallowed back some feeling. 'Growing up, if I ever thought about being a man, what it takes to be a *good* one, I'd think of him.'

Would a good man be holding innocent strangers hostage? Aaliyah thought, though she kept it to herself.

They climbed out of the bunker and walked together back into the kitchen, where a sombre quiet had taken over.

The men perked up, though, when they saw Andrew.

'They have lacto-free!' said one of the boys, who looked younger than the rest, wearing a Scout's uniform. He took a long swig from the UHT carton and grinned.

Mum grabbed the supplies from Aaliyah and gave her a conspiratorial look. Checking if she was okay. Aaliyah nodded and waited for her moment, watching her mother clean and dress the injured man's wound.

Eventually, as the intruders crowded around Dennis, Aaliyah managed to pull our mother into the hallway. 'I need to go,' she said quietly.

'Where?' Kim asked, alarmed.

'To get more formula.'

'Lia, no.'

But Aaliyah had already thought about it. How she would start walking to the relief centre now and hopefully make it there by sunrise.

'Mum, I *have* to.'

'Not on your own,' she said.

'I'll be fine. If I get there and back quickly, then hopefully Hero won't suffer for too long. You'll be okay,' she said quietly, looking around at the boys in the kitchen, gathered around their fallen leader. 'Just stick with Gabriel.'

Kim gritted her teeth and grabbed Aaliyah's wrist. She said, more seriously, 'You don't have to do this.'

Aaliyah shook herself free. 'I do, though. Carmen asked me to look after her. Hero's my responsibility. I can't just sit here and watch her starve.'

Our mother winced. She opened her mouth as if to say something, but Aaliyah just handed her the baby and ran upstairs. She grabbed a hoodie to wear on top of her pyjamas, found a pair of trainers and headed out into the night.

She returned home, half a day later, to find even more strange men in the house. They were putting their muddy feet on the sofa, drinking beer, playing with an old Monopoly set. Some were in the kitchen, feasting on junk food that had been stored in the pantry.

Aaliyah's feet were blistered from the walk in the heat. She had trekked to two different relief centres until a mother had overheard her desperate begging and had given her some of the formula she had left in her bag. 'He's exclusively breastfed, but ...' She pointed to her six-month-old boy. 'I kept it just in case.'

Aaliyah's head ached and the skin on the back of her neck was itchy from hours of sun exposure. But the entire time, her chest had been tight with obsessive worry about Hero. It had felt strange being away from the baby for so long, with no access to information to add to her mental tally of naps and nappy changes.

She clutched the paper bag of formula tightly and looked around for them.

'Where's my mum?' Aaliyah asked Mohawk, who was playing some game with a shuttlecock and paper cups on the dining table. There was a sticky dust of formula on everything in the kitchen. Some mixed with blood under the table, congealed to jelly. 'Where's the baby?'

'Upstairs, I think,' Mohawk said.

'I thought you were ... going?' Aaliyah asked him, trying to sound indifferent.

'Dex, Kevin and Andrew took Mr C up to the relief centre. I told them I'd stay here, hold the fort until they returned.' A roil of impotent rage twisted her stomach, and she glared at him.

'You've got a great set-up here.' Crossbow was sitting on the counter and eating Nutella with a spoon. 'Be a shame to waste it.'

'We *weren't* wasting it,' Aaliyah said through gritted teeth.

'And pass up on your great hospitality?' Crossbow smiled, a glitter of menace in his eyes.

Aaliyah headed upstairs, where she found a man in threadbare battle fatigues asleep on her bed. 'Hey!' she shouted, startling him awake. 'This is *my* room.'

He rubbed his eyes and just looked at her as if she was being unreasonable. She fought the urge to throw something at him, to make him leave, then remembered her purpose. *Find Mum, feed Hero.*

As she climbed up the stairs, she heard Kim. Our mother was softly singing the nonsense song she used to sing to Chantale. 'A-tisket, a-tasket, a green-and-yellow basket ...'

Aaliyah was relieved that Hero wasn't bawling hysterically

from half a day of no food. There was a quick inhale of surprise when she pushed open their bedroom door.

Kimona was topless on the bed, Hero in her arms, nursing.

Aaliyah stared at her in surprise and some revulsion.

'What are you doing?'

Mum scrabbled for the crochet throw blanket and draped it over her shoulders. Opening her mouth.

The memory came to Aaliyah suddenly. Chantale at four, her long legs splayed on the sofa, rolling a toy car across Kim's shoulder blades as she fed. The way she'd cry before nap times in the car, Kim pulling over to feed her. Our dad had said, 'She's too old,' but Mum had told us that '*stillen*', the German word for breastfeeding, also meant 'to satisfy' or 'to comfort'. 'She's not getting anything from that teat anymore,' Gladys from church had remarked disdainfully when she'd seen Chantale napping in her mother's arms, a rill of milk dribbling down her chin. Except maybe what she was getting couldn't be weighed on a kitchen scale. Kim had made noises about stopping when Chantale had started school, and Aaliyah had never cared to ask.

Our mother had once called pregnancy 'the ghost train'. Aaliyah still remembered watching her grow round and varicose-veined, watching her skin split with stretch marks and her molars crumble. But, she thought now, this was what Kim loved about motherhood, the animal part, surrendering to it, letting her body trundle ahead on its journey and come out changed. Not the other parts, not working to change, to accommodate another will. *She would have loved us best if we'd all stayed seven. No, if we'd remained as helpless as Hero forever.*

'You know what?' Aaliyah hissed, real venom in her voice as she slammed the formula down on the dresser, making her mother's costume jewellery clatter. She was leaving. 'I never asked for any of this, anyway.'

BRIAR MINTON – 7 DAYS AFTER

I didn't sleep at all that night. I just lay crying, watching dust motes swirl in Hero's blueish light. Digit nuzzled next to me, the musty smell of her fur reminding me of home.

I wanted to leave then. But I felt stranded. Not least because I'd lost my map somehow, but also because the world outside the walls of the estate seemed suddenly menacing. The thought of venturing out there alone, even with Digit for company, filled me with dread.

We gathered to the sound of the drums the next morning. By then, word had spread about Soo-Jin's death, and Freya led us all in a quiet meditation before we ate.

We had managed to return with a feast, in spite of everything. I watched as the others enjoyed crackers and chutney, pickles and boiled potatoes. Even Digit munched happily on the bones and scraps that the Group indulgently threw her. I was too disconsolate to eat. Soo-Jin had been my one ally. Not only because we shared the same secret ambition – to uncover what had happened to Ruby – but I believed that her presence had exerted a rationalizing force on the Group. She'd been the one to suggest that we didn't fast longer than forty-eight hours and that no one should give up water. She was always ready with an answer or a plan. Without her, I feared some essential psychic balance had already been lost.

The tables were arranged in a U-shape out on the patio. Freya presided in the centre. Raising her arms, she said, 'Although we are grateful that some facets of the minds of the Celestial Ones have been revealed to us, there is still so much we are yet to uncover. Like how they will return our dead to us and what hour the Reunion will occur.'

This was the part of their philosophy that appealed to almost everyone in the Group. That the Tau, over millennia of scientific advancement, had developed a way to reverse entropy and death. A way to recover lost cells and quicken minds from beyond the grave. They spoke often of the Reunion. It might be one of the first ways we'd know that the benevolent reign of the Tau had begun.

Freya continued, 'We thank Cato, Briar, Isaac, Laurie, Min-ho, Jacob and Ishaan for this sustenance. And we eat it in honour of Soo-Jin. Sharp-minded, phlegmatic, she who sought to crack her heel on the truth.'

Everyone raised their glasses, which were filled with a currant juice that Charlie had made. 'To Soo-Jin,' they toasted and drank.

'It could have been any of us,' Laurie said. Quiet then.

Freya told us, 'We will suffer without her, but our weeping will turn to laughter when the ones we mourn quicken from their long sleep, shake the dirt from their hair, pull the mortician's wax from their eyes, greet us. Smile with all their teeth.'

I'd been lucky until then, as I hadn't previously lost anyone I cared about – though I did keep myself awake some nights worrying about death. More so after the Event, when a member of the Group would say something and I'd be reminded urgently of my anxiety about my sisters and Dad. It actually was a comfort to me then to believe that there might be something beyond what my father had taught – the certain abyss, the final void. The notion of my mind shutting off like an engine, my memories unspooling in a coffin as my brain cells turned themselves over to the dirt, had always filled me with a suffocating terror.

'When will it be?' Martha asked. Another silence, then whispers falling into the stunned quiet. She'd voiced what we'd all been saying but only in secret, to each other and never to Freya.

'I'm excited for it,' Martha hedged, noticing the chill at the tables, 'but . . .' She pointed up at Hero, which was huge in the sky. This was the morning of its closest approach to Earth. The planet was clear to see in the day by then, and its reflection had been so bright that we could eat by it at night and barely needed any torches. 'I guess I thought it would have happened by now.'

Beth shot her a venomous look. 'Martha—'

'No,' Freya interrupted, holding her palm out towards Beth and looking sympathetically at Martha. 'I understand your longing, I share it. I've spent the past few weeks in anxious petition for a sign. But I've tried to remind myself that the Tau do not move by clocks or calendars.'

'They will come when we are ready to receive Them!' another follower shouted from the far end of the table.

Freya nodded. 'They regard us as a species, a collective consciousness still learning. Their moment of revelation must be perfect. It will mark a turning point for the entire galaxy. Soon, humans, enlightened with Their knowledge, will utilize Their tools to create intergalactic empires.' The Group stared at her, faces raised in rapturous attention. She could hold a crowd like no one I knew, except for perhaps my grandfather.

'When will the hour be? I can't say. But I do know that it is not for us to demand Their presence but to *prepare* for it.'

Although Martha nodded, I could tell she was unsatisfied.

Amy cleared her throat. 'No one has had an "experience" for a while, either,' she said. Although the Tau had been known to communicate via dreams and visions, despite our fasting and meditations, the last time the Tau had made any contact with us had been five days ago, when Cato had attempted to drown me in the river.

'Perhaps,' offered Beth delicately, 'we need to . . . provoke one.' She looked around, and a couple of people exchanged glances.

Axel shook his head vehemently. 'We said we weren't doing that anymore.'

'But Cato already did.' She pointed at me. 'He induced an NDE in Briar, and They spoke to her.' Everyone's eyes were on me. Whispers rose in the Group. I deliberately avoided looking at Cato, but I could imagine his smirk of unearned pride at the mention.

'It's too dangerous,' said Edith.

Freya seemed to agree. 'Look at the stars. They burn for eons. Let them teach us patience. The Tau will come when we are ready to receive Them and not at our urging.'

Charlie chimed in. 'We need to work together now to ensure that when They reveal Themselves, we are ready for Their gifts.'

As if neither of them had spoken, Beth said, '*I'll* do it.'

Laurie swung around in horror. 'No!'

'Laurie—' she protested.

'Not *you*.'

'I'll do it,' volunteered Martha.

'I will.' Isaac stood and raised his hand.

'Choose me!' shouted Charlie.

'Me!' said Amy, along with a couple of others in the Group.

'Enough!' Freya shouted above the din. She sounded, for the first time, as if she might be losing patience.

In the resulting silence, Beth continued, 'I've been giving it some thought. We could replicate the conditions of my first experience.'

'No . . .' Laurie was blanched.

'Pine nuts.'

'So I watch your throat swell up again? Watch you die this time? No fucking way.'

'But my EpiPen . . .' Beth said.

'No, Beth!' he shouted.

'You know how to use it.' She reached for his hand to calm him down and stared deeply into his eyes. 'When I'm close, you bring me back.'

Axel shook his head. 'This sounds . . .'

'Like a good idea,' said Cato. He was staring at Beth with an intensity that frightened me. It reminded me of how calmly he'd put down Soo-Jin, as if she was nothing more than an ageing pet. And his dark eyes on me as I'd climbed down from the tree where I'd been hiding the night before. 'The weak and the botched shall perish,' he'd whispered. 'And one should help them to do so.'

Beth was encouraged by Cato's support.

'Laurie, I *want* to do this.' He still looked horror-stricken. 'I'm not like you. The Tau don't haunt my dreams.

I saw Them once and once only, and it was so long ago now. What if …' She was slightly tearful then. 'What if I died like Soo-Jin and never saw Them again? I would rather die now and—'

'But you won't,' Cato said. 'The EpiPen. It's ingenious. More precise than drowning.' He looked at me, and I shivered at the memory.

'Exactly,' Beth agreed.

'And you would do it?' Martha said. 'You really *want* to?'

'It would be my honour.'

'And what if it doesn't work?' Laurie asked. 'What if you die in the attempt?'

'Death is only the beginning,' Beth told him.

'And we already understand the logic of this world,' Cato said. 'Revelation comes at a price. Which is paid in blood.'

TANICE MINTON – 7 DAYS AFTER

Tanice couldn't remember ever being happier to see our house. Even with Marcus and the Pastor's help, it had taken almost three full days on foot to finally reach it, she and Chantale were still weak after days of dehydration. They'd stopped overnight at a relief centre along the way, where there had been a pile of discarded clothes. Tanice had been grateful to exchange her strappy wedding stilettos for a pair of worn-out trainers, her torn and bloodied tulle dress for someone else's jeans.

She woke, that first night in the relief centre, gasping, her rickety camp bed shaking under her. She'd had a dream that the air was poisonous and woke remembering that there had been no bomb after all. That the danger in the cellar hadn't come from outside, but from within – from the photographer, his paranoia, his violence.

Through the centre's high windows, she could see Hero, the clouds making a halo around it, and she felt the weight of the lie collapse inside her. *I had to do it,* she'd remind herself. She had killed him. *I had to do it to escape.* She hadn't needed to save herself or her sister from radiation or fallout – but she'd had to save them from him.

The next afternoon, Tanice, Chantale and Marcus parted with our grandfather at the ruin of Clapham Junction station. He told them that he needed to head to Providence House to see how he could help. Tanice was sad to see him go, but the sight of some of the old landmarks – the Clapham Grand, St Mark's Church, the Common – calmed her a little.

Tanice had seen that the city hadn't been burned or irradiated, though it was broken. The roads were choked with debris, and the half-leveled skyline was now jagged and unfamiliar. At the end of our street, the wind picked up, bringing with it the exhaust, garbage fires, rotting rubbish and sewage. But, Tanice reminded herself, she was free. The cellar was behind her. And while the world she'd stepped into was different, London had survived. And so had she.

Tanice's elation at the sight of our house was short-lived, though. As the three of them approached, they all could sense that something was wrong. Marcus fell quiet as they walked up the driveway. The bay window next to the front door was smashed, and there were strange voices coming from inside. Some bikes lay abandoned in the driveway.

Marcus's hand flickered to the altered pocket in his trousers, where Tanice knew he kept a knife.

'You know what,' he said quietly, an affected calm in his voice. 'Let's go around back.'

They took the little alley around the side of the house, where more bikes and scooters were abandoned. Marcus poked his head around the tall garden gate before gesturing my sisters through it.

When they reached the bunker, Dad said, 'You get in

there. I'll be back as soon as I find out what's happening.' He didn't wait for a response, just crept across the parched grass and disappeared inside.

Tanice froze. The sight of the bunker door – metal and half-buried, its bolts like staring eyes – sent a jolt of panic through her chest. She might be free of the suffocating dark of the wine cellar, but she had only to descend the ladder and her mind would take her back there. Suddenly the air smelled of it again – human waste, Paris's body, bile and fruitcake. Her breath quickened and her palms turned clammy. The idea of closing herself into another underground room made her knees tremble.

'I . . . I can't,' she whispered.

Chantale turned to her, eyes wide. 'What do you mean? We have to go in.'

But Tanice couldn't move. Her feet were planted like roots. Even with sunlight still on her skin, the panic had already sunk its talons into her.

She backed away, shaking her head. 'I can't go down there again.'

She didn't know what that meant for her safety. Only that she'd rather face whatever waited above ground than be entombed again.

'We'll wait up here, then,' Chantale said, but she darted a nervous glance at the kitchen window, where they could both hear raised voices, our father's drowned out by those of strange men.

'Do you think Mum's in there?' she asked, and both their eyes floated up to the window of her bedroom.

'Probably,' Tanice said. She couldn't wait to see Aaliyah, me and our mother again, but another urgent concern had been pressing on her mind as the days had passed, and she realized that, while Marcus was distracted, now was the perfect chance to attend to it.

'What are you doing?' Chantale hissed. Tanice found the gym bag she had abandoned on the porch over a week ago. It had her – admittedly slightly smelly – basketball uniform in it, which, she decided, was better than what she was wearing now and would have to do for a change of clothes.

In the shadow behind the house, Tanice changed quickly, exposing little skin. The deft way that changing for years in girls' locker rooms had taught her. 'Wait in the bunker. I'll be back soon,' she told Chantale.

'What should I tell Dad?' our little sister asked, looking worried. In the house, the argument was continuing.

'That I went to see Kezhia,' Tanice said.

She'd walked down this street only once before, but she knew it when she found it. Recognized it because of the children's playground in the centre of the road – the one with the now-mangled monkey bars and ripped Astroturf scattering green and black crumbs down the pavement. Knew it because of the tinfoil taped to one of the upper flat windows. He'd told her that he'd turned his bedroom into a darkroom.

Was she crazy? Tanice shook away the doubt.

A few teen boys sat on the steps inside the gloomy entrance of the council estate, guarding the building like sphinxes before a temple. Tanice attempted to stride past them, but they moved together to block her.

'Where you off to?' the first asked. He looked only a little older than her, in shorts and a hoodie. Tanice hesitated, then wondered if saying a name would help her.

'Do you know Sydney Walker?'

'Depends ...' the first boy said.

'Who's asking?' said the second, a younger boy with ripped jeans and elaborately patterned cornrows.

'I'm ... his girlfriend?' Tanice ventured. They looked at each other.

'He never mentioned a girl,' said the third, rolling his heel lazily over a battered football.

Tanice shrugged and tried to hide her hurt.

'I wanted to see if he's okay,' she said honestly.

'Where you from?' the first asked. Was there a right answer to this? Tanice knew better than to say her actual address, which, she had been told, was 'bougie'.

'Doddington,' she lied.

'Oh yeah? We've had enough beef with them Doddington lot!' said the footballer. The boys closed ranks and regarded her with new suspicion.

'Please?' Tanice pleaded.

'No, and if you see Eb and Ty—'

'Tell them to fuck off.'

'Yeah. They ain't welcome here!'

Tanice turned and headed back outside into the June sun. She thought she could recognize some old signs of a fight. A broken bike tyre, scuffs on the wall, a brown spatter on the asphalt, which could have been anything but could also have been blood.

She shaded her eyes and looked back up at the window covered in tinfoil. The thought of Sydney, so close after so long, filled her with desperation.

Her father had counselled her that, post-collapse, they would have to barter for everything they wanted. She cursed herself for leaving the house without any money or food. Put her hands in the deep pockets of her basketball shorts and found her locker key and some headbands, Airwaves gum and a nail file she'd often – walking home in the dark – comforted herself that she could use as a weapon, a tiny tub of Vaseline and a fifty-pence coin. Nothing she could bargain with.

She gazed at the boys, who had sat back down on the staircase, chatting. If she left now, she might never get a chance to see Sydney again. She regarded them with frustration, watched as one of them rolled the ball under his foot and then lost control of it. It span towards her.

Tanice imagined herself in her familiar role of shooting guard, seeking to penetrate their defences and make a successful shot.

Without thinking too much about it, Tanice ran, dived for the football and pitched it just above their heads. The acoustics of the stairwell made her shot ring out with a loud *bang* as the ball collided with the concrete steps. The sound startled the boys, who scattered with shouts of surprise. The first dived out of the way, the second dropped to the floor and the third pressed himself against the wall, leaving a clear opening for Tanice to career past them, sprinting as fast as she could up the stairs.

She was already two flights up before they began to follow her. Tanice tried to remember how far up Sydney's window had been. Five flights? Four?

They were gaining on her, their voices echoing.

'Get her!'

'That bitch!'

She was at the fourth floor and launched herself through the staircase door to find herself on a long outdoor walkway, doors stretching along the left-hand side. In her haste, she tripped on an abandoned scooter. Fell so hard, the concrete slamming into her shin was enough to bring tears to her eyes. She pulled herself to her feet shakily.

Which door was it? She was too flustered to orientate herself. One had a mezuzah on the lintel. She was pretty sure it wasn't that one.

'Up here! I can hear her!'

She took a wild guess and pushed open a door that gave against her weight just in time to hear the feet of the boys thunder up the stairs outside.

She realized immediately that she was in the wrong house. This one smelled of menthol and urine. There was a gasp down the hall, and Tanice pressed herself against the front door as she heard the boys shouting upstairs.

'Excuse me?' An elderly man, she guessed. A skinny cat bounced towards her, and she started. The window was open, and through it she heard a voice she recognized. One flight up. *Sydney*, she thought, with a flash of relief. He was alive.

'You better sort out your girl,' one of the boys shouted at him.

'My who . . . ?' Sydney said.

'Excuse me?' With some effort, the old man entered the hallway. He was shaking, holding on to a cane. 'Take anything you want.'

'I'm sorry,' Tanice said. She could see stains on his trousers. He looked as if he hadn't changed or bathed in days.

'What more do you want from me!' She couldn't tell if that was a pathological tremble in his voice or if he was on the edge of tears. 'I don't have anything!'

'I'm going . . .' Tanice whispered.

Thankfully, the boys didn't seem to have heard her. She waited a moment as the sound of their footsteps clattered back down the staircase. She hoped they were returning to their post. The old man stared at her, wary.

'I'm sorry.' Tanice threw her hands up to show him that she meant no harm.

But he just cried, 'I don't have anything else!'

She turned and fumbled for the door, mumbling apologies. She took care to slip out without letting the cat escape. And then – leaning hard on the banister as her shins squealed in pain – she went upstairs and knocked on Sydney's door.

He'd told her that he'd never taken the Christmas decorations down after his father died, had kept the wreath on the door. She should have known to look for it. It was shabbier than she had imagined. A real one, made of fir clippings and prickled holly leaves that had curled and shed themselves in the heat. Desiccated berries, their red long faded.

When she knocked, Sydney shouted, 'Malik, I already said—!'

'It's me,' Tanice said timidly.

The door wasn't locked; it was a simple thing to push it open. The floor in the dark hall was scattered with shoes. The air carried the vinegary smell of photo developer.

In the gloom, she could see photos on the wall, school pictures: Sydney at seven, missing teeth. At nine, with a wrinkled shirt collar. Eleven, with a tweenage bashfulness in his smile. And there, his father, Ezekiel Walker. Whose face she'd only seen in pictures. A darkly handsome man, with some of Sydney's features, a noble jaw and thoughtful eyes. Here, in his wedding photo, he was confetti-strewn and smiling. And there was one she recognized as Sydney's work, in black and white, his eyes closed, about to say something.

'Nicey ...' A weak voice came from the living room. 'Don't ...'

She entered to find him curled on the sofa. She'd wondered why he hadn't come to the door, but realized why as his body jolted forward and he retched into a plastic bowl.

After her torturous days in the wine cellar, Tanice wasn't fazed by the sight or the smell. Only sorry for him.

'I didn't want you to see—' He leaned over and gagged again, but this time not much came out. He wiped his mouth.

'What's wrong?' she said, walking slowly towards him.

'I don't know. The water maybe ...'

Tanice knew this was part of the collapse. Those who didn't die during the first Event would die in the coming days and weeks of previously curable illnesses: cholera, minor infections, waterborne diseases.

The small living room also made her feel sorry for him. The polyvinyl Christmas tree next to the television, with plastic baubles filmed in dust. Empty crisp packets on the carpet, a chicken bone in a cardboard box plastered with ketchup.

She hated to imagine how he'd been living.

'Don't you have ... somewhere else to go?'

He snorted. 'My dad's all I have. Had ...'

There were more photographs on the folding dining table that caught Tanice's eye. The underside of a car in the sky, captured from above. Sparks flying up from a powerline. Auroras. A bike levitating against fiery clouds.

'Are these ... How did you take these?'

'Leica M3,' he said, a hint of pride at his ingenuity audible in his voice. 'It's fully mechanical. It didn't have a microchip that melted.'

'But wasn't it … snatched up into the air?'

'I took those from the window. It wasn't easy.'

Tanice imagined Sydney clinging on to the camera as he was pulled up to the ceiling.

'You know what my dream is?' he said weakly. 'To photograph the big one. First contact. The moment they appear in the sky. Or when the ship comes down in front of the Houses of Parliament.'

'You think … you think it's aliens?'

'It's obviously aliens, Nicey! Where have you been?'

Imprisoned in a wine cellar, she thought.

'But imagine if it was me,' he continued wistfully. 'Think of Hiroshima, Vietnam, the moon landings. How many world events are represented by just one picture? What if that picture was mine?'

'You'd be …'

'Famous.' A word Tanice loved.

'So you're alien hunting?' she asked with a smile.

Sydney rubbed his stomach and winced, visibly fighting the urge to vomit.

'Not right now. Now I'm just … surviving.'

He leaned over, his face creased in discomfort.

Tanice hated to feel sorry for people. For her, it was the death knell of almost any relationship. The opposite of affection, it triggered something closer to revulsion in her. And her sympathy for Sydney was almost crushing. He was such a sad sight, in his boxers, glazed with sweat, in this dingy flat he lived in by himself. He was all alone in the world because of Marcus. And if she left, he would probably die here like the old man would, become another number among the numberless dead.

Her first impulse was to run. To thunder down the stairs

and race home and forget about him. But since killing the photographer, she'd promised to prove to herself that she was not a bad person. *What would a good person do?*

'Come home with me?'

'Sure,' Sydney snorted.

'Sydney, we have water and medicine. Imodium, maybe, electrolyte drinks. Food.' His eyes glittered at that word. 'Lots of food. Beans and preserved meat and sweets.'

He caught himself. 'Your dad, though.'

'He doesn't have to know.'

His eyes narrowed in suspicion.

'I mean, you don't even have to come into the house, if you don't want to. Just wait around the back, and I'll bring you the things you need. The meds, a water canister, enough food for a couple of weeks.'

She knelt down beside him and stroked his clammy cheek with the back of her hand. He let his fingers brush over hers.

'You'd do that for me?'

She liked this feeling. *What would a good person say?*

'It's the least I can do.'

It was a thirty-minute walk back to the house, and fifteen minutes in Tanice realized what a mistake she had made. Sydney was barely well enough to stand, let alone walk. Every now and then, she hinted that they could turn back, but by the time they reached the station, she was sure that if she sent him home, he would die. His skin was waxy, he was limping and he had to stop regularly to lean on something and catch his breath or to vomit. Tanice felt completely out of her depth.

He stopped again to lean on a low wall as they approached the house, struggling to climb up the hill. 'Are you . . . ?' Tanice ventured for the hundredth time.

'Just . . . catching my breath,' he promised. His eyes flitted up the road. 'Which one is yours?'

Tanice pointed up to the three-storey townhouse in the middle of the road. Sydney let out a low whistle. 'That's big.'

'I guess.' The house was always so full of people – our family of six, our grandad often, clucking church ladies, cousins and friends for sleepovers – that it had always felt a little cramped to Tanice. But she could have fitted Sydney's entire flat on the ground floor. She told him the spiel: 'It's technically my grandad's house. We just live in it, and he lives in the annexe of his church. My grandparents bought it for, like, a thousand pounds in the Seventies. They say this whole area was nothing like it is now. It's changed a lot in three generations.' Her mum was always listing the problems with it that they couldn't afford to fix. The roof, the crack in that wall, the toolshed in the garden.

'My family never owned anything,' Sydney said. Tanice shifted uncomfortably. 'Didn't you say you were from Doddington?'

'Yeah . . .' Tanice said and looked away. It was clear that was a lie. 'I used to be embarrassed of it.' The houses of the girls at St Clotilde's had always seemed so impeccable. Big and luxurious. Window boxes of hydrangeas that their gardeners drenched in water, chaise longues covered in duck-feather cushions, TVs as big as walls, second homes with stables.

'I used to cycle up here, on my way to the Common,' said Sydney. 'I'd look in the big windows of these houses and just think, "One day."'

Tanice shaded her eyes from the sun and looked back at the house. She'd spent so long being ashamed of everything about her life. It was hard to imagine anyone wanting it.

'We should head,' she said. 'Get you out of the sun.'

They crept towards the house via the back alley, ducking between bins and climbing carefully over fences. By the time they reached the back garden gate, Tanice knew that Sydney wouldn't have the strength to make the journey again – not anytime soon.

'Stay the night?' she suggested gently.

'No fucking way,' he groaned, propping himself up against the wall, sweat pouring from his hair. His breathing was laboured, as though each inhalation took enormous effort.

'Or rest, at least.'

He gave her a doubtful look. 'Where?'

Tanice looked back at the house. It seemed to be quiet. Whatever argument had been happening when she'd left, it was over now.

'The attic,' she said. 'We can get in without anyone noticing.'

Sydney looked at her sceptically. 'How?'

'Follow me,' Tanice whispered. She led him quietly around the side of the house, pointing up to the wooden trellis.

'Can you climb?' she asked quietly.

Sydney didn't answer at first, just nodded, gathering what little strength he had left. Tanice went first, grabbing firmly onto the wooden lattice, testing each foothold carefully before pulling herself upwards. Her heart raced at the familiar creaking sounds the trellis made, but it seemed sturdy enough for now.

Tanice had lost count of how many times she'd climbed it, sneaking out after curfew under the cover of darkness. Several times, she'd used this very route to slip away unnoticed and meet Sydney. Now, thick clusters of ivy wound up the lattice, some leaves brown and brittle from the relentless heat. It was strange how familiar it felt, climbing it now with him behind her – though this time it was to save his life rather than to steal secret hours together beneath the stars.

She glanced down to check Sydney's progress. He was moving painfully slowly, pausing frequently to wipe the sweat from his forehead. His jaw was clenched in determination. At any moment, her parents might poke their heads from a window or the door of the bunker and she'd be in more trouble than she likely already was. But she knew better than to hurry him.

When Tanice reached the first floor window ledge, she shuffled carefully sideways, guiding Sydney towards a thick stone sill that jutted out just enough to support their feet. From there, they had to cross carefully to the drainpipe, then step up onto the narrow edge of brickwork that encircled her second-floor bedroom window.

The window was partially open in the June heat, but she hesitated before pushing it wider, straining her ears for movement inside. Satisfied there was none, she pressed the frame upwards, holding her breath as the old wood groaned. She slipped in first, then reached back out to help Sydney climb inside.

Just as his trainers touched the carpet, they heard heavy footsteps on the landing outside.

Tanice grabbed Sydney's arm, pulling him behind her wardrobe. The bedroom door swung open. Through the narrow gap, Tanice saw one of the intruders – a boy barely older than her, his head shaved unevenly. He paused, glancing suspiciously around the room.

Tanice held her breath. Beside her, Sydney tried to keep as still as possible. After what felt like forever, the boy turned around and left, slamming the door behind him.

It was only when she heard his footsteps fading down the stairs that Tanice exhaled. For the first time, she took in the state of her bedroom. Muddy boot prints tracked across the carpet, her favourite duck-egg blue throw blanket was crumpled on the floor, a half-eaten packet of crisps had been left on her desk chair, oil spotting the fabric. Her drawers had been rifled through, underwear spilling out, and the mirrored jewellery box on her desk had been opened, its contents scattered – fake gold earrings and a few beaded friendship bracelets.

Trying to contain her fury, Tanice quickly reached beneath her bed, relieved to find her GOOD bag still hidden below the soiled mattress, miraculously untouched. Pulling it free, she slung it over her shoulder.

'Come on,' she whispered to Sydney as she ushered him quickly into the hallway, then towards the ladder leading to the attic. She reached up, tugging at the cord until the ladder unfolded onto the carpet. Carefully, she helped Sydney climb up, closing the hatch behind them with trembling hands.

Tanice could count on one hand the number of times she'd ever been up there. Sunlight filtered through a small, grimy dormer window, illuminating motes of dust and the cobwebs that fluttered in the corners. It was difficult to stand upright without knocking her head against the sloping ceiling beams, and even harder for Sydney. The room was piled high with cardboard boxes labelled with things like 'Outerwear 4–5 years' or 'Camping stuff'.

She opened that one and pulled out a crumpled sleeping

bag. Some tent poles. A couple of uneaten energy bars that – a quick examination revealed – were only a year past their best-before dates. She offered one to Sydney, and he devoured it so ravenously that she felt her heart clench.

Tanice opened her GOOD bag, pulling out a plastic water bottle filled with clean water. She produced some antiseptic wipes, handing him a couple for his hands and face, and another energy bar.

She took a moment to study him. He still looked ill, but at least he was safe. For now.

'You rest here,' she said. 'I'll be back as soon as I can.'

Sydney's eyes widened in alarm. 'No, wait – where are you going?'

'I have to go and get you some medication. And some more food. And I have to explain to my parents where I've been. They'll be livid. I'll be as quick as I can, I promise.'

He looked away, uncertain.

'I'll come back,' Tanice said, leaning forward so he could see the sincerity in her face. But even as she spoke, she felt the weight of her words. Why should he trust her, after everything? 'I swear.'

Sydney nodded, though doubt lingered plainly in his expression. He turned away, curling onto the sleeping bag, too exhausted to protest further.

Tanice crept back towards the hatch, her stomach tightening with worry and determination. She would return, she told herself. She would prove that she was worthy of his trust.

MARCUS MINTON – 7 DAYS AFTER

People would call it the Night of Awe, the night when Hero was as close to the Earth as it would ever be. Awe in the old sense of the word: dread and wonder. Its blue light seemed to set pollen aglow, creating an otherworldly 'dream light' that bathed the street as Marcus walked, looking for his children.

He'd returned home like travel-weary Odysseus, only to find his sanctuary overrun by intruders. When he'd first entered our family home, Crossley's group had greeted him with knives and crossbows. Marcus had discovered Dennis lounging on his sofa. The man had remained smug despite the crude bandages across his side.

Marcus's chest burned with impotent fury at their invasion. He had wanted to fight, but he knew that he was outnumbered. By his count, there were five boys in the garden and two more in the kitchen, judging by the voices. At least another six inside the house. And all of them armed.

Crossley claimed that they had nowhere else to go. 'We were nearly overrun at the Asda. One of the boys – Tommy – he's fifteen – he got his ear cut clean off.'

'That's not my problem,' Marcus said. Except they could both see that now it was.

Crossley calmly explained how Marcus's home, with its stockpiles, fuel reserves and medical supplies, was the perfect refuge for them.

'I have to congratulate you,' he said. 'When you mentioned you were prepping, I didn't imagine how extensive it was.'

Marcus felt like a fool for accidentally breaking one of the cardinal rules: he'd failed to keep his prepping a secret. Crossley and his boys knew exactly what we had, because Marcus had been careless enough to tell them. He'd practically invited them to invade.

All he'd ever wanted was for his family to be safe. Our father had imagined us weathering the collapse of society as we might a stormy weekend. Locked in the house together, protected. He hadn't considered that his prepping would make us a target.

In the end, it was Crossley who'd suggested the pragmatic truce. Marcus and our family would stay out of sight, underground in the bunker, while Crossley and his gang would occupy the house above. They could share resources, fuel, food and supplies, but they would keep away from each other's territory. Marcus was humiliated. A defeated general, forced to sign away his stronghold while the enemy camped on his lawn and raided his stores. We had been relegated to the cellar, tolerated only because we were useful, not dangerous.

And the indignity might have been bearable – just barely – if he hadn't returned home with two of his daughters, only to discover that the other two were missing.

*

Marcus's heart leapt when he spotted Aaliyah on a swing in the park. He'd recognized her by the slope of her back, by her elegant fingers on the chains.

'How did you find me?' she asked.

'I walked around for a long time, calling your name and checking every swing set.' It was a place he'd discovered her retreating a couple of times when she was upset, even long after she'd outgrown playgrounds.

'Oh, Dad.' Aaliyah reached out to hug him. 'I'm so glad you're back. I feel like ... everything's fallen apart without you.'

'Your mum said ...' Where to begin?

'Carmen died and ...' Aaliyah started crying again. 'And she left me with this baby and ... you know I've never wanted children.'

'You say that now ...'

'No!' Aaliyah had been sure about few things in her life, but this had been one of them.

'You know, your mother thought that at first, but then—'

'She cried every day and then went to Guatemala.'

'Yes, well,' Marcus conceded.

'Motherhood doesn't end,' Aaliyah said.

'That's the good part, though,' Marcus said, sitting on the swing next to hers. Aaliyah looked at him quizzically. 'When you leave the hospital with a newborn baby, all you hear about is cot death and safe sleeping. It is scary, but one nurse told me that statistically all my children were likely to outlive me. Live into the next century, maybe. What thing have I loved that will be here even after I die? You lot. I'd hoped that you could be like the temple I built in the dust. That you're what will survive of me. None of the other stuff.'

He rocked absent-mindedly forwards and then back-wards, pushing his shoes against the Astroturf. The soles of his feet remembered how often he used to come here. The endless rotation of parks. The heavy all-consuming years, the ones he was warned by every parent on the bus to savour, were almost over now. He'd gone decades in his early adulthood never noticing a playground, and then there was a period of his life where every one in the vicinity was staked, in his mental map, with a fluorescent pin. He could almost see it now. Chantale on her hand-me-down scooter, which lit up on only one wheel. The tooth that Tanice had lost in the sandpit, the way she'd cried on the way home when they couldn't find it ('I had big plans for that tooth fairy money.'). Me on my knees with a magnifying glass, hunting for tardigrades in the brambles. Aaliyah hanging off the monkey bars. 'You're so brave!' he'd shouted. 'I'm not brave,' she'd replied, searching for the word in her starter vocabulary. 'I'm ... happy.' He'd smiled because, for years, that was all he'd wanted her to be.

Aaliyah said then, 'I want to be a good person.'

'You are,' Marcus said automatically. By 'good', he meant well-spoken and mostly law-abiding.

'I wasn't to Carmen,' Aaliyah whispered.

'You don't owe her the rest of your life,' he said, 'looking after this baby. You don't have to do it if you don't want to.' Her eyes filled up with tears.

As he reached a hand towards her, Marcus's senses alerted him to something moving in the shadows. He thought he saw a child near the bushes looking at him. When he turned fully, though, she was gone.

'Do you remember the Junior semis?' Aaliyah asked.

'No,' Marcus joked, 'remind me again?'

She meant the semi-finals of Junior Wimbledon. Marcus could still taste the excitement in the air that day, and his pride at her. He remembered how he'd taken Aaliyah out to the tennis court every weekend and had promised her a Coke float at Wimpy if she ever managed to beat him. The day she had, he'd watched her ice cream dissolve into jet bubbles and told her that most people had ordinary lives, lived and died within thirty miles of where they were born. Not her, though: Aaliyah was 'glory-bound'. That was the term he'd used. He'd dreamed of a gilded life for her, and that semi-final match was the first time he'd felt that dream becoming a reality.

'Do you remember that Carmen dropped out the night before the match?' Aaliyah asked.

Marcus had actually forgotten that detail, but after she jogged his memory, he said, 'Oh yeah, it was a real stroke of luck.' She'd been a formidably strong player. 'I mean,' he caught himself quickly, 'yeah – you could have beaten her, but ... the timing.'

Aaliyah grimaced.

'Failed drugs test, wasn't it?' The memory glimmered distantly.

'No,' Aaliyah said strongly, 'no evidence of drugs ... in the end.'

'But I heard ...'

'A rumour.' She paused for a moment. 'I spread it,' she said quietly.

'What?' Marcus turned to her, trying to hide his disgust. 'She was your friend! Why would you do that?'

Aaliyah squirmed, too ashamed to look at him. 'I don't know. The stress of everything got to me? I felt like I was poised on a knife edge. Either I won and I made it in life, or I failed, missed "glory" and slumped back into obscurity.'

'Aaliyah ...' Marcus's mind swam. Had he created this need in her?

'And Carmen ... I was certain she'd beat me. She won every match we played against each other for eighteen months leading up to that tournament. And I *hated* her for it. I wanted her life. Her looks, her money, her raw fucking talent. I felt as if I had to grind and grind for all the things I had, and ... I never felt bad about what I did ...'

Marcus thought he saw it again, out of the corner of his eye. A girl in a purple rainbow trench coat with matching jelly shoes. No older than Chantale. She seemed to be alone. He turned and stared at her, wondering if Aaliyah could see her, too, but she was deep in her own recollection, head in her hands.

'Until now, I wanted everything she had. Everything but her baby.'

'Look,' Marcus sighed, 'dwelling on it – on any of it – is only going to upset you. There's nothing you can do now. Carmen is gone.'

'But what do I owe her?' Aaliyah asked.

Marcus didn't know how to answer that.

He turned to the mysterious girl. 'Hey, do you have ... somewhere to be?' he asked, eyeing the street for her parents.

'Dad,' Aaliyah hissed, 'I'm talking.'

He was worried about this child, though. Where had she come from?

'Where are your parents?' he asked. She turned on her heels with a terrified look on her face, grabbed her scooter and ran. As she went, one of the wheels flashed red and green.

'Dad,' Aaliyah demanded, 'who are you ... ?'

'You didn't see her?' he asked. 'She looked a bit like ... '

Aaliyah's brow wrinkled in worry. 'It's been happening to me, too,' she said, 'the past couple of hours. Like déjà vu?'

'No.' Marcus rubbed fiercely at his eyes, trying to clear the shadows dancing across his vision. 'This seemed ... real.'

'I thought I saw Hugo earlier. I followed him up here, and then he vanished into the air. I guess it must have been someone who looked like him. I miss him so much. I'd hoped that when you came back with Tanice and Chantale, he might be with you.'

Marcus just shook his head. Everything felt hazy, wrong.

'Let's get back,' Aaliyah said. Jumping off the swing, she lost her balance for a moment. 'Oooh.' She caught herself. 'I feel a bit lightheaded.' A shimmering mist had begun drifting through the streets, catching Hero's light like dry ice. The two of them looked at each other.

'We need to get back to the bunker,' Marcus said.

They hurried back down Battersea Rise, the mist thickening with every step. People outside stood staring up at the sky or at their hands. A man on a bench was sobbing, another was crouching, terrified, in the shadow of a tree.

A woman rushed up the street, looking harrowed, shivering despite her fur-lined coat. Mascara ran like navy oil slicks down her pale cheeks.

Her eyes lit up when she saw Marcus. 'Oh, officer!' she cried with relief. She almost fell into him, grabbing his arms for support. He could tell, even before smelling the vomit in her locks, that she was drunk. 'That man is following me.' She pointed behind her. 'He's off his head.'

In the shadows, Marcus saw the outline of a tall man, his lanky frame hunched over, coming towards them with an unsteady gait, his eyes fixed on the woman. 'I thought he was going to hit me.'

As the stranger approached, Marcus lifted his other hand and said, 'All right, sir, I need you to step away from this young lady and calm down.'

The man looked up, his bloodshot eyes narrowing.

'Calm down?' he slurred. 'You have no fucking idea.'

Marcus bristled. This was just the start of another night for him. Before sunrise, he'd probably break up a fight outside a kebab shop or a night club. He'd be spat on by addicts, flashed by drunks or threatened by abusers with knives. He'd raid a trap-house, his boots would trample through broken glass, urine and vomit. He'd see the worst of humanity. This was only the beginning.

'She started shouting at me first,' the man claimed. 'I did nothing. I just wanted—'

Marcus could sense the aggression in his tone. 'You need to lower your voice and step back.' He prided himself on his ability to sense trouble before it started, the shift in energy when a man's stance turned predatory, when a shout dropped into a snarl. There was a rhythm to the chaos. Years of it had sanded down the edges of his empathy. Every interaction seemed to spin into the same tired loop. Same accusations. Same pleas. Same nights, same stench, same bruises on his ribs.

The man barked a bitter laugh. 'You already believe her, don't you?'

'You're shouting in a public place,' Marcus said, 'and causing a disturbance.'

The man stabbed the air over Marcus's shoulder.

'*She's* causing the fucking disturbance,' he said. 'What did I even do, huh? Walk too close? Exist?'

The woman let out a soft sob, her shoulders shaking. 'He came right up to me. Right up to my *face*.'

'Is that right?' the man said, his voice cracking with rage.

'I was frightened!' she shouted back.

'Frightened of what? Me breathing? Me looking at you? You don't even know me.'

Marcus took a deliberate step forward, voice low and forceful. 'Enough. Calm down and move on. You're clearly drunk—'

'What are you gonna do? Arrest me? Go on, then, arrest me!' He swung forwards. 'Big man with a badge, protecting the poor little white lady. Is that what you want?'

The man was close then, swaying on his heels, and Marcus caught the scent of something on his breath, like nail polish remover or something fruity like pear drops.

'Pear drops,' Marcus whispered then, heart hammering.

It snapped him out of the hallucination. Hadn't he learned, during his first aid training at Hendon Police College, that a sign that diabetics were experiencing low insulin – a life-threatening condition called diabetic ketoacidosis – was that their breath would smell of pear drops? They might seem drunk – slurred speech, confusion, aggression – he'd been warned, but the officers had been instructed to treat it as a medical emergency. 'Suspect overdose, suspect DKA, never assume drunkenness'. Except that he had.

'Dad!'

When Marcus turned, the woman behind him was Aaliyah.

'Something's wrong,' she gasped, clutching her throat. 'Do you feel it, too?'

When he turned again, he still saw the man, Ezekiel Walker. Marcus stepped back, his chest tight.

'Dad!' Aaliyah sounded panicked. 'Are you okay?'

Ezekiel Walker, single father, worked two jobs to pay the rent for his tiny flat. How often had Marcus pictured this moment and then pushed it away? But he was spiralling towards it now.

Suddenly, the street vanished and he was back in the patrol car, Ezekiel Walker behind him. Marcus had arrested Walker for drunk and disorderly conduct, and in the car on the way to the station, the man shouted, 'Hey, officer!' Marcus glanced into the rear-view mirror. The man was sweating, face drained of colour. 'Pull over ... I'm sick ...'

Marcus laughed bitterly, dismissive. 'Yeah, heard it before, mate.'

'Please, I need help. You got anything to eat? Anything? Sweets, a biscuit? Twix?'

Marcus rolled his eyes. 'You wish.'

And finally, Ezekiel said, 'Look, I'm diabetic ...'

'Sure,' Marcus scoffed. 'Pull the other one.'

By the time they put him in his cell, he was vomiting. 'Wasted,' Marcus told the other officers, and they rolled their eyes. Just another Friday night in London. A couple of hours later, as Marcus processed the paperwork, a constable on desk duty would call out, 'Minton, your guy – he's out cold.'

He'd never be able to justify the time it took to call the ambulance. They found Ezekiel in his cell, the blood around his mouth like coffee grounds. By the time he arrived in A&E, he had already slipped into a coma. Marcus heard about his death the next afternoon.

'Dad!'

Marcus snapped back violently to reality. He dropped to

his knees, pulling at the collar of his T-shirt, working hard
to breathe. The guilt he felt was almost a physical weight.
He had killed a man. Not with malice, not with force – but
with negligence. With apathy worn into him by years of
routine. Ezekiel had needed help, and Marcus had laughed.
There had been a moment – maybe two – when he could
have saved a life and he hadn't.

Aaliyah gripped our father's arm, her eyes brimming with
tears. 'We need to get you home – now!'

There was something sickening in the air. Marcus's vision
swam as he stumbled along the street, Aaliyah's hand
clutched tightly in his own. Dr Sengupta's warning echoed
in his head: an alien substance capable of crossing the
blood–brain barrier. He thought he could see it in the
moonlight, like motes of dust wafting on currents of hot
air. He could almost taste it, he thought, a sickly-sweet
flavour, like fruit on the edge of rotting. Marcus pulled up
his shirt to cover his mouth and instructed Aaliyah to do
the same. She pulled off her thin cardigan and bunched it
in front of her face.

The world took on an unfamiliar menace. The tarmac
beneath his feet began to grow viscous, rippling like the
surface of a pond. Shadows darted at the corners of his
eyes, and he could hear whispers of people he knew. His
brothers and father lurked in the shadows. Around them,
the street had descended into chaos. People stumbled aim-
lessly, some collapsing onto the ground, others clawing at
the air as if to fend off invisible assailants. A man raved
about flames consuming his hands, while a woman argued
with ghosts.

'Dad, keep going!' Aaliyah's voice was sharp, her fear

cutting through the fog in his mind. He tightened his grip, forcing his feet to move. Each step felt like wading through syrup, and his legs trembled with the effort.

Finally, the house came into view. Marcus staggered into the garden, gasping for air that offered no relief. His trembling fingers jabbed at the keypad, and after a moment, the airlock door hissed open. He shoved Aaliyah inside and followed, climbing shakily down the ladder.

The change was immediate. The air inside the bunker stifled the fire in his lungs. Marcus coughed violently, his vision swimming with spots of light. Through the haze, he could see Kim rushing forward, her face taut with worry.

'What happened?' she demanded, steadying him as he struggled to sit up. He dimly recognized that this was the first time she'd touched him since he'd returned home.

'The air ...' he croaked, his voice seeming to ring distantly in his ears. His head throbbed, and the room swayed. The walls were pulsing, expanding and contracting as if the bunker itself was breathing.

'On the way back, he just ... lost it,' Aaliyah said, her voice trembling. 'He kept talking about things that weren't there. Everyone is going crazy outside. I don't know why it's not affecting me ...' Then, suddenly, she burst into hysterical laughter, her eyes wide and unfocused.

'Do you think it's an asthma attack?' Kim asked, her voice tense.

'No,' Chantale said, her eyes narrowing as she rifled through her mental inventory of terrors and finally identified the right one. 'Poisonous gas.'

'It's something alien ...' Marcus managed to choke out. Kim frowned in confusion. 'Scientists told me.'

Chantale rummaged around in a storage box and pulled

out one of the gas masks Dad had urged us to wear for one of his drills, its butyl rubber straps dangling in her hand.

'From now on,' Marcus demanded, coughing still, 'no one is to go outside without one of those.'

'Okay, okay ... You lie down,' Kim said, with a tenderness Marcus wasn't used to. She helped him onto the lower bunk and dabbed at the sweat on his forehead.

When he blinked, she was nineteen again. She wore her hair in braids. Before she'd paid for Invisalign to fix it, she'd had a cute gap between her two front teeth, which Tanice and Chantale had inherited. Before university had rounded it out, she'd pronounced some words with a hard Nigerian emphasis. He'd loved how determined she was, how ambitious and clever. He'd been dazzled by her beauty and impeccable style. He'd wanted to marry her as soon as he saw her. He'd wanted this life.

'I could fall in love with you all over again,' Marcus murmured.

Kim's lip curled on one side. She said, 'Only make that mistake once.'

BRIAR MINTON – 7 DAYS AFTER

The last time we sang 'No One Is Alone' was for the dress rehearsal of *Into the Woods*. It's the penultimate song, the one that always brings tears to my eyes. Little Red discovers that the giantess has killed her grandmother, and Jack finds that his mother has died. The Baker loses his wife and must raise his child alone, though he is fearful that he doesn't know how to be a father.

When practising for the school's production, back in the 'old normal', our musical director had said, 'Your childhood ends when you have a child or when you lose your parents.'

I fought back the tears now, listening to everyone's voices in the gloaming. It had only been a day since Soo-Jin had died. She'd helped us build a lot of the set, turning a broken wardrobe into Rapunzel's tower, tearing curtains and table-cloths into capes and gowns. We'd all agreed to dedicate the show to her.

'Do you think Jack was the first person to discover that there are giants in the sky?' Martha asked, as we tidied up. She was playing Little Red. Her interpretation struck the perfect balance between naïve and annoying. She played it like a girl who had a kind of optimism that time would probably rub away.

'Maybe not?' I offered. 'It's likely the Witch knew. Or the Witch's mother. That's why she's so angry when she loses the beans.'

Axel said, 'I always think of it like ... the first time you fall in love. It's like a revelation. It feels like the first time anyone has *ever* been in love.'

'Except that Jack upset the whole order of the universe,' I reminded him. 'Giants aren't meant to walk among us.'

'Yeah,' said Laurie, a cardboard crown on his head, 'they kill half the cast.'

I've seen pictures of the giant feet that hung off the facade of the Martin Beck Theatre during the 1987 run of *Into the Woods* – one of the earliest. I would have loved to have seen it. Not least because I often wonder how big Sondheim imagined the giants were. In the songs, their footprints are forty feet, about the size of a double-decker bus. According to the internet, the length of a foot is fifteen per cent of a person's height, which, I calculated long ago, would make Sondheim's giants around two hundred and sixty-seven feet tall. Slightly shorter than the Statue of Liberty. A terrifying prospect.

'All right, everyone, listen up,' Axel said after the last rehearsal. 'Tomorrow is it. Our moment. Tomorrow, we bring *Into the Woods* to life.'

'The woods are dangerous,' I told them, 'but they are also a place of discovery. Transformation.' I thought of Rapunzel's prince escaping with blood dripping from his eyes. 'No one emerges from the woods the same. Neither can we.'

As we dispersed for dinner, Axel said to me, 'It's going to be good,' his voice a mixture of hope and relief.

I squeezed his shoulder and said, 'Can you imagine telling past us,' meaning the sickly kids on the Eating Disorders Ward, 'that we'd do this? Put on a play at the end of the world?' I remembered the first song I'd shared with him in the bathroom stall.

He said, 'I think I could have endured anything if you'd told me I'd make it here.'

If Axel had lived, he'd be famous. Maybe some leaked audition tape would have gone viral, and you could have seen it. When he sang 'Giants in the Sky', it was as if he really had seen them, as if he'd really pulled back the fabric of everything and beheld something spectacular and dreadful.

I've told the story of that night only once. Though I've heard rumours. In some retellings, there was a pentagram on the floor, ceremonial dresses and chanting. In some, Beth was naked, pinned down, and Freya presided above her like a priestess.

In fact, Freya wasn't there at all. That night, over dinner, she'd implored Beth not to go through with it, had said that the Tau would not come when forced.

'The path to the divine is not paved with recklessness, but with faith, patience and reverence for the gift of life.' A couple of the other Tauans had dissented as well, but Beth was firm in her resolve.

She repeated Cato's words. 'Revelation comes at a cost.'

After our final rehearsal, I had gone to bed early, and woke when Martha shook me, an urgent thrill in her voice.

'It's time.'

She led me down to the dining room, where the Group was gathered.

'These aren't the same conditions as last time,' Laurie was arguing. 'What if it doesn't work?'

It had been Boxing Day when Beth had died before. Laurie told us that he could still remember the paper Christmas cracker crown she had been wearing, the purple of her lips.

'Should we bring in a Christmas tree?' Cato asked derisively. 'Let a pot of mulled wine go to waste on the stove?'

'I'm just saying,' Laurie hissed. He agreed with Freya that none of this should be happening, but of course he had to be here. He clutched the green pouch that contained her EpiPen the way a bishop might clutch a Bible.

Beth sat in the centre of the room with the plate of pine nuts – foraged by Charlie – in front of her.

Martha was close by, and so were Cato and Charlie. There were two others, Isaac and another Tauan whose name I can't remember. A bald woman with tattoos.

And me. I keep wondering why I went. I like to think it's because I was worried about Beth. But maybe it's also because my curiosity got the better of me. I wanted to witness a visitation from the Tau.

'Are you ready?' Martha asked. Beth nodded. I thought of Socrates holding the chalice of hemlock to his mouth.

'You don't have to do this,' Laurie reminded her a final time. He sounded desperate.

But Beth just smiled at him.

'I love you, Laurie.' She took a deep breath, grabbed a handful of pine nuts and chewed vigorously.

In the quiet that followed, Cato said, 'What if They're not kind? The Tau. Take the long view of history, and isn't tyranny the norm?'

As he spoke, I watched a faint flush creep up Beth's neck. She pulled at her collar as if she was too hot.

'What does it take to span a galaxy? What forces must you bend to your will?'

Beth's skin was glistening with sweat, her lips looked wasp-stung and her eyelids grew heavy and taut. I had to look away.

'Maybe on M31, it's the same as here. Maybe it's the same in a thousand years and in higher dimensions. Red in tooth and claw.'

Even as I fixed my eyes on the radiating oriental motif on the rug beneath my feet, I could hear Beth straining to breathe, her wheezing growing louder.

'Okay.' Laurie's voice was firm. 'That's enough now.' He unzipped the EpiPen case.

'No!' Martha hissed at him. I pushed my back against the door. It was like a witch's spell, how quickly Beth's beautiful face erupted in hive-like welts.

Digit, who had followed me downstairs, started whining.

'She said she'd give the signal when it was time,' Martha told him.

The muscles in Beth's neck strained for air.

'She can't give any signal, look at her!' Laurie cried. 'It's time.' He moved towards Beth with the EpiPen, but Martha lunged reflexively to block him. It slipped from his hand, and, with a shout of fury, Laurie pushed Martha at the wall. She was ready for his attack, though, and only lost her balance slightly, stumbling backwards.

In the dim light, we only heard it: the crack of plastic, the pen under her heel, its spring mechanism pinging apart, its lifesaving contents a wet slick on her sandal.

Digit was barking furiously now.

Laurie shouted in horror, his eyes going immediately to

Beth, who was terrifying to see, clawing at the collar of her shirt as if it was a noose. Her lips had turned blue.

'I'm sorry!' Martha gasped.

'She has another, right?' Isaac urged. It jogged a memory in Laurie, who was on the edge of despair, tears glistening in his eyes.

'Right, yeah. She ...' He gasped, holding his chest, almost as pale as his sister.

'Someone shut that dog up!' Cato grunted.

I pulled Digit by the harness and tried to calm her by stroking her.

Laurie was shaking himself, trying to remember. 'It's somewhere safe. Where she keeps things safe.'

Martha was panicking, too. 'Laurie, where is that?!'

'Her bedroom?' he guessed.

'Where?'

He thought for a moment, his eyes swivelling in horror. Then, 'Her dresser, her music box! I think ...'

I remembered the altar I'd seen on it. I could tell that Laurie didn't want to leave her, and I didn't want to sit there and watch someone die.

'I'll get it,' I offered.

I ran through the house in a blur, my heart pounding. I felt sick, responsible; why hadn't I stopped it? I'd done nothing to save Soo-Jin, though I could have tried to, and now, if Beth died, I would never forgive myself.

Up the rickety stairs, the stumble of my feet disturbed the birds nesting in the roof. Beth's room was dark. I had to strain to see using the faint glow of Hero's light from the window. Soo-Jin's telescope was still there, pointed at the window. Dimly, I wondered how many of us were going to die here?

Suddenly, the Tau seemed impossibly distant to me. Dispassionate and fickle. What if our efforts to call Them were for nothing?

Beth's music box had a little spring-loaded ballet dancer that chimed when I unsettled it. There was a shallow shelf of brushed velvet inside, but when I shook it, it popped out and revealed the treasures underneath. Wads of money fastened with brightly coloured hairbands. A necklace of dusty amber beads, a couple of rings. A velvet coin pouch, the string of which my finger caught on as I rummaged. I wondered if it could contain the spare EpiPen.

Pulling it out, I loosened the tie and scattered its contents onto the dresser.

For a second, I thought I was dreaming, as they spilled out like a string of loose pearls. I squinted in the darkness, and then my heart stopped. Teeth. A bag of teeth.

Whose? My immediate thought was of Ruby, of the way she had smiled at me the morning she'd saved me from that oncoming car. With her weight on my chest, I had seen her fillings, her little canines, narrow as fangs.

The moonlight glittered off the patches of silver amalgam in the molars. And there ... two little canines, their roots like icebergs dusted in flesh. They looked as if they had been pulled out of a mouth with force.

I stepped back, shaking all over, and vomited on the carpet.

Over the sound of blood crashing in my ears, I heard the thunder of feet. The door flew open, and I saw Laurie. 'What the fuck are you doing?' he barked at me, more furious than I'd ever seen him.

I was too overcome to speak. Laurie pushed past me and grabbed the EpiPen from the bottom of the box, then stormed out again. I stumbled after him, down the stairs and into the hall.

By the time I reached the dining room, I could already hear Beth gasping for air. Laurie was sobbing.

I lingered by the door and watched them, as Digit came and cowered behind my legs.

'Never! Never!' Laurie shouted, 'Never do that to me again!' Beth's face was still swollen. 'I would die if you died.' He cradled her in his arms as if unaware that he had an audience. 'I mean it.' And then he kissed her on the lips. Deeply, passionately. Isaac started in alarm, but Cato only smirked as if a long-held suspicion of his had been confirmed. I turned away.

'What did you see?' Martha asked finally, offering Beth a glass of water. Beth was still shivering too much to hold it. 'Did you hear from the Tau?'

Beth nodded.

With Laurie's help, she took a gentle sip of water.

'Hero,' Beth strained to say through her swollen throat, 'is a beacon. Hero has a message.'

In some of my dreams, I thought I had seen it. Thousands of Heros launched in a spiral formation from a planet, sent like spores to skim the universe.

'What is it?' Martha asked eagerly.

'The Tau . . .' Beth swallowed, then winced. 'The Tau are in danger. Their sun is dying. They need us to save Them.'

PART THREE

Fallout

BRIAR MINTON – 7 DAYS AFTER

I tried to leave that night. The Group suddenly seemed more dangerous to me than anything I might encounter in the forest. My mind kept returning to the cracked remains of the EpiPen on the carpet, to Beth's bulging eyes and what I'd discovered in her music box. I'd have to run. As soon as Beth returned to her room, her heel would sink into a puddle of vomit on her floor, and she'd see Ruby's teeth like scattered beads on her dresser. They would know it was me.

After Beth delivered her message from the Tau, I rushed back to my room, my heart pounding her name: *Ruby, Ruby*. They'd killed her, probably. Killed her here. Her body could be buried somewhere out in the woods near Soo-Jin's. Or sunk in the river. And now, if it was ever found, it wouldn't be identifiable by dental records. The coldness of the act astonished me.

Why did they do it? I kept wondering. Because their gods were hungry and demanded blood? Because she'd angered them in some way? Soo-Jin had suggested that Ruby had uncovered some evidence about Freya, that she was going to write something damning about the Group. Was it for protection, then? Or spite?

Before Martha returned to our room, I started packing up my things – what few of them there were. Dirty clothes, some camping supplies, though most of them had been repurposed by the Group. My tent was pitched outside, serving as the Witch's house for the play. Looking around I discovered, with despair, that my boots had disappeared. I squeezed my feet into a flimsy pair of canvas shoes that Beth had offered me, two sizes too small. After abandoning my saxophone case, I managed to shove most of the body of the instrument into my big backpack, though the brass neck stuck out and I would be peeling cotton from under its keys for days if I made it home unscathed.

Quietly, I zipped up my hoodie and crept over to the door, careful to avoid the floorboards I knew creaked. I picked Digit up in my arms and bundled her out with me. Then into the hall, where I could still hear the raised voices of Cato, Laurie and the others in the dining room, and onto the patio, where a thin band of light illuminated the great house.

How awed I'd been by Midacre when I first beheld it. How haunted it seemed to me now.

'Mischief!' I tried not to start. Someone emerged behind me from the house. I turned around.

Axel wore a bright yellow Pikachu onesie and my pink Dr. Martens.

'Those belong to me,' I hissed. He looked down as if he'd only just noticed them on his feet.

'But they look so good on me,' he said, twirling. 'I've been thinking that our feet must be the same size for a reason. So that I could have these.'

Was it worth fighting over? My eyes darted to the

double-storeyed window of the dining room where the
Group were gathered. I hoped they couldn't hear us. I
turned and began to head towards the river.

'Where are you going?' Axel asked.

'Home,' I said.

'Briar.' His tone suddenly changed, all seriousness returning
to his voice. He rushed ahead to block my path. 'You can't.'

I stared at him. Even in the gloom, his cheekbones and
high, translucent forehead seemed to reflect what little light
there was. He was the palest person I've ever known.

'We have a play to do,' he said. After that evening's
events, the play had fallen so far down in my concerns.

'There isn't going to be a play,' I said.

'What? Why?'

'Did Beth kill Ruby?'

Axel froze. His expression told me all I needed to know.
I pushed past him and started walking away. He followed.

'It wasn't what you think,' he added hastily.

'Why?' I stopped and faced him again.

'It was an accident,' Axel said.

'How did it happen?' But he went quiet and just slowly
shook his head. He didn't want to relive it. 'Did *you*—?' I
ventured.

'No!' He frowned. 'Ruby wasn't like you – she was a liar.'

'What?'

'Turned out she'd joined us to write some kind of hit piece
about Freya. For her zine. All lies, of course ...'

'What were the lies?'

'She claimed that while Freya was missing, those years
she spent with the Tau, she was actually a patient at High
Tower.' I blinked at him.

'Is that true?' I wondered what ward she would have been

on. How do you help a girl who felt compelled to gouge out her own eyes?

'I don't . . .' Axel fumbled for the right words. 'It doesn't matter, anyway. What matters is that the things Freya says and everything that happened to us were real. Ruby was spreading rumours, trying to convince people to leave the Group. She wasn't like you. She hadn't seen the Tau for herself, and she hadn't received a revelation.' His eyes flickered back over his shoulder. I should have run then, but I wanted to hear what he had to say. 'It was Beth's idea to try to . . . "provoke" one in her.'

'How?' My fingers turned cold.

Axel shook his head.

'But it didn't work,' I concluded.

He couldn't look at me.

'Maybe she . . . wasn't worthy of Them.' Those sounded like Freya's words. 'But you are! Briar, the Tau—'

'The Tau are gone.' I was surprised that tears came to my eyes as I said it. Just as suddenly, all my belief crumbled. Axel looked horrified. He shook his head adamantly.

'I've seen Them.' He gestured around. 'All of us have. *You* have.'

I wasn't so sure anymore. 'Maybe I saw . . . what I wanted to see.'

Axel gestured to Hero, hanging in the sky above us. 'Then what is *that*?'

'Beth said that Hero is a beacon. That they sent it to Earth to ask us to help them. But at the rate it's travelled, they would have sent it millions of years ago.' It seemed obvious to me now.

'Maybe They did. They're outside of time.'

'Or maybe they're gone. Maybe they've been gone for

longer than we've known there was anything out there. Maybe we've been alone all this time.'

Axel was enraged. 'You shut up!' he shouted furiously. 'I've felt Them. They're out there, I know They are.'

I made a move to leave, but he blocked me again. 'Don't go. Please.' I felt sorry for him then. He seemed as small as he had when I'd first met him in High Tower, a frail boy singing alone.

'Come with me?' I offered. He recoiled.

'To where?'

'My house. My mum and dad, my sisters . . .' It suddenly seemed like the safest place in the world.

'There's nothing for me out there. Or you. How will you even get back?' He was right, I had no map or guide. The usual geographical markers I might have used to signpost me had been torn apart.

'I don't know,' I admitted.

'You'll probably be killed out there.' He said it with a mean relish, as if it would be what I deserved. It hurt to see but only reminded me of my purpose.

I called for Digit, who came bounding over to me, tail wagging and oblivious, and started walking away.

'They won't let you go!' Axel shouted after me. 'If they know you know . . .'

I kept walking.

Then, as I reached the treeline, he stepped back towards the patio, where the acoustics were better, and screamed at the top of his lungs:

'Mischief! Mischief!'

The sound made me panic. I started to run.

My breath burned in my throat as I pushed myself forward. In my flimsy, too-tight shoes, I could feel every stone and root in the damp earth and had to take extra care not to slip. I had maybe only a minute's head start before the Group began searching the woods for me. I didn't want to die like Soo-Jin in the shade of the pines.

Somewhere ahead, Digit moved like a shadow, her black coat catching the occasional dagger of light. Her ears flapped wildly as she darted through the undergrowth. Was she frightened, too? Could she sense that we were in danger?

The clouds overhead were thick, threatening rain, and the night felt swollen with it. Behind me, faintly, voices rang out – sharp, excited and getting closer. I risked a glance over my shoulder, catching the faint glow of torches flickering between the gnarly oaks. I didn't slow.

A flicker of movement to my left snapped my head around. Figures emerged from the trees: Cato with the bow and arrow he used for hunting, I guessed Isaac, maybe Laurie? Their torches cast twisted light on the forest floor. I felt like a roe deer in the sights of hunters. I bolted, turning right, listening eagerly for the sound of the river. Digit barked, startled, then veered sharply to follow. The forest closed in again as we ran, branches whipping against my arms and snagging my clothes.

I heard a hiss, a cut through the air like a wasp. An arrow buried itself into the tree beside me with a dull thud. I froze for half a second, then turned my head slowly, dread curling in my stomach. Through the trees, I saw Cato, his long silhouette lit faintly by the torchlight behind him. He was drawing another arrow from the quiver strapped to his back, his movements deliberate, his face calm.

I threw myself sideways just as the next arrow zipped past my shoulder. The sound was sharp and terrifyingly close. I hit the ground hard, and my hands sank into the damp earth.

Digit barked again, frantic, before vanishing into the undergrowth. I struggled to scramble to my feet, my knees stinging. I took off. My feet screamed in protest, but I pushed them harder, zigzagging through the trees to make myself a more difficult target. An arrow embedded itself in my backpack, the bundled clothes and equipment acting as a shield. Another arrow shot past, missing me by inches. I didn't dare look back. Cato was skilled – I had seen the bloodied bodies of pheasants and rabbits he'd presented us for dinner. He wouldn't miss forever.

Ahead, the forest began to thin again. Behind soaring pine and conifer trees, the river growled. I guessed that I was close to the bridge by then, but the ground was treacherous, with roots jutting like jagged teeth from the wet loam. I felt a spark of elation when I saw Hero's light bouncing off the water ahead, but at the same moment an arrow pierced my left calf. The pain was so sharp and sudden that it sent me sprawling to the ground. I cried out, clutching at the wound. My fingers came away slick with blood. Gritting my teeth, I forced myself upright, stumbling forward with a limp. I tripped once, catching myself against a tree, my palms scraping the bark.

I was going to die if I didn't get to the river. I started running again, my chest burning, forcing the impact of every bound onto my right leg. I reached the edge of the trees and stopped short. The bridge loomed ahead, swaying slightly in the wind, the wood slick with moss and the ropes frayed. It was my only escape.

Close behind, Cato shouted something – I couldn't hear what over the rush of the river – and I turned to see him moving closer, his bow raised. He hadn't spotted me. If I stepped out onto the bridge, I would make myself a clear target.

Slinking back, I ducked behind some bushes. Pain seared through my calf as I did, my nerves shrieking, but I bit my cheek to stop myself from crying out. I hid among the leaves, each breath ragged. I felt clumsy and overburdened with my backpack, but when I debated abandoning it to run, I remembered the arrow sunk deep into it. It offered me some protection, at least.

A couple of metres away, Cato slowed and lowered his weapon. He scanned the river and the bridge, eyes narrowing as he searched for me. Deeper in the forest behind us, Digit barked again, a sharp, panicked sound. Cato's head whipped around to identify the noise, and he raised his bow again, drawing back the string. My heart twisted. I couldn't lose Digit! Horror gripped me as I imagined the arrow skewering her soft little body.

It was then that I remembered the fireworks Beth had given me – 'In case you get lost,' she'd said. I'd stored them in the side pocket of my rucksack.

Now I fumbled for the lighter I kept in my pocket, my hands trembling as its wheel bit into my thumb. The flame flared to life, momentarily blinding me. I shoved it against the fuse of the first firework and hurled it at Cato.

It exploded in a burst of red and gold, lighting up the forest. I heard Digit yelp in surprise and Cato curse loudly, the flash illuminating his sharp-featured face and the bow in his hands. I lit another and aimed for his head. The second firework exploded with a deafening crack, sparks scattering across the ground. Cato roared and stumbled backwards. I could see blood on his face. I seized my chance, darting towards the river as quickly as I dared, though my injured leg throbbed relentlessly and my vision blurred from the pain.

I sprinted for the bridge, my canvas shoes slipping on the wet wood as I crossed. The river churned beneath me, black and merciless, the sound almost drowning the shouts from Isaac and Laurie, Freya and Axel, who were gathering by the bank. The bridge rocked violently, but I didn't dare slow down. I could hear Cato shouting, his voice razor-edged with fury.

As I reached the far riverbank, I threw myself forward, landing hard in the mud. Pain flared through me as another arrow struck me, this time slicing through my shoulder.

I cried out. Stars exploded in my vision. The pain felt catastrophic. I scrambled behind a nearby tree, my breaths sharp and uneven as I clutched at the wound, warm blood seeping between my fingers.

'There's nothing out there,' Cato called after me from the other side of the bridge. His voice was getting closer. 'Without the light of our gods, humanity will spiral into disaster. It's already happening. We can save you from it. We chosen few. The Tau, when They come, will save us from it.'

'The Tau aren't coming!' I yelled back.

'We've seen Them,' Freya said. 'Felt Their healing power.'

I never would completely understand everything I'd seen, but the memory of it seemed to me then as hollow as anything else I had ever placed my hopes in. I stepped out from behind the tree, stared into Cato's cold eyes as he made his way slowly across the bridge.

I said, 'You get the gods you deserve.'

The final firework was in my hands. I lit it and hurled it at the bridge. It exploded mid-air, the sparks raining down onto the wooden planks, onto Cato, who stumbled backwards, the bow falling from his hands as he shielded his face.

Now was my chance to flee, but I couldn't leave yet, not without my dog. 'Digit!' I roared.

My heart hammered as I scanned the woods on the other side, desperate for a sign of her. For a horrifying moment, it stopped as I saw her leap into the river, her small body braving the churning current. The water threatened to sweep her away. 'No! Digit!' I cried, stumbling towards the riverbank, feeling helpless. I watched as she paddled furiously with her ears pinned back and her eyes fixed on me. Then she made it, her paws scrabbling at the muddy bank until she pulled herself out, dripping and shaking. Relief coursed through me, but there was no time to rest. I reached for her, shouting, 'Come on!' before we turned and ran, the roar of the river and the Group's shouts fading behind us.

TANICE MINTON – 7 DAYS AFTER

Tanice waited for Aaliyah to fall asleep before she tried to sneak away.

For the rest of that day, her every other thought had been of Sydney, alone and sick in the attic. When she'd climbed back down into the garden, our parents had been furious at her for running away. Marcus had shouted, and Kim had wept, both overwhelmed by the thought of losing another daughter so soon after I'd disappeared. Their hysteria had frightened Tanice, reminding her of the fragile safety of this new reality.

She had burst into tears and explained everything that had happened in the wine cellar to our mother. She confessed that the darkness, the damp and the claustrophobic walls reminded her too much of being buried alive in there. Kim, her face tight with anguish, reluctantly convinced Marcus to let Tanice sleep in the small toolshed at the garden's edge. But only if someone stayed with her.

The toolshed itself was nothing like the sturdy, well-stocked bunker. It was small and cramped, with a roof of corrugated metal that rattled faintly in the breeze. Rusting

spades and dented watering cans lined its splintered wooden
walls next to crooked shelves stacked with long-expired
pots of paint and fertilizer. A single grimy window let in
weak moonlight, and a dusty smell of compost lingered in
the air. Yet, even in discomfort, Tanice preferred this to
the suffocating weight of earth above the bunker's ceiling.
At least here she could glimpse the sky and hear the owls
hooting.

That night, Tanice lay awake for hours, staring through
the smudged visor of her mask at the whey-faced moon,
anxiously wondering if Sydney had given up waiting for her.
Her stomach churned at the thought of him alone, fighting
for breath in the poisoned air.

Finally, around midnight, she sensed her chance when she
heard Aaliyah's breathing – muffled by her respirator – grow
steady and even. Getting to her feet and grabbing her bag
of stolen supplies, Tanice reached for the toolshed door, her
heart hammering.

At the hinge's faint creak, Aaliyah jolted awake, her voice
sleepy but edged with panic. 'Tanice,' she gasped, 'where're
you going?' In the dark, Tanice could only see the whites
of her sister's eyes behind her visor. 'The air – remember?'

'It's fine,' Tanice whispered. 'I'm just going to get something from the bunker.'

Aaliyah propped herself up weakly, still groggy from the
lingering effects of whatever she'd inhaled.

'You're wearing your mask?' she asked anxiously.

'Yes,' Tanice reassured her, tugging on its rubber straps.
'I'll be safe.'

Aaliyah's head sank back onto her sleeping bag, eyes
fluttering closed again. 'Just ... check on Mum and Hero,
please?' she whispered softly.

'I will,' Tanice said, grateful that our sister was too dazed to argue further.

Outside, Tanice sprinted up the garden path, her steps muffled by sprouting weeds. Hero hung ominously in the sky, a spectral presence, almost twice the size of the moon by then and so bright that a couple of confused birds were still singing – no doubt mistaking the light for dawn. Tanice slowed for a moment and beheld its face with a shiver. It was so close now that she could see the symmetrical craters etched across it.

She approached the house carefully, ducking out of eyeline to avoid being spotted. Brief glimpses through the windows made her worried, though. One boy knelt on the kitchen floor, vomiting violently. Another stood, arms flailing, screaming at shadows only he could see. In the dining room, two of the men were in the middle of a panicked brawl, clawing at each other. Tanice recoiled, heart pounding, hoping that Sydney wasn't in as bad a shape as they were.

Hurrying to the side of the house, she gripped the familiar wooden trellis tightly and climbed up, her fingers finding the divots and grooves she'd long ago memorized. She moved swiftly from the trellis to the drainpipe, then stepped carefully onto the narrow brick ledge beneath her bedroom window. She tugged at the window frame – shut tight now – and nearly lost her grip when it resisted. With a surge of desperate strength, she finally shoved it open and scrambled inside.

A shadow lunged at her immediately. Tanice gasped, frozen, as a boy with a mohawk grabbed her shoulders. He stared at her with wide, feverish eyes.

'Emily?' he whispered hoarsely, voice choked with grief. 'It's you, isn't it?'

'No – I'm—' Tanice stammered, then stopped, seeing tears spill down his cheeks.

'I'm sorry,' Mohawk sobbed. 'It was my fault. I should have believed you the first time!'

Tanice stared at him, her heart thudding, worried that this was some kind of trick. But the boy just sank to his knees, shaking with sobs, beside himself.

'Hey ...' Despite her better judgement, Tanice leaned down and touched his shoulder. His skin was clammy, and he was shivering. When he looked up at her, she saw that his pupils were impossibly wide. 'I forgive you,' she told him.

Relief flooded his face. Tanice didn't wait another second – as soon as he let go of her, she bolted out into the hall and scrambled for the attic ladder.

Once her vision adjusted to the dark, she discovered Sydney curled on the floor, his eyes closed, and for an awful moment she feared that she was too late. That he'd died up here in the night, unwittingly poisoned by an alien toxin.

Rushing to his side, Tanice pushed her hand against his stained T-shirt and discovered that his heart was beating, fast and shallow.

At her touch, his eyes fluttered open. 'Dad?' he murmured softly. 'I thought – I thought you were gone.'

Tanice's chest tightened at that. Tears blurred her vision. 'It's me, Sydney. It's Tanice.'

He blinked slowly. ''m sorry ...' he slurred.

'For what?' Tanice asked.

'Skipped college,' Sydney replied. 'You said, "You'll never make anything of yourself" and I was like, "What, like you?"' Sydney had once alluded to the final argument he'd had with his father on the night the man had died, but he'd never told Tanice the details.

She swallowed hard, unable to speak. She didn't feel as if she could lie to him the way she had to the boy downstairs. Instead, she said what she had wanted to say the first time she ever saw him, on the news, a desolate pallbearer at his father's funeral.

'I'm so sorry.' Some guilt she hadn't been able to shake.

Sydney's eyes closed again, and Tanice came to her senses.

'Hey,' she hissed, 'wake up,' as she rifled through the rucksack she had brought with her. She quickly unpacked her bag, pressing water, painkillers and electrolyte tablets into his shaking hands. She coaxed him into drinking, then she guided the spare gas mask over his face and instructed him to breathe deeply.

Sydney was shivering. Tanice looked around for the sleeping bag to wrap around him. 'Don't leave?' he asked plaintively.

Her eyes flitted to the little attic window. She needed to get back before our parents or Aaliyah realized that she was gone. But Sydney reached for her and wrapped his arms around her.

'Please, don't leave?' he asked again. Tanice hesitated but then relented, curling beside him.

His touch was familiar to her. Reminded her of the initial thrill of their secret meetings. Their playful DMs that had turned into whispers behind fences and in the sodium halo of the street lamps. She remembered the night that they'd leapt over the fence of a private park and scared the ducks before lying back on the damp grass to stargaze. Taking the train across town to an art-house cinema – he'd convinced her to watch a black-and-white film with no dialogue, and they'd made out through the entire thing. They'd first said 'I love you' in a Tesco car park, their breath clouding in the cold. Those stolen moments in their short shared history were even more dear to her now that they seemed to be slipping away.

Tanice felt out of her depth. Sydney was clearly too sick to climb down the trellis, but what if he died up here in the attic? The image of Paris's body rotting in the wine cellar shot a cold jolt of adrenaline through her. She tried to shake it away.

As the night wore on, Sydney seemed to improve, though. His breathing grew deeper and his pulse less shallow. By the time the sky started to turn pink, he wasn't shivering anymore.

Tanice thought she didn't sleep at all, but she must have. Because suddenly the mechanical click of a shutter woke her. She blinked and realized that the sky outside was light.

Sydney was standing over her with his camera.

'What—?' She squeezed her finger under her mask to rub her eyes and then panicked. Was it morning? Had her parents woken? 'What are you doing?'

'There's something in the air,' Sydney said, his voice muffled by his respirator. 'I wanted to see what it'll look like when I develop these.'

Tanice was heartened to hear how much better he sounded. He smiled sadly at her, then lowered his head, looking at the camera in his hands.

'I have to go home,' he said weakly.

'The air outside is poisoned,' Tanice told him. 'People are acting strangely. It's not safe.' Even as she said it, though, she felt a twinge of guilt, knowing it'd be less stressful if he left, if she didn't have to worry about him anymore.

Sydney's brow wrinkled as he glanced out of the window. She could tell that he was frightened, too.

'I have a mask now, though, thanks to you. What else do I do, stay here?'

Tanice winced. Some part of her was becoming distantly certain that if he left, they'd never see each other again.

'How about I check it's safe, and then you go?' she suggested. 'And ...' She offered him some of the food she had brought up with her. Crisps and a KitKat, canned beans and sausages. He lifted his mask and ate ecstatically with the spork she'd packed. 'You were pretty sick yesterday,' she told him. 'At least if you stay a couple more hours, you can recover your strength some more, and I won't have to worry that you'll collapse on the way home.'

Sydney nodded reluctantly. 'Just a couple more hours,' he said, 'until I feel better. Then I'm going.'

'Sure,' Tanice agreed. Thinking of our parents, she said goodbye to him and headed for the hatch.

When she reached it, though, Sydney said, 'Hey, Nicey.' She looked back at his sunken eyes. Saw the pain in them. 'Did you ever really ...' He winced and looked away. 'Did you ever really care about me?'

'Syd, of course I did. *Do.*' She bit her lip. He looked unconvinced. 'The first time I saw you, I thought I could love you,' she continued.

'When?'

'In the videos I saw of the funeral. In your black suit, with your hair up. How brave you looked, but also how alone.'

He didn't answer for a moment. 'Was that love, though? Or was it just pity? Or worse, some kind of guilt?'

Tanice swallowed, a hard knot in her throat.

'What's the difference?'

BRIAR MINTON – 7 DAYS AFTER

For a short while, panic and adrenaline fuelled me. Digit and I were able to make it a mile or two before the pain really set in. I managed to limp on another half a mile before wild starbursts of it began shafting through my nerves at every step.

When I stumbled to the ground – sick with agony – I knew I wouldn't be able to get up again.

The second arrow had entered at an angle and lodged under my right shoulder blade. Almost any movement of my arm sent pain radiating down my back and to my elbow. I had to lie down on my front, pine needles pricking at my cheek.

With some effort, I rolled onto my side to examine my leg. The sight of the arrow buried deep into my muscles made me dizzy, the way I had felt when Tanice had dislocated her shoulder falling off the trampoline. It was the nauseating sight of something where it shouldn't be, her bone jutting out.

I did what you're not supposed to do: I gripped the arrow's carbon fibre shaft with both hands and, gritting my teeth, pulled it out. I howled so loudly then that birds in the canopy above erupted into the sky in a sudden explosion of feathers and leaves.

Removing the arrow made a jet of blood gurgle from the wound. It pulsed down to my ankles and soaked my shoes. I felt my hands grow cold and start to shake. A discordant trill began in my ears. Digit growled low in her throat, her body tense beside me, but as I lay trembling on the forest floor, I could do nothing to try to calm her. I don't think I've ever cried as much as I did then. From pain and terror, from blood loss and despair.

When I opened my eyes again, the forest was dark and cold. I woke at the sound of a girl sobbing, her breath misting on the air, red moonlight spearing the canopy above and illuminating her face. Ruby.

She was shivering, falling to her knees on the ground, where frosted leaves and iced twigs snapped under her weight. She was wearing the green hoodie she had worn in that Polaroid. She turned in terror as she heard a group approach behind her. Beth, Charlie, Cato, Isaac and a couple of others. It was difficult to see their faces in the shadows.

'Please!' Ruby shouted desperately.

'You know,' said Cato. He was standing back, a dark silhouette in the trees, though I could see his quiver strapped to his back and his eyes glimmering in the light. '"Apocalypse" comes from a Greek word that means to uncover or reveal. Though we think it means catastrophe.' Ruby was staring at him, confused. 'It involves a peeling back, a revelation of the true order of things, the present, the future, the other worlds.'

'Receive this as a gift,' said Beth with a smile. 'An opportunity for your eyes to be opened as ours were.'

'No.' Ruby shook her head. 'You're delusional. None of this is real!'

'This is a favour we're doing you,' said Isaac, clutching something in his hands. As he approached her, I saw that it was a heavy-duty bike chain.

The bald woman with the tattoos picked Ruby up underneath her armpits and pinned her against an oak tree.

'No!' Ruby cried again as she stumbled backwards. 'What are you doing?' She winced as the cold bark pressed sharply into her back, struggling to push herself free. Beth, Martha and Charlie moved with a practised determination.

'Hold her still,' the tattooed woman barked as Isaac approached with the bike chain. Together, they looped it once around her waist and the oak. It was loose enough to sit just above her hips, but without enough give for her to free herself if she tried. Ruby thrashed, struggling to twist away, as Charlie snapped the padlock shut with a sharp metallic clink. Beth grabbed her wrists and yanked them above her head, while Martha pinned her shoulders against the trunk.

'Let me go! Please!' Ruby screamed, her voice cracking. Her breath came in frantic clouds, visible in the freezing air. She kicked out, her blue Air Jordans scraping the ground, but the girls were relentless. Charlie pulled a frayed rope from her backpack and bound Ruby's hands together tightly, the coarse fibres biting into her skin.

Beth stepped back. 'You'll meet Them in the darkness,' she said, 'on the edge of oblivion.'

'You can't leave me here!' Ruby yelled. She twisted and tugged, but the lock held firm.

'You won't be alone,' Martha promised, leaning forward to kiss Ruby on the cheek.

Ruby gritted her teeth and spat at the girl.

'I'm almost jealous of you,' Isaac said. 'Of what you'll see. When Freya saw the Tau, They were so beautiful, she plucked her eyes out.'

'Freya is a fraud,' Ruby hissed. 'She's a sick person. A liar!'

The Group exchanged glances, then turned as one, their boots crunching on the frosty ground. Ruby's pleas followed them as they walked away.

Cato lingered for only a moment in the trees, watching her.

'Please!' Ruby was so frightened that she had wet herself, dark stains seeping down her trousers. 'If I say I saw Them, will you let me go? If I promise to believe?' He didn't reply, only smiled into the darkness. I saw his teeth gleaming, like the mouth of a wolf. 'Please!' The snap of the undergrowth as he turned away. She was frantic. 'Don't leave me out here, it's freezing. I'll die!'

As the sound of their footsteps faded, the forest seemed to close in, the towering trees casting long shadows in the weak light. Ruby's heart hammered as the chill seeped through her clothes. She tugged and strained against the bike lock and the rope, but they didn't budge. Her fingers, already numbed by the cold, fumbled uselessly at the knots.

She closed her eyes, maybe willing herself to calm down. I could feel it myself, the merciless cold, gnawing through my dungarees and settling deep into my bones. Ruby's teeth chattered uncontrollably.

'Help!' she screamed, over and over again, her voice becoming hoarse and thin. Tears welled in her eyes as the realization sank in: no one was coming.

The vision faded for me then, but I'd learned from my father how long it takes for a person to die of hypothermia.

Even in the UK, it's surprisingly quick. An hour or two in, she'd have been shivering uncontrollably and confused. If she was left overnight, her heart would have stopped. Would she have seen the Tau in the moment before the end? Or would she have only seen herself? The short life she'd lived, everyone she'd ever loved or who had loved her, as if watching a moonlit city recede from the back of an express train.

They might have found her slumped against that oak in the morning, her mouth hanging open, sunrise light glimmering off her molars as her head lolled on her shoulders. Cato would have pressed two fingers to her throat and shaken his head. Would some of them have been frightened? Would Charlie have suggested they'd gone too far? If so, the others would have stifled the notion: *Revelation comes at a cost. The universe is red in tooth and claw.*

Who suggested pulling out all her teeth?

Some things would turn out to be true. Records would demonstrate that Freya did spend a couple of months as a patient in High Tower after claiming that aliens had compelled her to cut out her eyes. Though there are years of her life that no one will ever be able to account for.

There are a lot of things I'll never know. Like how Freya knew the things she knew, about me, about my mum. Could she really heal people? Were they completely imaginary, the things I saw: the planet, the voices of celestial gods?

I would tell anyone who would listen what had happened to Ruby. But at the end of it all, the only evidence I had was a bag full of teeth scattered in a house I'd escaped. A confession only I heard. A vision. And they never did find her body.

KIMONA MINTON – 8 DAYS AFTER

The morning after the Night of Awe, Kim and Marcus put on their masks and returned to their house to discover Dennis Crossley dead in the kitchen, keeled over in a dining chair. He looked like a waxwork. His skin was bone-pale, his lips the colour of sea foam, eyes glass beads.

An eerie silence had settled over the house, which looked as if it had been trashed by a three-day party. There was a tear in the chaise longue, stuffing pouring out of it. Finger marks all over the wallpaper and curtains. The rug in the TV room was stained with mud and ash from hastily constructed fires. 'COLLAPSE IS HERE' someone had spray-painted on the shower curtain. Broken glass and shattered dishes littered the kitchen floor, while flies buzzed around rotting food festering on the counters.

The intruders had all died in the night. Marcus and Kim counted nine of them. Four were crumpled in the TV room, their faces discoloured. Some had bloody streaks trailing from their mouths, noses and ears. One young man lay in the foetal position on a beanbag, looking like he'd just curled up to rest. There weren't any signs of a struggle; they all looked as if they'd died in their sleep.

In the bedrooms, there were more men on duvets or in sleeping bags on the carpet. Andrew Griggs had died on his belly on their four-poster.

Through the visor of Kim's mask, she thought she could see the alien particles floating in the air. She was terrified. Whatever had killed them was still in their house.

'I can't ... I can't look at them, Marcus. This is too much.' Kim stifled a sob, and he reached out to hold her. His touch was reassuring, and she relaxed into it.

'At least,' he said with a sigh, 'we have our house back now.'

Kim pulled away, tears fogging up her visor. 'How can you say that?'

'What?' Marcus replied, his tone a little defensive.

'They were *people*,' Kim sniffed. 'Some of them were younger than our children!'

'Oh, come on. They were probably going to kill us, Kim. This is the best-case scenario. At least now it's over.'

'Over? Is it? Because I don't feel safe, Marcus. This house – our *home* – is filled with death. This air, these bodies ... It's unbearable.'

'We'll burn them,' Marcus said, 'in the garden. Then we'll seal the house, make it safe.'

Kim stepped back. 'Burn them? I can't even *touch* them!'

'It's fine, I'll do it. We don't have a choice. It's summer, we can't just let them rot here.'

Kim stared at him. Even though he had spent the last few years preparing us all for something like this, she was still baffled by his resolve, by his calmness in the face of all this death.

The two of them jumped when they heard a banging. Kim snapped into action almost reflexively, rushing down the stairs. Marcus thundered after her. As she reached to pull back one of the bolts on the front door, he pushed her away.

'What are you doing?' Kim asked him. He ignored her, an arm protectively over her chest.

'Who is it?' Marcus barked.

'Hey,' a voice said from outside. 'It's Gabe ...' He waited for a response, but then added uncertainly, 'Your neighbour?' Marcus squinted through the peep hole.

'What do you want?' he asked.

'Are you okay?' Kim shouted.

'Well ... no, I have Hannah with me—'

'Hi ...' Her voice was faint. The sound of a crying baby echoed through the door, and Kim had a brief moment of panic before she remembered that Hero was safe in the bunker.

'We're all falling sick and ... we hate to be a burden but ...'

'Do you have any food?' Hannah begged. 'Anything. Anything you could spare?'

'Or water?' Gabriel said.

Kim reached out her hand to pull back the lock, but Marcus smacked it away.

'Sorry,' he said firmly. 'We can't help.'

'*Please?*' The desperation in Hannah's voice wrenched Kim's heart.

'Marcus!' she hissed at him.

'No!' he shouted, his eyes flashing furiously.

Gabriel was cautious. 'Maybe you could just ...'

'No!' Marcus yelled again. 'We can't help you. Don't come back here.'

Kim was desperate to let them in. She reached again for the handle of the door, but Marcus was ready, turning and pushing her so hard that she fell backwards, her head clipping the edge of the console table. She saw stars.

Marcus listened for the sound of their footsteps disappearing and then turned to help Kim off the floor.

'Don't you touch me!' she snapped. 'Don't you *dare* touch me.'

Marcus looked a little remorseful as he watched Kim pull herself up to her feet, rubbing her head. The tears in her eyes were from shock and fury more than anything.

'You're just like your father!' she spat and limped into the kitchen, where the sight of someone else's vomit in the sink made her want to throw up herself.

'How can you say that?' Marcus asked as he followed her. One Halloween, early in their marriage, Kim had asked him what his worst fear was. She'd joked that no one ever dressed up as commitment or failure. He'd told her that he never wanted to look in the mirror and see his father.

'You're controlling. You're selfish . . .' She listed the items on her fingers.

'Oh, *I'm* selfish? You're the one who left our children to live your best life.'

'Are you going to bring that up in every argument forever? I was *working*. And when I came back, I found that you'd been fucking our babysitter. Which is just so unoriginal. Men are so lazy.'

'You *poisoned* me. With mushrooms.'

'You said, "What do I have to do for you to forgive me?"'

'So you made me pay?'

Kim screamed in frustration. 'You're a malevolent presence

in this house. When you were gone, it was like we could finally all *breathe*.'

'All I've ever done is try to protect this family.'

Kim pointed at the front door. 'They're going to die out there.'

'You already let a gang of strangers waltz into our house like it was theirs. Do you want to do that again?'

'How was I supposed to stop a gang of armed men? Anyway, Gabe and Hannah aren't strangers, Marcus, they're our neighbours.'

'You've spoken to Gabriel, what, once ever? And all of a sudden, you want him to move in with us?' Kim felt herself blush a little at that.

'Hannah has no one. She's a single mum. With a baby.'

'If we let them in, we're risking everything. We don't know what pathogens they'll spread. And we only have enough supplies for our family, you know that. I'm doing this for our daughters. I'm doing it for *us*.'

'Us? Don't say that like it means anything. There hasn't been an "us" for years. I wanted out, Marcus. You made sure I couldn't leave, and now you want to shut the door on everyone else, too.'

'I didn't make this happen, Kim!' he yelled back at her, breath fogging up his mask. 'The world fell apart, and I did what I had to do! You think I'm some kind of monster for keeping this family alive? What about some fucking gratitude for everything I've done? I'm the one who built the bunker, I'm the one who stockpiled supplies. I bought the mask you're wearing, I hiked across a post-apocalyptic city to rescue our daughters and your father, and all you ever did was call me paranoid!'

'Because you never asked anyone else!' Kim fired back.

'You always do what you want. You just unilaterally decided to turn our home into your fortress, and you drove us hundreds of thousands of pounds into debt to do it. You've always been like this. Smothering. You don't love us, Marcus. You want to *own* us. You don't listen to me or our children or anyone else. You don't care about our needs. Or our lived experience.'

'What does that mean?'

'You just see allies and enemies. Strangers or blood. You don't see *people*. You didn't see Ezekiel—'

'Don't you dare.' His voice went cold.

'You didn't see him as a human being. You let him die when he begged for your help, and now you're doing that again.' Kim saw the tightening in his jaw.

'How can you bring that up? You were nowhere to be found when it happened. You didn't even defend me when the press got involved and called me racist!'

'Black people are more likely to die in police custody!'

Marcus roared in frustration at that. 'You sound like *them*!' A caged bear, he clenched his fingers, blood rising in his face. He plunged his fist so hard into the wall next to her that the plaster crumbled under his knuckles.

Marcus turned, his hand covered in blood and dust. Kim slid to the floor and started sobbing. He watched her, breathing heavily.

'It didn't used to be like this. You and me.' His voice cracked a little. 'You let the world get to you.'

They used to make easy banter about race – jollof rice versus Yorkshire puddings, her father's half-day-long, charismatic services compared to the dry hymns Marcus was used to. It had felt open and low stakes. Marcus loved Nigerian food. Kim was more at home in London than anywhere else in the world. He'd looked kingly in the purple embroidered agbada he'd worn at their wedding reception, and he'd been honoured to wear it. And underneath it all, they'd loved each other, loved everything that made their spouse *them*. They were overwhelmingly proud of the family they'd built together.

But Kim wondered now if she'd been naïve to think that their marriage could change anything about the world. Now, whenever she mentioned race, Marcus regarded it with defensive suspicion, something foul she'd dragged into the house. *Leave your 'politics' outside*. Kim believed that her life would be so much easier if she *could*.

Marcus said, 'Everyone always acted like I was so lucky you agreed to marry me.' He had asked three times before Kim finally said yes. 'I always felt like you were holding out for some better option to come along.'

'That's not true . . .' Kim said feebly.

'You were so unhappy when the girls were little. So you wanted this PhD, fine, you had to travel across the world to do it, fine. I thought, if that's what you need, if that's what you need to come back and be happy, then fine. But actually, maybe you'll *never* be happy.'

'I *was* happy,' Kim said, 'until you broke it. Us. This whole project of the life we wanted to build together.'

A tear rolled down the side of Marcus's face then. 'I made a *mistake*,' he said. 'Have you never made a mistake?'

'This one cost someone their life.'

He hung his head in shame. 'So what do I have to do now?' he asked, gritting back a sob. 'What do I have to do now . . . to be forgiven?'

Kim sighed shakily. Her father's face came to her mind then. Pastor Abiola had always been convinced that there

TEMI OH

weren't many men out there for her. He'd remind Kim, after her mother died, when she refused to let Gladys teach her how to cook, that she'd never find a husband that way. 'So I'll find a man who can cook,' she'd stated, as if it were the easiest solution in the world. She used to believe that if she'd dreamed up a husband for herself, she would have dreamed up Marcus.

It had been her father who had convinced Kim to finally say yes. She had been holding out hope for someone like Chijioke, the worship leader at Providence House who was an analyst for Deloitte. It had been her father who said, 'But this boy really *loves* you.' Kim saw that Marcus loved her and would always love her. Would be kind, would be a good father. But she'd always harboured the stifling sense that he would never be great. And that, if she stayed with him, she knew exactly what the rest of her life would look like. Would she die just like her mother had, stuck in this house?

She adjusted her mask and tilted her head back. Something caught her eye, a glimmer in the wall.

'Hey,' she said then, looking up at the hole Marcus had made. 'What's that?'

In the light, it looked like a soap bubble the size of a tennis ball, with rainbow colours refracted across it. Marcus frowned. Kim got to her feet, and they both peered at it. The shape bulged behind the plaster and little specks of gypsum floated across its translucent surface.

Marcus reached a hand out to touch it, but stopped when Kim said sharply, 'No!' Something about the sight of it made her feel ill.

Marcus searched for a hammer and a pair of gloves in the 'miscellaneous stuff' drawer and, after pulling them on, bashed another hole in the kitchen wall, half a metre away from the first. There were more bubbles, a little spray of them, swelling together in clusters. Kim felt a shiver go down her spine. It reminded her of the time she had lifted up the bedroom rug to find a shoal of silverfish batting their wingless bodies between the floorboards.

With gloved hands, Marcus started to pull away the plaster, tossing it into the dirty sink. Kim watched as the wall crumbled away.

Behind it was an infestation. Strange rainbow bubbles swirled in tight fractal spirals that resembled nautilus shells or florets of Romanesco broccoli. Clusters and blisters pulsated unevenly as though gasping for air, refracting light into a sickly kaleidoscope.

Kim leaned back on the table behind her, feeling a little dizzy. 'What is it?' she asked.

Black liquid oozed from the bigger ones. Marcus grabbed a fork and did what Kim almost longed to do – he pricked one. With a hiss of expelled air, it deflated like bubblegum, huffing little glittery motes into the room.

They both jolted away from it, but the specks spread, drifting lazily towards them with an inevitability that terrified her.

'Is that it?' Kim asked in horror. 'The thing in the air? The thing that's killing everyone?' The idea was terrible. 'It's coming from our house?'

MARCUS MINTON – 8 DAYS AFTER

It took Marcus a couple of years to guess that Kim had poisoned him. It was when he'd started his class on urban foraging and learned about which mushrooms could kill (*Amanita phalloides*, the death cap) and which ones caused nausea, cramps and vomiting (*Russula emetica*, the sickener). Was he misremembering the reddish tinge to the mushrooms she'd served him, and him alone, that morning on his crepes?

Since then, Marcus had come to a wary respect for fungi. He learned that they were in a kingdom all of their own, one more closely related to animals than to plants. *Mycena chlorophos* could glow in the dark; he'd seen pictures of its pale green mushrooms fruiting under logs. He'd heard that the largest living organism on Earth was a subterranean fungus in Oregon, estimated to weigh as much as thirty-five thousand tonnes. The shaggy ink cap mushroom was strong enough to break through asphalt and concrete pavement. Penicillin had been isolated by accident when Alexander Fleming noticed that his colony of bacteria had been destroyed by a chance growth of mould.

The curly-haired mycologist who'd guest-lectured that class had said that aliens, viewing Earth, might believe that it was ruled by fungi. After all, lichen covered about eight per cent of the planet's surface and lived everywhere from the Artic tundra to bare volcanic rock.

'They're mushrooms,' Marcus guessed that day, after they'd pulled away much more of the plaster to find clusters of fat, undulating bubbles spread behind the walls. Every now and then, one would explode with a wet sucking noise, releasing what Marcus guessed were spores into the air. 'The mushroom is the fruiting body of a fungus.'

Kim shuddered, her eyes rolling behind her visor. 'Almost every one of those words was disgusting.'

These ones reminded Marcus of a picture he had seen of *Pilobolus* – a kind of fungi that often grew in animal dung. Its spore-producing organs were like glass bulbs. He'd read that when they ruptured, they would scatter spores with ballistic force, with an acceleration more than ten thousand times that of a space shuttle.

'They release spores into the air, which allow the fungi to reproduce.' It made sense now; of course this might be how an extraterrestrial civilization would choose to communicate! Spores were some of the hardiest cells, capable of surviving extreme temperatures, UV radiation and even the vacuum of space. Some fungal spores could remain dormant for centuries until favourable conditions arose – the right level of moisture, temperature and nutrient availability – making them ideal intergalactic messengers.

'Do you think this is what's been making everyone sick?' Kim asked, waving her hand shakily through the glittering dust in the air.

'I mean, black mould makes people ill,' Marcus said.

'And if it's just in our house, then the spores are most concentrated here, which would explain why our neighbours are sick but not dead.'

'But,' Kim said, 'it looks like this stuff is releasing spores every second. There'll be more and more in the air, and people will get sicker—'

'And they'll reproduce and grow more fungi elsewhere, in other houses, if that hasn't happened already.'

Marcus and Kim's logic was trundling forward on the same terminal tracks. They stared at each other.

'How do we stop it?' Kim asked.

A sound outside the room made their heads snap to the doorway.

Tanice stood in the hall, wearing her gas mask, tears running down her face behind it. 'Mum? Dad? What's going on?'

'Where did you come from?' Marcus asked, looking at both the sealed front and back doors.

'Upstairs,' she said.

'How did you get upstairs?' Marcus frowned. But she shook her head.

'Why are there dead bodies all over our house?' she demanded.

As Kim explained their discovery to Tanice, taking her back out into the garden, Marcus bashed his hammer through more of the house. He cracked through the plasterboard on the staircase and next to our pinboard of family pictures on the landing. He looked behind the spinning solar system mobile in Chantale's bedroom. If not quite at the level of the thickly bubbling mass on the ground floor, little globules and sprays of the fungus were beginning to expand almost everywhere he looked.

Most fungi were composed of a network of tiny cylindrical threads called hyphae, which made up the body of the fungus, the mycelium. Marcus knew that the mycelium grew through the substrate – which could be soil or wood or apparently his *house* – allowing the fungus to colonize large areas. The mushroom was like the tip of the iceberg, the relatively small, temporary part of the fungus that appeared on the surface for reproduction. So wherever he found the bubbles, it was likely that there was already a vast infestation of the organism.

As he worked through the first floor, Dr Sengupta's words came back to him. The spores must have been the 'xeno-biological substance' her scientists had detected on his body the previous week. Hadn't she warned that it could cross the blood–brain barrier, as he knew alcohol and psilocybin did? And hadn't she said that high temperatures would denature it?

'Kim!' he shouted then, but she was already coming up the stairs behind him.

'It's everywhere, isn't it?' she said, looking at the holes in the walls, wincing at the nauseating structure.

'As far as I can tell. And its mycelium – its roots – could be in everything.' He looked at Kim and glanced down the stairs. 'Where's Tanice?'

'I told her to tell Chantale, Aaliyah and Hero to stay in the bunker while we sort this out.' Kim turned to a shimmering nest of mushrooms that – in the time since Marcus had made the hole in the wall – had begun to ooze onto the banister. She said, 'We have to get rid of it.'

'I know.'

'Or way more people will probably die.'

'I know.'

'And we can't live here anymore.' The words pained her to say.

'Yes,' Marcus said, surprised by his own resolve. 'We have to burn the house down.'

BRIAR MINTON – 8 DAYS AFTER

Pain dredged me from my sleep. I woke to a body full of it, razoring my arm and leg, a fire in my lungs. The sound of metal in dirt tumbled into my consciousness.

When I opened my eyes, I assumed it was the early afternoon because of the way the sun was coming through the diamond-pane windows. The room was small and furnished like a monk's cell: white walls streaked with some water damage, a narrow wooden bed that I lay in, under a hand-stitched quilt. There were framed pressed forget-me-nots on the wall opposite, next to a cross crafted from twigs and twine. Within reach of the bed was a wooden dresser with an oil lamp on it. I eyed the books on the desk: there were a few on astronomy and a couple of gardening encyclopaedias, *Forgotten Fruits*, *Muck and Mind*, a hand-drawn star map draped over Martin Luther's *Commentary on Galatians*.

Looking down, I discovered that my wounds had been dressed. My arm was in a sling made from what seemed to be a torn bedsheet, and someone had bandaged my leg with strips of fabric. On the stool beside me was a cup of water and a wooden bowl containing what looked like a herbal poultice. The distinctive scent of garlic, pine and yarrow suffused the room.

Memories returned in flashes. Passing out in the forest, the coldness of the night, the prickle of acorns and pine needles on my face, tears in dirt, the barking of a dog.

'Digit!' I tried to shout, but my voice came out raspy.

It took some careful planning to manoeuvre myself out of bed, and then I had to lean on the dresser and take a couple of deep breaths just to control the pain. I sniffed the water glass suspiciously, then took a few gentle sips to soothe my dry throat.

For a nightmarish moment, I worried that the door would be locked, that I would be trapped in this little room. But it opened easily, onto a churchyard overgrown with wildflowers: clusters of meadowsweet swaying gently in the breeze, red campion, hardy lush ferns, seed-heavy grasses scattered with oxeye daisies, foxgloves dotted with bees. I had to shade my eyes as I emerged from the dim cottage and into the midsummer brilliance, temporarily sun-blind.

As my vision adjusted, I saw the dilapidated chapel. An ancient stone structure, honeysuckle climbed in efflorescent vines up one crumbling wall. The roof sagged slightly, and the half-collapsed bell tower cast a crooked shadow across the garden.

Digit came bounding towards me, trampling through an unruly bed of lady's mantle and iris, her tongue lolling, sending pollen spraying everywhere, delighted to see me. I leaned down to greet her – 'Hey, girl!' – though the sudden motion made me wince in pain.

I saw a woman then, kneeling in the shade of a dwarf tree – the gardener, I guessed from her olive overalls and broad-brimmed hat with its ugly neck flap. I limped over to her, and as I did, she put down her tools and turned to greet me.

'You're probably losing that leg,' was the first thing she said as I approached. I looked down at it. 'I did what I could, alcohol on the wound, garlic, yarrow and pine for their anti-microbial and anti-inflammatory properties, but I'm not a surgeon.' I'd later discover that she had stitched my wound together with dental floss.

'I probably would have died out there,' I said.

'No doubt about it,' she agreed. She looked a bit older than my mother – mid-fifties, I'd say – though her skin had the weathered texture of someone who had spent most of her life outdoors. 'It was the dog that saved you.' She jutted her chin at Digit, who was still bounding about my ankles, hoping for a treat. 'I heard her and went looking. There have been a couple of stray animals around, owners who haven't returned. And after I found her, she led me to you.'

I nodded, taking this in. I was astounded by her kindness, bringing me here, treating my wounds and letting me sleep on her bed. Overwhelmed by gratitude.

'Do you have a name?' she asked.

'Briar,' I said. For some reason, after all she had done, I felt I owed her my full name. 'Briar Rita Minton.'

'Rita ...' She said the word as if tasting an aged wine. '... of Cascia. Patron saint of impossible feats.' I hadn't actually known that. All I'd been told was that it was my grandmother's name. The one she'd had to adopt in order to go to school in colonial Nigeria.

'What are you doing?' I looked at the tree she'd been crouched beside.

'Grafting fruit trees,' she explained. She could clearly tell from my expression that I had no idea what that meant. She knelt down and gestured to a newly tied branch. 'This one's a Victoria plum – it'll give you the sweetest fruit, but only if it's paired with good, sturdy roots.' She pointed to one side of the tree. 'The rootstock's like the bones of the tree, strong enough to weather this stony soil and the seasons. The scion is where the magic happens. It carries the memory of the fruit, the sweetness of summers past. I join them like this, cut and bound, and they grow together, stronger than they were apart.'

It seemed strange to me, putting all this work into a garden outside a church that appeared long abandoned. Stranger still, considering everything that had happened, to put any effort into grafting trees that wouldn't bear good fruits for at least another season, maybe longer. A kind of wild hopefulness.

I wondered how much time had passed. 'How long was I . . . ?'

'A day, almost. What happened to you, anyway?' she asked. 'Did you get on the wrong side of a game hunter?'

'You could say that,' I mumbled.

'Where are you from?' she asked.

'South London,' I said. People used to say they could tell by my accent. 'Clapham.'

'You're a long way from home.'

'How far am I?'

'Half a day's walk, roughly.' She looked down at my leg, sceptical that it would carry me that far. 'Have you heard of the First Contact Committee?'

I nodded, remembering Astrid's face on the news the morning of the Event. It felt like a lifetime ago.

'I was a fellow with them for a few years.'

'You're a scientist?' I asked.

'Was,' she replied. 'Astrobiology. Interesting work, but too much time indoors for me. I radioed them to investigate an unusual natural phenomenon I witnessed in the woods. A couple of their agents are on their way. I could call in a favour and see if they could help get you home.'

'That would be amazing,' I said. But then, 'Astrobiology? That's like – searching for life on other planets?'

She nodded. 'And the origins of life on this one.'

'What was the "unusual phenomena"?'

Her eyes lit up at my question. 'The night before last, a couple of miles from here, I discovered some ghost orchids.' She paused as if waiting for me to gasp. 'Ghost orchids are Britain's rarest plants. They don't need sunlight to flower, so they have no leaves; they rely on fungi from the soil for nutrients and spend most of their life underground. They were declared extinct over a decade ago but then reappeared.'

'What does that have to do with the First Contact Committee?' I asked.

'It was something about the way I found them,' she said. 'They were growing in this strange spiral shape. In a pattern too precise to be random. Let me show you.' She dropped her spade and began walking back towards the cottage. I limped to follow her. 'The formation seemed to have a magical kind of symmetry. It made me think of molluscs, snowflakes, sunflower seed heads ...' She looked excited, glad to share her discoveries with someone. I'd read about spiral shapes in nature and listened to a podcast about how these structures demonstrated the golden ratio, which could be observed in everything from the nanoscopic structure of DNA to human faces. 'I thought,' she said, 'that it looked like a galaxy.'

Returning from the sunlight and into the dark cottage made my vision cloud with shadows. 'These are the flowers.' She pulled out a hard-backed encyclopaedia and pointed to an open page headed *Epipogium aphyllum*. When my vision cleared, I could see the delicate little bone-pale orchid clearly. She explained that they bloomed at night to attract moths. I imagined how astounding it must have been to stumble across their ghostly faces in a twilit clearing.

'This is a map I drew of their formation. It would have been easier if I'd had a camera.' She spread out the map she had drawn. 'Would you believe that they're growing in the shape of the Andromeda galaxy?' She'd rendered it as a cluster of asterisks, crosses and dots, indicating orchids and their corresponding stars at various stages in their life cycle. From the map, I could see a prominent spiral structure, with bright, well-defined arms. Its central swell was dense with old stars, surrounding a supermassive black hole.

She believed that some atmospheric disturbance caused by the Event had triggered the ghost orchids to grow in a way that communicated this map.

'Hero must have triggered it,' she said. 'Maybe this pattern is appearing in different ways all over the country – the world, even.'

'Could it be a message?' I asked.

'It must be.' She flipped excitedly through her sketches and star maps then, and said, 'I only noticed the differences when I compared it to my old books. The stars on this map don't match Andromeda as we see it today.' She noted that bright stars, whose light we marvel at in our current skies, were fading red giants in the plant map, or else, disappeared entirely, collapsed into black holes. White dwarfs slowly cooled, clustered young stars had drifted apart on galactic tides. Most intriguingly, the spiral arms of the galaxy were subtly displaced.

'I began comparing this orchid map to our current star charts,' she said. She hinted at how long it had taken to calculate the shifts in stellar positions and the rotation of Andromeda's arms. 'The result? This map doesn't show Andromeda as it is. It shows Andromeda as it *will be* ... two million years in the future.

'I think the map tells a story. I believe that the civilization who sent it were based around here.' She pointed to a patch she'd marked in red pen on the map. 'AF Andromedae.' This was a name I'd heard before. The Group believed that this was the Tau's closest star; hearing this old scientist confirm it made my pulse race. Stoked at the dying embers of my hope. Had the group been right about everything after all? Were the Tau real? Were They coming to save us?

She continued, 'In our sky, this is an extremely massive and unstable star. In this map, it's entered a late, dying phase. I think they were trying to tell us that it was about to explode, swallowing all the nearby planets with it.'

'What?' I whispered, my throat dry. *The Tau are in danger,* Beth's voice rattled urgently in my head, *Their sun is dying.*

'This likely already happened,' she said with a sad shrug.

'H-how can you tell?'

She explained that it could take two million years for us to know for sure. That, although in our sky AF Andromedae is burning bright, it is a massive star, and big stars burn through their fuel quickly, they fizzle out into red giants and then, within a few hundred thousand years, they explode spectacularly in supernovae. Her guess was that any life forms in that star system were likely wiped out five hundred thousand years ago.

When she turned, she could see the look in my eyes. Despair hit me like a fist in the solar plexus. 'Are we really alone, then?' I asked.

'In cosmic time,' she said, 'half a million years is the blink of an eye but for us, it's everything.'

For a couple of weeks, we'd had company: Hero. But now we knew that Hero was only a ghost ship, pitched through the stars. An ebbing relic from a civilization long dead. Worse, gone before we could ever have hoped to reach it, likely vanquished before our species even walked the Earth.

'We were always alone,' I said, feeling the ground crumble under my feet.

The universe seemed desolate to me, then. As enchanted as a clockwork train trundling through aeons on certain tracks. On its fringes, stars were birthed and then exploded in spectacular power, and no sentient eye would ever be awed or astonished by them.

With the promise of the Tau, I had hoped I was intimately loved. Completely known. I'd felt that love like a hum at the back of my consciousness. I'd felt as if it had always been there, waiting for me to attend to it.

I collapsed in tears on the bed, pain and exhaustion overcoming me. Disenchantment. It felt good to share some of what I had been through now I was free of the group. 'For a while, they convinced that my life mattered.' More tears welled in my eyes. 'I thought I was part of some bigger plan.'

'Hey,' the gardener said. She knelt beside me, put her hand on my shoulder and smiled. 'Briar Minton,' she said, 'you always have been.'

KIMONA MINTON – 8 DAYS AFTER

There's a kind of relief that comes from losing something you were terrified to lose.

Marcus gave her an hour to pack up everything they would ever need. Things that were important: our birth certificates and passports. Art we'd made. Miniature models of the Damocles spaceship I'd lovingly fashioned from cereal boxes and toilet roll, using empty pill packets as buttons. A sheet of old sugar paper with Tanice's handprints on it in the shape of a sunflower and the scrawled words, '*Dear Daddy, thank u for helping me grow.*'

Things that were irreplaceable: a few of Aaliyah's most valued tennis trophies and her signed racket. Tanice asked for her prom dress and diaries. Chantale wanted her Girl Guides uniform with all its badges. My mother had to guess at what I would have wanted. She packed for me, hoping against hope that I would return home. Kim picked my worn 'I'm with Sondheim' canvas tote (which I love her for), some music books and photographs. Every now and then, for a couple of years, something new would occur to me. The comfort blanket Nan Minton had knitted for me, the one with my name carefully embroidered into it. Tanice's 'soul' – a small scrap of paper with her signature on it – which she'd sold to me for a KitKat when she was eight and which I kept in my dresser drawer. That sweet-smelling shea butter moisturiser Aaliyah used to make, and the book with the recipe. All the things our grandmother, Kim's mother, ever touched . . .

When they were finally ready, Kim crouched by the front door, watching spores glint in the air as Marcus knelt, arranging supplies: several battered jerry cans of the kerosene they'd been using for their lanterns, blue canisters of butane they usually stored by the stove, half-empty bottles of paint thinner, acetone and white spirit that he'd managed to root out from the DIY cupboard. Behind his mask, he looked sallow but determined.

'We'll be quick,' he said, his voice low. 'Start upstairs, work down. Once it's burning, we're out. No second guesses.'

Kim nodded, though her hands trembled. She followed him up the creaking staircase to the third floor. The master bedroom was first. Kim paused at the door, staring at their gorgeous four-poster, with its blush pink and champagne gold duvet, embroidered cushions and lace-edged pillows.

Marcus used to say that it was her bed, adding, 'Do you think, if I wasn't married to you, I would live in this room?' Then he'd gesture at everything, the cream-tasselled lamps, the blue swallows flocking across their intricately illustrated wallpaper, the baroque overmantel and silk damask curtains.

'Isn't marriage supposed to change you?' she'd tease.

'True,' he'd concede, 'but if you weren't married to me, this is *exactly* the room you'd live in.'

'Are you ready?' Marcus asked her now. Kim looked up at the wall behind the bed's elaborately carved finials. The wallpaper was bubbling up as if something behind it was respiring. Kim knew that if they knocked through the wall, they would find more colonies of the fungus, pushing its tendrils under the carpet and up through the wooden studs behind the plasterboard.

As if in response, Kim uncapped a jerry can of kerosene and shook it out onto the mattress; she watched it drip down the turned posts and pool on the carpet.

Marcus stepped into their closet and did the same. Kim imagined those sightless polystyrene heads going up in flames, all her lovely, expensive wigs.

In mine and Chantale's bedroom, they followed the same routine, pouring accelerant on each of the bunks, on the grimy shag carpet and blackout curtains. I'd always resented that I had to share a room (because Chantale was too terrified to sleep on her own and Tanice was too argumentative to share), but I do feel a pang when I imagine my mum glancing up for the final time at the glow-in-the-dark stars that twinkled across our ceiling.

The two split up to do the other bedrooms. Marcus took Tanice's, and Kim went to Aaliyah's. It was a faded collage of her childhood. There, the wilting floral wallpaper Kim had struggled to hang at eight months pregnant. The worn nursing chair in the corner, covered in clothes. Collages from magazines festooned the walls. Graffiti in pink Sharpie above the bed read, *Tanice* ~~hates~~ *Aaliyah*. The kente cloth phase Aaliyah went through. She'd made a banner from one which read: *Non-violence is fine, as long as it works.* In the ensuite to the side, Hero had been born. That was the bed that Carmen woke up in the morning she died. In the corner was Aaliyah's bloodstained and singed wedding dress – once Kim's.

'You done?' Marcus asked.

'How much is enough?' Kim replied. Marcus shrugged.

'I've never done this before.' He shook his can. 'Obviously, we need to make sure we have enough for it all to ignite. Maybe we open some windows to increase oxygen flow. Hopefully, the stairs will take care of themselves.'

Marcus littered what paper he could find – school reports and magazine subscriptions they'd cancelled too late – across the floor.

By the time they reached the ground floor, Kim's gloves were slick, and though she wore her respirator, she could imagine the sharp scent of the fumes rising. My mother ignored her lightheadedness and pressed on.

Marcus poured rubbing alcohol over the bodies of the intruders that he'd dragged into a pile in the living room. Kim watched as the liquid evaporated almost instantly. She uncapped a second bottle and dripped it along the edges of the chaise longue, watching it soak into the fabric. Marcus emptied the last of the paint thinner over an old armchair in the corner.

'That's it,' Kim said, her voice tight. They shared a glance before returning to the kitchen, where the spores seemed to have multiplied even in the time they'd been gone. Bubbles dripped onto the counter, where they'd clone themselves, splitting into two wobbling masses. *Burn them, burn them,* Kim thought at the sight.

Marcus doused the kitchen table where Kim had left her wedding and engagement rings over a week ago. The rings were gone, she saw, probably stolen by one of the men or dropped through a crack in the floor. More things, Kim thought sorrowfully, to list among the many she'd lost.

'What about the butane?' Kim asked, glancing at the small canisters in Marcus's pack.

'Controlled burn,' he said. 'Not for spreading fire. For making it hotter.' He punctured the canisters and placed one carefully in the centre of the dining table – the one she'd lovingly decorated for every Christmas of her life. 'Once the flames reach these, it'll blow fast enough to take out the spores.'

Kim hesitated. 'Are we sure this will work?'

Marcus turned to her, his eyes hard. 'It has to. It's this or the fungus spreads to the whole street.'

She nodded, swallowing her fear. 'Let's finish it.'

The Molotov cocktail was crude but effective. Marcus had fashioned it from an empty bottle of Supermalt filled with kerosene and stuffed with a torn dishcloth soaked in rubbing alcohol. Kim held it tightly, her fingers trembling.

'You light it,' she said as they stood in the kitchen.

Marcus struck a match, the flame flickering to life. He touched it to the rag, which flared instantly with a *whoooosh!*

'Throw it into the hall!' – where Marcus had stacked a pile of Kim's old romance novels – 'We need it to catch first.'

Kim took a deep breath and hurled the bottle. It shattered on impact, and the kerosene ignited with a roar. Flames engulfed the books in seconds, leaping across the rug and licking at the curtains. The heat was immediate and suffocating.

'Go!' Marcus urged, grabbing her arm.

They fled, stumbling out through the garden door as smoke billowed from the windows. The butane canisters inside hissed and exploded, sending shards of glass raining onto the back patio. Kim imagined, with grim satisfaction, the mushrooms writhing in panic, blackening and disintegrating.

She clung to Marcus as the blaze roared. 'It's done,' she whispered, though her voice wavered. He hugged her. And behind his visor, she saw that he was crying.

'I loved it, too,' she told him.

'I didn't realize I did,' he said, 'until now.'

'We did what we had to,' she said, repeating what he had said to her earlier. Marcus nodded and composed himself as well as he could. With the house, Kim felt, their whole past was gone. All the dreams they'd conjured together. *Maybe we make new ones?* she said to herself.

Marcus looked at her. Kim saw her own despair reflected in his eyes. He reached into his pocket and brought something out.

Her rings. The ones she'd left on the table. Her wedding band, a buttery yellow in the twilight. And her engagement ring, with that old European cut diamond which floated in a bed of seed pearls. They'd bought it for almost nothing from a vintage store run by a man with no teeth. At Marcus's bargaining, the man had offered it to them for half and then a quarter of the price, which only served to make Marcus more suspicious. Was it actually worth nothing at all? It had lasted, though the band was dented and scratched, and almost all of its little stones had fallen out, leaving blackened holes that winked like blinded eyes. Every now and then, when it looked as if they might come into some money, he'd promised to upgrade it, but that had never happened.

Kim held it up in her gloved hand. Its facets sparkled with a warm, fiery brilliance. Marcus watched her intently, a

desperate question in his eyes: *What do I have to do now …
to be forgiven?*

'No!' Behind them, Tanice screamed. Over the roar of
the fire, they hadn't heard the rattle of the toolshed door
opening. '*No!*' Her face was twisted in horror. 'What did
you do?!' Tears ran down her cheeks, and she shook all over.

'I'm so sorry, sweetheart,' Kim said, with a pang of guilt
at seeing her daughter's pain. They'd agreed it would be
better not to tell my sisters what they were planning to do.

'Tanice, put on your mask!' Marcus ordered.

Tanice screamed again. 'You said we had to leave the
house! You didn't say that you'd *burn it down*!' She was
still in her old basketball jersey; the flames reflected off the
black-and-pink polyester lettering at the front.

'Mask. Now!' our father yelled at her.

'This is crazy,' Tanice whispered, ignoring him.

'Yeah.' Aaliyah emerged from the bunker in her pyjamas, Hero in her arms. 'You love that house, Mum.' When
Aaliyah had complained that, statistically, Black families
had a tenth of the wealth of white families, Kim had reminded her of their home. 'You told me it was the only
valuable thing we owned.'

'We couldn't waste any time,' Marcus explained again.
'Every second, that thing was releasing more spores.'

Behind them, a window on the second floor exploded,
and Kim saw the polka dot curtains on the landing ignite.
Tanice looked wan, like she was going to be sick.

'Dad, you have to stop it!' she pleaded.

'We can't now,' Marcus replied, the radiant heat from the
fire making him sweat behind his mask.

'*We have to go back in!*' Tanice lunged towards the
house, but Kim grabbed her.

'What are you doing?'

'Are you crazy?!' Marcus roared at her. Tanice collapsed to her knees on the grass, howling.

'*Someone's in there!*'

Kim frowned in confusion, her arms around Tanice now. 'They were all already dead. Dennis, Andrew . . . those other boys.'

'But he was *alive* when I left him. I sneaked him Briar's mask, so the spores couldn't kill him.'

'Who?' Kim asked.

Tanice sobbed, 'Sydney Walker.'

'*What?*' Marcus's blue eyes flashed.

'He's in the attic. He's been there since yesterday.' Tanice made another move towards the house, but Kim held her daughter firmly. She and Marcus exchanged a look.

'You can't,' she told him. Marcus exhaled deeply and closed his eyes.

'I have to,' he said.

'It's suicide,' Kim told him.

Marcus turned. 'You guys get back,' he ordered. He grabbed a crowbar and a towel hanging on the washing line, which he doused with water from one of the plastic bottles by the rocket stove.

Then he wrapped it around his fist to open the door. 'Get back!' he shouted at them again, shielding his own face as flames and black smoke poured out. Kim watched in horror, her heart in her throat, as her husband disappeared inside the house.

MARCUS MINTON – 8 DAYS AFTER

Marcus had never been more terrified than he was when he ventured back into that house. He felt as if he was choosing to dive into a dragon's flaming maw, and every instinct told him to flee. He tried to remember what his training had taught him about entering a burning building, but when he stepped over the threshold and the heat slammed his body, fear struck all thoughts from his mind.

One glance over his shoulder, and he saw Kim and Tanice on the grass, their bodies shimmering like a mirage behind the haze. Marcus draped the wet towel over his head and shoulders, its dampness offering fleeting relief.

The kitchen was unrecognisable: the dining table a bed of flames, which also rushed in blue jets across the counters. Through the smoke, Marcus thought he could see the mushrooms melting into black liquid. The respirator strapped to his face made breathing bearable at first, but as the rubber seals softened in the intense heat, sour wisps of smoke seeped through, making his eyes water.

He moved quickly but cautiously, using his crowbar to sweep debris out of the way. He took care to keep low, trying to preserve his breathing through the rising smoke. But when he entered the hall, a beam above him groaned. Marcus looked up to see it suddenly collapse, sending sparks and plaster flying. He ducked, but not quickly enough; the edge of it cracked off his shoulder, searing through his shirt and sending a jolt of pain lancing down his arm. He bit back a cry, temporarily knocked to his knees, crawling beneath fallen debris, propellant smearing his rubber gloves. The sharp pain in his shoulder throbbed with every movement, but he kept moving, dragging himself up to the foot of the stairs.

'Sydney!' he shouted, his voice hoarse and cracking. There was no response except the roar of the fire. *Maybe he's already dead*, Marcus thought. But picturing it made him feel so desperate that he moved even more quickly up the staircase, testing each step before putting his weight on it, his heart hammering against his ribs.

The heat wrapped around him, an oppressive, living thing. Sweat poured down his back and pooled in the visor of his failing mask, which wasn't designed to withstand this. By the time he reached the first-floor landing, he could barely see. The rubber in his gloves was melting, and he had to pull off his mask just to heave for air.

Marcus threw it down and let the flames on the rug engulf it. Instead, he held the wet towel up to his mouth, though it felt warm to him now.

Above him, the ceiling sagged dangerously, ash raining like black snow. How long until the floor crumbled underneath his feet?

Aaliyah's bedroom was already a cauldron; as he tiptoed past, a fresh plume of smoke and flames roared from the door. Coughing, tears in his eyes, Marcus tried shouting again. 'Sydney!' But there was no answer.

Fear clawed at his mind. He thought of the cool air outside. His family. Safety. But he forced himself onward, each step a battle against the primal instinct to flee.

'Sydney!' he called again, louder this time. He thought he heard a banging, two flights up. *Sydney must be trapped*, Marcus thought, remembering the attic door and its tendency to jam.

His hope renewed, he pushed himself harder, clawing his way to the second floor. The hallway was an inferno where the fire seethed along the rug and burst up the walls, making the photographs blacken in their picture frames, causing the glass to pop and crack. Marcus had to duck as a canister of butane blasted a jet of fire right at him. Although he dived out of the way, he felt it catch his right leg. Pain roared up his calf, and though he batted it out with the wet towel, his nose was filled with the smell of his own scorched flesh.

He limped on. Further down the hall was the attic hatch. Grabbing the pull cord, Marcus tugged it hard, but the mechanism didn't budge. As he'd suspected, the door was swollen shut, its edges warped from the heat.

Marcus slammed the crowbar into the gap, leveraging all his strength to pry it open. With a groan of splintering wood, the hatch gave way and the ladder unfurled.

Coughing, he climbed into the attic, his shoulder and leg sending thunderbolts up his nerves with every motion.

'Help!' Though the room was filled with smoke, the flames hadn't reached it yet. Marcus could see Sydney, wide-eyed and terrified, pressed up against the open dormer window. The boy must have considered leaping from it but then baulked at the height – three storeys down to the street, enough to kill him.

'You,' he said then, turning to Marcus in stunned recognition. '*You* came for me?'

Marcus was coughing too much to say anything. He crouched low on the ground and took some desperate lungfuls of air. 'Need ... to get out,' he rasped. He could see embers rising up through the floorboards beneath them. The wood was beginning to crackle and hiss. If they stayed here much longer, the floor would collapse under them and all their escape routes would be incinerated – if they hadn't been already.

As Sydney came towards him, Marcus wrapped his singed towel over his shoulders. 'Stay close to me.'

The steel ladder was already hot to the touch, and the pair descended quickly and crashed onto the second-floor landing. Marcus shielded Sydney with his body as debris fell around them.

'Which way?' Sydney asked, panicked at the sight and proximity of the flames.

'The stairs!' Marcus said, pointing to them. Sydney leapt forward but stopped when he saw that Marcus wasn't following. He was in too much pain – his lungs scalded, his vision turning black, his seared muscles screaming with every motion.

'Come on!' Sydney shouted.

'You go!' Marcus said. Sydney turned to leave, but then hesitated and turned back again, grabbing Marcus's arm.

'Come on!' he shouted again, pulling my father, sweat pouring down his face. Marcus staggered past their burning bedroom, leaning heavily on Sydney's arm as the two of them braced for the next step. But then – 'Get down!'

A ruptured butane tank detonated. A searing wall of heat blasted upward, scorching their exposed skin. Both Marcus and Sydney howled.

Flames had surged up the stairwell, engulfing their path and cutting off escape. *We're going to die here*, Marcus thought.

'Is there another way?' Sydney asked. Marcus couldn't see him as embers rained down. His ears were ringing. Every nerve in his body was a Roman candle.

'Our bedroom.' Marcus crawled towards it, his desperate movements powered by sheer survival instinct.

The bedroom was a blazing tomb. White paint blistered and flaked off the popping mahogany skeleton of their charred bed. One of the crossbeams between the posts had splintered on the carpet. Clothes hanging in the wardrobe burned, sending smoke spiralling to the ceiling. The cream silk curtains at the window crumpled like brittle rice paper as fire rushed up them.

The heat here was unbearable, pressing on Marcus's chest like a weight. Once they neared the window, Sydney gripped his good arm and helped him to his feet.

'We'll climb,' Sydney said as flames clawed at their heels. The window was open, smoke pouring out into the sky. Marcus helped Sydney through first and watched as he balanced precariously on the window ledge. Then he reached back to steady Marcus as he followed.

'We're almost there,' Sydney said, his voice hoarse but firm. The cool air outside was a blessed relief to Marcus's lungs – almost painful. He coughed and gasped all at once, his eyes watering as he watched Sydney pull himself along the ledge.

The two men clung to the drainpipe, their hands slick with sweat and soot. Marcus moved carefully sideways, listening to the sounds of destruction in the house behind him. His muscles trembled, and then voices floated up to him.

'Dad!'

'Syd!'

'Marcus!'

Sydney took the lead, shimmying down to the slatted
trellis. Marcus followed after, the cool night air on his back.
He was almost safe.

But the flimsy willow structure could not support both
their weights. The last thing he felt was the wood splintering
under his fingers. The last thing he saw was the night sky,
spangled with embers, a second-floor window blowing like
a lightbulb. Kim's face, her dark mane haloed by the light,
her cheekbones and nose, her philtrum and brow like a
mountain range he'd been grateful to map.

KIMONA MINTON – 8 DAYS AFTER

My mother told me once about the afternoon she lost me. A couple of months after my thirteenth birthday, I'd gone out to collect something from the corner shop. But forty-five minutes passed, and Kim looked up from her iPad to find that I hadn't returned. Everyone else was out. Aaliyah was travelling, Tanice was at a party, Chantale was on a walk with Marcus. In the silence, the house rang in her ears like a radio tuned to a dead channel.

She tried to concentrate for another fifteen minutes, but her eyes kept flitting to the door, poised for the sound of my key in the lock. For the sight of me chewing on a strawberry lace and shielding my eyes from the sun.

I'd left my phone by my ink-stained pencil case at the opposite end of the dining table. Another twenty minutes and Kim's stomach twisted with dread. Something was wrong. She couldn't stop thinking that something had happened to her daughter. What if I was lying on the road, my ribcage ripped open by the hood of a car? What if I'd been dragged into an alley? Panic prickled up her body. My mother abandoned her chair, looped her keys around her finger and rushed outside, where midday light bleached her eyes.

They were calling it an Indian summer on the radio. London glittered in the heat haze. Kim could see all the way down the road. There were people on the streets, talking over hoods of cars, playing music, dogs barking. No sign of me, though she made the trip to the shop in record time, looking around.

'Have you seen my daughter?' she asked the man in the turban behind the counter. He shook his head. She left in blind panic.

Where could I have gone without my phone? With only a five-pound note that I'd scrunched in my hand? Kim ran, asking everyone she passed. Around the block, under the neglected overpass where cats went to die, through the labyrinth of council flats, the brutalist tower blocks on the opposite side of the road, into the spartan playgrounds at the centre of their courtyards, where a group of young mothers was gathered on the bench watching their infants. By that point, Kim had tears in her eyes, was teetering on the edge of certainty that I was gone forever.

'Have you seen my daughter?' she asked, breathless in her despair.

All the women shook their heads. 'What does she look like, love?'

'She has this gap between her teeth that's just like mine. She has brown freckles on her nose.' And even as she sputtered the other details, she saw, in the concern in all of their eyes, that now was the time to call the police.

'We'll look for you,' said one of the women. Kim had been surprised but so deeply grateful for their assistance. They galvanized their children and took different streets, back under the overpass, through the neglected alleys behind the houses, calling my name – *Bri-ar, Bri-ar* – and Kim believed that if anyone could help her find me, it would be these determined women. These mothers.

So when they returned fifteen minutes later empty-handed, her heart broke again. 'We'll keep looking,' said one of the women, 'but I think you should probably call the police now.'

'Yeah,' agreed another, 'the sooner, the better, really.'

Kim fumbled for her mobile, cursing the time she'd already lost, the hour she'd spent doubting and searching. Her daughter could be dead already or on the back of a truck to France. A girl on their street had been raped in broad daylight, Kim had heard, and her body rocked with nausea.

'Bri-ar, Bri-ar,' some of the children were still chanting as if they thought it was a game, a gibberish string of syllables they sang as they skipped over the hot cracks in the pavement.

'Yeah? Mum?'

She said that my voice was like a bell in her ears. When she looked up, there I was, hand in hand with Chantale, our dad behind us, emerging from the afternoon heat like a mirage. Three people as beautiful as any Kim could have imagined. Her heart burst.

There was friction in the moment before she realized that I was alive. Kim had felt as if she'd come to a sudden stop at the edge of a cliff, rocks skittering off into the nothingness below, momentum threatening to send her over the edge. There it was; for just a moment, she really saw it, the unfathomed depths of her love for me. Of course, it had always been there. But those years were some of the hardest between us. Fights over the dinner table, her begging me to eat, everything a power struggle.

The disaster had shaken Kim, humbled her and then embarrassed her, as I looked around at the crowd, which had already begun to disperse.

'I met Dad on the way back,' I said, confusion in my face, 'and we went for a walk.'

The memory of that day returned to Kim, the panic and then the relief, as she watched Marcus and Sydney emerge from the fire. Neighbours had gathered to watch the inferno, the largest crowd that Kim had seen in a while, people pouring out into the streets, seemingly dazzled by the flames. Our house was detached, so, with luck, the fire wouldn't spread.

Kim ran over to tend to Marcus and Sydney, who lay sprawled on the grass. Marcus's arms and chest were severely burned, his skin charred in places and peeling deeply enough to expose raw, glistening tissue beneath. Sydney's face was swollen and blistering, his hands trembling uncontrollably. He refused to meet anyone's eyes, breathing heavily through gritted teeth.

'I'm sorry!' Tanice was in tears, reaching for Sydney, but he just stared bitterly at Marcus and ignored her completely.

Kim steadied her daughter. 'Tanice, listen, go down into the bunker. Get gauze, antiseptic cream, we'll need more clean water and bandages – everything we have.' Tanice nodded, seemingly relieved to have something to do.

Marcus groaned in pain, and Kim's heart lurched at the sight of his suffering.

'If you think we're even now,' Sydney told Marcus finally, his eyes blazing despite his injuries, 'you're wrong.'

Kim began initial first aid on Marcus, pouring bottled water over his blistered skin to reduce the heat and pain. Though he cried out in discomfort, she peeled away his singed shirt, trying her best not to disturb the damaged flesh beneath. When Tanice returned, Kim instructed her to do the same for Sydney.

Marcus's wounds were terrible, the type of damage that – in the old normal – would have warranted a skin graft. Hard to imagine how he would make it through the night without strong painkillers, and the scars would be disfiguring.

'Hey?' The voice behind her was Gabriel. 'I saw the fire and . . .' He was still taking it in, stunned. 'Show me what I can do to help.'

Kim and Gabriel repositioned Sydney and Marcus to ease their breathing and shield their wounds from further contamination. Gabriel helped Tanice apply the bandages. They worked for what felt like almost an hour to stabilize the men, before Hero's crying echoed up from the bunker.

Aaliyah emerged with the baby and put her hand on her mother's shoulder, glancing nervously at our father and Sydney. 'I think she's hungry,' she whispered. Kim was reluctant to leave, but by then, Marcus and Sydney both seemed more stable.

'Also, I hope it's okay,' Aaliyah told Kim, 'but I invited Hannah and Hudson down to the bunker for some food.'

At the back of the garden, Kim saw that Chantale, determined to help in her own way, had set up a tent on the grass with quiet efficiency, preparing a safe space for Marcus and Sydney to eventually rest, as both men were too injured to descend into the bunker.

Kim retreated into the tent to quietly nurse Hero. As she

settled back against the canvas, exhaustion took hold of her. 'Mum?' She heard Chantale's voice at the little entrance. 'Can I come in?' she asked as she pushed inside.

'Are you okay?' Kim said. Chantale's curls were dusted with ash, and Kim couldn't shake off an icky sense of betrayal as her youngest daughter watched her feed the new baby. Kim thought back to the night before the Event, when she had cradled Chantale in the same way as she was holding Hero now.

The thing she hadn't realized about motherhood was that her daughters would constantly be moving away from her. Never mind that they'd unfurled like jasmine flowers inside her, that she'd built them from her bones, that they were sustained for months by her body alone. They would move away, and they probably wouldn't even consider those early years when they did their accounting. Kim had worried that once she weaned Chantale, it would be the beginning of the end for the two of them. And in a way, she was right.

Chantale stared quietly for a moment but then reached out to stroke the baby's hair. 'It's for Hero now,' she said. *Was that the last time?* Kim wondered, conjuring the bunk bed, the room which had gone up in smoke.

Now they were both ready, she said, 'It is.'

Later that night, some commotion in front of the house motivated Kim to walk around to the front to see what was going on.

A man in a high-vis jacket with the peaked black cap of a police officer had just dismounted a horse, his boots crunching against the gravel. 'Mrs Minton?' he said. 'Do you remember me?'

She squinted through the smoke and dim light. He was tall and pallid, young, with a greasy mop of blonde hair and teeth too large for his mouth. 'No,' she said honestly.

'We only met once. At the work Christmas do. I think you were pregnant then ... ?'

'Oh ...' A distant glimmer in her recollection. 'Sergeant Cooper?' she hazarded. He grinned, and his teeth looked as if they might all pop out of his mouth.

'Vincent now.' He patted the horse's flank absently. 'We're not much for titles anymore. Heard about the fire over the radio and came to see if anyone needed help.' Kim thought she could hear the static buzz of it in his pocket. 'Recognized the address. Is Sergeant Minton ... ?'

'He made it out,' Kim said. 'He's injured, but ...' Vincent nodded, his gaze following the dizzy blizzard of embers as they were whipped up by the wind.

'It's like this everywhere,' he said. 'Trying to put out fires where we find them. But stretched too thin and coming too late.'

'We?' Kim asked.

'The Post-Collapse Task Force. We're kind of a local community-led group. Some emergency service workers partnering with relief centres, volunteers ... anyone willing to lend a hand. But honestly? It feels like trying to stop a flood with a bucket.' Kim noted that Vincent didn't seem to be trying to stop the fire with anything at all.

They spoke for a while. Vincent told her about where he'd been when the collapse had happened – on the way to a music festival – and how he had diverted home. He wanted to do what he could to help. He told her some of the things he had seen, the fights he'd broken up, the people he had reunited. But he also hinted at the vast scale of the tragedy.

How disappointed and inspired he'd been by humanity in equal measure.

Kim was only half-listening. She kept glancing back at the house, paying attention to the sound of the first floor as it collapsed. Smoke billowed out through the windows.

Maybe no one will know, Kim thought ruefully, *that we saved everyone.*

'And then yesterday, on the radio, thirty people, mostly teenagers ...' Vincent shook his head sadly. 'Mass suicide, it looked like.' The words filtered into Kim's awareness, and her head snapped to him.

'Wait,' she grilled him, 'what? Who?'

'Some posh kids in a mansion, out in the Surrey Hills. I mean, tragic, really. And not so far from here.'

'Kids, who?'

'I didn't catch all of their names. But a couple of girls from the local school.'

Kim's hand flew to her mouth. 'Which school?' she whispered, hoping it wouldn't be true.

'St Something ... Catherine?'

'Clotilde's?'

'That's the one!'

A ringing in her ears. That old dread. The bone-deep terror at the prospect of losing a child. Kim couldn't breathe, clawed at her chest, panicked. *Bri-ar*, she thought. She heard it again in that sing-song way those children had called it out when I went missing all those years before.

Her mind kept tumbling back, recalling in horror the last things she'd said to me in the kitchen. She made the old deals she used to make with God. *If Briar returns*, she thought, *I'll never ask for anything else.*

Looking back at the house, Kim came to see, in the

moment it was burning, that there was no such thing as choosing the right or the wrong life. She had only ever had one, and she decided that night to love it for however long it might last.

Kim would later hear that the spores caused the human mind to perceive the world in five dimensions, the way the aliens could. The past looked to them like a sun scorched canyon, and the future was clearly visible in the distance, beyond mountains of millions of years. She discovered that if she viewed the house the way they could, it would be a palimpsest. She would be seven, walking through its empty hall hours after she first arrived in the UK from Lagos in her warmest dress, which was all wrong for the English winter. She would be fifteen, crying over her dead mother in the living room. Kim would be laughing and watching Marcus wipe vernix from Chantale's face just minutes after she was born unexpectedly on the kitchen floor. They would be seventeen, listening to Pink Floyd. And she would be telling him she'd *never* marry him, standing at the top of the same staircase that she would descend in her wedding dress on the day she finally did. They would be fighting, and they would be in love. She would grow up and grow old, but also, the house would always, always be burning.

BRIAR MINTON – 9 DAYS AFTER

I would hear about what happened to Freya and the Group in the coming days. Their bodies were discovered by the house manager at Midacre the day after the Night of Awe, at the trestle table where once we'd agreed that – thanks to the technology which would be granted to us by the Tau – we would soon live forever.

He'd taken his bike up to a nearby relief centre and reported the incident. A couple of members of the Post-Collapse Task Force had followed him back to investigate.

Belladonna poisoning, a coroner would eventually conclude. I'd think about the afternoon we'd found the deadly nightshade in the woods at the edge of the estate. How I'd shaken the black berries from Martha's hands – she'd laughed then, 'And I almost baked them into a pie.'

Why did they do it? Had it been, like Ruby's death, an attempt to force the Tau to respond? Or had they grown tired of waiting?

I think often about what might have happened if I'd been there. Sometimes I convince myself that I would have been the sole voice of reason. I imagine how heroically I would have spoken up and brought them all to their senses. But then I remember what it was like: the almost physical force the vortex of their communal beliefs exerted on me. The way that being trapped with them in Midacre had warped reality. I remember that I never spoke up, not really. Not after Cato broke my phone or tried to drown me. Not when I was faint from fasting. Not when the Tau seemed to go silent. Not as I watched my hair tumble into the dirt under Beth's razor. Not after Soo-Jin's death.

I still have dreams where I wake in Midacre, chasing Cato or Axel or Martha down its double-storeyed halls. In them, Axel smiles at me and then turns on his heel, the rubber soles of my boots flashing Pepto-Bismol pink as he vanishes. Martha is dancing in the Little Red riding cape that Soo-Jin made for her from an old jacquard curtain. Cato looks down at his hands and spreads his fingers as if surprised to find that there is nothing in them.

If I ever reach them, I ask, through sobs, 'Why?' And they never tell me.

They'd signed a logbook with their names on the final day.

Cato had been the last: *You'll meet Them in the darkness. C.*

I reached my house by sunrise, in the back of the First Contact Committee's horse-drawn wagon. A large group of their agents organized to clear the area. They evacuated the local buildings and blocked off the street. They hosed down smouldering embers and began trampling through the wreckage, looking for any final traces of fungal fruiting bodies and spore samples beneath the charred timbers.

I had been devastated to discover my home imploded like

a star, but my despair transformed quickly into relief when I hobbled around the side of the house to find Tanice curled on a blanket laid over blackened grass.

'What happened to you ...?' she said. The gardener had fashioned a crutch for me out of a broken chair. Tanice looked up at me, rubbing her eyes as if hoping she wasn't dreaming. She ran to me, nearly knocking me off balance with the strength of her embrace. She held tight, her fingers clutching at my filthy hoodie, her face pressed against my shoulder. 'Everything fell apart,' she told me, 'without you.'

Aaliyah emerged from the toolshed, holding baby Hero in her arms. She had the wild-eyed look of someone who hadn't had an unbroken night of sleep for a while, but at the sight of me she gasped in relief, 'Oh, Briar!' A sob caught in her throat, and she carefully shifted Hero to one arm to pull me into a trembling hug. 'Thank God you're alive.'

'Never leave,' Tanice said, kissing my cheek.

'I won't.' My face was hot and prickling. 'I'm sorry, I never should have.'

The sound – bare feet and palms slapping against metal – of Chantale scrabbling up the bunker's ladder made us all turn around. She leapt towards me shouting, 'I knew you'd come back! I knew everything would be all right!'

There was a tent at the back of the garden, and movement there caught my eye. My dad struggled up from the stretcher where he'd been sleeping, his movements deliberate, a tightness in his jaw as if every step pained him. He limped towards me. 'Dad—' I began, but he cut me off with a shaking hand, cupping my cheek gently.

Losing me had been his nightmare. 'I didn't imagine ...' he said, eyes glistening above the gauze.

'I found my way home,' I told him, and he nodded with pride.

When I looked up, I saw my mother, lingering back a little. Her hair had turned suddenly grey with fallen ash. She opened her mouth, as if fighting to form words.

'Briar,' she said, 'I shouldn't have ...' Then her chest heaved with sobs as she rushed forward to pull me close. Her grip made a jolt of pain shoot up my calf, and I flinched. She pulled back, shame in her eyes. 'I love you,' she said quietly. When Kim stepped back, I regarded her in a way I never had before, with pity and love, as a creature like myself. Only human. When she told me that she loved me, I believed her the first time and experienced an unfamiliar lightness, the inward release of pain that followed me deciding, finally, to forgive her.

The agents from the First Contact Committee took us in for questioning. They combed through our hair and hosed us down. They gave us all comprehensive medical exams and several MRIs. Most of what I know, I gathered from their reports and the extensive interviews they conducted with every member of my family.

The gardener was right. I did lose my leg. The Committee's medical staff performed the surgery in their underground facility, and I was grateful for it, for the anaesthesia. My dad, too, was badly and permanently scarred by his burns, and his lungs would never fully recover from the damage they sustained in the fire. But really, none of us emerged unscathed.

Our whole family was kept under observation in the First Contact Committee's facility for almost a month. During that time, we watched live feeds of the sky. Watched as

Hero began accelerating away from the Earth. By July, it was invisible to the naked eye, and then it vanished almost as swiftly as it had appeared.

The scientists shared what they could with us about the nature of the aliens. Based on human interaction with the spores, which allowed us to witness past events with impossible precision, it was hypothesized that the Andromedans – as the Committee referred to them – had experienced the universe in five dimensions.

The working theory was that they had predicted the death of their sun many millions of years before it happened and had launched probes into neighbouring galaxies which crashed into planets, burying pods like seeds in the ground. The Andromedans had left one of these pods on Earth sometime in the Palaeolithic period like a sleeper cell, designed to send us a message at some point in the future. In the holograms the scientists conjured, this reconstructed alien object looked like a honeycomb wrapped around a ball, with dormant fungi caged in a strange structure made with an extraterrestrial element that responded to magnetic force. It seemed that the pod had been programmed to rupture when triggered by a signal from a satellite – Hero.

More than a million years later, our house had been built right on top of this alien artefact. Hero's massive magnetic pulse had pulled the pod up through layers of sediment and earth and caused it to rupture under the foundations of the building, whereupon dormant spores in the alien object, activated by Hero, had begun multiplying furiously. After the fire, the scientists had uncovered its shattered hull just under the building. It was assumed that the spores had been their way of trying to speak to us, influencing our neurobiology in a way that allowed us to glimpse the past and contemplate their fate. All around the city, during the Night of Awe, people had reported dreaming the same dreams, of exploding stars, vaporised planets, obliterated outer worlds and distant moons sterilized by radiation. Nowhere to flee.

I wondered if something about the pod's latent presence had been affecting my family for years. Had it caused our father to start digging into the ground, tormented by visions of our planet's collapse? Had it made our mother compulsively foresee our house's destruction? Had it made my mind pliable in a way that allowed me to visualize the Tau when prompted? No one knew the answers to these questions.

'Did they think we might respond to their message?' I asked Dr Sengupta when I met her in the facility a couple of days before our release. Dr Astrid Juma was there, too – it was disorientating to see her in the flesh and not projected ten feet tall on a screen or as a talking head on the news.

'It's hard to know exactly what their intentions were,' Dr Sengupta said.

'Maybe it was a warning,' Dad suggested, 'or an act of war.'

I came to their defence. 'Maybe they didn't know, at this stage in our history, how much that level of magnetic force would devastate us.' Although the cities were starting to rebuild, working to restore electricity, many predicted that it would take a generation to regain all we had lost.

'Hero's message was clearly an invitation,' Dr Sengupta said. 'I believe they wanted us to visit them.' The same map of Andromeda that the gardener had discovered had appeared suddenly all over the world, in spiral formations of night-blooming ghost orchids, patterns in sand dunes and ice crystals, crop circles and mosses. Hero's magnetic waves had created the atmospheric disturbances that had caused these phenomena to take place within the same few days.

The doctor continued, 'Given the distance between Andromeda and here, we assume that their civilization is long gone now. Some of my colleagues believe that they buried their pods hoping that they would be triggered at a time they were in need of rescue.'

'An SOS,' Mum said, 'to a species that could never save them?'

'According to this theory, they likely sent others,' Dr Sengupta said, 'to different planets in other galaxies as well.'

'But if they could see the future—' I began.

'We don't know how clear their foresight was, though,' interrupted Dr Juma. 'Maybe they could see it the way we can see a faraway monument, the details muddled by distance.'

'But if they had some foreknowledge of their own destruction, wouldn't they have also glimpsed the futility of their plans?' I asked. 'I mean, like Mum said, we could never have saved them.'

'Maybe, in another millennium or two, we'd have had that capability . . .' Dr Sengupta suggested.

'Or maybe,' said Dr Juma, 'it was never about being rescued. Maybe they only wanted to be known.'

BRIAR MINTON – 3 MONTHS AFTER

The wedding was beautiful. It was organized for almost nothing in the garden of Providence House. With its overgrown grass and vibrant blooms, it didn't need much decoration, but my mum stayed up late the night before to hang ribbons between the trees and string up faded paper lanterns. She and Chantale had spent a week folding origami cranes, which they draped in pretty garlands from the rafters.

Aaliyah wore a cotton sateen dress from the 'free closet', with delicate little flowers that Gladys had embroidered along the neckline. Her veil was crafted from an old lace lectern cover that had been tucked away in the church's storage room. I'd spent the morning with my sisters, gathering wildflowers and early autumn leaves from the garden, which we tied into little bouquets and corsages, laughing and singing as we worked. I wove gold and rust-coloured chrysanthemums with hawthorn berries and tiny star-shaped asters to make a crown for Aaliyah.

Tanice, of course, had helped with makeup. As I placed my crown lightly on my sister's veil, Tanice gently ran her thumb over Mum's brows and said sorrowfully, 'You know, I don't think they ever recovered from the Nineties.' Mum laughed. After the fire, she'd stopped caring about such things. She wore her afro without a care. She let herself go grey.

The medical examinations from the First Contact Committee had revealed that somehow the alien spores had made the cancerous cells in Kim's temporal lobe shrink for good. She was collaborating with the research fellows, hoping that their discovery would lead to a breakthrough in cancer treatment.

Aaliyah regarded herself in the mirror. 'These are happy tears,' she told us.

'Are they?' I pressed. 'Are you *really* happy to marry Hugo?'

After we were released from the Committee's headquarters, we moved to Providence House to live with Grandad. It was there that Hugo found her.

'He searched the whole city for me,' she said softly. He'd been frantic and he had suffered so much along the way. Aaliyah told us, for the first time, about how she'd met him – at Carmen and Paris's shotgun wedding. She said it had been an act of self-harm to attend, heartbroken as she was. 'But then Hugo was there, and he was so kind to me.'

Aaliyah told us that, for months, she kept thinking back to her accident and replaying the moment of the turn, the precise angle of the fall. Why hadn't she braced herself? For a while, she thought that maybe it was her fear of failure resurfacing all over again – the panic that had led her to spread that damaging rumour about Carmen. Perhaps she had been scared of the upcoming season, of competing in Wimbledon. But after Hugo had proposed, she wondered if it was because some part of her was already done with tennis. With competing and striving. With constantly pushing for *more*. With Hugo, she felt loved and centred and ... enough.

'But what about Paris?' Tanice pressed. Tanice had told Aaliyah about Paris's death, about how he had bravely saved her and Chantale, and our eldest sister had burst into devastated tears. When Hugo had arrived, like a beacon of hope, Aaliyah believed that she owed him the truth. Finally, she admitted to Hugo that she had loved his cousin. 'I know,' he said sadly. 'I always knew.'

'Paris never loved me,' Aaliyah told us now. 'He never chose me.'

I played 'Sorry-Grateful' on the saxophone as Aaliyah walked up the aisle between Mum and Dad, and when she and Hugo read out their vows, I had to hold back tears.

Grandad officiated. He told us, 'Now we reach the centre of the centre of the scroll ... the sixteenth book. The Day of Atonement. "Kippur", the Hebrew word for atonement, means two things – to cover and to reconcile ... In marriage, this is not a single act but a daily practice ...'

I delivered my speech over the wedding breakfast. 'For a while, we weren't alone, and then we always were.' We sat at a long trestle table for the meal, which Dad had taken great pride in preparing with the help of people from the community. It was a marvel – a testament to his culinary ingenuity and determination to turn humble, long-life

ingredients into a gourmet feast fit for the occasion. The
starter was a smoked mackerel pâté, which he served with
crispbread crackers that someone had bartered for and a
garnish of pickled onions and capers. For the main course,
he slow-cooked a stew using tinned beef in gravy, canned
mushrooms and dehydrated vegetables, serving it over a bed
of instant mashed potatoes.

Chantale was in charge of the dessert, and she and
Hannah baked a cake with flour and powdered milk. She'd
cut out little paper dolls of Aaliyah and Hugo and placed
them on top with a scattering of dried lavender and mari-
golds from the garden.

'Who should we be now?' I asked the group, as we ate
the food we'd gathered and grown together. Our father had
become a leader in our local branch of the Post-Collapse
Task Force. Using his prepping skills to help plan how to
grow and redistribute supplies, he had earned the trust of
our neighbours, who began to look to him for guidance.
He coordinated efforts to rebuild our shattered community,
from setting up sustainable gardens in abandoned lots to
establishing bartering networks for essential goods, offering
us all some measure of hope amid the uncertainty.

Tanice and Aaliyah devoted themselves to the food-
bank. Tanice helped the volunteers at Providence House to
manage the daily redistribution of food, while Aaliyah took
on the challenge of devising sustainable, long-term solutions
for the community. She worked with Hugo to think of ways
to use Glassford House and its surrounding estate, with its
fertile land and access to water, to help grow seasonal crops
and bring them into the city.

'It could be easy to let disaster define us,' I said, looking
out at the gathered crowd, my family, and Aaliyah in her

headdress of autumn flowers and Hugo in his second-hand suit. People I'd come to know, Gladys, Vincent, Hannah and Gabriel, baby Hero gurgling in Chantale's arms.

After the fire, Sydney would never speak to any of us again. But the pictures he took would become famous. You've probably seen the iconic one of Tanice in our attic. He'd saved the roll of film in his pocket when he escaped from the fire. It's the only photographic evidence that exists of the alien spores, which, in the picture, float like stars about her head.

'For a while, I did. Even now, I still dream about the Andromedans and their decimated home world. What we'd see if we ever travelled there. After hundreds of thousands of years, is every trace of every civilization utterly wiped away? And what about us? I keep wondering what will remain of us . . .'

Once dinner was over, my family would scatter onto the dancefloor. Hugo and Aaliyah would sway, their eyes locked together. Tanice would teach Grandad some forgotten viral dance moves. Chantale would spin around, carefully hold-ing Hero in her arms.

I would watch Mum and Dad embrace each other, his hand on her back, her head on his chest, wedding rings glittering on her finger.

I said, 'I hope it's love.'

Acknowledgements

Sincere thanks go to everyone at Greene and Heaton and to my agent, Judith Murray. To my editor Charlotte Trumble, it was such a joy to work with you, and I feel so lucky for the opportunity. Thank you for your encouragement and quick edits against our two hard deadlines.

This book would not exist without everyone who looked after my children so I could write it. For that reason, I'm particularly indebted to Ellakeche, who has steadfast and selflessly provided me with the time to work for three years and is the reason I have been able to travel for work. I'm incredibly grateful to both of our mothers and to Professor Sionaidh Douglas-Scott, who has inspired me throughout my adult life. And, most of all, to Dr Sheila Obim, I could not have finished this book without you. I love you so much! You are a wonderful mother, my vital support and friend.

To beautiful, talented Ruth, who brings the whole family joy. Thank you for the care you took in helping me and for all of your encouragement when I've needed it. My love to Che, who is a blessing to us. And to Grandma – without you, there is no us.

My love and thanks to Nanci Gilliver, who was the first person to read this story in full and made me feel brave about sharing it with the world. To Stella Fielder, who demonstrated a shoulder press with a doll for me on Zoom. To Ella Sparks, who is the gardener I hope to meet at the end of the world. To my other sister, Natasha Djukic, who can brighten any day or task with her delightful self. I've been lucky to grow up with you and hope to grow old with you.

My love to Alexander and Venetia Douglas-Scott. To Anne Alfred and Dr. Michael Douglas-Scott.

Thank you to Sarah at The Tram Stop for providing a warm and lovely place to work that isn't my windowless office!

For Victory, my heart's delight and the greatest thing that happened to us this year. Jubilee, who we longed for. To Benedict Douglas-Scott, always, for everything. If I write about a good man, I'm writing about you.

For God, my help and my sole hope, the shade at my right hand and the lifter of my head.

Discover more from Temi Oh ...

AVAILABLE NOW

There are far better things ahead
than what we leave behind ...